D0644072

Dumped

Dumped

An Anthology

Edited by
B. Delores Max

Grove Press
New York

Published simultaneously in Canada
Printed in the United States ofAmerica

FIRST EDITION

Library of Congress Cataloging-in-Publication Data

Dumped : an anthology / edited by B. Delores Max.
p. cm.
ISBN 0-8021-3961-2
1. Rejection (Psychology)—Fiction. 2. Separation (Psychology)—Fiction. 3. Marital conflict—Fiction. 4. Separated people—Fiction 5. Divorced people—Fiction. 6. Divorce—Fiction. 7. Short stories, American. 8. Short stories, English. I. Max, B. Delores.
PS648.R43 D86 2003
813'.5080353—dc21 2002035449

Grove Press
841 Broadway
New York, NY 10003

03 04 05 06 07 10 9 8 7 6 5 4 3 2 1

Contents

Introduction
ix

The Zagat History of My Last Relationship
NOAH BAUMBACH
1

The Spanish Lady
ALICE MUNRO
5

Access to the Children
WILLIAM TREVOR
21

Willing
LORRIE MOORE
41

From *Sense and Sensibility*
JANE AUSTEN
61

The Male Gaze
LUCINDA ROSENFELD
83

From *This Boy's Life*
TOBIAS WOLFF
91

UFO in Kushiro
HARUKI MURAKAMI
99

How to Love a Republican
STEVE ALMOND
117

The Fourth State of Matter
JO ANN BEARD
143

Under the Radar
RICHARD FORD
163

From *Herzog*
SAUL BELLOW
175

A Telephone Call
DOROTHY PARKER
179

Over the Hill
ANDRE DUBUS
185

From *Open House*
ELIZABETH BERG
199

Final Touches
DAN O'BRIEN
213

My Stuff
ROGER HART
223

The End of the Relationship
WILL SELF
235

Making Arrangements
ELIZABETH BOWEN
263

Marching Through Delaware
BRUCE JAY FRIEDMAN
275

Lamb to the Slaughter
ROALD DAHL
281

The Camping Ground
DALLAS ANGGUISH
293

Fever
RAYMOND CARVER
309

Introduction

B. DELORES MAX

If you are thinking of leaving or have just left your lover or spouse, drop this book, or perhaps simply use caution. This isn't for you. It's for that heart you broke. It's for every heart you ever broke, but then, you've had your heart broken, too, haven't you?

If, on the other hand, you have just been left, or dumped, by your lover or spouse, pull up a chair, or settle into your couch, or, better yet, your bed. Prepare for catharsis, for temporary immersion in a community of like-left souls. And this community is vast; there is no one alive who has not been, at one time, lovelorn, the unrequited lover, the broken-hearted, the *dumped.*

Of the many levels of being dumped, the most innocuous is what I call the *uplifting dump,* as by the blind date years ago with an investment banker at the Italian restaurant from which I walked home fifty-five blocks. He had offered half-heartedly to hail me a cab, but I hadn't wanted to give him the satisfaction of having done a single honorable thing. It's also true that I didn't have enough money in my purse to pay the driver. So I walked the date out of my system, walked off the wine, walked off the veal and garlic spinach, walked off the uninspired conversation, walked off the shroud of humiliation of not being escorted home—no matter that I wouldn't have wanted to spend another minute in this guy's company, wouldn't have wanted to go back to his plush apartment on Central Park West to see his collection of abstract expressionism. I wanted none of that—just to be home in my shabby studio apartment with my shedding cat and my sparse and thrift-shop-purchased furnishings and a tattered copy of *Emma*, bought on Astor Place for a dime. Nothing like rejection to make what is wholly yours seem sweet and right. This kind of dumping is purifying—it's good for you. It purges greed, money-lust, and envy from a bruised heart. It makes even those with eroded self-esteem feel virtuous and wise. Hell, if every bloated, overpaid ego were dumped like that on a regular basis, the world would be a better place. It would have to be on a regular basis, though, because the effects are not long-lasting.

And then there is the *annoying dump*. This dump makes you angrier at yourself than at the dumper. Like the time the guy I was dating (or, more accurately, sleeping with, though I was then too optimistic to make the distinction) went out in the morning and returned with an Egg McMuffin and a cup of coffee for himself. I got out of bed, stomach growling, and rummaged through the paper bag only to find a nest of ketchup packets and crumpled napkins. He was reading the newspaper when I inquired, hating myself for the tremulous tone in my voice, whether he had thought to get me anything. "No," he said, hardly looking up. "Sorry." Then he stuffed the rest of his Egg McMuffin into his mouth. I stomped around his apartment barely noticed, collecting my shoes and other stray articles of clothing as my rage built.

"Th-that's it," I stammered, like an inarticulate twelve-year-old. "I'm outa here."

"Wha-?" he said with his mouth full. "Christ, it's only breakfast."

Sure, the actual dumping was more passive than overt. But a dumping can be subtle. And this brand of rejection fills you with a deep loathing: for yourself and for all of humanity. Fortunately, the effects of this type are also short-lived. Your friends say, *Jeez, what an asshole. Not even a donut? Good riddance. You should have dumped his coffee on his head / in his shoe / down his pants . . .*

And then there is the *crushing dump*. As when your boyfriend or girlfriend of four to six years fails to make eye contact while muttering that he or she: needs to talk / is in a rut / doesn't know what's wrong with him- or herself / woke up one morning dissatisfied / needs a "break" (which means "break-up") / needs some space / wants to see other people. Or worse: You begin to suspect and then find incontrovertible evidence that there is someone else. . . . Oh sure, you knew the relationship had lately had its troubles. You had sensed your lover was preoccupied, withdrawn, and making more and more reflexive gestures of contempt, but you had thought it was just a rough patch. It is this kind of dumping that knocks the wind out of you at first and that's the good part. Later comes the hollowed-out feeling in your gut; the sense of massacre-scale tragedy; the uncontrolled weeping; the disbelieving; the repeated groveling; and the catatonia.

And if that is the crushing-blow variety of being dumped, then that leaves the sort that is just shy of the death knell: the unexpected departure of the heretofore-believed-to-be soul mate and life partner. One person suddenly takes off, burning rubber, down the highway of life and the other person is like unto roadkill.

In this anthology are short stories and excerpts from novels by writers including Raymond Carver, Alice Munro, Richard Ford, Dorothy Parker, Tobias Wolff, Lorrie Moore, Elizabeth Bowen, Saul Bellow, Haruki Murakami, Andre Dubus, and William Trevor. These masters of the art of fiction render the anguish of being left so truthfully that there is no one among us who will not recognize these characters in our exes, in ourselves.

These stories range in intensity from the unreciprocated crush to the devastation of divorce, each exploring the emotional terrain scorched by pain and longing. On the lighter side of being left there is Noah Baumbach's hilarious satire "The Zagat History of My Last Relationship." In Lucinda Rosenfeld's "The Male Gaze" the dumping is symptomatic of the hollow, postmodern notions of intimacy, lust, sex—and love doesn't even enter into the picture. Contrast this with the nineteenth-century sensibility of Jane Austen's Marianne Dashwood as she is misused by Willoughby. Everything has changed in two hundred years except the tactics of rejection.

We naturally sympathize with the one who has been left, but sometimes it's more complicated than that, as in William Trevor's "Access to the Children," which is actually a triple dumped story. When the husband takes a mistress (implicit dumping #1), almost randomly destroying his perfectly happy marriage, his wife gives him ample time to reconsider. When he cannot seem to leave his mistress, even though he is in love with his wife, his wife demands a divorce (dumping #2). After his wife has left him, his mistress follows suit (dumping #3). He returns to beg his wife to take him back, but she has moved on by then, and it is too late. We pity him, even though it was his own damn fault to begin with.

After all, a relationship becomes a living thing in and of itself, and the death of this being is to be mourned no matter who has left whom. In Will Self's "The End of the Relationship" the relationship as living organism takes on almost literal meaning as the protagonist becomes a twisted version of Typhoid Mary, unwittingly spreading dissent like a relationship-wrecking virus.

In Raymond Carver's "Fever," a man's wife has dumped him for a friend and left him with their two children. Our hearts ache for Carlyle, and we weep with him when he reaches a kind of resolution in an awesome testament to the resilience of the human spirit. Yet it is not easy to demonize his wife, either, for all her misguided psychic attempts at soothing his pain over the telephone. Only in Richard Ford's scathing story "Under the Radar" do we feel unmitigated disdain for the leaver. Then, too, in "Making Arrangements" by Elizabeth Bowen, we are exceedingly gratified when an older man, who is left by his young frivolous wife, exacts his revenge.

Sometimes a dumping is ambiguous, as in Steve Almond's "How to Love a Republican," and in Lorrie Moore's "Willing," wherein both parties are victims of their incompatibility.

What makes these stories so fulfilling and so disturbing at the same time is that they are as like life as any real story you know. In real life, though, in the thick of heartache, in the chaos of grief, it is often impossible to make sense of anything. But because these are works of fiction, controlled by their authors, precisely crafted, they contain the keen insight and wisdom we all desire.

Whether you have been recently dumped and are still reeling from the shock, or whether you are nursing an older wound, you will find within these stories solace and truth. Two things all hearts, broken or mended, require.

Dumped

The Zagat History of My Last Relationship

NOAH BAUMBACH

AASE'S

Bring a "first date" to this "postage stamp"-size bistro. Tables are so close you're practically "sitting in the laps" of the couple next to you, but the lush décor is "the color of love." Discuss your respective "dysfunctional families" and tell her one of your "fail-safe" stories about your father's "cheapness" and you're certain to "get a laugh." After the "to die for" soufflés, expect a good-night kiss, but don't push for more, because if you play your cards right there's a second date "right around the corner."

BRASSERIE PENELOPE

"Ambience and then some" at this Jamaican-Norwegian hybrid. Service might be a "tad cool," but the warmth you feel when you gaze into her baby blues will more than compensate for it. Conversation is "spicier than the jerk chicken," and before you know it you'll be back at her one-bedroom in the East Village, quite possibly "getting lucky."

THE CHICK & HEN

Perfect for breakfast "after sleeping together," with "killer coffee" that will "help cure your seven-beer/three-aquavit hangover." Not that you need it—your "amplified high spirits" after having had sex for the first time in "eight months" should do the trick.

DESARCINA'S

So what if she thought the movie was "pretentious and contrived" and you felt it was a "masterpiece" and are dying to inform her that "she doesn't know what she's talking about"? Remember, you were looking for a woman who wouldn't "yes" you all the time. And after one bite of chef Leonard Desarcina's "duck manqué" and a sip of the "generous" gin Margaritas you'll start to see that she might have a point.

GORDY'S

Don't be ashamed if you don't know what wine to order with your seared minnow; the "incredibly knowledgeable" waiters will be more than pleased to assist. But if she makes fun of "the way you never make eye contact with people," you might turn "snappish" and end up having your first "serious fight," one where feelings are "hurt."

PANCHO MAO

"Bring your wallet," say admirers of Louis Grenouille's pan Asian-Mexican-style fare, because it's "so expensive you'll start to wonder why she hasn't yet picked up a tab." The "celeb meter is high," and "Peter Jennings" at the table next to yours might spark an "inane political argument" where you find yourself "irrationally defending

Enron" and finally saying aloud, "You don't know what you're talking about!" Don't let her "stuff herself," as she might use that as an excuse to go to sleep "without doing it."

RIGMAROLE

At this Wall Street old boy's club, don't be surprised if you run into one of her "ex-boyfriends" who works in "finance." Be prepared for his "power play," when he sends over a pitcher of "the freshest-tasting sangria this side of Barcelona," prompting her to visit his table for "ten minutes" and to come back "laughing" and suddenly critical of your "cravat." The room is "snug," to say the least, and it's not the best place to say, full voice, "What the fuck were you thinking dating him?" But don't overlook the "best paella in town" and a din "so loud" you won't notice that neither of you is saying anything.

TATI

Prices so "steep" you might feel you made a serious "career gaffe" by taking the "high road" and being an academic rather than "selling out" like "every other asshole she's gone out with." The "plush seats" come in handy if she's forty-five minutes late and arrives looking a little "preoccupied" and wearing "a sly smile."

VANDERWEI'S

Be careful not to combine "four dry *sakes*" with your "creeping feeling of insecurity and dread," or you might find yourself saying, "Wipe that damn grin off your face!" The bathrooms are "big and glamorous," so you won't mind spending an hour with your cheek pressed against the "cool tiled floor" after she "walks out." And the hip East Village location can't be beat, since her apartment is "within walking distance," which makes it very convenient if you should choose to "lean on her buzzer for an hour" until she calls "the cops."

ZACHARIA AND SONS & CO.

This "out of the way," "dirt cheap," "near impossible to find," "innocuous" diner is ideal for "eating solo" and insuring that you "won't run into your ex, who has gone back to the bond trader." The "mediocre at best" burgers and "soggy fries" will make you wish you "never existed" and wonder why you're so "frustrated with your life" and unable to sustain a "normal," "healthy" "relationship."

The Spanish Lady

ALICE MUNRO

Dear Hugh and Margaret,

I have been by myself a good deal these past weeks and have been able to think about us all and have reached several interesting though not perhaps original conclusions:

1) Monogamy is not a natural condition for men and women.

2) The reason that we feel jealous is that we feel abandoned. This is absurd, because I am a grown-up person capable of looking after myself. I cannot, literally, be abandoned. Also we feel jealous—I feel jealous—because I reason that if Hugh loves Margaret he is taking something away from me and giving it to her. Not so. Either he is giving her extra love—in addition to the love he feels for me—or he does not feel love for me but does for her. Even if the latter is true it does not mean that I am unlovable. If I can feel strong and happy in myself then Hugh's love is not necessary for my self-esteem. And if Hugh loves Margaret I should be glad, shouldn't I, that he has this happiness in his life? Nor can I make any demands on him—

Dear Hugh and Margaret,

The thing that makes me suffer is not just that you were having an affair but that you deceived me so skillfully. It is terrible when you find out that your idea of reality is not the real reality. Surely having Margaret at the house all the time and having us three go out together and Margaret pretending to be my friend was unnecessary treachery? How often you must have been laughing at me exchanging your careful heartless glances when we were together, it was all a show put on for your own cruel amusement and my being such a dupe and a fool of course lent spice to your lovemaking. I despise you both. I could never do that. I could never make a fool of someone I had loved and been married to or even someone who had been good to me and was my friend—

I tear those letters off, both of them, crumple them and put them in the tiny receptacle for waste paper. Everything in the roomette is well-planned, adequate. In this cubicle of metal and upholstery a human being could without real inconvenience or discomfort pass a life. The train is westbound out of Calgary. I sit watching the brown oceanic waves of dry country rising into the foothills and I weep monotonously, seasickly. Life is not like the dim ironic stories I like to read, it is like a daytime serial on television. The banality will make you weep as much as anything else.

Girlfriend. Mistress. Nobody says mistress any more, that I know of. Girlfriend sounds brash, yet has a spurious innocence, is curiously evasive. The possibilities of mystery and suffering that hung around the old-fashioned word have entirely disappeared. Violetta could never have been anybody's girlfriend. But Nell Gwyn could, she was more modern.

Elizabeth Taylor: mistress.

Mia Farrow: girlfriend.

This is exactly the sort of game Hugh and Margaret and I would have taken up in our old evenings together, or more likely Margaret and I would have taken it up, amusing then irritating Hugh with our absorption in it.

Neither word would hang well on Margaret.

Last spring we went downtown to buy her a new dress. I was amused and touched by her thriftiness, her cautious taste. She is a rich girl, she lives in the Uplands with her old mother, but she drives a six-year-old Renault, dented along one side, she carries sandwiches to school, she wishes not to give offense.

I tried to persuade her to buy a long straight dress, heavy dark green cotton with gold and silver embroidery.

"It makes me feel like a courtesan," she said. "Or like somebody trying to look like a courtesan, which is worse."

We left the shop and went to a department store where she bought a rose-colored wool with three-quarter sleeves and self-covered buttons and belt, the sort of dress she always wore, in which her tall flat-chested figure appeared as usual dry, shy, unyielding. Then we went to a secondhand bookshop, and decided to buy each other presents. I bought her *Lala Rookh* and she bought me a copy of *The Princess,* from which we recited to each other as we walked down the street:

Tears, idle tears, I know not what they mean. . . .

We were often giddy, like high school girls. Was this normal, when you come to think of it? We made up stories about people we saw on the street. We laughed so hard we had to sit down on a bus-stop bench, and the bus came, and we still laughed, waving it on. The edge of hysteria. We were attracted to each other because of the man, or to the man because of each other. I used to go home worn out from talking, from laughing, and say to Hugh, "It's ridiculous. I haven't had a friend like this in years."

Sitting at the dinner table with us, where she so often sat, she told us she wanted to be called Margaret, not Marg any more. Marg is what most people call her, what the other teachers call her. She teaches English and Physical Education at Hugh's school, the school where Hugh is Principal. Marg Honecker, they say, she's a great girl when you get to know her, really Marg is a wonderful *person,* and you know from the way they say it that she isn't pretty.

"*Marg* is so gawky, in fact it's just like me. I think *Margaret* would make me feel more graceful," she said at the dinner table, surprising me with the modest hope behind the droll tone. I was concerned for her as I would have been for a daughter and I always remembered, afterwards, to say Margaret. But Hugh did not bother, he said Marg.

"Margaret has quite nice legs. She should wear her skirts shorter."

"Too muscular. Too athletic."

"She should grow her hair."

"She has got hair growing. On her face."

"What a mean thing to say."

"I didn't pass judgment on it, I stated a fact."

It is a fact. Margaret has a soft down growing in front of her ears, at the corners of her mouth. She has the face of a fair, freckled, twelve-year-old boy. Alert, intelligent, bony in a delicate way, often embarrassed. There is something very attractive about Margaret, I would often say, and Hugh would say yes, she was just the sort of woman about whom other women would say there was something very attractive. And why did they say that? he asked. Because she was no threat.

No threat.

Why is it a surprise to find that people other than ourselves are able to tell lies?

We entertained the young teachers. Young men in jeans, young girls in jeans too, or tiny leather skirts. Longhaired, soft-spoken, passive but critical. Teachers have changed. Margaret wore her knee-length rose wool, sat on a hassock for which her legs were too long, helped with the coffee, did not say twenty words all evening. I was in one of my long, peacock dresses, I tried for rapport. I was not above congratulating myself on my flexibility, my *au-courant*-ness, yes, my un-middle-aged style. I was flaunting myself in front of somebody. Margaret? Hugh? Hugh's real pleasure came from Margaret, when everybody had gone.

"The trouble is I just don't know if I *relate.* I don't know if I relate to all this interpersonal re*lat*ing. I mean, sometimes I think all I am is head tripping—"

I laughed at her too, I was proud of her in the perverse way a parent will be proud of a demure child who imitates self-important guests after they have gone home. But it was between Hugh and Margaret, really, that such bracing airs of boundless skepticism blew. He loved her for her wit, her cynicism, her deceptions. Less than lovable these seem to me now. They are both shy, Hugh and Margaret, they are socially awkward, easily embarrassed. But cold underneath, you may be sure, colder than us easy flirts with our charms and conquests. They do not reveal themselves. They will never admit to anything, never have to talk about anything, no, I could claw their skin and it would be my own fingers that would bleed. I could scream at them till my throat bursts and never alter their self-possession, change the look of their sly averted faces. Both blond, both easy blushers, both cold mockers.

They have contempt for me.

That is rubbish of course. Nothing for me. All for each other. *Love.*

I am coming back from visiting relatives in various parts of the country. These are people to whom I feel bound by irritable, almost inexpressible, bonds of sympathy, and whose deaths I dread nearly as much as I do my own. But I cannot tell them anything and they cannot do anything for me. They took me fishing and out to dinner and to see the view from high buildings, what else could they do? They never want to hear bad news from me. They value me for my high spirits and my good looks and my modest but tangible success—I have translated a collection of short stories and some children's books from French into English, they can go into libraries and find my name on the book jackets—and the older and unluckier among them, particularly, feel that I have an obligation to bring them these things. My luck and happiness is one of the few indications they have now that life is not entirely a downhill slide.

So much for kin, so much for visiting.

Suppose I come back to the house and they are both there, I come in and find them in bed, just as in the Dear Abby letters in the paper (at which I do not intend to laugh again)? I go to the closet and take out my remaining clothes, I begin to pack, I talk diplomatically to the bed.

"Would you like a cup of coffee, I imagine you're awfully tired?"

To make them laugh. To make them laugh as if they were reaching out their arms to me. Inviting me to sit on the bed.

On the other hand, perhaps I go into the bedroom and without a word pick up everything I can find—a vase, a bottle of lotion, a picture off the wall, shoes, clothes, Hugh's tape recorder—and hurl these things at the bed, the window, the walls; then grab and tear the bedclothes and kick the mattress and scream and slap their faces and beat their bare bodies with the hairbrush. As the wife did in *God's Little Acre,* a book I read aloud to Hugh, with a comic accent, during a long dusty car trip across the prairies.

We may have told her that. Many anecdotes, of our courtship and even our honeymoon, were trotted out for her. Showing off. I was. What Hugh was doing I have no way of knowing.

A howl comes out, out of me, amazing protest.

I put my arm across my open mouth and to stop the pain I bite it, I bite my arm, and then I get up and lower the little sink and wash my face at it, and put on blusher and comb my hair, and smooth my eyebrows and go out.

The cars in the train are named after explorers, or mountains or lakes. I often traveled by train when the children were small, and Hugh and I were poor, because the train allowed children under six to ride free. I remember the names written on the heavy doors, and how I used to have to push the doors and hold them open and urge the scrambling unsteady children through. I was always nervous between cars, as if the children could fall off somehow, though I knew they couldn't. I had to sleep close beside them at night and sit with them climbing around me in the daytime; my body felt bruised by their knees and elbows and feet. I did think then that it would be lovely to be a woman traveling alone, able to sit after a meal drinking coffee and looking out the window, able to go to the club car and have a drink. Now one of my daughters is hitchhiking in Europe and the other is a counselor at a camp for handicapped children, and all that time of care and confusion that seemed as if it would never end seems as if it never was.

Somehow without my noticing it we have got into the mountains. I ask for a gin and tonic. The glass catches the sunlight, reflecting a circle of light on the white mat. This makes the drink seem pure and restorative to me, like mountain water. I drink thirstily.

From the club car a little staircase goes up to the dome, where people have been sitting no doubt since Calgary, waiting for the mountains. Latecomers hoping for seats climb part way up the stairs, crane their necks, come down disgruntled.

"Them that's up there's going to stay for a week," says a fat woman in a turban, turning around to address a procession of what may be grandchildren. Her bulk fills the whole stairway. Many of us smile, as if the size and loudness and innocent importance of this old woman were being offered to us, as encouragement.

A man sitting by himself, further down the car with his back to the window, looks at me, smiling. His face reminds me of the face of some movie star of a past era. Outdated good looks, a willed and conscious, yet easily defeated, charm. Dana Andrews. Somebody like that. I have an unpleasant impression of mustard-colored clothes.

He does not come and sit beside me, but keeps looking at me from time to time. When I get up and leave the car I feel him watching. I wonder if he will follow me. What if he does? I haven't time for him, not now, I can't spare him attention. I used to be ready for almost any man. When I was in my teens, and later too, when I was a young wife. Any man looking at me in a crowd, any teacher letting his eyes pause on me in a classroom, a stranger at a party, might be transformed, some time when I was alone, into the lover I was always searching for—somebody passionate, intelligent, brutal, kind—and made to play opposite me in those simple, satisfactory, explosive scenes everybody knows about. Later on, a few years married, I took steps to solidify fantasies. At parties, with my push-up brassiere, my tousled Italian cut, my black dress with the shoestring straps, I kept on the lookout for some man to fall in love with me, involve me in a volcanic affair. That did happen, more or less. You see it is not so simple, not so plain a case as my grieving now, my sure sense of betrayal, would lead anybody to believe. No. Men have left marks on me which I did not have to worry about hiding from Hugh, since there are parts of my body at which he has never looked. I have lied as well as I have been lied to. Men have expressed ravenous appreciation of my nipples and my appendix scar and the moles on my back and have also said to me, as it is proper for them to do, "Now don't make too big a thing of this," and even, "I really do love my wife." After a while I gave up on this sort of thing and went secretly to see a psychiatrist who led me to understand that I had been trying to get Hugh's attention. He suggested I get it instead by kindness, artfulness, and sexiness around the house. I was not able to argue with him, nor could I share his optimism. He seemed to me to have a poor grasp on Hugh's character, assuming that certain refusals were simply the result of not having been properly asked. To me they seemed basic, absolute. I could not imagine what tactics could alter them. But he was shrewd enough. He said he assumed I wanted to stay with my husband. He was right; I could not think, I could not bear to think, of an alternative.

The train stops at Field, just inside the British Columbia border. I get off and walk beside the tracks, in a hot wind.

"Nice to get off the train for a bit, isn't it?"

I almost fail to recognize him. He is short, as I believe those handsome movie stars often were, too. His clothes really are mustard-colored. That is, the jacket and pants are; his open shirt is red, his shoes burgundy. He has the voice of somebody whose dealings bring him into daily and dependent contact with the public.

"I hope you don't mind me asking. Are you a Leo?"

"No."

"I asked you because I'm an Aries. An Aries can usually recognize a Leo. Those signs are sympathetic ones to each other."

"I'm sorry?"

"I thought you looked like you would be an interesting person to talk to."

I go and shut myself into my roomette and read my magazine, down to the ads for liquor and men's shoes. But I feel sorry. Probably he meant nothing more than he said. I am an interesting person to talk to. The reason is that I will listen to anything. It may be because of those articles in magazines I used to read as a teenager (when any title with the word popularity in it could both chill and compel me), urging the development of this receptive social art. I don't mean to do it. But face to face with anyone who has a conviction, a delusion—which most people have—or only a long procession of dim experiences to share, I feel something like amazement, enough to paralyze me. You ought to get up and walk away, Hugh says, that's what I would do.

"Asking you were you a Leo, that was just for something to say. What I wanted to ask you was different but I didn't know how to put it. As soon as I saw you I knew I'd seen you before."

"Oh, I don't think so. I don't think you have."

"I believe that we lead more than one life."

Diverse experiences, many lives in one, is that what he means? Perhaps he is about to justify unfaithfulness to his wife, if he has a wife.

"I believe it. I have been born before and I have died before. It's true."

You see? I say to Hugh, already starting a story for him, about this man, in my mind. *They always find me.*

"Did you ever hear of the Rosicrucians?"

"Are they the ones who advertise about the mastery of life?"

Irony may be wasted but he can detect flippancy. The boring reproachfulness of the convert hardens his tone.

"Six years ago I saw one of those ads. I was in a bad way. My marriage had broken up. I was drinking more than was good for me. But that wasn't all the trouble. You know? That wasn't the real trouble. I just used to sit and think, why am I here anyway. Like religion—I'd given all that up. I couldn't tell if there was such a thing as a soul. But if not, what the hell? You know what I mean?

"Then I wrote in and got some of their literature and started going to their meetings. First time I went, I was scared it was going to be a bunch of nuts. I didn't know what to expect, you know? What a shock I got when I saw the kind of people there. Influential people. Wealthy people. Professional people. All cultured and educated top-drawer people. This is not crackpot stuff. It is known, scientifically proven."

I don't dispute.

"One hundred and forty-four years. That is the span from the start of one life to the next. So if you or I dies at, say, seventy, that's what—seventy-four years, seventy-four years to the start of the next life when our soul is born again."

"Do you remember?"

"From the one life to the next, you mean? Well, you know yourself, the ordinary person doesn't remember a thing. But once your mind is opened up, once you know what is going on, why, then you start to remember. Only one life I myself know about for sure. In Spain and in Mexico. I was one of the conquistadors. You know the conquistadors?"

"Yes."

"A funny thing. I always knew I could ride horseback. I never did, you know, city kid, we never had any money. Never was on a horse. Just the same I knew. Then at a meeting couple of years ago, Rosicrucian conference in the Hotel Vancouver, a fellow came up to me, older man, he was from California, and he says, *You were there. You were one of them,* he says. I didn't know what he was talking about. *In Spain,* he says. *We were together.* He said I was one of the ones that went out to Mexico and he was one of the ones that stayed behind. He knew my face. And you want to know the strangest thing of all? Just as he was bending over to speak to me, I had got the impression that he was wearing a hat. Which he wasn't. You know the plumed kind of hat. And I got the impression his hair was dark and long, instead of gray and short. All before he ever said a word of this to me. Isn't that a remarkable thing?"

Yes. A remarkable thing. But I have heard things before. I have heard from people who regularly see astral bodies floating around just under the ceiling, people who rule all their days by astrology, who have changed their names and moved to new addresses so that the numerical values of the new letters will bless them. These are the ideas people live with in this world. And I can see why.

"What do you want to bet you were there too?"

"In Spain?"

"In Spain. I thought as soon as I saw you. You were a Spanish lady. You probably stayed behind, too. That explains what I see. When I look at you—and I don't mean any offense, you're a very attractive woman—I see you younger than you are now. That is probably because when I left you behind in Spain you were only twenty, twenty-one years old. And I never saw you again in that life. You don't mind me saying that?"

"No. No, it's very pleasant, really, to be seen like that."

"I always knew, you know, there has to be something more to life. I'm not a materialistic person. Not by nature. That's why I'm not much of a success. I'm a real estate salesman. But I guess I don't give it the attention you've got to give it, if you want to be a success. It doesn't matter. I've got nobody but myself."

Me too. I've got nobody but myself. And can't think what to do. I can't think what to do with this man except to make him into a story for Hugh, a curiosity, a joke for Hugh. Hugh wants life seen that way, he cherishes a dry tone. Bare feelings he must pass over, like bare flesh.

"Do you love me, do you love Margaret, do you love us both?"

"I don't know."

He was reading a magazine. He reads whenever I speak to him. He said those words in a bored, exhausted, barely audible voice. Blood from a stone.

"Will I divorce you, do you want to marry her?"

"I don't know."

Margaret approached on the subject managed to turn the conversation to some ceramic mugs she had just bought us, as a present, and to hope that I would not throw them out, in my rage, because she, Margaret, would find them useful should she ever move in. Hugh smiled to hear that, he was grateful. If we make jokes we can all survive. I wonder.

The happiest moment in our marriage I have no trouble deciding on. It was in Northern Michigan, on a trip when the children were small. A shoddy carnival, under gray skies. They rode on a miniature train. We wandered off together and stopped in front of a cage with a chicken in it. A sign said that this chicken could play the piano. I said that I wanted to hear it play the piano, and Hugh dropped a dime. What happened was that when the dime dropped, a trap door opened, a kernel of corn descended on the keys of the toy piano, and the chicken, pecking at the corn, produced a tinny note. I was shocked and called it a fraud; for some reason I had believed the sign, I had believed that the chicken would actually *play the piano.* But it was Hugh's act, his dropping the dime, such uncharacteristic frivolity, that seemed so amazing, an avowal of love, more than anything he did or said at any other time, any high point of need or satisfaction. That act was like something startling and temporary—a very small bird, say, with rare colors—sitting close by, in a corner of your vision, that you dare not look at openly. In that moment our kindness to each other was quite unclouded, not tactical, our struggles seemed unreal. A gate had opened, very likely. But we did not get past.

The unhappiest moment I could never tell you. All our fights blend into each other and are in fact re-enactments of the same fight, in which we punish each other—I with words, Hugh with silence—for being each other. We never needed any more than that.

He is the one person I would not mind seeing suffer. I would not mind seeing him drawn out, beads of pain on his face, so that I could say, *Now you know, don't you, now you see.* Yes. In his extremest pain I would show him my little, satisfied, withdrawing smile. I would show it.

"When I came to understand about this it was like I had been given a fresh start."

People believe in fresh starts, nowadays. Right up to the end of their lives. It has to be allowed. To start again with a new person, your old selves known only to yourself; nobody can stop anyone from doing that. Generous people throw the doors open and provide blessings. Why not? It will happen anyway.

The train is beyond Revelstoke, in the gradually diminishing mountains. The coffee car is empty and has been empty for some time, except for me and the Rosicrucian. The waiters have cleaned up.

"I must go back."

He does not try to stop me.

"It's been a great pleasure talking to you and I hope you don't think I'm crazy."

"No. No, I don't."

He takes several pamphlets from his inside pocket. "You might want to look at these if you find the time."

I thank him.

He rises, he even bows to me slightly, with a Spanish dignity.

I walked into the Vancouver station alone, carrying my suitcase. The Rosicrucian has disappeared somewhere, he has vanished as if I had invented him. Perhaps he did not come as far as Vancouver, perhaps he got off at one of the Fraser Valley towns, in the chilly early morning.

Nobody to meet me, nobody knew I was coming. Part of the interior of the station appears to be boarded up, closed off. Even now, one of the two times in the day when there is sure to be some activity in it, this place looks cavernous, deserted.

Twenty-one years ago Hugh met me here, at this time in the morning. A noisy crowded place then. I had come west to marry him. He was carrying flowers which he dropped when he saw me. Less self-possessed in those days, though not more communicative. Red-faced, comically severe-looking, full of emotion which he bore staunchly, like a private affliction. When I touched him, he would never loosen. I could feel the stiff cords in his neck. He would shut his eyes and proceed, by himself. He may have foreseen things; the embroidered dresses, the enthusiasms, the infidelities. And I was not often ready to be kind. Annoyed to see the flowers drop, wishing to be greeted in other than comic-book style, dismayed to face his innocence which seemed even greater than my own, I did not mind letting him see a corner of my dissatisfaction. There are layers on layers in this marriage, mistakes in timing, wrongs on wrongs, nobody could get to the bottom of it.

But we went straight to each other; we grabbed hold and hung on. We crushed the retrieved unappreciated flowers, we clung like people surfacing, miraculously rescued. And not for the last time. That could happen again; it could happen again and again. And it would always be the same mistake.

Aooh.

A cry fills the railway station, a real cry, coming from outside myself. I can see that other people have stopped, have heard it too. The cry is like that of an invader, full of terrible grievances. People look toward the open doors, toward Hastings Street, as if they expect vengeance to come rushing in on them. But now it can be seen that the cry comes from one old man, from an old man who has been sitting with other old men on a bench at one end of the station. There used to be several benches; now there is just one, with old men sitting on it, no more noticed than old newspapers. The old man has risen to his feet to let out this cry, which is more a cry of rage, of conscious rage and terrorization, than a cry of pain. As the cry fades out he half turns, staggers, tries to hang on to the air with fully raised arms and open fingers, falls, and lies on the floor, twitching. The other old men sitting on the bench do not bend over to help him. Not one of them has risen, in fact they hardly look at him, but continue reading the papers or staring at their feet. The twitching stops.

He is dead, I know it. A man in a dark suit, some manager or official, comes out to inspect him. Some people continue with their baggage as if not a thing has happened. They do not look in that direction. Others like me approach the place where the old man is lying, and then stop; approach and stop, as if he were giving out some dangerous kind of ray.

"Must've been his heart."

"Stroke."

"Is he gone?"

"Sure. See the guy putting aside his coat?"

The official stands now in his shirtsleeves. His jacket will have to go to the cleaners. I turn away with difficulty, I walk toward the station entrance. It seems as if I should not leave, as if the cry of the man dying, now dead, is still demanding something of me, but I cannot think what it is. By that cry Hugh, and Margaret, and the Rosicrucian, and I, everybody alive, is pushed back. What we say and feel no longer rings true, it is slightly beside the point. As if we were all wound up a long time ago and were spinning out of control, whirring, making noises, but at a touch could stop, and see each other for the first time, harmless and still. This is a message; I really believe it is; but I don't see how I can deliver it.

Access to the Children

WILLIAM TREVOR

Malcolmson, a fair, tallish man in a green tweed suit that required pressing, banged the driver's door of his ten-year-old Volvo and walked quickly away from the car, jangling the keys. He entered a block of flats that was titled—gold engraved letters on a granite slab—The Quadrant.

It was a Sunday afternoon in late October. Yellow-brown leaves patterned grass that was not for walking on. Some scurried on the steps that led to the building's glass entrance doors. Rain was about, Malcolmson considered.

At three o'clock precisely he rang the bell of his ex-wife's flat on the third floor. In response he heard at once the voices of his children and the sound of their running in the hall. "Hullo," he said when one of them, Deirdre, opened the door. "Ready?"

They went with him, two little girls, Deirdre seven and Susie five. In the lift they told him that a foreign person, the day before, had been trapped in the lift from eleven o'clock in the morning until teatime. Food and cups of tea had been poked through a grating to this person, a Japanese businessman who occupied a flat at the top of the block. "He didn't get the hang of an English lift," said Deirdre. "He could have died there," said Susie.

In the Volvo he asked them if they'd like to go to the Zoo and they shook their heads firmly. On the last two Sundays he'd taken them to the Zoo, Susie reminded him in her specially polite, very quiet voice: you got tired of the Zoo, walking round and round, looking at all the same animals. She smiled at him to show she wasn't being ungrateful. She suggested that in a little while, after a month or so, they could go to the Zoo again, because there might be some new animals. Deirdre said that there wouldn't be, not after a month or so: why should there be? "Some old animals might have died," said Susie.

Malcolmson drove down the Edgware Road, with Hyde Park in mind.

"What have you done?" he asked.

"Only school," said Susie.

"And the news cinema," said Deirdre. "Mummy took us to a news cinema. We saw a film about how they make wire."

"A man kept talking to Mummy. He said she had nice hair."

"The usherette told him to be quiet. He bought us ice cream, but Mummy said we couldn't accept them."

"He wanted to take Mummy to a dance."

"We had to move to other seats."

"What else have you done?"

"Only school," said Susie. "A boy was sick on Miss Bawden's desk."

"After school stew."

"It's raining," said Susie.

He turned the windscreen-wipers on. He wondered if he should simply bring the girls to his flat and spend the afternoon watching television. He tried to remember what the Sunday film was. There often was something suitable for children on Sunday afternoons, old films with Deanna Durbin or Nelson Eddy and Jeanette MacDonald.

"Where're we going?" Susie asked.

"Where d'you want to go?"

"*A Hundred and One Dalmatians.*"

"Oh, please," said Susie.

"But we've seen it. We've seen it five times."

"Please, Daddy."

He stopped the Volvo and bought a *What's On.* While he leafed through it they sat quietly, willing him to discover a cinema, anywhere in London, that was showing the film. He shook his head and started the Volvo again.

"Nothing else?" Deirdre asked.

"Nothing suitable."

At Speakers' Corner they listened to a Jehovah's Witness and then to a woman talking about vivisection. "How horrid," said Deirdre. "Is that true, Daddy?" He made a face. "I suppose so," he said.

In the drizzle they played a game among the trees, hiding and chasing one another. Once when they'd been playing this game a woman had brought a policeman up to him. She'd seen him approaching the girls, she said; the girls had been playing alone and he'd joined in. "He's our daddy," Susie had said, but the woman had still argued, claiming that he'd given them sweets so that they'd say that. "Look at him," the woman had insultingly said. "He needs a shave." Then she'd gone away, and the policeman had apologized.

"The boy who was sick was Nicholas Barnet," Susie said. "I think he could have died."

A year and a half ago Malcolmson's wife, Elizabeth, had said he must choose between her and Diana. For weeks they had talked about it; she knowing that he was in love with Diana and was having some kind of an affair with her, he caught between the two of them, attempting the impossible in his effort not to hurt anyone. She had given him a chance to get over Diana, as she put it, but she couldn't go on forever giving him a chance, no woman could. In the end, after the shock and the tears and the period of reasonableness, she became bitter. He didn't blame her: they'd been in the middle of a happy marriage, nothing was wrong, nothing was lacking.

He'd met Diana on a train; he'd sat with her, talking for a long time, and after that his marriage didn't seem the same. In her bitterness Elizabeth said he was stupidly infatuated: he was behaving like a murderer: there was neither dignity nor humanity left in him. Diana she described as a flat-chested American nymphomaniac and predator, the worst type of woman in the world. She was beautiful herself, more beautiful than Diana, more gracious, warmer, and funnier: there was a sting of truth in what she said; he couldn't understand himself. In the very end, after they'd been morosely drinking gin and lime juice, she'd suddenly shouted at him that he'd better pack his bags. He sat unhappily, gazing at the green bottle of Gordon's gin on the carpet between his chair and hers. She screamed; tears poured in a torrent from her eyes. "For God's sake go away!" she cried, on her feet, turning away from him. She shook her head in a wild gesture, causing her long fair hair to move like a horse's mane. Her hands, clenched into fists, beat at his cheeks, making bruises that Diana afterward tended.

For months after that he saw neither Elizabeth nor his children. He tried not to think about them. He and Diana took a flat in Barnes, near the river, and in time he became used to the absence of the children's noise in the mornings, and to Diana's cooking and her quick efficiency in little things, and the way she always remembered to pass on telephone messages, which was something that Elizabeth had always forgotten to do.

Then one day, a week or so before the divorce was due, Diana said she didn't think there was anything left between them. It hadn't worked, she said; nothing was quite right. Amazed and bewildered, he argued with her. He frowned at her, his eyes screwed up as though he couldn't properly see her. She was very poised, in a black dress, with a necklace at her throat, her hair pulled smooth and neatly tied. She'd met a man called Abbotforth, she said, and she went on talking about that, still standing.

"We could go to the Natural History Museum," Deirdre said. "Would you like to, Susie?"

"Certainly not," said Susie.

They were sitting on a bench, watching a bird that Susie said was a yellow-hammer. Deirdre disagreed: at this time of year, she said, there were no yellow-hammers in England, she'd read it in a book. "It's a little baby yellow-hammer," said Susie. "Miss Bawden said you see lots of them."

The bird flew away. A man in a raincoat was approaching them, singing quietly. They began to giggle. *"Sure, maybe some day I'll go back to Ireland,"* sang the man, *"if it's only at the closing of my day."* He stopped, noticing that they were watching him.

"Were you ever in Ireland?" he asked. The girls, still giggling, shook their heads. "It's a great place," said the man. He took a bottle of VP wine from his raincoat pocket and drank from it.

"Would you care for a swig, sir?" he said to Malcolmson, and Malcolmson thanked him and said he wouldn't. "It would do the little misses no harm," suggested the man. "It's good, pure stuff." Malcolmson shook his head. "I was born in County Clare," said the man, "in 1928, the year of the Big Strike." The girls, red in the face from containing their laughter, poked at one another with their elbows. "Aren't they the great little misses?" said the man. "Aren't they the fine credit to you, sir?"

In the Volvo on the way to Barnes they kept repeating that he was the funniest man they'd ever met. He was nicer than the man in the news cinema, Susie said. He was quite like him, though, Deirdre maintained: he was looking for company in just the same way, you could see it in his eyes. "He was staggering," Susie said. "I thought he was going to die."

Before the divorce he had telephoned Elizabeth, telling her that Diana had gone. She hadn't said anything, and she'd put the receiver down before he could say anything else. Then the divorce came through and the arrangement was that the children should remain with Elizabeth and that he should have reasonable access to them. It was an extraordinary expression, he considered: reasonable access.

The Sunday afternoons had begun then, the ringing of a doorbell that had once been his own doorbell, the children in the hall, the lift, the Volvo, tea in the flat where he and Diana had lived and where now he lived on his own. Sometimes, when he was collecting them, Elizabeth spoke to him, saying in a matter-of-fact way that Susie had a cold and should not be outside too much, or that Deirdre was being bad about practicing her clarinet and would he please speak to her. He loved Elizabeth again; he said to himself that he had never not loved her; he wanted to say to her that she'd been right about Diana. But he didn't say anything, knowing that wounds had to heal.

Every week he longed more for Sunday to arrive. Occasionally he invented reasons for talking to her at the door of the flat, *after* the children had gone in. He asked questions about their progress at school, he wondered if there were ways in which he could help. It seemed unfair, he said, that she should have to bring them up single-handed like this; he made her promise to telephone him if a difficulty arose; and if ever she wanted to go out in the evenings and couldn't find a baby-sitter, he'd willingly drive over. He always hoped that if he talked for long enough the girls would become so noisy in their room that she'd be forced to ask him in so that she could quieten them, but the ploy never worked.

In the lift on the way down every Sunday evening he thought she was more beautiful than any woman he'd ever seen, and he thought it was amazing that once she should have been his wife and should have borne him children, that once they had lain together and loved, and that he had let her go. Three weeks ago she had smiled at him in a way that was like the old way. He'd been sure of it, positive, in the lift on the way down.

He drove over Hammersmith Bridge, along Castelnau and into Barnes High Street. No one was about on the pavements; buses crept sluggishly through the damp afternoon.

"Miss Bawden's got a black boyfriend," Susie said, "called Eric Mantilla."

"You should see Miss Bawden," murmured Deirdre. "She hasn't any breasts."

"She has lovely breasts," shouted Susie, "and lovely jumpers and lovely skirts. She has a pair of earrings that once belonged to an Egyptian empress."

"Flat as a pancake," said Deirdre.

After Diana had gone he'd found it hard to concentrate. The managing director of the firm where he worked, a man with a stout red face called Sir Gerald Travers, had been sympathetic. He'd told him not to worry. Personal troubles, Sir Gerald had said, must naturally affect professional life; no one would be human if that didn't happen. But six months later, to Malcolmson's surprise, Sir Gerald had suddenly suggested to him that perhaps it would be better if he made a move. "It's often so," Sir Gerald had said, a soft smile gleaming between chubby cheeks. "Professional life can be affected by the private side of things. You understand me, Malcolmson?" They valued him immensely, Sir Gerald said, and they'd be generous when the moment of departure came. A change was a tonic; Sir Gerald advised a little jaunt somewhere.

In reply to all that, Malcolmson said that the upset in his private life was now over; nor did he feel, he added, in need of recuperation. "You'll easily find another berth," Sir Gerald Travers replied, with a wide, confident smile. "I think it would be better."

Malcolmson had sought about for another job, but had not been immediately successful: there was a recession, people said. Soon it would be better, they added, and because of Sir Gerald's promised generosity Malcolmson found himself in a position to wait until things seemed brighter. It was always better, in any case, not to seem in a hurry.

He spent the mornings in the Red Lion, in Barnes, playing dominoes with an old-age pensioner, and when the pensioner didn't turn up owing to bronchial trouble Malcolmson would borrow a newspaper from the landlord. He slept in the afternoons and returned to the Red Lion later. Occasionally when he'd had a few drinks he'd find himself thinking about his children and their mother. He always found it pleasant then, thinking of them with a couple of drinks inside him.

"It's *The Last of the Mohicans,*" said Deirdre in the flat, and he guessed that she must have looked at the *Radio Times* earlier in the day. She'd known they'd end up like that, watching television. Were they bored on Sundays? he often wondered.

"Can't we have *The Golden Shot*?" demanded Susie, and Deirdre pointed out that it wasn't on yet. He left them watching Randolph Scott and Binnie Barnes, and went to prepare their tea in the kitchen.

On Saturdays he bought meringues and brandy-snaps in Frith's Patisserie. The elderly assistant smiled at him in a way that made him wonder if she knew what he wanted them for; it occurred to him once that she felt sorry for him. On Sunday mornings, listening to the omnibus edition of *The Archers,* he made Marmite sandwiches with brown bread and tomato sandwiches with white. They loved sandwiches, which was something he remembered from the past. He remembered parties, Deirdre's friends sitting around a table, small and silent, eating crisps and cheese puffs and leaving all the cake.

When *The Last of the Mohicans* came to an end they watched *Going for a Song* for five minutes before changing the channel for *The Golden Shot.* Then Deirdre turned the television off and they went to the kitchen to have tea. "Wash your hands," said Susie, and he heard her add that if a germ got into your food you could easily die. "She kept referring to death," he would say to Elizabeth when he left them back. "D'you think she's worried about anything?" He imagined Elizabeth giving the smile she had given three weeks ago and then saying he'd better come in to discuss the matter.

"Goody," said Susie, sitting down.

"I'd like to marry a man like that man in the park," said Deirdre. "It'd be much more interesting, married to a bloke like that."

"He'd be always drunk."

"He wasn't drunk, Susie. That's not being drunk."

"He was drinking out of a bottle—"

"He was putting on a bit of flash, drinking out of a bottle and singing his little song. No harm in that, Susie."

"I'd like to be married to Daddy."

"You couldn't be married to Daddy."

"Well, Richard then."

"Ribena, Daddy. Please."

He poured drops of Ribena into two mugs and filled them up with warm water. He had a definite feeling that today she'd ask him in, both of them pretending a worry over Susie's obsession with death. They'd sit together while the children splashed about in the bathroom; she'd offer him gin and lime juice, their favorite drink, a drink known as a Gimlet, as once he'd told her. They'd drink it out of the green glasses they'd bought, years ago, in Italy. The girls would dry themselves and come to say good night. They'd go to bed. He might tell them a story, or she would. "Stay to supper," she would say, and while she made risotto he would go to her and kiss her hair.

"I like his eyes," said Susie. "One's higher than another."

"It couldn't be."

"It is."

"He couldn't see, Susie, if his eyes were like that. Everyone's eyes are—"

"He isn't always drunk like the man in the park."

"Who?" he asked.

"Richard," they said together, and Susie added: "Irishmen are always drunk."

"Daddy's an Irishman and Daddy's not always—"

"Who's Richard?"

"He's Susie's boyfriend."

"I don't mind," said Susie. "I like him."

"If he's there tonight, Susie, you're not to climb all over him."

He left the kitchen and in the sitting room he poured himself some whiskey. He sat with the glass cold between his hands, staring at the gray television screen. "Sure, maybe some day I'll go back to Ireland," Deirdre sang in the kitchen, and Susie laughed shrilly.

He imagined a dark-haired man, a cheerful man, intelligent and subtle, a man who came often to the flat, whom his children knew well and were already fond of. He imagined him as he had imagined himself ten minutes before, sitting with Elizabeth, drinking Gimlets from the green Italian glasses. "Say good night to Richard," Elizabeth would say, and the girls would go to him and kiss him good night.

"Who's Richard?" he asked, standing in the kitchen doorway.

"A friend," said Deirdre, "of Mummy's."

"A nice friend?"

"Oh, yes."

"I love him," said Susie.

He returned to the sitting room and quickly poured himself more whiskey. Both of his hands were shaking. He drank quickly, and then poured and drank some more. On the pale carpet, close to the television set, there was a stain where Diana had spilt a cup of coffee. He hated now this memory of her, he hated her voice when it came back to him, and the memory of her body and her mind. And yet once he had been rendered lunatic with the passion of his love for her. He had loved her more than Elizabeth, and in his madness he had spoilt everything.

"Wash your hands," said Susie, close to him. He hadn't heard them come into the room. He asked them, mechanically, if they'd had enough to eat. "She hasn't washed her hands," Susie said. "I washed mine in the sink."

He turned the television on. It was the girl ventriloquist Shari Lewis, with Lamb Chop and Charley Horse.

Well, he thought under the influence of the whiskey, he had had his fling. He had played the pins with a flat-chested American nymphomaniac and predator, and he had lost all there was to lose. Now it was Elizabeth's turn: why shouldn't she have, for a time, the dark-haired Richard who took another man's children on to his knee and kissed them good night? Wasn't it better that the score should be even before they all came together again?

He sat on the floor with his daughters on either side of him, his arms about them. In front of him was his glass of whiskey. They laughed at Lamb Chop and Charley Horse, and when the program came to an end and the news came on he didn't want to let his daughters go. An electric fire glowed cozily. Wind blew the rain against the windows, the autumn evening was dark already.

He turned the television off. He finished the whiskey in his glass and poured some more. "Shall I tell you," he said, "about when Mummy and I were married?"

They listened while he did so. He told them about meeting Elizabeth in the first place, at somebody else's wedding, and of the days they had spent walking about together, and about the wet, cold afternoon on which they'd been married.

"February the 24th," Deirdre said.

"Yes."

"I'm going to be married in summertime," Susie said, "when the roses are out."

His birthday and Elizabeth's were on the same day, April 21st. He reminded the girls of that; he told them of the time he and Elizabeth had discovered they shared the date, a date shared also with Hitler and the Queen. They listened quite politely, but somehow didn't seem much interested.

They watched *What's in a Game?* He drank a little more. He wouldn't be able to drive them back. He'd pretend he couldn't start the Volvo and then he'd telephone for a taxi. It had happened once before that in a depression he'd begun to drink when they were with him on a Sunday afternoon. They'd been to Madame Tussaud's and the Planetarium, which Susie had said frightened her. In the flat, just as this time, while they were eating their sandwiches, he'd been overcome with the longing that they should all be together again. He'd begun to drink and in the end, while they watched television, he'd drunk quite a lot. When the time came to go he'd said that he couldn't find the keys of the Volvo and that they'd have to have a taxi. He'd spent five minutes brushing his teeth so that Elizabeth wouldn't smell the alcohol when she opened the door. He'd smiled at her with his well-brushed teeth but she, not then being over her bitterness, hadn't smiled back.

The girls put their coats on. Deirdre drank some Ribena; he had another small tot of whiskey. And then, as they were leaving the flat, he suddenly felt he couldn't go through the farce of walking to the Volvo, putting the girls into it and then pretending he couldn't start it. "I'm tired," he said instead. "Let's have a taxi."

They watched the Penrhyn Male Voice Choir in *Songs of Praise* while they waited for it to arrive. He poured himself another drink, drank it slowly, and then went to the bathroom to brush his teeth. He remembered the time Deirdre had been born, in a maternity home in the country because they'd lived in the country then. Elizabeth had been concerned because she'd thought one of Deirdre's fingers was bent and had kept showing it to nurses who said they couldn't see anything the matter. He hadn't been able to see anything the matter either, nor had the doctor. "She'll never be as beautiful as you," he'd said and quite soon after that she'd stopped talking about the finger and had said he was nice to her. Susie had been born at home, very quickly, very easily.

The taxi arrived. "Soon be Christmas," said the taxi man. "You chaps looking forward to Santa Claus?" They giggled because he had called them chaps. "Fifty-six more days," said Susie.

He imagined them on Christmas Day, with the dark-haired Richard explaining the rules of a game he'd bought them. He imagined all four of them sitting down at Christmas dinner, and Richard asking the girls which they liked, the white or the brown of the turkey, and then cutting them small slices. He'd have brought, perhaps, champagne, because he was that kind of person. Deirdre would sip from his glass, not liking the taste. Susie would love it.

He counted in his mind: if Richard had been visiting the flat for, say, six weeks already and assuming that his love affair with Elizabeth had begun two weeks before his first visit, that left another four months to go, allowing the affair ran an average course of six months. It would therefore come to an end at the beginning of March. His own affair with Diana had lasted from April until September. "Oh darling," said Diana, suddenly in his mind, and his own voice replied to her, caressing her with words. He remembered the first time they had made love and the guilt that had hammered at him and the passion there had been between them. He imagined Elizabeth naked in Richard's naked arms, her eyes open, looking at him, her fingers touching the side of his face, her lips slightly smiling. He reached forward and pulled down the glass shutter. "I need cigarettes," he said. "There's a pub in Shepherd's Bush Road, the Laurie Arms."

He drank two large measures of whiskey. He bought cigarettes and lit one, rolling the smoke around in his mouth to disguise the smell of the alcohol. As he returned to the taxi, he slipped on the wet pavement and almost lost his balance. He felt very drunk all of a sudden. Deirdre and Susie were telling the taxi man about the man in Hyde Park.

He was aware that he walked unsteadily when they left the taxi and moved across the forecourt of the block of flats. In the hall, before they got into the lift, he lit another cigarette, rolling the smoke about his mouth. "That poor Japanese man," said Deirdre.

He rang the bell, and when Elizabeth opened the door the girls turned to him and thanked him. He took the cigarette from his mouth and kissed them. Elizabeth was smiling: if only she'd ask him in and give him a drink he wouldn't have to worry about the alcohol on his breath. He swore to himself that she was smiling as she'd smiled three weeks ago. "Can I come in?" he asked, unable to keep the words back.

"In?" The smile was still there. She was looking at him quite closely. He released the smoke from his mouth. He tried to remember what it was he'd planned to say, and then it came to him.

"I'm worried about Susie," he said in a quiet voice. "She talked about death all the time."

"Death?"

"Yes."

"There's someone here actually," she said, stepping back into the hall. "But come in, certainly."

In the sitting room she introduced him to Richard who was, as he'd imagined, a dark-haired man. The sitting room was much the same as it always had been. "Have a drink," Richard offered.

"D'you mind if we talk about Susie?" Elizabeth asked Richard. He said he'd put them to bed if she liked. She nodded. Richard went away.

"Well?"

He stood with the familiar green glass in his hand, gazing at her. He said:

"I haven't had gin and lime juice since—"

"Yes. Look, I shouldn't worry about Susie. Children of that age often say odd things, you know—"

"I don't mind about Richard, Elizabeth, I think it's your due. I worked it out in the taxi. It's the end of October now—"

"My due?"

"Assuming your affair has been going on already for six weeks—"

"You're drunk."

He closed one eye, focusing. He felt his body swaying and he said to himself that he must not fall now, that no matter what his body did his feet must remain firm on the carpet. He sipped from the green glass. She wasn't, he noticed, smiling any more.

"I'm actually not drunk," he said. "I'm actually sober. By the time our birthday comes round, Elizabeth, it'll all be over. On April the 21st we could have family tea."

"What the hell are you talking about?"

"The future, Elizabeth. Of you and me and our children."

"How much have you had to drink?"

"We tried to go to *A Hundred and One Dalmatians*, but it wasn't on anywhere."

"So you drank instead. While the children—"

"We came here in a taxi. They've had their usual tea, they've watched a bit of *The Last of the Mohicans* and a bit of *Going for a Song* and all of *The Golden Shot* and *The Shari Lewis Show* and—"

"You see them for a few hours and you have to go and get drunk—"

"I am not drunk, Elizabeth."

He crossed the room as steadily as he could. He looked aggressively at her. He poured gin and lime juice. He said:

"You have a right to your affair with Richard, I recognize that."

"A *right?*"

"I love you, Elizabeth."

"You loved Diana."

"I have never not loved you. Diana was nothing—nothing, nothing at all."

"She broke our marriage up."

"No."

"We're divorced."

"I love you, Elizabeth."

"Now listen to me—"

"I live from Sunday to Sunday. We're a family, Elizabeth; you and me and them. It's ridiculous, all this. It's ridiculous making Marmite sandwiches with brown bread and tomato sandwiches with white. It's ridiculous buying meringues and going five times to *A Hundred and One Dalmatians* and going up the Post Office Tower until we're sick of the sight of it, and watching drunks in Hyde Park and poking about at the Zoo—"

"You have reasonable access—"

"Reasonable access, my God!" His voice rose. He felt sweat on his forehead. Reasonable access, he shouted, was utterly no good to him; reasonable access was meaningless and stupid; a day would come when they wouldn't want to go with him on Sunday afternoons, when there was nowhere left in London that wasn't an unholy bore. What about reasonable access then?

"Please be quiet."

He sat down in the armchair that he had always sat in. She said:

"You might marry again. And have other children."

"I don't want other children. I have children already. I want us all to live together as we used to—"

"Please listen to me—"

"I get a pain in my stomach in the middle of the night. Then I wake up and can't go back to sleep. The children will grow up and I'll grow old. I couldn't begin a whole new thing all over again: I haven't the courage. Not after Diana. A mistake like that alters everything."

"I'm going to marry Richard."

"Three weeks ago," he said, as though he hadn't heard her, "you smiled at me."

"Smiled?"

"Like you used to, Elizabeth. Before—"

"You made a mistake," she said, softly. "I'm sorry."

"I'm not saying don't go on with your affair with this man. I'm not saying that, because I think in the circumstances it'd be a cheek. D'you understand me, Elizabeth?"

"Yes, I do. And I think you and I can be perfectly good friends. I don't feel sour about it any more: perhaps that's what you saw in my smile."

"Have a six-month affair—"

"I'm in love with Richard."

"That'll all pass into the atmosphere. It'll be nothing at all in a year's time—"

"No."

"I love you, Elizabeth."

They stood facing one another, not close. His body was still swaying. The liquid in his glass moved gently, slopping to the rim and then settling back again. Her eyes were on his face: it was thinner, she was thinking. Her fingers played with the edge of a cushion on the back of the sofa.

"On Saturdays," he said, "I buy the meringues and the brandysnaps in Frith's Patisserie. On Sunday morning I make the sandwiches. Then I cook sausages and potatoes for my lunch, and after that I come over here."

"Yes, yes—"

"I look forward all week to Sunday."

"The children enjoy their outings, too."

"Will you think about it?"

"About what?"

"About all being together again."

"Oh, for heaven's sake!" She turned away from him. "I wish you'd go now," she said.

"Will you come out with me on our birthday?"

"I've told you." Her voice was loud and angry, her cheeks were flushed. "Can't you understand? I'm going to marry Richard. We'll be married within a month, when the girls have had time to get to know him a little better. By Christmas we'll be married."

He shook his head in a way that annoyed her, seeming in his drunkenness to deny the truth of what she was saying. He tried to light a cigarette; matches dropped to the floor at his feet. He left them there.

It enraged her that he was sitting in an armchair in her flat with his eyelids drooping through drink and an unlighted cigarette in his hand and his matches spilt all over the floor. They were his children, but she wasn't his wife: he'd destroyed her as a wife, he'd insulted her, he'd left her to bleed and she had called him a murderer.

"Our birthday," he said, smiling at her as though already she had agreed to join him on that day. "And Hitler's and the Queen's."

"On our birthday if I go out with anyone it'll be Richard."

"Our birthday is beyond the time—"

"For God's sake, there is no beyond the time. I'm in love with another man—"

"No."

"On our birthday," she shouted at him, "on the night of our birthday Richard will make love to me in the bed you slept in for nine years. You have access to the children. You can demand no more."

He bent down and picked up a match. He struck it on the side of the empty box. The cigarette was bent. He lit it with a wobbling flame and dropped the used match on to the carpet. The dark-haired man, he saw, was in the room again. He'd come in, hearing her shouting like that. He was asking her if she was all right. She told him to go away. Her face was hard; bitterness was there again. She said, not looking at him:

"Everything was so happy. We had a happy marriage. For nine years we had a perfectly happy marriage."

"We could—"

"Not ever."

Again he shook his head in disagreement. Cigarette ash fell on to the green tweed of his suit. His eyes were narrowed, watching her, seemingly suspicious.

"We had a happy marriage," she repeated, whispering the words, speaking to herself, still not looking at him. "You met a woman on a train and that was that: you murdered our marriage. You left me to plead, as I am leaving you to now. You have your Sunday access. There is that legality between us. Nothing more."

"Please, Elizabeth—"

"Oh for God's sake, stop." Her rage was all in her face now. Her lips quivered as though in an effort to hold back words that would not be denied. They came from her, more quietly but with greater bitterness. Her eyes roved over the green tweed suit of the man who once had been her husband, over his thin face and his hair that seemed, that day, not to have been brushed.

"You've gone to seed," she said, hating herself for saying that, unable to prevent herself. "You've gone to seed because you've lost your self-respect. I've watched you, week by week. The woman you met on a train took her toll of you and now in your seediness you want to creep back. Don't you know you're not the man I married?"

"Elizabeth—"

"You didn't have cigarette burns all over your clothes. You didn't smell of toothpaste when you should have smelt of drink. You stand there, pathetically, Sunday after Sunday, trying to keep a conversation going. D'you know what I feel?"

"I love—"

"I feel sorry for you."

He shook his head. There was no need to feel sorry for him, he said, remembering suddenly the elderly assistant in Frith's Patisserie and remembering also, for some reason, the woman in Hyde Park who peculiarly had said that he wasn't shaved. He looked down at his clothes and saw the burn marks she had mentioned. "We think it would be better," said the voice of Sir Gerald Travers unexpectedly in his mind.

"I'll make some coffee," said Elizabeth.

She left him. He had been cruel, and then Diana had been cruel, and now Elizabeth was cruel because it was her right and her instinct to be so. He recalled with vividness Diana's face in those first moments on the train, her eyes looking at him, her voice. "You have lost all dignity," Elizabeth had whispered, in the darkness, at night. "I despise you for that." He tried to stand up but found the effort beyond him. He raised the green glass to his lips. His eyes closed and when he opened them again he thought for a drunken moment that he was back in the past, in the middle of his happy marriage. He wiped at his face with a handkerchief.

He saw across the room the bottle of Gordon's gin so nicely matching the green glasses, and the lime juice, a lighter shade of green. He made the journey, his legs striking the arms of chairs. There wasn't much gin in the bottle. He poured it all out; he added lime juice, and drank it.

In the hall he could hear voices, his children's voices in the bathroom, Elizabeth and the man speaking quietly in the kitchen. "Poor wretch," Elizabeth was saying. He left the flat and descended to the ground floor.

The rain was falling heavily. He walked through it, thinking that it was better to go, quietly and without fuss. It would all work out; he knew it; he felt it definitely in his bones. He'd arrive on Sunday, a month or so before their birthday, and something in Elizabeth's face would tell him that the dark-haired man had gone forever, as Diana had gone. By then he'd be established again, with better prospects than the red-faced Sir Gerald Travers had ever offered him. On their birthday they'd both apologize to one another, wiping the slate clean: they'd start again. As he crossed the Edgware Road to the public house in which he always spent an hour or so on Sunday nights, he heard his own voice murmuring that it was understandable that she should have taken it out on him, that she should have tried to hurt him by saying he'd gone to seed. Naturally, she'd say a thing like that; who could blame her after all she'd been through? At night in the flat in Barnes he watched television until the programs closed down. He usually had a few drinks, and as often as not he dropped off to sleep with a cigarette between his fingers: that was how the burns occurred on his clothes.

He nodded to himself as he entered the saloon bar, thinking he'd been wise not to mention any of that to Elizabeth. It would only have annoyed her, having to listen to a lot of stuff about late-night television and cigarettes. Monday, Tuesday, Wednesday, he thought, Thursday, Friday. On Saturday he'd buy the meringues and brandy-snaps, and then it would be Sunday. He'd make the sandwiches listening to *The Archers,* and at three o'clock he'd ring the bell of the flat. He smiled in the saloon bar, thinking of that, seeing in his mind the faces of his children and the beautiful face of their mother. He'd planted an idea in Elizabeth's mind and even though she'd been a bit shirty she'd see when she thought about it that it was what she wanted, too.

He went on drinking gin and lime juice, quietly laughing over being so upset when the children had first mentioned the dark-haired man who took them on to his knee. Gin and lime juice was a Gimlet, he told the barmaid. She smiled at him. He was celebrating, he said, a day that was to come. It was ridiculous, he told her, that a woman casually met on a train should have created havoc, that now, at the end of it all, he should week by week butter bread for Marmite and tomato sandwiches. "D'you understand me?" he drunkenly asked the barmaid. "It's *too* ridiculous to be true—that man will go because none of it makes sense the way it is." The barmaid smiled again and nodded. He bought her a glass of beer, which was something he did every Sunday night. He wept as he paid for it, and touched his cheeks with the tips of his fingers to wipe away the tears. Every Sunday he wept, at the end of the day, after he'd had his access. The barmaid raised her glass, as always she did. They drank to the day that was to come, when the error he had made would be wiped away, when the happy marriage could continue. "Ridiculous," he said. "Of course it is."

Willing

LORRIE MOORE

How can I live my life without committing an
act with a giant scissors?
—JOYCE CAROL OATES,
"An Interior Monologue"

In her last picture, the camera had lingered at the hip, the naked hip, and even though it wasn't her hip, she acquired a reputation for being willing.

"You have the body," studio heads told her over lunch at Chasen's.

She looked away. "Habeas corpus," she said, not smiling.

"Pardon me?" A hip that knew Latin. Christ.

"Nothing," she said. They smiled at her and dropped names. Scorsese, Brando. Work was all playtime to them, playtime with gel in their hair. At times, she felt bad that it *wasn't* her hip. I should have been her hip. A mediocre picture, a picture queasy with pornography: these, she knew, eroticized the unavailable. The doctored and false. The stand-in. Unwittingly, she had participated. Let a hip come between. A false, unavailable, anonymous hip. She herself was true as a goddamn dairy product; available as lunch whenever.

But she was pushing forty.

She began to linger in juice bars. Sit for entire afternoons in places called I Love Juicy or Orange-U-Sweet. She drank juice and, outside, smoked a cigarette now and then. She'd been taken seriously—once—she knew that. Projects were discussed: Nina. Portia. Mother Courage with makeup. Now her hands trembled too much, even drinking juice, *especially* drinking juice, a Vantage wobbling between her fingers like a compass dial. She was sent scripts in which she was supposed to say lines she would never say, not wear clothes she would never not wear. She began to get obscene phone calls, and postcards signed, "Oh yeah, baby." Her boyfriend, a director with a growing reputation for expensive flops, a man who twice a week glowered at her Fancy Sunburst guppy and told it to get a job, became a Catholic and went back to his wife.

"Just when we were working out the bumps and chops and rocks," she said. Then she wept.

"I know," he said. "I know."

And so she left Hollywood. Phoned her agent and apologized. Went home to Chicago, rented a room by the week at the Days Inn, drank sherry, and grew a little plump. She let her life get dull—dull, but with Hostess cakes. There were moments bristling with deadness, when she looked out at her life and went *"What?"* Or worse, feeling interrupted and tired, "Wha—?" It had taken on the shape of a terrible mistake. She hadn't been given the proper tools to make a real life with, she decided, that was it. She'd been given a can of gravy and a hairbrush and told, "There you go." She'd stood there for years, blinking and befuddled, brushing the can with the brush.

Still, she was a minor movie star, once nominated for a major award. Mail came to her indirectly. A notice. A bill. A Thanksgiving card. But there was never a party, a dinner, an opening, an iced tea. One of the problems with people in Chicago, she remembered, was that they were never lonely at the same time. Their sadnesses occurred in isolation, lurched and spazzed, sent them spinning fizzily back into empty, padded corners, disconnected and alone.

She watched cable and ordered in a lot from a pizza place. A life of obscurity and radical calm. She rented a piano and practiced scales. She invested in the stock market. She wrote down her dreams in the morning to locate clues as to what to trade. *Disney,* her dreams said once. *St. Jude's Medical.* She made a little extra money. She got obsessed. The words *cash cow* nestled in the side of her mouth like a cud. She tried to be original—not a good thing with stocks—and she began to lose. When a stock went down, she bought more of it, to catch it on the way back up. She got confused. She took to staring out the window at Lake Michigan, the rippled slate of it like a blackboard gone bad.

"Sidra, *what* are you doing there?" shrieked her friend Tommy long distance over the phone. "Where are you? You're living in some state that borders on North Dakota!" He was a screenwriter in Santa Monica and once, a long time ago and depressed on Ecstasy, they had slept together. He was gay, but they had liked each other very much.

"Maybe I'll get married," she said. She didn't mind Chicago. She thought of it as a cross between London and Queens, with a dash of Cleveland.

"Oh, *please,*" he shrieked again. "What are you *really* doing?"

"Listening to seashore and self-esteem tapes," she said. She blew air into the mouth of the phone.

"Sounds like dust on the needle," he said. "Maybe you should get the squawking crickets tape. Have you *heard* the squawking crickets tape?"

"I got a bad perm today," she said. "When I was only halfway through with the rod part, the building the salon's in had a blackout. There were men drilling out front who'd struck a cable."

"How awful for you," he said. She could hear him tap his fingers. He had made himself the make-believe author of a make-believe book of essays called *One Man's Opinion,* and when he was bored or inspired, he quoted from it. "I was once in rock band called Bad Perm," he said instead.

"Get out." She laughed.

His voice went hushed and worried. "What *are* you *doing* there?" he asked again.

Her room was a corner room where a piano was allowed, it was L-shaped, like a life veering off suddenly to become something else. It had a couch and two maple dressers and was never as neat as she might have wanted. She always had the DO NOT DISTURB sign on when the maids came by, and so things got a little out of hand. Wispy motes of dust and hair the size of small heads bumped around in the corners. Smudge began to darken the moldings and cloud the mirrors. The bathroom faucet dripped, and, too tired to phone anyone, she tied a string around the end of it, guiding the drip quietly into the drain, so it wouldn't bother her anymore. Her only plant, facing east in the window, hung over the popcorn popper and dried to a brown crunch. On the ledge, a jack-o'-lantern she had carved for Halloween had rotted, melted, froze, and now looked like a collapsed basketball—one she might have been saving for sentimental reasons, one from the *big game!* The man who brought her room service each morning—two poached eggs and a pot of coffee—reported her to the assistant manager, and she received a written warning slid under the door.

On Fridays, she visited her parents in Elmhurst. It was still hard for her father to look her in the eyes. He was seventy now. Ten years ago, he had gone to the first movie she had ever been in, saw her remove her clothes and dive into a pool. The movie was rated PG, but he never went to another one. Her mother went to all of them and searched later for encouraging things to say. Even something small. She refused to lie. "I liked the way you said the line about leaving home, your eyes wide and your hands fussing with your dress buttons," she wrote. "That red dress was so becoming. You should wear bright colors!"

"My father takes naps a lot when I visit," she said to Tommy.

"Naps?"

"I embarrass him. He thinks I'm a whore hippie. A hippie whore."

"That's ridiculous. As I said in *One Man's Opinion,* you're the most sexually conservative person I know."

"Yeah, well."

Her mother always greeted her warmly, puddle-eyed. These days, she was reading thin paperback books by a man named Robert Valleys, a man who said that after observing all the suffering in the world—war, starvation, greed—he had discovered the cure: hugs.

Hugs, hugs, hugs, hugs, hugs.

Her mother believed him. She squeezed so long and hard that Sidra, like an infant or a lover, became lost in the feel and smell of her—her sweet, dry skin, the gray peach fuzz on her neck. "I'm so glad you left that den of iniquity," her mother said softly.

But Sidra still got calls from the den. At night, sometimes, the director phoned from a phone booth, desiring to be forgiven as well as to direct. "I think of all the things you might be thinking, and I say, 'Oh, Christ.' I mean, do you think the things I sometimes think you do?"

"Of course," said Sidra. "Of course I think those things."

"*Of course! Of course* is a term that has no place in this conversation!"

When Tommy phoned, she often felt a pleasure so sudden and flooding, it startled her.

"God, I'm so glad it's you!"

"You have no right to abandon American filmmaking this way!" he would say affectionately, and she would laugh loudly, for minutes without stopping. She was starting to have two speeds: Coma and Hysteria. Two meals: breakfast and popcorn. Two friends: Charlotte Peveril and Tommy. She could hear the clink of his bourbon glass. "You are too gifted a person to be living in a state that borders on North Dakota."

"Iowa."

"Holy bejesus, it's worse than I thought. I'll bet they say that there. I'll bet they say 'Bejesus.'"

"I live downtown. They don't say that here."

"Are you anywhere near Champaign-Urbana?"

"No."

"I went there once. I thought from its name that it would be a different kind of place. I kept saying to myself, 'Champagne, ur*bah*na, *champagne,* ur*bah* na! Champagne! Urbana!'" He sighed. "It was just this thing in the middle of a field. I went to a Chinese restaurant there and ordered my entire dinner with *extra* MSG."

"I'm in Chicago. It's not so bad."

"Not so bad. There are no movie people there. Sidra, what about your *acting talent?"*

"I have no acting talent."

"Hello?"

"You heard me."

"I'm not sure. For a minute there, I thought maybe you had that dizziness thing again, that inner-ear imbalance."

"Talent. I don't have *talent.* I have willingness. What *talent?"* As a kid, she had always told the raunchiest jokes. As an adult, she could rip open a bone and speak out of it. Simple, clear. There was never anything to stop her. Why was there never anything to stop her? "I can stretch out the neck of a sweater to point at a freckle on my shoulder. Anyone who didn't get enough attention in nursery school can do that. Talent is something else."

"Excuse me, okay? I'm only a screenwriter. But someone's got you thinking you went from serious actress to aging bimbo. That's ridiculous. You just have to weather things a little out here. Besides, I think willing yourself to do a thing is brave, and the very essence of talent."

Sidra looked at her hands, already chapped and honeycombed with bad weather, bad soap, bad life. She needed to listen to the crickets tape. "But I *don't* will myself," she said. "I'm just already willing."

She began to go to blues bars at night. Sometimes she called Charlotte Peveril, her one friend left from high school.

"Siddy, how are you?" In Chicago, Sidra was thought of as a hillbilly name. But in L.A., people had thought it was beautiful and assumed she'd made it up.

"I'm fine. Let's go get drunk and listen to music."

Sometimes she just went by herself.

"Don't I know you from the movies?" a man might ask at one of the breaks, smiling, leering in a twinkly way.

"Maybe," she'd say, and he would look suddenly panicked and back away.

One night, a handsome man in a poncho, a bad poncho—though was there such a thing as a good poncho? asked Charlotte—sat down next to her with an extra glass of beer. "You look like you should be in the movies," he said. Sidra nodded wearily. "But I don't go to the movies. So if you *were* in the movies, I would never have gotten to set my eyes on you."

She turned her gaze from his poncho to her sherry, then back. Perhaps he had spent some time in Mexico or Peru. "What do you do?"

"I'm an auto mechanic." He looked at her carefully. "My name's Walter. Walt." He pushed the second beer her way. "The drinks here are okay as long as you don't ask them to mix anything. Just don't ask them to mix anything!"

She picked it up and took a sip. There was something about him she liked: something earthy beneath the act. In L.A., beneath the act you got nougat or Styrofoam. Or glass. Sidra's mouth was lined with sherry. Walt's lips shone with beer. "What's the last movie you saw?" she asked him.

"The last movie I saw. Let's see." He was thinking, but she could tell he wasn't good at it. She watched with curiosity the folded-in mouth, the tilted head: at last, a guy who didn't go to the movies. His eyes rolled back like the casters on a clerk's chair, searching. "You know what I saw?"

"No. What?" She was getting drunk.

"It was this cartoon movie." Animation. She felt relieved. At least it wasn't one of those bad art films starring what's-her-name. "A man is asleep, having a dream about a beautiful little country full of little people." Walt sat back, looked around the room, as if that were all.

"And?" She was going to have to push and pull with this guy.

"'And?'" he repeated. He leaned forward again. "And one day the people realize that they are only creatures in this man's dream. Dream people! And if the man wakes up, they will no longer exist!"

Now she hoped he wouldn't go on. She had changed her mind a little.

"So they all get together at a town meeting and devise a plan," he continued. Perhaps the band would be back soon. "They will burst into the man's bedroom and bring him back to a padded, insulated room in the town—the town of his own dream—and there they will keep watch over him to make sure he stays asleep. And they do just that. Forever and ever, everyone guarding him carefully, but apprehensively, making sure he never wakes up." He smiled. "I forget what the name of it was."

"And he never wakes up."

"Nope." He grinned at her. She liked him. She could tell he could tell. He took a sip of his beer. He looked around the bar, then back at her. "Is this a great country or what?" he said.

She smiled at him, with longing. "Where do you live," she asked, "and how do I get there?"

"I met a man," she told Tommy on the phone. "His name is Walter."

"A forced relationship. You're in a state of stress—you're in a *syndrome,* I can tell. You're going to force this romance. What does he do?"

"Something with cars." She sighed. "I want to sleep with someone. When I'm sleeping with someone, I'm less obsessed with the mail."

"But perhaps you should just be alone, be by yourself for a while."

"Like you've ever been alone," said Sidra. "I mean, have you *ever* been alone?"

"I've been alone."

"Yeah, and for how long?"

"Hours," said Tommy. He sighed. "At least it felt like hours."

"Right," she said, "so don't go lecturing me about inner resources."

"Okay. So I sold the mineral rights to my body years ago, but, hey, at least *I* got good money for mine."

"I got some money," said Sidra. "I got some."

Walter leaned her against his parked car. His mouth was slightly lopsided, paisley-shaped, his lips anneloid and full, and he kissed her hard. There was something numb and on hold in her. There were small dark pits of annihilation she discovered in her heart, in the loosening fist of it, and she threw herself into them, falling. She went home with him, slept with him. She told him who she was. A minor movie star once nominated for a major award. She told him she lived at the Days Inn. He had been there once, to the top, for a drink. But he did not seem to know her name.

"Never thought I'd sleep with a movie star," he did say. "I suppose that's every man's dream." He laughed—lightly, nervously.

"Just don't wake up," she said. Then she pulled the covers to her chin.

"Or change the dream," he added seriously. "I mean, in the movie I saw, everything is fine until the sleeping guy begins to dream about something else. I don't think he wills it or anything; it just happens."

"You didn't tell me about that part."

"That's right," he said. "You see, the guy starts dreaming about flamingos and then all the little people turn into flamingos and fly away."

"Really?" said Sidra.

"I *think* it was flamingos. I'm not too expert with birds."

"You're *not?"* She was trying to tease him, but it came out wrong, like a lizard with a little hat on.

"To tell you the truth, I really don't think I ever saw a single movie you were in."

"Good." She was drifting, indifferent, no longer paying attention.

He hitched his arm behind his head, wrist to nape. His chest heaved up and down. "I think I may of *heard* of you, though,"

Django Reinhardt was on the radio. She listened, carefully. "Astonishing sounds came from that man's hands," Sidra murmured.

Walter tried to kiss her, tried to get her attention back. He wasn't that interested in music, though at times he tried to be. "'Astonishing sounds'?" he said. "Like this?" He cupped his palms together, making little pops and suction noises.

"Yeah," she murmured. But she was elsewhere, letting a dry wind sweep across the plain of her to sleep. "Like that."

He began to realize, soon, that she did not respect him. A bug could sense it. A doorknob could figure it out. She never quite took him seriously. She would talk about films and film directors, then look at him and say, "Oh, never mind." She was part of some other world. A world she no longer liked.

And now she was somewhere else. Another world she no longer liked.

But she was willing. Willing to give it a whirl. Once in a while, though she tried not to, she asked him about children, about having children, about turning kith to kin. How did he feel about all that? It seemed to her that if she were ever going to have a life of children and lawn mowers and grass clippings, it would be best to have it with someone who was not demeaned or trivialized by discussions of them. Did he like those big fertilized lawns? How about a nice rock garden? How did he feel deep down about those combination storm windows with the built-in screens?

"Yeah, I like them all right," he said, and she would nod slyly and drink a little too much. She would try then not to think too strenuously about her *whole life*. She would try to live life one day at a time, like an alcoholic—drink, don't drink, drink. Perhaps she should take drugs.

"I always thought someday I would have a little girl and name her after my grandmother." Sidra sighed, peered wistfully into her sherry.

"What was your grandmother's name?"

Sidra looked at his paisley mouth. "Grandma. Her name was Grandma." Walter laughed in a honking sort of way. "Oh, thank you," murmured Sidra. "Thank you for laughing."

Walter had a subscription to *AutoWeek*. He flipped through it in bed. He also liked to read repair manuals for new cars, particularly the Toyotas. He knew a lot about control panels, light-up panels, side panels.

"You're so obviously wrong for each other," said Charlotte over tapas at a tapas bar.

"Hey, please," said Sidra. "I think my taste's a little subtler than that." The thing with tapas bars was that you just kept stuffing things into your mouth. "Obviously wrong is just the beginning. That's where *I always* begin. At obviously wrong." In theory, she liked the idea of mismatched couples, the wrangling and retangling, like a comedy by Shakespeare.

"I can't imagine you with someone like him. He's just not special." Charlotte had met him only once. But she had heard of him from a girlfriend of hers. He had slept around, she'd said. "Into the pudding" is how she phrased it, and there were some boring stories. "Just don't let him humiliate you. Don't mistake a lack of sophistication for sweetness," she added.

"I'm supposed to wait around for someone special, while every other girl in this town gets to have a life?"

"I don't know, Sidra."

It was true. Men could be with whomever they pleased. But women had to date better, kinder, richer, and bright, bright, bright, or else people got embarrassed. It suggested sexual things. "I'm a very average person," she said desperately, somehow detecting that Charlotte already knew that, knew the deep, dark, wildly obvious secret of that, and how it made Sidra slightly pathetic, unseemly—inferior, when you got right down to it. Charlotte studied Sidra's face, headlights caught in the stare of a deer. Guns don't kill people, thought Sidra fizzily. Deer kill people.

"Maybe it's that we all used to envy you so much," Charlotte said a little bitterly. "You were so talented. You got all the lead parts in the plays. You were everyone's dream of what *they* wanted."

Sidra poked around at the appetizer in front of her, gardening it like a patch of land. She was unequal to anyone's wistfulness. She had made too little of her life. Its loneliness shamed her like a crime. "Envy," said Sidra. "That's a lot like hate, isn't it." But Charlotte didn't say anything. Probably she wanted Sidra to change the subject. Sidra stuffed her mouth full of feta cheese and onions, and looked up. "Well, all I can say is, I'm glad to be back." A piece of feta dropped from her lips.

Charlotte looked down at it and smiled. "I know what you mean," she said. She opened her mouth wide and let all the food inside fall out onto the table.

Charlotte could be funny like that. Sidra had forgotten that about her.

Walter had found some of her old movies in the video-rental place. She had a key. She went over one night and discovered him asleep in front of *Recluse with Roommate.* It was about a woman named Rose who rarely went out, because when she did, she was afraid of people. They seemed like alien life-forms—soulless, joyless, speaking asyntactically. Rose quickly became loosened from reality. Walter had it freeze-framed at the funny part, where Rose phones the psych ward to have them come take her away, but they refuse. She lay down next to him and tried to sleep, too, but began to cry a little. He stirred. "What's wrong?" he asked.

"Nothing. You fell asleep. Watching me."

"I was tired," he said.

"I guess so."

"Let me kiss you. Let me find your panels." His eyes were closed. She could be anybody.

"Did you like the beginning part of the movie?" This need in her was new. Frightening. It made her hair curl. When had she ever needed so much?

"It was okay," he said.

"So what is this guy, a race-car driver?" asked Tommy.

"No, he's a mechanic."

"Ugh! Quit him like a music lesson!"

"Like *a music lesson?* What is this, *Similes from the Middle Class? One Man's Opinion?*" She was irritated.

"Sidra. This is not right! You need to go out with someone really smart for a change."

"I've been out with smart. I've been out with someone who had two Ph.D.'s. We spent all of our time in bed with the light on, proofreading his vita," She sighed. "Every little thing he'd ever done, every little, little, little. I mean, have you ever seen a vita?"

Tommy sighed, too. He had heard this story of Sidra's before. "Yes," he said. "I thought Patti LuPone was great."

"Besides," she said. "Who says he's not smart?"

The Japanese cars were the most interesting. Though the Americans were getting sexier, trying to keep up with them. *Those Japs!*

"Let's talk about my world," she said.

"What world?"

"Well, something I'm interested in. Something where there's something in it for me."

"Okay." He turned and dimmed the lights, romantically. "Got a stock tip for you," he said.

She was horrified, dispirited, interested.

He told her the name of a company somebody at work invested in. AutVis.

"What is it?"

"I don't know. But some guy at work said buy this week. They're going to make some announcement. If I had money, I'd buy."

She bought, the very next morning. A thousand shares. By the afternoon, the stock had plummeted 10 percent; by the following morning, 50. She watched the ticker tape go by on the bottom of the TV news channel. She had become the major stockholder. The major stockholder of a dying company! Soon they were going to be calling her, wearily, to ask what she wanted done with the forklift.

"You're a neater eater than I am," Walter said to her over dinner at the Palmer House.

She looked at him darkly. "What the hell were you thinking of, recommending that stock?" she asked. "How could you be such an irresponsible idiot?" She saw it now, how their life would be together. She would yell; then he would yell. He would have an affair; then she would have an affair. And then they would be gone and gone, and they would live in that gone.

"I got the name wrong," he said. "Sorry."

"You what?"

"It wasn't AutVis. It was AutDrive. I kept thinking it was vis for vision."

"'Vis for vision,'" she repeated.

"I'm not that good with names," confessed Walter. "I do better with concepts."

"'Concepts,'" she repeated as well.

The concept of anger. The concept of bills. The concept of flightless, dodo love.

Outside, there was a watery gust from the direction of the lake. "Chicago," said Walter. "The Windy City. Is this the Windy City or what?" He looked at her hopefully, which made her despise him more.

She shook her head. "I don't even know why we're together," she said. "I mean, why are we even together?"

He looked at her hard. "I can't answer that for you," he yelled. He took two steps back, away from her. "You've got to answer that for yourself!" And he hailed his own cab, got in, and rode away.

She walked back to the Days Inn alone. She played scales soundlessly, on the tops of the piano keys, her thin-jointed fingers lifting and falling quietly like the tines of a music box or the legs of a spider. When she tired, she turned on the television, moved through the channels, and discovered an old movie she'd been in, a love story/murder mystery called *Finishing Touches*. It was the kind of performance she had become, briefly, known for: a patched-together intimacy with the audience, half cartoon, half revelation; a cross between shyness and derision. She had not given a damn back then, sort of like now, only then it had been a style, a way of being, not a diagnosis or demise.

Perhaps she should have a baby.

In the morning, she went to visit her parents in Elmhurst. For winter, they had plastic-wrapped their home—the windows, the doors—so that it looked like a piece of avant-garde art. "Saves on heating bills," they said.

They had taken to discussing her in front of her. "It was a movie, Don. It was a movie about adventure. Nudity can be art."

"That's not how I saw it! That's not how I saw it at all!" said her father, red-faced, leaving the room. Naptime.

"How are you doing?" asked her mother, with what seemed like concern but was really an opening for something else. She had made tea.

"I'm okay, really," said Sidra. Everything she said about herself now sounded like a lie. If she was bad, it sounded like a lie; if she was fine—also a lie.

Her mother fiddled with a spoon. "I was envious of you." Her mother sighed. "I was always so envious of you! My own daughter!" She was shrieking it, saying it softly at first and then shrieking. It was exactly like Sidra's childhood: just when she thought life had become simple again, her mother gave her a new portion of the world to organize.

"I have to go," said Sidra. She had only just gotten there, but she wanted to go. She didn't want to visit her parents anymore. She didn't want to look at their lives.

She went back to the Days Inn and phoned Tommy. She and Tommy understood each other. "I *get* you," he used to say. His childhood had been full of sisters. He'd spent large portions of it drawing pictures of women in bathing suits—Miss Kenya from Nairobi!—and then asking one of the sisters to pick the most beautiful. If he disagreed, he asked another sister.

The connection was bad, and suddenly she felt too tired. "Darling, are you okay?" he said faintly.

"I'm okay."

"I think I'm hard of hearing," he said.

"I think I'm hard of talking," she said. "I'll phone you tomorrow."

She phoned Walter instead. "I need to see you," she said.

"Oh, really?" he said skeptically, and then added, with a sweetness he seemed to have plucked expertly from the air like a fly, "Is this a great country or what?"

She felt grateful to be with him again. "Let's never be apart," she whispered, rubbing his stomach. He had the physical inclinations of a dog: he liked stomach, ears, excited greetings.

"Fine by me," he said.

"Tomorrow, let's go out to dinner somewhere really expensive. My treat."

"Uh," said Walter, "tomorrow's no good."

"Oh."

"How about Sunday?"

"What's wrong with tomorrow?"

"I've got. Well, I've gotta work and I'll be tired, first of all."

"What's second of all?"

"I'm getting together with this woman I know."

"Oh?"

"It's no big deal. It's nothing. It's not a date or anything."

"Who is she?"

"Someone whose car I fixed. Loose mountings in the exhaust system. She wants to get together and talk about it some more. She wants to know about catalytic converters. You know, women are afraid of getting taken advantage of."

"Really!"

"Yeah, well, so Sunday would be better."

"Is she attractive?"

Walter scrinched up his face and made a sound of unenthusiasm. "Enh," he said, and placed his hand laterally in the air, rotating it up and down a little.

Before he left in the morning, she said, "Just don't sleep with her."

"Sidra," he said, scolding her for lack of trust or for attempted supervision—she wasn't sure which.

That night, he didn't come home. She phoned and phoned and then drank a six-pack and fell asleep. In the morning, she phoned again. Finally, at eleven o'clock, he answered.

She hung up.

At 11:30, her phone rang. "Hi," he said cheerfully. He was in a good mood.

"So where were you all night?" asked Sidra. This was what she had become. She felt shorter and squatter and badly coiffed.

There was some silence. "What do you mean?" he said cautiously.

"You know what I mean."

More silence. "Look, I didn't call this morning to get into a heavy conversation."

"Well, then," said Sidra, "you certainly called the wrong number." She slammed down the phone.

She spent the day trembling and sad. She felt like a cross between Anna Karenina and Amy Liverhaus, who used to shout from the fourth-grade cloakroom, "I just don't feel *appreciated.*" She walked over to Marshall Field's to buy new makeup. "You're much more of a cream beige than an ivory," said the young woman working the cosmetics counter.

But Sidra clutched at the ivory. "People are always telling me that," she said, "and it makes me very cross."

She phoned him later that night and he was there. "We need to talk," she said.

"I want my key back," he said.

"Look. Can you just come over here so that we can talk?"

He arrived bearing flowers—white roses and irises. They seemed wilted and ironic; she leaned them against the wall in a dry glass, no water.

"All right, I admit it," he said. "I went out on a date. But I'm not saying I slept with her."

She could feel, suddenly, the promiscuity in him. It was a heat, a creature, a tenant twin. "I already know you slept with her."

"How can you know that?"

"Get a life! What am I, an idiot?" She glared at him and tried not to cry. She hadn't loved him enough and he had sensed it. She hadn't really loved him at all, not really.

But she had liked him a lot!

So it still seemed unfair. A bone in her opened up, gleaming and pale, and she held it to the light and spoke from it. "I want to know one thing." She paused, not really for effect, but it had one. "Did you have oral sex?"

He looked stunned. "What kind of question is that? I don't have to answer a question like that."

"You don't have to answer a question like that? You don't have any rights here!" she began to yell. She was dehydrated. "You're the one who did this. Now I want the truth. I just want to know. Yes or no!"

He threw his gloves across the room.

"Yes or no," she said.

He flung himself onto the couch, pounded the cushion with his fist, placed an arm up over his eyes.

"Yes or no," she repeated.

He breathed deeply into his shirtsleeve.

"Yes or no."

"Yes," he said.

She sat down on the piano bench. Something dark and coagulated moved through her, up from the feet. Something light and breathing fled through her head, the house of her plastic-wrapped and burned down to tar. She heard him give a moan, and some fleeing hope in her, surrounded but alive on the roof, said perhaps he would beg her forgiveness. Promise to be a new man. She might find him attractive as a new, begging man. Though at some point, he would have to stop begging. He would just have to be normal. And then she would dislike him again.

He stayed on the sofa, did not move to comfort or be comforted, and the darkness in her cleaned her out, hollowed her like acid or a wind.

"I don't know what to do," she said, something palsied in her voice. She felt cheated of all the simple things—the radical calm of obscurity, of routine, of blah domestic bliss. "I don't want to go back to L.A.," she said. She began to stroke the tops of the piano keys, pushing against one and finding it broken—thudding and pitchless, shiny and mocking like an opened bone. She hated, hated her life. Perhaps she had always hated it.

He sat up on the sofa, looked distraught and false—his face badly arranged. He should practice in a mirror, she thought. He did not know how to break up with a movie actress. It was boys' rules: don't break up with a movie actress. Not in Chicago. If *she* left *him,* he would be better able to explain it, to himself, in the future, to anyone who asked. His voice shifted into something meant to sound imploring. "I know" was what he said, in a tone approximating hope, faith, some charity or other. "I know you might not *want* to."

"For your own good," he was saying. "Might be willing . . ." he was saying. But she was already turning into something else, a bird—a flamingo, a hawk, a flamingo-hawk—and was flying up and away, toward the filmy pane of the window, then back again, circling, meanly, with a squint.

He began, suddenly, to cry—loudly at first, with lots of *ohs,* then tiredly, as if from a deep sleep, his face buried in the poncho he'd thrown over the couch arm, his body sinking into the plush of the cushions—a man held hostage by the anxious cast of his dream.

"What can I do?" he asked.

But his dream had now changed, and she was gone, gone out the window, gone, gone.

From *Sense and Sensibility*

JANE AUSTEN

CHAPTER 27

"If this open weather holds much longer," said Mrs. Jennings, when they met at breakfast the following morning, "Sir John will not like leaving Barton next week; 'tis a sad thing for sportsmen to lose a day's pleasure. Poor souls! I always pity them when they do; they seem to take it so much to heart."

"That is true," cried Marianne in a cheerful voice, and walking to the window as she spoke, to examine the day. "I had not thought of *that*. This weather will keep many sportsmen in the country."

It was a lucky recollection, all her good spirits were restored by it. "It is charming weather for *them* indeed," she continued, as she sat down to the breakfast table with a happy countenance. "How much they must enjoy it! But" (with a little return of anxiety) "it cannot be expected to last long. At this time of year, and after such a series of rain, we shall certainly have very little more of it. Frosts will soon set in, and in all probability with severity. In another day or two perhaps; this extreme mildness can hardly last longer—nay, perhaps it may freeze tonight!"

"At any rate," said Elinor, wishing to prevent Mrs. Jennings from seeing her sister's thoughts as clearly as she did, "I dare say we shall have Sir John and Lady Middleton in town by the end of next week."

"Aye, my dear, I'll warrant you we do. Mary always has her own way."

"And now," silently conjectured Elinor, "she will write to Combe by this day's post."

But if she *did,* the letter was written and sent away with a privacy which eluded all her watchfulness to ascertain the fact. Whatever the truth of it might be, and far as Elinor was from feeling thorough contentment about it, yet while she saw Marianne in spirits, she could not be very uncomfortable herself. And Marianne was in spirits; happy in the mildness of the weather, and still happier in her expectation of a frost.

The morning was chiefly spent in leaving cards at the houses of Mrs. Jennings's acquaintance to inform them of her being in town; and Marianne was all the time busy in observing the direction of the wind, watching the variations of the sky and imagining an alteration in the air.

"Don't you find it colder than it was in the morning, Elinor? There seems to me a very decided difference. I can hardly keep my hands warm even in my muff. It was not so yesterday, I think. The clouds seem parting too, the sun will be out in a moment; and we shall have a clear afternoon."

Elinor was alternately diverted and pained; but Marianne persevered, and saw every night in the brightness of the fire, and every morning in the appearance of the atmosphere, the certain symptoms of approaching frost.

The Miss Dashwoods had no greater reason to be dissatisfied with Mrs. Jennings's style of living, and set of acquaintance, than with her behavior to themselves, which was invariably kind. Every thing in her household arrangements was conducted on the most liberal plan, and excepting a few old city friends, whom, to Lady Middleton's regret, she had never dropped, she visited no one, to whom an introduction could at all discompose the feelings of her young companions. Pleased to find herself more comfortably situated in that particular than she had expected, Elinor was very willing to compound for the want of much real enjoyment from any of their evening parties, which, whether at home or abroad, formed only for cards, could have little to amuse her.

Colonel Brandon, who had a general invitation to the house, was with them almost every day; he came to look at Marianne and talk to Elinor, who often derived more satisfaction from conversing with him than from any other daily occurrence, but who saw at the same time with much concern his continued regard for her sister. She feared it was a strengthening regard. It grieved her to see the earnestness with which he often watched Marianne, and his spirits were certainly worse than when at Barton.

About a week after their arrival it became certain that Willoughby was also arrived. His card was on the table, when they came in from the morning's drive.

"Good God!" cried Marianne, "he has been here while we were out." Elinor, rejoiced to be assured of his being in London, now ventured to say, "Depend upon it he will call again tomorrow." But Marianne seemed hardly to hear her, and on Mrs. Jennings's entrance, escaped with the precious card.

This event, while it raised the spirits of Elinor, restored to those of her sister, all, and more than all, their former agitation. From this moment her mind was never quiet; the expectation of seeing him every hour of the day, made her unfit for anything. She insisted on being left behind, the next morning, when the others went out.

Elinor's thoughts were full of what might be passing in Berkeley-street during their absence; but a moment's glance at her sister when they returned was enough to inform her, that Willoughby had paid no second visit there. A note was just then brought in, and laid on the table.

"For me!" cried Marianne, stepping hastily forward.

"No, ma'am, for my mistress."

But Marianne, not convinced, took it instantly up.

"It is indeed for Mrs. Jennings; how provoking!"

"You are expecting a letter then?" said Elinor, unable to be longer silent.

"Yes, a little—not much."

After a short pause, "You have no confidence in me, Marianne."

"Nay, Elinor, this reproach from *you*—you who have confidence in no one!"

"Me!" returned Elinor in some confusion; "indeed, Marianne, I have nothing to tell."

"Nor I," answered Marianne with energy, "our situations then are alike. We have neither of us anything to tell; you, because you do not communicate, and I, because I conceal nothing."

Elinor, distressed by this charge of reserve in herself, which she was not at liberty to do away, knew not how, under such circumstances, to press for greater openness in Marianne.

Mrs. Jennings soon appeared, and the note being given her, she read it aloud. It was from Lady Middleton, announcing their arrival in Conduit-street the night before, and requesting the company of her mother and cousins the following evening. Business on Sir John's part, and a violent cold on her own, prevented their calling in Berkeley-street. The invitation was accepted: but when the hour of appointment drew near, necessary as it was in common civility to Mrs. Jennings, that they should both attend her on such a visit, Elinor had some difficulty in persuading her sister to go, for still she had seen nothing of Willoughby; and therefore was not more indisposed for amusement abroad, than unwilling to run the risk of his calling again in her absence.

Elinor found, when the evening was over, that disposition is not materially altered by a change of abode, for although scarcely settled in town, Sir John had contrived to collect around him, nearly twenty young people, and to amuse them with a ball. This was an affair, however, of which Lady Middleton did not approve. In the country, an unpremeditated dance was very allowable; but in London, where the reputation of elegance was more important and less easily attained, it was risking too much for the gratification of a few girls, to have it known that Lady Middleton had given a small dance of eight or nine couples, with two violins, and a mere side-board collation.

Mr. and Mrs. Palmer were of the party; from the former, whom they had not seen before since their arrival in town, as he was careful to avoid the appearance of any attention to his mother-in-law, and therefore never came near her, they received no mark of recognition on their entrance. He looked at them slightly, without seeming to know who they were, and merely nodded to Mrs. Jennings from the other side of the room. Marianne gave one glance round the apartment as she entered; it was enough, *he* was not there—and she sat down, equally ill-disposed to receive or communicate pleasure. After they had been assembled about an hour, Mr. Palmer sauntered toward the Miss Dashwoods to express his surprise on seeing them in town, though Colonel Brandon had been first informed of their arrival at his house, and he had himself said something very droll on hearing that they were to come.

"I thought you were both in Devonshire," said he.

"Did you?" replied Elinor.

"When do you go back again?"

"I do not know." And thus ended their discourse.

Never had Marianne been so unwilling to dance in her life, as she was that evening, and never so much fatigued by the exercise. She complained of it as they returned to Berkeley-street.

"Aye, aye," said Mrs. Jennings, "we know the reason of all that very well; if a certain person who shall be nameless, had been there, you would not have been a bit tired: and to say the truth it was not very pretty of him not to give you the meeting when he was invited."

"Invited!" cried Marianne.

"So my daughter Middleton told me, for it seems Sir John met him somewhere in the street this morning." Marianne said no more, but looked exceedingly hurt. Impatient in this situation to be doing something that might lead to her sister's relief, Elinor resolved to write the next morning to her mother, and hoped by awakening her fears for the health of Marianne, to procure those inquiries which had been so long delayed; and she was still more eagerly bent on this measure by perceiving after breakfast on the morrow, that Marianne was again writing to Willoughby, for she could not suppose it to be to any other person.

About the middle of the day, Mrs. Jennings went out by herself on business, and Elinor began her letter directly, while Marianne, too restless for employment, too anxious for conversation, walked from one window to the other, or sat down by the fire in melancholy meditation. Elinor was very earnest in her application to her mother, relating all that had passed, her suspicions of Willoughby's inconstancy, urging her by every plea of duty and affection to demand from Marianne, an account of her real situation with respect to him.

Her letter was scarcely finished, when a rap foretold a visitor, and Colonel Brandon was announced. Marianne, who had seen him from the window, and who hated company of any kind, left the room before he entered it. He looked more than usually grave, and though expressing satisfaction at finding Miss Dashwood alone, as if he had somewhat in particular to tell her, sat for some time without saying a word. Elinor, persuaded that he had some communication to make in which her sister was concerned, impatiently expected its opening. It was not the first time of her feeling the same kind of conviction; for more than once before, beginning with the observation of "your sister looks unwell today," or "your sister seems out of spirits," he had appeared on the point, either of disclosing, or of inquiring, something particular about her. After a pause of several minutes, their silence was broken, by his asking her in a voice of some agitation, when he was to congratulate her on the acquisition of a brother? Elinor was not prepared for such a question, and having no answer ready, was obliged to adopt the simple and common expedient, of asking what he meant? He tried to smile as he replied, "Your sister's engagement to Mr. Willoughby is very generally known."

"It cannot be generally known," returned Elinor, "for her own family do not know it."

He looked surprised and said, "I beg your pardon, I am afraid my inquiry has been impertinent; but I had not supposed any secrecy intended, as they openly correspond, and their marriage is universally talked of."

"How can that be? By whom can you have heard it mentioned?"

"By many—by some of whom you know nothing, by others with whom you are most intimate, Mrs. Jennings, Mrs. Palmer, and the Middletons. But still I might not have believed it, for where the mind is perhaps rather unwilling to be convinced, it will always find something to support its doubts, if I had not, when the servant let me in today, accidentally seen a letter in his hand, directed to Mr. Willoughby in your sister's writing. I came to inquire, but I was convinced before I could ask the question. Is every thing finally settled? Is it impossible to—? But I have no right, and I could have no chance of succeeding. Excuse me, Miss Dashwood. I believe I have been wrong in saying so much, but I hardly know what to do, and on your prudence I have the strongest dependence. Tell me that it is all absolutely resolved on, that any attempt, that in short concealment, if concealment be possible, is all that remains."

These words, which conveyed to Elinor a direct avowal of his love for her sister, affected her very much. She was not immediately able to say anything, and even when her spirits were recovered, she debated for a short time, on the answer it would be most proper to give. The real state of things between Willoughby and her sister was so little known to herself, that in endeavoring to explain it, she might be as liable to say too much as too little. Yet as she was convinced that Marianne's affection for Willoughby, could leave no hope of Colonel Brandon's success, whatever the event of that affection might be, and at the same time wished to shield her conduct from censure, she thought it most prudent and kind, after some consideration, to say more than she really knew or believed. She acknowledged, therefore, that though she had never been informed by themselves of the terms on which they stood with each other, of their mutual affection she had no doubt, and of their correspondence she was not astonished to hear.

He listened to her with silent attention, and on her ceasing to speak, rose directly from his seat, and after saying in a voice of emotion, "to your sister I wish all imaginable happiness; to Willoughby that he may endeavor to deserve her,"—took leave, and went away.

Elinor derived no comfortable feelings from this conversation, to lessen the uneasiness of her mind on other points; she was left, on the contrary, with a melancholy impression of Colonel Brandon's unhappiness, and was prevented even from wishing it removed, by her anxiety for the very event that must confirm it.

CHAPTER 28

Nothing occurred during the next three or four days, to make Elinor regret what she had done, in applying to her mother; for Willoughby neither came nor wrote. They were engaged about the end of that time to attend Lady Middleton to a party, from which Mrs. Jennings was kept away by the indisposition of her youngest daughter; and for this party, Marianne, wholly dispirited, careless of her appearance, and seeming equally indifferent whether she went or staid, prepared, without one look of hope, or one expression of pleasure. She sat by the drawing-room fire after tea, till the moment of Lady Middleton's arrival, without once stirring from her seat, or altering her attitude, lost in her own thoughts and insensible of her sister's presence; and when at last they were told that Lady Middleton waited for them at the door, she started as if she had forgotten that any one was expected.

They arrived in due time at the place of destination, and as soon as the string of carriages before them would allow, alighted, ascended the stairs, heard their names announced from one landing-place to another in an audible voice, and entered a room splendidly lit up, quite full of company, and insufferably hot. When they had paid their tribute of politeness by curtseying to the lady of the house, they were permitted to mingle in the crowd, and take their share of the heat and inconvenience, to which their arrival must necessarily add. After some time spent in saying little and doing less, Lady Middleton sat down to Casino, and as Marianne was not in spirits for moving about, she and Elinor luckily succeeding to chairs, placed themselves at no great distance from the table.

They had not remained in this manner long, before Elinor perceived Willoughby, standing within a few yards of them, in earnest conversation with a very fashionable looking young woman. She soon caught his eye, and he immediately bowed, but without attempting to speak to her, or to approach Marianne, though he could not but see her; and then continued his discourse with the same lady. Elinor turned involuntarily to Marianne, to see whether it could be unobserved by her. At that moment she first perceived him, and her whole countenance glowing with sudden delight, she would have moved towards him instantly, had not her sister caught hold of her.

"Good heavens!" she exclaimed. "He is there—he is there—Oh! why does he not look at me? Why cannot I speak to him?"

"Pray, pray be composed," cried Elinor, "and do not betray what you feel to every body present. Perhaps he has not observed you yet."

This however was more than she could believe herself; and to be composed at such a moment was not only beyond the reach of Marianne, it was beyond her wish. She sat in an agony of impatience, which affected every feature.

At last he turned round again, and regarded them both; she started up, and pronouncing his name in a tone of affection, held out her hand to him. He approached, and addressing himself rather to Elinor than Marianne, as if wishing to avoid her eye, and determined not to observe her attitude, inquired in a hurried manner after Mrs. Dashwood, and asked how long they had been in town. Elinor was robbed of all presence of mind by such an address, and was unable to say a word. But the feelings of her sister were instantly expressed. Her face was crimsoned over, and she exclaimed in a voice of the greatest emotion, "Good God! Willoughby, what is the meaning of this? Have you not received my letters? Will you not shake hands with me?"

He could not then avoid it, but her touch seemed painful to him, and he held her hand only for a moment. During all this time he was evidently struggling for composure. Elinor watched his countenance and saw its expression becoming more tranquil. After a moment's pause, he spoke with calmness.

"I did myself the honor of calling in Berkeley-street last Tuesday, and very much regretted that I was not fortunate enough to find yourselves and Miss Jennings at home. My card was not lost, I hope."

"But have you not received my notes?" cried Marianne in the wildest anxiety. "Here is some mistake I am sure—some dreadful mistake. What can be the meaning of it? Tell me, Willoughby; for heaven's sake tell me, what is the matter?"

He made no reply; his complexion changed and all his embarrassment returned; but as if, on catching the eye of the young lady with whom he had been previously talking, he felt the necessity of instant exertion, he recovered himself again, and after saying, "Yes, I had the pleasure of receiving the information of your arrival in town, which you were so good as to send me," turned hastily away with a slight bow and joined his friend.

Marianne, now looking dreadfully white, and unable to stand, sank into her chair, and Elinor, expecting every moment to see her faint, tried to screen her from the observation of others, while reviving her with lavender water.

"Go to him, Elinor," she cried, as soon as she could speak, "and force him to come to me. Tell him I must see him again—must speak to him instantly.—I cannot rest—I shall not have a moment's peace till this is explained—some dreadful misapprehension or other.—Oh go to him this moment."

"How can that be done? No, my dearest Marianne, you must wait. This is not a place for explanations. Wait only till tomorrow."

With difficulty however could she prevent her from following him herself; and to persuade her to check her agitation, to wait, at least, with the appearance of composure, till she might speak to him with more privacy and more effect, was impossible; for Marianne continued incessantly to give way in a low voice to the misery of her feelings, by exclamations of wretchedness. In a short time Elinor saw Willoughby quit the room by the door toward the staircase, and telling Marianne that he was gone, urged the impossibility of speaking to him again that evening, as a fresh argument for her to be calm. She instantly begged her sister would entreat Lady Middleton to take them home, as she was too miserable to stay a minute longer.

Lady Middleton, though in the middle of a rubber, on being informed that Marianne was unwell, was too polite to object for a moment to her wish of going away, and making over her cards to a friend, they departed as soon as the carriage could be found. Scarcely a word was spoken during their return to Berkeley-street. Marianne was in a silent agony, too much oppressed even for tears; but as Mrs. Jennings was luckily not come home, they could go directly to their own room, where hartshorn restored her a little to herself. She was soon undressed and in bed, and as she seemed desirous of being alone, her sister then left her, and while she waited the return of Mrs. Jennings, had leisure enough for thinking over the past.

That some kind of engagement had subsisted between Willoughby and Marianne she could not doubt; and that Willoughby was weary of it, seemed equally clear; for however Marianne might still feed her own wishes, *she* could not attribute such behavior to mistake or misapprehension of any kind. Nothing but a thorough change of sentiment could account for it. Her indignation would have been still stronger than it was, had she not witnessed that embarrassment which seemed to speak a consciousness of his own misconduct, and prevented her from believing him so unprincipled as to have been sporting with the affections of her sister from the first, without any design that would bear investigation. Absence might have weakened his regard, and convenience might have determined him to overcome it, but that such a regard had formerly existed she could not bring herself to doubt.

As for Marianne, on the pangs which so unhappy a meeting must already have given her, and on those still more severe which might await her in its probable consequence, she could not reflect without the deepest concern. Her own situation gained in the comparison; for while she could *esteem* Edward as much as ever, however they might be divided in future, her mind might be always supported. But every circumstance that could embitter such an evil seemed uniting to heighten the misery of Marianne in a final separation from Willoughby—in an immediate and irreconcileable rupture with him.

CHAPTER 29

Before the housemaid had lit their fire the next day, or the sun gained any power over a cold, gloomy morning in January, Marianne, only half dressed, was kneeling against one of the window seats for the sake of all the little light she could command from it, and writing as fast as a continual flow of tears would permit her. In this situation, Elinor, roused from sleep by her agitation and sobs, first perceived her; and after observing her for a few moments with silent anxiety, said, in a tone of the most considerate gentleness,

"Marianne, may I ask?—"

"No, Elinor," she replied, "ask nothing; you will soon know all."

The sort of desperate calmness with which this was said, lasted no longer than while she spoke, and was immediately followed by a return of the same excessive affliction. It was some minutes before she could go on with her letter, and the frequent bursts of grief which still obliged her, at intervals, to withhold her pen, were proofs enough of her feeling how more than probable it was that she was writing for the last time to Willoughby.

Elinor paid her every quiet and unobtrusive attention in her power; and she would have tried to soothe and tranquilize her still more, had not Marianne entreated her, with all the eagerness of the most nervous irritability, not to speak to her for the world. In such circumstances, it was better for both that they should not be long together; and the restless state of Marianne's mind not only prevented her from remaining in the room a moment after she was dressed, but requiring at once solitude and continual change of place, made her wander about the house till breakfast time, avoiding the sight of every body.

At breakfast she neither ate, nor attempted to eat anything; and Elinor's attention was then all employed, not in urging her, not in pitying her, nor in appearing to regard her, but in endeavoring to engage Mrs. Jennings's notice entirely to herself.

As this was a favorite meal with Mrs. Jennings, it lasted a considerable time, and they were just setting themselves, after it, round the common working table, when a letter was delivered to Marianne, which she eagerly caught from the servant, and, turning of a deathlike paleness, instantly ran out of the room. Elinor, who saw as plainly by this, as if she had seen the direction, that it must come from Willoughby, felt immediately such a sickness at heart as made her hardly able to hold up her head, and sat in such a general tremor as made her fear it impossible to escape Mrs. Jennings's notice. That good lady, however, saw only that Marianne had received a letter from Willoughby, which appeared to her a very good joke, and which she treated accordingly, by hoping, with a laugh, that she would find it to her liking. Of Elinor's distress, she was too busily employed in measuring lengths of worsted for her rug, to see any thing at all; and calmly continuing her talk, as soon as Marianne disappeared, she said,

"Upon my word I never saw a young woman so desperately in love in my life! *My* girls were nothing to her, and yet they used to be foolish enough; but as for Miss Marianne, she is quite an altered creature. I hope, from the bottom of my heart, he won't keep her waiting much longer, for it is quite grievous to see her look so ill and forlorn. Pray, when are they to be married?"

Elinor, though never less disposed to speak than at that moment, obliged herself to answer such an attack as this, and, therefore, trying to smile, replied, "And have you really, Ma'am, talked yourself into a persuasion of my sister's being engaged to Mr. Willoughby? I thought it had been only a joke, but so serious a question seems to imply more; and I must beg, therefore, that you will not deceive yourself any longer. I do assure you that nothing would surprise me more than to hear of their being going to be married."

"For shame, for shame, Miss Dashwood! How can you talk so! Don't we all know that it must be a match, that they were over head and ears in love with each other from the first moment they met? Did not I see them together in Devonshire every day, and all day long;

and did not I know that your sister came to town with me on purpose to buy wedding clothes? Come, come, this won't do. Because you are so sly about it yourself, you think nobody else has any senses; but it is no such thing, I can tell you, for it has been known all over town this ever so long. I tell every body of it and so does Charlotte."

"Indeed, Ma'am," said Elinor, very seriously, "you are mistaken. Indeed, you are doing a very unkind thing in spreading the report, and you will find that you have, though you will not believe me now."

Mrs. Jennings laughed again, but Elinor had not spirits to say more, and eager at all events to know what Willoughby had written, hurried away to their room, where, on opening the door, she saw Marianne stretched on the bed, almost choked by grief, one letter in her hand, and two or three others lying by her. Elinor drew near, but without saying a word; and seating herself on the bed, took her hand, kissed her affectionately several times, and then gave way to a burst of tears, which at first was scarcely less violent than Marianne's. The latter, though unable to speak, seemed to feel all the tenderness of this behavior, and after some time thus spent in joint affliction, she put all the letters into Elinor's hands; and then covering her face with her handkerchief, almost screamed with agony. Elinor, who knew that such grief, shocking as it was to witness it, must have its course, watched by her till this excess of suffering had somewhat spent itself, and then turning eagerly to Willoughby's letter, read as follows:

Bond Street, January.

My Dear Madam,

I have just had the honor of receiving your letter, for which I beg to return my sincere acknowledgments. I am much concerned to find there was any thing in my behavior last night that did not meet your approbation; and though I am quite at a loss to discover in what point I could be so unfortunate as to offend you, I entreat your forgiveness of what I can assure you to have been perfectly unintentional. I shall never reflect on my former acquaintance with your family in Devonshire without the most grateful pleasure, and flatter myself it will not be broken by any mistake or misapprehension of my actions. My esteem for your whole family is very sincere; but if I have been so unfortunate as to give rise to a belief of more than I felt, or meant to express, I shall reproach myself for not having been more guarded in my professions of that esteem. That I should ever have meant more you will allow to be impossible, when you understand that my affections have been long engaged elsewhere, and it will not be many weeks, I believe, before this engagement is fulfilled. It is with great regret that I obey your commands of returning the letters, with which I have been honored from you, and the lock of hair, which you so obligingly bestowed on me.

I am, dear Madam,
Your most obedient
humble Servant,
JOHN WILLOUGHBY.

With what indignation such a letter as this must be read by Miss Dashwood, may be imagined. Though aware, before she began it, that it must bring a confession of his inconstancy, and confirm their separation forever, she was not aware that such language could be suffered to announce it; nor could she have supposed Willoughby capable of departing so far from the appearance of every honorable and delicate feeling—so far from the common decorum of a gentleman, as to send a letter so impudently cruel: a letter which, instead of bringing with his desire of a release any professions of regret, acknowledged no breach of faith, denied all peculiar affection whatever—a letter of which every line was an insult, and which proclaimed its writer to be deep in hardened villainy.

She paused over it for some time with indignant astonishment; then read it again and again; but every perusal only served to increase her abhorrence of the man, and so bitter were her feelings against him, that she dared not trust herself to speak, lest she might wound Marianne still deeper by treating their disengagement, not as a loss to her of any possible good but as an escape from the worst and most irremediable of all evils, a connection, for life, with an unprincipled man, as a deliverance the most real, a blessing the most important.

In her earnest meditations on the contents of the letter, on the depravity of that mind which could dictate it, and, probably, on the very different mind of a very different person, who had no other connection whatever with the affair than what her heart gave him with every thing that passed, Elinor forgot the immediate distress of her sister, forgot that she had three letters on her lap yet unread, and so entirely forgot how long she had been in the room, that when on hearing a carriage drive up to the door, she went to the window to see who could be coming so unreasonably early, she was all astonishment to perceive Mrs. Jennings's chariot, which she knew had not been ordered till one. Determined not to quit Marianne, though hopeless of contributing, at present, to her ease, she hurried away to excuse herself from attending Mrs. Jennings, on account of her sister being indisposed. Mrs. Jennings, with a thoroughly good-humored concern for its cause, admitted the excuse most readily, and Elinor, after seeing her safe off, returned to Marianne, whom she found attempting to rise from the bed, and whom she reached just in time to prevent her from falling on the floor, faint and giddy from a long want of proper rest and food; for it was many days since she had any appetite, and many nights since she had really slept; and now, when her mind was no longer supported by the fever of suspense, the consequence of all this was felt in an aching head, a weakened stomach, and a general nervous faintness. A glass of wine, which Elinor procured for her directly, made her more comfortable, and she was at last able to express some sense of her kindness, by saying,

"Poor Elinor! How unhappy I make you!"

"I only wish," replied her sister, "there were any thing I *could* do, which might be of comfort to you."

This, as every thing else would have been, was too much for Marianne, who could only exclaim, in the anguish of her heart, "Oh! Elinor, I am miserable indeed," before her voice was entirely lost in sobs.

Elinor could no longer witness this torrent of unresisted grief in silence.

"Exert yourself, dear Marianne," she cried, "if you would not kill yourself and all who love you. Think of your mother; think of her misery while *you* suffer; for her sake you must exert yourself."

"I cannot, I cannot," cried Marianne; "leave me, leave me, if I distress you; leave me, hate me, forget me! But do not torture me so. Oh! how easy for those who have no sorrow of their own to talk of exertion! Happy, happy Elinor, *you* cannot have an idea of what I suffer."

"Do you call *me* happy, Marianne? Ah! if you knew!—And can you believe me to be so, while I see you so wretched!"

"Forgive me, forgive me," throwing her arms round her sister's neck; "I know you feel for me; I know what a heart you have; but yet you are—you must be happy; Edward loves you—What, oh! What can do away such happiness as that?"

"Many, many circumstances," said Elinor, solemnly.

"No, no, no," cried Marianne wildly, "he loves you, and only you. You *can* have no grief."

"I can have no pleasure while I see you in this state."

"And you will never see me otherwise. Mine is a misery which nothing can do away."

"You must not talk so, Marianne. Have you no comforts? No friends? Is your loss such as leaves no opening for consolation? Much as you suffer now, think of what you would have suffered if the discovery of his character had been delayed to a later period—if your engagement had been carried on for months and months, as it might have been, before he chose to put an end to it. Every additional day of unhappy confidence, on your side, would have made the blow more dreadful."

"Engagement !" cried Marianne, "there has been no engagement."

"No engagement?"

"No, he is not so unworthy as you believe him. He has broken no faith with me."

"But he told you that he loved you?"

"Yes—no—never absolutely. It was every day implied, but never professedly declared. Sometimes I thought it had been—but it never was."

"Yet you wrote to him?"—

"Yes—could that be wrong after all that had passed?—But I cannot talk."

Elinor said no more, and turning again to the three letters which now raised a much stronger curiosity than before, directly ran over the contents of all. The first, which was what her sister had sent him on their arrival in town, was to this effect.

Berkeley Street, January.

How surprised you will be, Willoughby, on receiving this; and I think you will feel something more than surprise, when you know that I am in town. An opportunity of coming hither, though with Mrs. Jennings, was a temptation we could not resist. I wish you may receive this in time to come here tonight, but I will not depend on it. At any rate I shall expect you tomorrow. For the present, adieu.

M.D.

Her second note, which had been written on the morning after the dance at the Middletons,' was in these words:—

I cannot express my disappointment in having missed you the day before yesterday, nor my astonishment at not having received any answer to a note which I sent you above a week ago. I have been expecting to hear from you, and still more to see you, every hour of the day. Pray call again as soon as possible, and explain the reason of my having expected this in vain. You had better come earlier another time, because we are generally out by one. We were last night at Lady Middleton's, where there was a dance. I have been told that you were asked to be one of the party. But could it be so? You must be very much altered indeed since we parted, if that could be the case, and you not there. But I will not suppose this possible, and I hope very soon to receive your personal assurance of its being otherwise.

M.D.

The contents of her last note to him were these:—

What am I to imagine, Willoughby, by your behavior last night? Again I demand an explanation of it. I was prepared to meet you with the pleasure which our separation naturally produced, with the familiarity which our intimacy at Barton appeared to me to justify. I was repulsed indeed! I have passed a wretched night in endeavoring to excuse a conduct which can scarcely be called less than insulting; but though I have not yet been able to form any reasonable apology for your behavior, I am perfectly ready to hear your justification of it. You have perhaps been misinformed, or purposely deceived, in something concerning me, which may have lowered me in your opinion. Tell me what it is, explain the grounds on which you acted, and I shall be satisfied, in being able to satisfy you. It would grieve me indeed to be obliged to think ill of you; but if I am to do it, if I am to learn that you are not what we have hitherto believed you, that your regard for us all was insincere, that your behavior to me was intended only to deceive, let it be told as soon as possible. My feelings are at present in a state of dreadful indecision; I wish to acquit you, but certainty on either side will be ease to what I now suffer. If your sentiments are no longer what they were, you will return my notes, and the lock of my hair which is in your possession.

M.D.

That such letters, so full of affection and confidence, could have been so answered, Elinor, for Willoughby's sake, would have been unwilling to believe. But her condemnation of him did not blind her to the impropriety of their having been written at all; and she was silently grieving over the imprudence which had hazarded such unsolicited proofs of tenderness, not warranted by anything preceding, and most severely condemned by the event, when Marianne, perceiving that she had finished the letters, observed to her that they contained nothing but what any one would have written in the same situation.

"I felt myself," she added, "to be as solemnly engaged to him, as if the strictest legal covenant had bound us to each other."

"I can believe it," said Elinor; "but unfortunately he did not feel the same."

"He *did* feel the same, Elinor—for weeks and weeks he felt it. I know he did. Whatever may have changed him now, (and nothing but the blackest art employed against me can have done it,) I was once as dear to him as my own soul could wish. This lock of hair, which now he can so readily give up, was begged of me with the most earnest supplication. Had you seen his look, his manner, had you heard his voice at that moment! Have you forgot the last evening of our being together at Barton? The morning that we parted too! When he told me that it might be many weeks before we meet again—his distress—can I ever forget his distress!"

For a moment or two she could say no more; but when this emotion had passed away, she added, in a firmer tone,

"Elinor, I have been cruelly used; but not by Willoughby."

"Dearest Marianne, who but himself? By whom can he have been instigated?"

"By all the world, rather than by his own heart. I could rather believe every creature of my acquaintance leagued together to ruin me in his opinion, than believe his nature capable of such cruelty. This woman of whom he writes—whoever she be—or any one, in short, but your own dear self, Mama, and Edward, may have been so barbarous to bely me. Beyond you three, is there a creature in the world whom I would not rather suspect of evil than Willoughby, whose heart I know so well?"

Elinor would not contend, and only replied, "Whoever may have been so detestably your enemy, let them be cheated of their malignant triumph, my dear sister, by seeing how nobly the consciousness of your own innocence and good intentions supports your spirits. It is a reasonable and laudable pride which resists such malevolence."

"No, no," cried Marianne, "misery such as mine has no pride. I care not who knows that I am wretched. The triumph of seeing me so may be open to all the world. Elinor, Elinor, they who suffer little may be proud and independent as they like—may resist insult, or return mortification—but I cannot. I must feel—I must be wretched—and they are welcome to enjoy the consciousness of it that can."

"But for my mother's sake and mine—"

"I would do more than for my own. But to appear happy when I am so miserable—Oh! who can require it?"

Again they were both silent. Elinor was employed in walking thoughtfully from the fire to the window, from the window to the fire, without knowing that she received warmth from one, or discerning objects through the other; and Marianne, seated at the foot of the bed, with her head leaning against one of its posts, again took up Willoughby's letter, and after shuddering over every sentence, exclaimed—

"It is too much! Oh! Willoughby, Willoughby, could this be yours! Cruel, cruel—nothing can acquit you. Elinor, nothing can. Whatever he might have heard against me—ought he not to have suspended his belief? ought he not to have told me of it, to have given me the power of clearing myself? 'The lock of hair, (repeating it from the letter,) which you so obligingly bestowed on me'—That is unpardonable. Willoughby, where was your heart, when you wrote those words? Oh! barbarously insolent!—Elinor, can he be justified?"

"No, Marianne, in no possible way."

"And yet this *woman*—who knows what her art may have been—how long it may have been premeditated, and how deeply contrived by her!—Who is she?—Who can she be?—Whom did I ever hear him talk of as young and attractive among his female acquaintance?—Oh! no one, no one—he talked to me only of myself."

Another pause ensued; Marianne was greatly agitated, and it ended thus.

"Elinor, I must go home. I must go and comfort Mama. Cannot we be gone tomorrow?"

"Tomorrow, Marianne!"

"Yes; why should I stay here? I came only for Willoughby's sake—and now who cares for me? Who regards me?"

"It would be impossible to go tomorrow. We owe Mrs. Jennings much more than civility; and civility of the commonest kind must prevent such a hasty removal as that."

"Well, then, another day or two, perhaps; but I cannot stay here long, I cannot stay to endure the questions and remarks of all these people. The Middletons and Palmers—how am I to bear their pity? The pity of such a woman as Lady Middleton! Oh! what would he say to that!"

Elinor advised her to lie down again, and for a moment she did so; but no attitude could give her ease; and in restless pain of mind and body she moved from one posture to another, till growing more and more hysterical, her sister could with difficulty keep her on the bed at all, and for some time was fearful of being constrained to call for assistance. Some lavender drops, however, which she was at length persuaded to take, were of use and from that time till Mrs. Jennings returned, she continued on the bed quiet and motionless.

The Male Gaze

LUCINDA ROSENFELD

Sometimes she felt like hot shit, sometimes just like shit. It changed by the hour, or even by the minute. City life had that effect on Phoebe: spontaneous self-aggrandizement degenerated into self-disgust at the smallest provocation. The insistent bass line of a teenager's boom box, the sickly sweet smell of chicken wings on the subway, the sight of other women taller and thinner and more gorgeous than she would ever be could render the stories that she told herself about herself pure fiction. So it was that while she rode the elevator up to a party that Susan Kenny was throwing at her Pearl Street apartment a fleeting glance at her hair (too flat!) and her face (too puffy!) in the polished-copper ceiling, the reflective surface of which was as unforgiving as a fluorescent-lit mirror in a public rest room, left Phoebe suddenly dejected and wondering if she ought to turn back.

But she hated to miss things. And since she'd come all this way, invested all that time in separating her eyelashes, styling her hair, moisturizing her cheeks, and lining her lips, she opened the door. A barrage of static heat, exaggerated laughter, and stale smells made her feel daunted all over again. She'd never seen so many people packed into such a small space. She didn't recognize a single one. She elbowed her way through the crowd in search of the hostess.

She finally found Susan Kenny sitting cross-legged on the kitchen counter nursing a Corona.

"Susan!" Phoebe squealed in relief. (That she could perform giddy exuberance even at her most defeated—Phoebe had always taken this quality of hers for granted.)

"Phoebe!" Susan chimed, matching Phoebe's exultant tone as she descended from her perch and enveloped Phoebe in an overblown bear hug—as if they actually liked each other, as if they hadn't seen each other in ten years when the truth was more like a year. "Ohmygod you look *so* great!"

"Thanks. So do you," Phoebe lied. In fact, she'd never seen Susan look worse. Her skin was blotchy. It was pretty obvious she'd gained weight. Susan, Phoebe thought with a combination of disdain and jealousy, but mostly just disdain, was one of those girls for whom mediocrity was its own reward.

"It's the craziest thing," Susan said, leaning into Phoebe's ear with her hot beer breath. "There are all these totally gorgeous guys here!"

"That's so crazy!" Phoebe said, distracted. She'd already spotted her gorgeous guy, standing over by a potted ficus. He was a tallish thing with streaks of platinum in his spiky brown hair, and he was wearing a brown suede fringed jacket and black leather pants. She had a feeling he was looking at her, too. She wasn't expecting him to admit it. But there he was, not three minutes later, standing next to her, saying, "I've been checking you out," one elbow leaned up against an Ikea bookcase filled with Susan's college psychology textbooks.

"Oh, really?" Phoebe said.

"Yeah, really," the gorgeous guy said and then smiled. He lifted a plastic cup to his lips. "You're very fuckable," he told her before he bent his head back and chugged.

Of all the affronts! But Phoebe could play this game, too. Which is why she asked him, "Do you really mean it?" all big eyes and faux grateful.

Except she was. That was the pathetic part. She couldn't help herself. When cocky assholes expressed interest in her, she felt alive. When nice guys hit on her, she had trouble caring. This was because she had become a living metaphor for her aspirations, for her quest for approval (and, invariably, for her history of disappointment). It had started in the fifth grade with Roger (Stinky) Mancuso, who mysteriously left town a week after their first kiss; in high school, it was Jason Barry Gold, the captain of the varsity lacrosse team, who informed Phoebe that she was "more of a challenge" than the other girls in her class because she was a virgin; then there were Spitty Clark, a frat boy and possible date rapist who lost his lunch in the middle of her first attempt to lose that virginity, and Humphrey Fung, a kilt-wearing anarchist who dumped her for an animal-rights activist, and, finally, Bruce Bledstone, a married professor of critical theory, who assured Phoebe, during one of several breakups, that though he couldn't express deeper feelings for her, she had "permanently eroticized the topography of his bedroom." It was little wonder that, by the time Phoebe arrived in New York with a B.A. in feminist film theory, she felt that sex was all she really had to offer.

"I mean it," he said. Then he extended an arm and introduced himself as Pablo Miles.

"Starla Chambers," she said, returning the favor—because it sounded like the kind of name that belonged to the kind of girl he'd want to know and she wanted to be.

Whereupon Pablo Miles got down on one knee, pressed his lips to the back of her hand, then his tongue.

"Gross!" She jerked her hand out of his grasp.

"You know you like it," he told her.

"I don't just like it, I need it," Phoebe corrected him.

"Nympho."

"Letch."

"I never said I wasn't."

She rolled her eyes. She lit a cigarette. She wasn't having a bad time.

Their first date was more like an appointment—to screw. Pablo Miles called her the very next morning. He arrived at her apartment at noon. They went to bed at one. But first he pushed her up against the door of her closet. "You have a really hot body," he told her.

"So do you," she was going to tell him, then changed her mind, thinking it sounded too aggressive. And because, despite the nympho jokes, he was the conqueror and she was the conquest. That was the arrangement.

"Thank you," she said instead, and smiled demurely.

Whereupon Pablo Miles reached under her skirt. In response, Phoebe made little breathy noises intended to imply her helplessness in the face of overwhelming desire. She didn't mean most of them. Maybe not any of them. Not because it didn't feel good. It felt plenty good. But it felt insignificant. Something like pissing. She was finding that sex could be like that—satisfying, but in only the most quotidian of ways. In fact, she could come at will. In ten seconds flat. With the right amount of pressure applied to the right places. At the same time, she was never entirely convinced that she'd come. Her orgasms frequently seemed too calculated to be believed.

It was like that with Pablo Miles.

After which point he asked her, "Do you want me to fuck you now?"

She told him, "OK."

Because it seemed like a nice thing to do—to let him fuck her after he'd brought her, if not to orgasm, then to something that loosely approximated one. And then he did. And she enjoyed it insofar as she enjoyed watching Pablo Miles enjoy himself. So she came again. Or, at least, she made noises to imply that she had. Because Pablo Miles was bound to be both flattered and impressed.

Afterward, he said, "A lot of girls can't come during intercourse."

To which Phoebe replied, "I'm not like other girls. I'm more like a man."

"You're like a man's fantasy," he told her.

She didn't argue with the assessment.

They showered. They dressed. They moseyed on over to some adorable little café with an Italian surname, on MacDougal Street, where they sat at a wrought-iron table out front, slurping the froth off their cappuccinos. They were both feeling high on themselves—the way people sometimes do after sex that leads to orgasm in a timely fashion. Pablo told Phoebe that he was destined to be recognized as the most important American artist of the post–Second World War period. In the meantime, he was getting his M.F.A. at Hunter. Phoebe told Pablo that she intended to make groundbreaking documentaries on the "male gaze." In the meantime, she was working as a two-hundred-dollar-a-week production assistant for an all-women documentary collective, currently shooting *Home Is Where the Husband Is,* a cinema vérité exploration of Filipino mail-order brides living in Queens.

Later, the talk turned to all the other guys/girls who were currently hot for the two of them. "There's this total dweeb named Robert who's always calling me, and I feel bad because he's really nice, but I'm totally not interested," Phoebe told Pablo.

"Believe me, I know what that's like," Pablo told Phoebe. "There's this girl at Hunter who's, like, obsessed with me. She's, like, this big fat girl. Ass like a truck. She's always writing me these love letters. Maybe I should fuck her. You know, just to be nice." (Smile, smile.)

"You're so bad." (Phoebe shaking her head; Pablo loving it; Phoebe loving it, too. What was more ego-enhancing than making dumb jokes at the expense of ugly women? Phoebe could never decide whom she hated more—other people or herself.)

Their second date was more of a date. They met for a late dinner at Rose of India on East Sixth Street, where they split an order of *chana saag* and talked about the past. "I hated guys like you in high school," Phoebe felt compelled to inform Pablo.

"How do you know what I was like in high school?" Pablo asked.

"I can just tell," she told him. "You probably wouldn't even have talked to me in high school."

"Were you hot?"

"Not particularly," she admitted.

"Then I probably wouldn't have talked to you," he agreed.

"See, I told you," she said, hating him just a little.

"But you're hot now," he said. "So what does it matter?"

She liked him again. She was easy to appease. She was even more eager to please. The only reason she went to the midnight showing of *Wings of Desire* at the Angelika Film Center was that Pablo wanted to. She dozed off halfway through. Pablo nudged her during the credits. "Come on, wake up," he whispered. "Unless you want me to fuck you while you're asleep."

"Rapist," she muttered under her breath.

"Baby, I'm a rape fantasy," he muttered back.

"I thought Alekan's use of chiaroscuro was pure genius," he volunteered in the taxi back to his Brooklyn digs—half a floor of an old turpentine factory that he shared with four other guys.

"Alex who?" she asked.

"Forget it," he said, scowling.

"No, why?"

"I thought you said you worked in film."

"I do."

"Alekan is only, like, the greatest cinematographer who ever lived."

"Well, I didn't know that!"

"Well, now you do."

His canvases hung from the makeshift walls of his bedroom. They were big and busy, with splattered oil paint half obscuring recognizable cartoon characters and free-floating female body parts. There was a quality to all of them that was, she had to admit, oppressively familiar. Phoebe was disappointed. She'd been thinking that Pablo Miles might be a great innovator for our times. Despondent, she stretched out on his futon and closed her eyes.

"What's the matter?" he asked, climbing onto the mattress next to her.

"Nothing," she answered.

"Are you horny?"

"Maybe."

"Do you want me to fuck you?"

Was it possible that she didn't know if she did? Phoebe often found herself unable to differentiate between what she wanted and what he wanted, whoever *he* happened to be at the time.

"I'll take that to mean yes," Pablo said, reaching for her zipper.

The next morning, over a portion of Stouffer's French Bread Pizza and some strawberry-flavored Carnation Instant Breakfast, he said, "I've got to be careful. I could get used to this life."

"I know what you mean," Phoebe said, jubilant at the thought that he might be growing attached to her. That she wasn't necessarily growing attached to him was beside the point. He was so handsome, and a painter. He'd even gone to Princeton. It was an impressive résumé, a romantic résumé.

She felt like hot shit just thinking about it.

"I want to go away with you," he told her on the phone the following day. "My family has a house near Killington. Nothing fancy. Just an old A-frame at the base of the mountain. Let's go up Friday morning. Just you and me. What do you say?"

The idea of going away with Pablo Miles worried Phoebe. After all, they'd met only a week before. And what if they ran out of things to talk about up there in the country with no distractions—no downtown Manhattan or bohemian Brooklyn to confuse with a context? She thought back to the only trip she'd taken with Humphrey the anarchist, a relationship-ending sojourn on an island off the coast of Maine. He'd spent the entire weekend lying on a flotation device off the dock, reading Simone de Beauvoir's *The Second Sex*—and ignoring Phoebe.

"We hardly know each other," she said.

"So?"

"It seems kind of soon."

"I want to fuck you in a sleeping bag."

The image excited her. Or maybe it was the sound of the word "fuck" on Pablo Miles's lips. On his lips, that word sounded like an imperative.

"The thing is, I have a shoot on Friday," Phoebe told him. "I mean, it's not my shoot . . ." Because she was just the grunt who unpacked the catered lunch, who separated the clear plastic wrap from the basket of premade sandwiches. "Let me see if I can get out of it."

And she did. She started packing the night before. All her cute clothes. The kind of clothes *Mademoiselle* suggested you pack for a romantic getaway. Puffy socks to pad around the fire in. An oversized chenille sweater with extra-long sleeves to hide your hands in when you're feeling coy. She was ready to go at ten. At quarter past, she looked at her watch. At half past, the phone rang. It was Pablo calling from the street. "Listen, Starla, I broke down on the Brooklyn Bridge," he shouted over honking horns and emergency-vehicle sirens.

"That's terrible!" Phoebe shouted back.

"Yeah, the radiator overheated or something. I'm gonna take Betty to the garage. I'll call you when I get home."

But he didn't. He didn't call the next day, either. And by that point it was pretty clear that he wasn't going to.

Phoebe was mostly just relieved. She didn't know how much longer she could have continued the experiment, in the end, that's all Pablo Miles was to her—a test case to see whom she could fool, and for how long, into thinking that she was someone she wasn't. If it ended now as opposed to later, he would never learn how neurotic and boring and essentially talentless she really was, and be forced to leave, disappointing them both. That was the problem with cocky assholes. In the end, they were good only for sex. In the end, you couldn't wait to get away, to get back to yourself—even if that self was a fraud, or a freak, or a fool.

From *This Boy's Life*

TOBIAS WOLFF

One day my mother and I went down to Alkai Point to watch a mock naval battle between the Odd Fellows and the Lions Club. This was during Seafair, when the hydroplane races were held. The park overlooked the harbor; we could just make out the figures on the two sailboats throwing water-balloons back and forth and trying to repel each other's boarding parties. There was a crowd in the park, and whenever one of these boarding parties got thrown back into the water everybody would laugh.

My mother was laughing with the rest. She loved to watch men goof around with each other: lifeguards, soldiers in bus stations, fraternity brothers having a car wash.

It was a clear day. Hawkers moved through the crowd, selling sun glasses and hats and Seafair souvenirs. Girls were sunning themselves on blankets. The air smelled of coconut oil.

Two men holding bottles of beer stood nearby. They kept turning and looking at us. Then one of them walked over, a pair of binoculars swinging from a strap in his hand. He was darkly tanned and wore tennis whites. He had a thin mustache and a crew cut. "Hey, Bub," he said to me, "want to give these a try?" While he adjusted the strap around my neck and showed me how to focus the lenses, the other man came up and said something to my mother. She answered him, but continued gazing out toward the water with her hand shielding her eyes. I brought the Lions and the Odd Fellows into focus and watched them push each other overboard. They seemed so close I could see their pale bodies and the expressions of fatigue on their faces. Despite the hearty shouts they gave, they climbed the ropes with difficulty and fell back as soon as they met resistance. Each time they hit the water they stayed there a while longer, paddling just enough to keep themselves afloat, looking wearily up at the boats they were supposed to capture.

My mother accepted a beer from the man beside her. The one who'd offered me the binoculars sensed my restlessness, maybe even my jealousy. He knelt down beside me and explained the battle as if I were a little kid, but I took the binoculars off and handed them back to him.

"I don't know," my mother was saying. "We should probably get home pretty soon."

The man she'd been talking with turned to me. He was the older of the two, a tall angular man with ginger-colored hair and a disjointed way of moving, as if he were always off balance. He wore Bermudas and black socks. His long face was sunburned, making his teeth look strangely prominent. "Let's ask the big fella," he said. "What say, big fella? You want to watch the fun from my place?" He pointed at a large brick house on the edge of the park.

I ignored him. "Mom," I said. "I'm hungry."

"He hasn't had lunch yet," my mother said.

"Lunch," the man said. "That's no problem. What do you like?" he asked me. "What's your absolute favorite thing to have for lunch?"

I looked at my mother. She was in high spirits and that made me even grimmer, because I knew they were not due to my influence. "He likes hamburgers," she told him.

"You got it," he said. He took my mother's elbow and led her across the park toward the house. I was left to follow along with the other man, who seemed to find me interesting. He wanted to know my name, where I went to school, where I lived, my mother's name, the whereabouts of my father. I was a sucker for any grown-up who asked me questions. By the time we reached the house I had forgotten to be sullen and told him everything about us.

The house was cavernous inside, hushed and cool. The windows had stained-glass medallions set within their mullioned panes. They were arched, and so were the heavy doors. The living room ceiling, ribbed with beams, curved to an arch high overhead. I sat down on the couch. The coffee table in front of me was crowded with empty beer bottles. My mother went to the open windows on the harbor side of the room. "Boy!" she said. "What a view!"

The sunburned man said, "Judd, take care of our friend."

"Come on, Bub," said the man I'd been talking to. "I'll rustle you up something to eat."

I followed him to the kitchen and sat at a counter while Judd pulled things out of the refrigerator. He slapped together a baloney sandwich and set it in front of me. He seemed to have forgotten about the hamburger. I would have said something, but I had a pretty good idea that even if I did there still wasn't going to be any hamburger.

When we came back to the living room, my mother was looking out the window through the binoculars. The sunburned man stood beside her, his head bent close to hers, one hand resting on her shoulder as he gestured with his beer bottle at some point of interest. He turned as we came in and grinned at us. "There's our guy," he said. "How's it going? You get some lunch? Judd, did you get this man some lunch?"

"Yes sir."

"Great! That's the ticket! Have a seat, Rosemary. Right over here. Sit down, Jack, that's the boy. You like peanuts? Great! Judd, bring him some peanuts. And for Christ's sake get these bottles out of here." He sat next to my mother on the couch and smiled steadily at me while Judd stuck his fingers into the bottles and carried them clinking away. Judd returned with a dish of nuts and left with the rest of the bottles.

"There you go, Jack. Dig in! Dig in!" He watched me eat a few handfuls, nodding to himself as if I were acting in accordance with some prediction he had made. "You're an athlete," he said. "It's written all over you. The eyes, the build. What do you play, Jack, what's your game?"

"Baseball," I said. This was somewhere in the neighborhood of truth. In Florida I'd played nearly every day, and gotten good at it. But I hadn't played much since. I wasn't an athlete and I didn't look like one, but I was glad he thought so.

"Baseball!" he cried. "Judd, what did I tell you?"

Judd had taken a chair on the other side of the room, apart from the rest of us. He raised his eyebrows and shook his head at the other man's perspicacity.

My mother laughed and said something teasing. She called the man Gil.

"Wait a minute!" he said. "You think I'm just shooting the bull? Judd, what did I say about Jack here? What did I say he played?"

Judd crossed his dark legs. "Baseball," he said.

"All right," Gil said. "All right, I hope we've got *that* straightened out. Jack. Back to you. What other activities do you enjoy?"

"I like to ride bikes," I said, "but I don't have one." I saw the good humor leave my mother's face, just as I knew it would. She looked at me coldly and I looked coldly back at her. The subject of bicycles turned us into enemies. Our problem was that I wanted a bike and she didn't have enough money to buy me one. She had no money at all. She had explained this to me many times. I understood perfectly, but not having a bike seemed too hard a thing to bear in silence.

Gil mugged disbelief. He looked from me to my mother and back to me. "No bike? A boy with no bike?"

"We'll discuss this later," my mother told me.

"I just said—"

"I know what you said." She frowned and looked away.

"Hold on!" Gil said. "Just hold on. Now what's the story here, Mom? Are you seriously telling me that this boy does not have a bicycle?"

My mother said, "He's going to have to wait a little longer, that's all."

"Boys can't wait for bikes, Rosemary. Boys need bikes now!"

My mother shrugged and smiled tightly, as she usually did when she was cornered. "I don't have the money," she said quietly.

The word *money* left a heavy silence in its wake.

Then Gil said, "Judd, let's have another round. See if there's some ginger ale for the slugger."

Judd rose and left the room.

Gil said, "What kind of bicycle would you like to have, Jack?"

"A Schwinn, I guess."

"Really? You'd rather have a Schwinn than an English racer?" He saw me hesitate. "Or would you rather have an English racer?"

I nodded.

"Well then, say so! I can't read your mind."

"I'd rather have an English racer."

"That's the way. Now what *kind* of English racer are we talking about?"

Judd brought the drinks. Mine was bitter. I recognized it as Collins mix.

My mother leaned forward and said, "Gil."

He held up his hand. "What kind, Jack?"

"Raleigh," I told him. Gil smiled and I smiled back.

"Champagne taste," he said. "Go for the best, that's the way. What color?"

"Red."

"Red. Fair enough. I think we can manage that. Did you get all that, Judd? One bicycle, English racer, Raleigh, red."

"Got it," Judd said.

My mother said thanks but she couldn't accept it. Gil said it was for me to accept, not her. She began to argue, not halfheartedly but with resolve. Gil wouldn't hear a word of it. At one point he even put his hands over his ears.

At last she gave up. She leaned back and drank from her beer. And I saw that in spite of what she'd said she was really happy at the way things had turned out, not only because it meant the end of these arguments of ours but also because, after all, she wanted very much for me to have a bicycle.

"How are the peanuts, Jack?" Gil asked.

I said they were fine.

"Great," he said. "That's just great."

Gil and my mother had a few more beers and talked while Judd and I watched the hydroplane qualifying heats on television. In the early evening Judd drove us back to the boardinghouse. My mother and I lay on our beds for a while with the lights off, feeling the breeze, listening to the treetops rustle outside. She asked if I would mind staying home alone that night. She had been invited out for dinner. "Who with?" I asked. "Gil and Judd?"

"Gil," she said.

"No," I said. I was glad. This would firm things up. The room filled with shadows. My mother got up and took a bath, then put on a full blue skirt and an off-the-shoulder Mexican blouse and the fine turquoise jewelry my father had bought her when they were driving through Arizona before the war. Earrings, necklace, heavy bracelet, concha belt. She'd picked up some sun that day; the blue of the turquoise seemed especially vivid, and so did the blue of her eyes. She dabbed perfume behind her ears, in the crook of her elbow, on her wrists. She rubbed her wrists together and touched them to her neck and chest. She turned from side to side, checking herself in the mirror. Then she stopped turning and studied herself head-on in a sober way. Without taking her eyes from the mirror she asked me how she looked. Really pretty, I told her.

"That's what you always say."

"Well, it's true."

"Good," she said. She gave herself one last look and we went downstairs.

Marian and Kathy came in while my mother was cooking dinner for me. They had her turn around for them, both of them smiling and exclaiming, and Marian pushed her away from the stove and finished making my dinner so she wouldn't get stains on her blouse. My mother was cagey with their questions. They teased her about this mystery man, and when the horn honked outside they followed her down the ball, adjusting her clothes, patting her hair, issuing final instructions.

"He should have come to the door," Marian said when they were back in the kitchen.

Kathy shrugged, and looked down at the table. She was hugely pregnant by this time and may have felt unsure of her right to decide the finer points of dating.

"He should have come to the door," Marian said again.

I slept badly that night. I always did when my mother went out, which wasn't often these days. She came back late. I listened to her walk up the stairs and down the hall to our room. The door opened and closed. She stood just inside for a moment, then crossed the room and sat down on her bed. She was crying softly. "Mom?" I said. When she didn't answer I got up and went over to her. "What's wrong, Mom?" She looked at me, tried to say something, shook her head. I sat beside her and put my arms around her. She was gasping as if someone had held her underwater.

I rocked her and murmured to her. I was practiced at this and happy doing it, not because she was unhappy but because she needed me, and to be needed made me feel capable. Soothing her soothed me.

She exhausted herself, and I helped her into bed. She became giddy then, laughing and making fun of herself, but she didn't let go of my hand until she fell asleep.

In the morning we were shy with each other. I somehow managed not to ask her my question. That night I continued to master myself, but my self-mastery seemed like an act; I knew I was too weak to keep it up.

My mother was reading.

"Mom?" I said.

She looked up.

"What about the Raleigh?"

She went back to her book without answering. I did not ask again.

UFO in Kushiro

HARUKI MURAKAMI

Five straight days she spent in front of the television, staring at crumbled banks and hospitals, whole blocks of stores in flames, severed rail lines and expressways. She never said a word. Sunk deep in the cushions of the sofa, her mouth clamped shut, she wouldn't answer when Komura spoke to her. She wouldn't shake her head or nod. Komura could not be sure the sound of his voice was even getting through to her.

Komura's wife came from way up north in Yamagata and, as far as he knew, she had no friends or relatives who could have been hurt in Kobe. Yet she stayed rooted in front of the television from morning to night. In his presence, at least, she ate nothing and drank nothing and never went to the toilet. Aside from an occasional flick of the remote control to change the channel, she hardly moved a muscle.

Komura would make his own toast and coffee, and head off to work. When he came home in the evening, he'd fix himself a snack with whatever he found in the refrigerator and eat alone. She'd still be glaring at the late news when he dropped off to sleep. A stone wall of silence surrounded her. Komura gave up trying to break through.

When he came home from work that Sunday, the sixth day, his wife had disappeared.

* * *

Komura was a salesman at one of the oldest hi-fi-equipment specialty stores in Tokyo's Akihabara "Electronics Town." He handled top-of-the-line stuff and earned a sizeable commission whenever he made a sale. Most of his clients were doctors, wealthy independent businessmen, and rich provincials. He had been doing this for eight years and had a decent income right from the start. The economy was healthy, real-estate prices were rising, and Japan was overflowing with money. People's wallets were bursting with ten-thousand-yen bills, and everyone was dying to spend them. The most expensive items were the first to sell out.

Komura was tall and slim and a stylish dresser. He was good with people. In his bachelor days he had dated a lot of women. But after getting married, at twenty-six, he found that his desire for sexual adventures simply—and mysteriously—vanished. He hadn't slept with any woman but his wife during the five years of their marriage. Not that the opportunity had never presented itself—but he had lost all interest in fleeting affairs and one-night stands. He much preferred to come home early, have a relaxed meal with his wife, talk with her for a while on the sofa, then go to bed and make love. This was everything he wanted.

Komura's friends and colleagues were puzzled by his marriage. Alongside him with his clean, classic good looks, his wife could not have seemed more ordinary. She was short with thick arms, and she had a dull, even stolid appearance. And it wasn't just physical: there was nothing attractive about her personality either. She rarely spoke and always wore a sullen expression.

Still, though he did not quite understand why, Komura always felt his tension dissipate when he and his wife were together under one roof; it was the only time he could truly relax. He slept well with her, undisturbed by the strange dreams that had troubled him in the past. His erections were hard; his sex life was warm. He no longer had to worry about death or venereal disease or the vastness of the universe.

His wife, on the other hand, disliked Tokyo's crowds and longed for Yamagata. She missed her parents and her two elder sisters, and she would go home to see them whenever she felt the need. Her parents operated a successful inn, which kept them financially comfortable. Her father was crazy about his youngest daughter and happily paid her round-trip fares. Several times, Komura had come home from work to find his wife gone and a note on the kitchen table telling him that she was visiting her parents for a while. He never objected. He just waited for her to come back, and she always did, after a week or ten days, in a good mood.

But the letter his wife left for him when she vanished five days after the earthquake was different: *I am never coming back,* she had written, then went on to explain, simply but clearly, why she no longer wanted to live with him.

The problem is that you never give me anything, she wrote. *Or to put it more precisely, you have nothing inside you that you* can *give me. You are good and kind and handsome, but living with you is like living with a chunk of air. It's not entirely your fault, though. There are lots of women who will fall in love with you. But please don't call me. Just get rid of all the stuff I'm leaving behind.*

In fact, she hadn't left much of anything behind. Her clothes, her shoes, her umbrella, her coffee mug, her hair dryer: all were gone. She must have packed them in boxes and shipped them out after he left for work that morning. The only things still in the house that could be called "her stuff" were the bike she used for shopping and a few books. The Beatles and Bill Evans CDs that Komura had been collecting since his bachelor days had also vanished.

The next day, he tried calling his wife's parents in Yamagata. His mother-in-law answered the phone and told him that his wife didn't want to talk to him. She sounded somewhat apologetic. She also told him that they would be sending him the necessary forms soon and that he should put his seal on them and send them back right away.

Komura answered that he might not be able to send them "right away." This was an important matter, and he wanted time to think it over.

"You can think it over all you want, but I know it won't change anything," his mother-in-law said.

She was probably right, Komura told himself. No matter how much he thought or waited, things would never be the same. He was sure of that.

Shortly after he had sent the papers back with his seal stamped on them, Komura asked for a week's paid leave. His boss had a general idea of what had been happening, and February was a slow time of the year, so he let Komura go without a fuss. He seemed on the verge of saying something to Komura, but finally said nothing.

Sasaki, a colleague of Komura's, came over to him at lunch and said, "I hear you're taking time off. Are you planning to do something?"

"I don't know," Komura said. "What *should* I do?"

Sasaki was a bachelor, three years younger than Komura. He had a delicate build and short hair, and he wore round, gold-rimmed glasses. A lot of people thought he talked too much and had a rather arrogant air, but he got along well enough with the easygoing Komura.

"What the hell—as long as you're taking the time off, why not make a nice trip out of it?"

"Not a bad idea," Komura said.

Wiping his glasses with his handkerchief, Sasaki peered at Komura as if looking for some kind of clue.

"Have you ever been to Hokkaido?" he asked.

"Never."

"Would you like to go?"

"Why do you ask?"

Sasaki narrowed his eyes and cleared his throat. "To tell you the truth, I've got a small package I'd like to send to Kushiro, and I'm hoping you'll take it there for me. You'd be doing me a big favor, and I'd be glad to pay for a round-trip ticket. I could cover your hotel in Kushiro, too."

"A small package?"

"Like this," Sasaki said, shaping a four-inch cube with his hands. "Nothing heavy."

"Something to do with work?"

Sasaki shook his head. "Not at all," he said. "Strictly personal. I just don't want it to get knocked around, which is why I can't mail it. I'd like you to deliver it by hand, if possible. I really ought to do it myself; but I haven't got time to fly all the way to Hokkaido."

"Is it something important?"

His closed lips curling slightly, Sasaki nodded. "It's nothing fragile, and there are no 'hazardous materials.' There's no need to worry about it. They're not going to stop you when they X-ray it at the airport. I promise I'm not going to get you in trouble. And it weighs practically nothing. All I'm asking is that you take it along the way you'd take anything else. The only reason I'm not mailing it is I just don't *feel* like mailing it."

Hokkaido in February would be freezing cold, Komura knew, but cold or hot it was all the same to him.

"So who do I give the package to?"

"My sister. My younger sister. She lives up there."

Komura decided to accept Sasaki's offer. He hadn't thought about how to spend his week off, and making plans now would have been too much trouble. Besides, he had no reason for not wanting to go to Hokkaido. Sasaki called the airline then and there, reserving a ticket to Kushiro. The flight would leave two days later, in the afternoon.

At work the next day, Sasaki handed Komura a box like the ones used for human ashes, only smaller, wrapped in manila paper. Judging from the feel, it was made of wood. As Sasaki had said, it weighed practically nothing. Broad strips of transparent tape went all around the package over the paper. Komura held it in his hands and studied it a few seconds. He gave it a little shake but he couldn't feel or hear anything moving inside.

"My sister will pick you up at the airport. And she'll be arranging a room for you," Sasaki said. "All you have to do is stand outside the gate with the package in your hands where she can see it. Don't worry, the airport's not very big."

Komura left home with the box in his suitcase, wrapped in a thick undershirt. The plane was far more crowded than he had expected.

Why were all these people going from Tokyo to Kushiro in the middle of winter? he wondered.

The morning paper was full of earthquake reports. He read it from beginning to end on the plane. The number of dead was rising. Many areas were still without water or electricity, and countless people had lost their homes. Each article reported some new tragedy, but to Komura the details seemed oddly lacking in depth. All sounds reached him as far-off, monotonous echoes. The only thing he could give any serious thought to was his wife as she retreated ever farther into the distance.

Mechanically he ran his eyes over the earthquake reports, stopped now and then to think about his wife, then went back to the paper. When he grew tired of this, he closed his eyes and napped. And when he woke, he thought about his wife again. Why had she followed the TV earthquake reports with such intensity, from morning to night, without eating or sleeping? What could she have seen in them?

Two young women wearing overcoats of similar design and color approached Komura at the airport. One was fair-skinned and maybe five feet six, with short hair. The area from her nose to her full upper lip was oddly extended in a way that made Komura think of short-haired ungulates. Her companion was more like five feet one and would have been quite pretty if her nose hadn't been so small. Her long hair fell straight to her shoulders. Her ears were exposed, and there were two moles on her right earlobe which were emphasized by the earrings she wore. Both women looked to be in their mid-twenties. They took Komura to a café in the airport.

"I'm Keiko Sasaki," the taller woman said. "My brother told me how helpful you've been to him. This is my friend Shimao."

"Nice to meet you," Komura said.

"Hi," Shimao said.

"My brother tells me your wife recently passed away," Keiko Sasaki said with a respectful expression.

Komura waited a moment before answering. "No, she didn't die."

"I just talked to my brother the day before yesterday. I'm sure he said quite clearly that you'd lost your wife."

"I did. She divorced me. But as far as I know she's alive and well."

"That's odd. I couldn't possibly have misheard something so important." She gave him an injured look. Komura put a small amount of sugar in his coffee and gave it a gentle stir before taking a sip. The liquid was thin, with no taste to speak of, more sign than substance. What the hell am I doing here? he wondered.

"Well, I guess I did mishear it. I can't imagine how else to explain the mistake," Keiko Sasaki said, apparently satisfied now. She drew in a deep breath and chewed her lower lip. "Please forgive me. I was very rude."

"Don't worry about it. Either way, she's gone."

Shimao said nothing while Komura and Keiko spoke, but she smiled and kept her eyes on Komura. She seemed to like him. He could tell from her expression and her subtle body language. A brief silence fell over the three of them.

"Anyway, let me give you the important package I brought," Komura said. He unzipped his suitcase and pulled the box out of the folds of the thick ski undershirt he had wrapped it in. The thought struck him then: I was supposed to be holding this when I got off the plane. That's how they were going to recognize me. How did they know who I was?

Keiko Sasaki stretched her hands across the table, her expressionless eyes fixed on the package. After testing its weight, she did as Komura had done and gave it a few shakes by her ear. She flashed him a smile as if to signal that everything was fine, and slipped the box into her oversize shoulder bag.

"I have to make a call," she said. "Do you mind if I excuse myself for a moment?"

"Not at all," Komura said. "Feel free."

Keiko slung the bag over her shoulder and walked off toward a distant phone booth. Komura studied the way she walked. The upper half of her body was still, while everything from the hips down made large, smooth, mechanical movements. He had the strange impression that he was witnessing some moment from the past, shoved with random suddenness into the present.

"Have you been to Hokkaido before?" Shimao asked.

Komura shook his head.

"Yeah, I know. It's a long way to come."

Komura nodded, then turned to survey his surroundings. "Funny," he said, "sitting here like this, it doesn't feel as if I've come all that far."

"Because you flew. Those planes are too damn fast. Your mind can't keep up with your body."

"You may be right."

"Did you want to make such a long trip?"

"I guess so," Komura said.

"Because your wife left?"

He nodded.

"No matter how far you travel, you can never get away from yourself," Shimao said.

Komura was staring at the sugar bowl on the table as she spoke, but then he raised his eyes to hers.

"It's true," he said. "No matter how far you travel, you can never get away from yourself. It's like your shadow. It follows you everywhere."

Shimao looked hard at Komura. "I'll bet you loved her, didn't you?"

Komura dodged the question. "You're a friend of Keiko Sasaki's?"

"Right. We do stuff together."

"What kind of stuff?"

Instead of answering him, Shimao asked, "Are you hungry?"

"I wonder," Komura said. "I feel kind of hungry and kind of not."

"Let's go and eat something warm, the three of us. It'll help you relax."

Shimao drove a small four-wheel-drive Subaru. It had to have way over a hundred thousand miles on it, judging from how battered it was. The rear bumper had a huge dent in it. Keiko Sasaki sat next to

Shimao, and Komura had the cramped rear seat to himself. There was nothing particularly wrong with Shimao's driving, but the noise in back was terrible, and the suspension was nearly shot. The automatic transmission slammed into gear whenever it down-shifted, and the heater blew hot and cold. Shutting his eyes, Komura felt as if he had been imprisoned in a washing machine.

No snow had been allowed to gather on the streets in Kushiro, but dirty, icy mounds stood at random intervals on both sides of the road. Dense clouds hung low and, although it was not yet sunset, everything was dark and desolate. The wind tore through the city in sharp squeals. There were no pedestrians. Even the traffic lights looked frozen.

"This is one part of Hokkaido that doesn't get much snow," Keiko Sasaki explained in a loud voice, glancing back at Komura. "We're on the coast and the wind is strong, so whatever piles up gets blown away. It's cold, though, *freezing* cold. Sometimes it feels like it's taking your ears off."

"You hear about drunks who freeze to death sleeping on the street," Shimao said.

"Do you get bears around here?" Komura asked.

Keiko giggled and turned to Shimao. "Bears, he says."

Shimao gave the same kind of giggle.

"I don't know much about Hokkaido," Komura said by way of explanation.

"I know a good story about bears." Keiko said. "Right, Shimao?"

"A *great* story!" Shimao said.

But their talk broke off at that point, and neither of them told the bear story. Komura didn't ask to hear it. Soon they reached their destination, a big noodle shop on the highway. They parked in the lot and went inside. Komura had a beer and a hot bowl of ramen noodles. The place was dirty and empty and the chairs and tables were rickety, but the ramen was excellent, and when he had finished eating, Komura did, in fact, feel a little more relaxed.

"Tell me, Mr. Komura," Keiko Sasaki said, "do you have something you want to do in Hokkaido? My brother tells me you're going to spend a week here."

Komura thought about it for a moment, but couldn't come up with anything he wanted to do.

"How about a hot spring? Would you like a nice, long soak in a tub? I know a little country place not far from here."

"Not a bad idea," Komura said.

"I'm sure you'd like it. It's really nice. No bears or anything."

The two women looked at each other and laughed again.

"Do you mind if I ask you about your wife?" Keiko said.

"I don't mind."

"When did she leave?"

"Hmm . . . five days after the earthquake, so that's more than two weeks ago now."

"Did it have something to do with the earthquake?"

Komura shook his head. "Probably not. I don't think so."

"Still, I wonder if things like that aren't connected somehow," Shimao said with a tilt of the head.

"Yeah," Keiko said. "It's just that you can't see how."

"Right," Shimao said. "Stuff like that happens all the time."

"Stuff like what?" Komura asked.

"Like, say, what happened with somebody I know," Keiko said.

"You mean Mr. Saeki?" Shimao asked.

"Exactly," Keiko said. "There's this guy—Saeki. He lives in Kushiro. He's about forty. A hair stylist. His wife saw a UFO last year, in the autumn. She was driving on the edge of town all by herself in the middle of the night and she saw a huge UFO land in a field. *Whoosh!* Like in *Close Encounters.* A week later, she left home. They weren't having any domestic problems or anything. She just disappeared and never came back."

"Into thin air," Shimao said.

"And it was because of the UFO?" Komura asked.

"I don't know why," Keiko said. "She just walked out. No note or anything. She had two kids in elementary school, too. The whole week before she left, all she'd do was tell people about the UFO. You couldn't get her to stop. She'd go on and on about how big and beautiful it was."

She paused to let the story sink in.

"My wife left a note," Komura said. "And we don't have any kids."

"So your situation's a little better than Saeki's," Keiko said.

"Yeah. Kids make a big difference," Shimao said, nodding.

"Shimao's father left home when she was seven," Keiko explained with a frown. "Ran off with his wife's younger sister."

"All of a sudden. One day," Shimao said, smiling.

A silence settled over the group.

"Maybe Mr. Saeki's wife didn't run away but was captured by aliens from the UFO," Komura said to smooth things over.

"It's possible," Shimao said with a somber expression. "You hear stories like that all the time."

"You mean like you're-walking-along-the-street-and-a-bear-eats-you kind of thing?" Keiko asked. The two women laughed again.

The three of them left the noodle shop and went to a nearby love hotel. It was on the edge of town, on a street where love hotels alternated with gravestone dealers. The hotel Shimao had chosen was an odd building, constructed to look like a European castle. A triangular red flag flew on its highest tower.

Keiko got the key at the front desk, and the three of them took the elevator to the room. The windows were tiny, compared with the absurdly big bed. Komura hung his down jacket on a hanger and went into the toilet. During the few minutes he was in there, the two women managed to run a bath, dim the lights, check the heat, turn on the television, examine the delivery menus from local restaurants, test the light switches at the head of the bed, and check the contents of the minibar.

"The owners are friends of mine," Keiko said. "I had them get their biggest room ready. It *is* a love hotel, but don't let that bother you. You're not bothered, are you?"

"Not at all," Komura said.

"I thought this would make a lot more sense than sticking you in a cramped little room in some cheap business hotel by the station."

"You may be right," Komura said.

"Why don't you take a bath? I filled the tub."

Komura did as he was told. The tub was huge. He felt uneasy soaking in it alone. The couples who came to this hotel probably took baths together.

When he emerged from the bathroom, Komura was surprised to find that Keiko Sasaki had left. Shimao was still there, drinking beer and watching TV.

"Keiko went home," Shimao said. "She wanted me to apologize and tell you that she'll be back tomorrow morning. Do you mind if I stay here a little while and have a beer?"

"Fine," Komura said.

"You're sure it's no problem? Like, you want to be alone or you can't relax if somebody else is around or something?"

Komura insisted it was no problem. Drinking a beer and drying his hair with a towel, he watched TV with Shimao. It was a news special on the Kobe earthquake. The usual images appeared again and again: tilted buildings, buckled streets, old women weeping, confusion and aimless anger. When a commercial came on, Shimao used the remote to switch off the TV.

"Let's talk," she said, "as long as we're here."

"Fine," Komura said.

"Hmm, what should we talk about?"

"In the car, you and Keiko said something about a bear, remember? You said it was a great story."

"Oh yeah," she said, nodding. "The bear story."

"You want to tell it to me?"

"Sure, why not?"

Shimao got a fresh beer from the minibar and filled both their glasses.

"It's a little raunchy," she said. "You don't mind?"

Komura shook his head.

"I mean, some men don't like hearing a woman tell certain kinds of stories."

"I'm not like that."

"It's something that actually happened to me, so it's a little embarrassing."

"I'd like to hear it if you're OK with it."

"I'm OK, if you're OK."

"I'm OK," Komura said.

"Three years ago—back around the time I entered junior college—I was dating this guy. He was a year older than me, a college student. He was the first guy I had sex with. One day the two of us were out hiking—in the mountains way up north."

She took a sip of beer.

"It was fall, and the hills were full of bears. That's the time of year when the bears are getting ready to hibernate, so they're out looking for food and they're really dangerous. Sometimes they attack people. They did an awful job on one hiker just three days before we went out. So somebody gave us a bell to carry—about the same size as a wind-bell. You're supposed to shake it when you walk so the bears know there are people around and won't come out. Bears don't attack people on purpose. I mean, they're pretty much vegetarians. They don't *have* to attack people. What happens is they suddenly bump into people in their territory and they get surprised or angry and they attack out of reflex. So if you walk along ringing your bell, they'll avoid you. Get it?"

"I get it."

"So that's what we were doing, walking along and ringing the bell. We got to this place where there was nobody else around, and all of a sudden he said he wanted to . . . do it. I kind of liked the idea, too, so I said OK and we went into this bushy place off the trail where nobody could see us, and we spread out a piece of plastic. But I was afraid of the bears. I mean, think how awful it would be to have some bear attack you from behind and kill you when you're having sex! I would never want to die that way. Would you?"

Komura agreed that he would not want to die that way.

"So there we were, shaking the bell with one hand and having sex. Kept it up from start to finish. *Ding-a-ling! Ding-a-ling!*"

"Which one of you shook the bell?"

"We took turns. We'd trade off when our hands got tired. It was so weird, shaking this bell the whole time we were doing it! I think about it sometimes even now, when I'm having sex, and I start laughing."

Komura gave a little laugh, too.

Shimao clapped her hands. "Oh, that's wonderful," she said. "You *can* laugh after all!"

"Of course I can laugh," Komura said, but come to think of it, this was the first time he had laughed in quite a while. When was the last time?

"Do you mind if I take a bath, too?" Shimao asked.

"Fine," he said.

While she was bathing, Komura watched a variety show emceed by some comedian with a loud voice. He didn't find it the least bit funny, but he couldn't tell whether that was the show's fault or his own. He drank a beer and opened a pack of nuts from the minibar. Shimao stayed in the bath for a very long time. Finally, she came out wearing nothing but a towel and sat on the edge of the bed. Dropping the towel she slid in between the sheets like a cat and lay there looking straight at Komura.

"When was the last time you did it with your wife?" she asked.

"At the end of December, I think."

"And nothing since?"

"Nothing."

"Not with anybody?"

Komura closed his eyes and shook his head.

"You know what *I* think," Shimao said. "You need to lighten up and learn to enjoy life a little more. I mean, think about it: tomorrow there could be an earthquake; you could be kidnapped by aliens; you could be eaten by a bear. Nobody knows what's going to happen."

"Nobody knows what's going to happen," Komura echoed.

"*Ding-a-ling,*" Shimao said.

After several failed attempts to have sex with Shimao, Komura gave up. This had never happened to him before.

"You must have been thinking about your wife," Shimao said.

"Yup," Komura said, but in fact what he had been thinking about was the earthquake. Images of it had come to him one after another, as if in a slide show, flashing on the screen and fading away. Highways, flames, smoke, piles of rubble, cracks in streets. He couldn't break the chain of silent images.

Shimao pressed her ear against his naked chest.

"These things happen," she said.

"Uh-huh."

"You shouldn't let it bother you."

"I'll try not to," Komura said. "Men always let it bother them, though."

Komura said nothing.

Shimao played with his nipple.

"You said your wife left a note, didn't you?"

"I did."

"What did it say?"

"That living with me was like living with a chunk of air."

"A chunk of air?" Shimao tilted her head back to look up at Komura. "What does *that* mean?"

"That there's nothing inside me, I guess."

"Is it true?"

"Could be," Komura said. "I'm not sure, though. I may have nothing inside me, but what would *something* be?"

"Yeah, really, come to think of it. What *would* something be? My mother was crazy about salmon skin. She always used to wish there were a kind of salmon made of nothing but skin. So there may be some cases when it's *better* to have nothing inside. Don't you think?"

Komura tried to imagine what a salmon made of nothing but skin would be like. But even supposing there were such a thing, wouldn't the skin itself be the *something* inside? Komura took a deep breath, raising and then lowering Shimao's head on his chest.

"I'll tell you this, though," Shimao said, "I don't know whether you've got nothing or something inside you, but I think you're terrific. I'll bet the world is full of women who would understand you and fall in love with you."

"It said that, too."

"What? Your wife's note?"

"Uh-huh."

"No kidding," Shimao said, lowering her head to Komura's chest again. He felt her earring against his skin like a secret object.

"Come to think of it," Komura said, "what's the *something* inside that box I brought up here?"

"Is it bothering you?"

"It wasn't bothering me before. But now, I don't know, it's starting to."

"Since when?"

"Just now."

"All of a sudden?"

"Yeah, once I started thinking about it, all of a sudden."

"I wonder why it's started to bother you now, all of a sudden?"

Komura glared at the ceiling for a minute to think. "I wonder."

They listened to the moaning of the wind. The wind: it came from someplace unknown to Komura, and it blew past to someplace unknown to him.

"I'll tell you why," Shimao said in a low voice. "It's because that box contains the *something* that was inside you. You didn't know that when you carried it here and gave it to Keiko with your own hands. Now, you'll never get it back."

Komura lifted himself from the mattress and looked down at the woman. Tiny nose, moles on the earlobe. In the room's deep silence, his heart beat with a loud, dry sound. His bones cracked as he leaned forward. For one split second, Komura realized that he was on the verge of committing an act of overwhelming violence.

"Just kidding," Shimao said when she saw the look on his face. "I said the first thing that popped into my head. It was a lousy joke. I'm sorry. Try not to let it bother you. I didn't mean to hurt you."

Komura forced himself to calm down and, after a glance around the room, sank his head into his pillow again. He closed his eyes and took a deep breath. The huge bed stretched out around him like a nocturnal sea. He heard the freezing wind. The fierce pounding of his heart shook his bones.

"Are you starting to feel a *little* as if you've come a long way?" Shimao asked.

"Hmm. Now I feel as if I've come a *very* long way," Komura answered honestly.

Shimao traced a complicated design on Komura's chest with her fingertip, as if casting a magic spell.

"But really," she said, "you're just at the beginning."

How to Love a Republican

STEVE ALMOND

I met Darcy Hicks early in the primary season, at a dive in Randolph, New Hampshire. She was sitting at the bar in a blue skirt, sipping from a tumbler and looking bored. The locals had hit on her already. But they were missing it. Her edges were too crisp for the room. Her makeup was nearly invisible.

The stool next to her opened up and I sat down. A Kenny Loggins tune came on the jukebox and the bartender began to sing along. Darcy glanced at her drink, trying to decide whether another would make matters better or worse. I'd had a miserable day and was feeling sorry for myself, lonely, a little reckless. I introduced myself and asked her please not to take offense if I bought her a drink.

Darcy turned slowly. In profile she had seemed dangerously icy. But straight on her face was sweet and a little flushed.

"Jack and ginger," she said.

I ordered two.

It turned out we were both in New Hampshire doing issue work. Darcy was pitching agricultural subsidies to the Republicans; I was pitching drug counseling to the Dems. I'd spent the past week trolling rehab centers, listening to earnest social workers and sad, unconvincing ex-junkies. At night, I squeezed into the tiny hotel bathtub and tried to wash the smoke out of my pores. Darcy was faring no better. She'd twisted her ankle that morning touring a derelict strawberry farm.

"Who farms here?" she said. "What would they farm, granite?"

"Maybe they thought they'd sent you to Vermont."

She shook her head. "There are no Republicans in Vermont."

The truth is, we were on the fringes of the campaign, miles from the action; our duties were more ceremonial than anything. But there was in each of us the bug of politics, a talky competitiveness, a desire to impose our sense of right on the world. We carried, along with our clattery Beltway cynicism and our Motorolas, a tremendous vulnerability to hope. And now, as we talked and drank, this vulnerability became shared property, like the pack of Camel Lights that lay between us, or the tales of Model UN coups, the geeky adolescent versions of our adult passion.

Outside, the December night was crisp. A fog had rolled in and lay draped over the pine barrens like gauze. We stood beside my rental car, shivering, swinging a little. Darcy was packed neatly into her blue cotton blend. Her hair was the color of wet straw and fell to her clavicle. A flower belonged behind her ear. Kissing her seemed the most uncomplicated decision I had made in years.

So there was that, an evening of esprit de corps, some very fine necking in the great hither and yon of the electorate. Back in D.C., the situation was a little less clear.

Darcy worked at the Fund For Tradition, a think tank devoted to—as the swanky, four-color pamphlets told it—*fiscal restraint and the defense of traditional values.* I was at Citizen Action, a relic of the LBJ era. We didn't have pamphlets. Our mission was to lobby the halls of power on behalf of the disenfranchised. To piss, in other words, up the mighty tree of capitalism.

We conducted the same basic life at a slightly different amplitude. The brutal hours of apprenticeship, the hasty lunches and reports whose sober facts gummed our thoughts. We were both involved with other people, people more like ourselves, who satisfied us in a placid way. I might never have seen her again. Except that I did.

She was standing alone in the Senate gallery. Congress was on break, the tourists gone. Darcy gazed down into the darkening well of the Senate. She was wearing a peacoat and a dark pillbox hat, which now, in my memory, I have affixed with a veil, though I'm certain this was not the case.

I circled the gallery and waited for her to notice me. When I called her name, she gasped and placed a hand over her heart.

"Oh Billy! It's you."

"I'm sorry. Did I startle you?"

"No," she said. "Not at all."

"You look beautiful," I said.

This wasn't what I'd meant to say. It was certainly too ardent for the setting. But it was the truest thing I was feeling, and anyway Darcy had this effect on me.

She shook her head a little, then blushed. "What are you doing here?" she said.

"I'm not sure. I was visiting a friend downstairs, a guy who works with Sarbanes. I just sort of wandered up here."

"I come here all the time," Darcy said. "It helps me think."

"About what?"

She pursed her lips. "Why we're here, I guess. The desire to effect good in an arena of civility."

"Is that Jefferson?"

"Not really. It's me."

The smell of the Senate rose from the empty well, old leather and something vaguely peppery, Brylcreem maybe. The place exuded a sense of quiet dignity, which was more than the absence of its usual clamor, seemed closer, in the end, to the calm we hoped to find at the center of our lives.

"Does that sound hokey, Billy?" Darcy said suddenly.

"Not at all."

"You don't think so?" Her face leapt from the dark fabric of her coat, sweetly arrayed in worry.

"Are you hungry?" I said.

Darcy opened her mouth but said nothing.

"Other plans?"

"Sort of. I should . . ." She looked at me for a moment. "Hold on."

"If you've got plans, I don't want to impose."

Darcy laughed, a bit lavishly. "I wouldn't let you impose," she said, and drew the cell phone from her coat pocket.

There are so many competing interests on the human heart. For those of us truly terrified of death, intent on leaving some kind of mark, plowing through our impatient twenties with an *agenda,* there are moments when chemistry—the chemistry between bodies, the chemistry of connection—seems no more than a sentimental figment. And then something happens, you meet a woman and you can't stop looking at her mouth. Everything she does, every word and gesture, stirs inside you, strikes the happy gong. The way she throws herself into a fresh field of snow. The delicacy of her sneezes, like a candle being snuffed. The sugary sting of whiskey on her tongue. Chemistry in its sensual aspects. Chemistry the ultimate single-issue voter.

We were both tipsy and tangled in my flannel sheets. We'd talked about not letting this happen, this sudden rush into the secret bodies. But Darcy, her neck, the length of her torso, the wisp of corn silk above her pelvic basin, and the gentle application of her hands, her generous, unfeigned devotions to my body—which I secretly loathed, which shamed me for its deficiencies of grace and muscle—and her hair reeling across my chest. . . . All these came at me in a tumble of violent emotion, stripped from me the language with which one crafts cautious deferrals, the *maybe I should go,* the sudden pause, the stuttered breath and step back, the gallant bonered retreat to the bathroom.

No. We made instead a ridiculous flying machine in two clamped parts. In the thick of our clumsy desire, pungent and shameless, we clutched one another by the cheeks, let the skin of our bellies smack briskly, and flew.

"So that's what it's like to love a Republican," I said.

"There are other ways, too." Darcy giggled. "Do you have cigarettes? I'd kill for a cigarette."

I reached into my bedside drawer.

"Why do we hide them?"

"They're an ugly habit."

She took a slow drag and blew the smoke at the ceiling. "Oh yeah."

Outside a light snow fell. The cars on the road made a sound like the surf. The moon lit Darcy's face. Her nose was a little blunt. One of her incisors pushed out dramatically from the neat band of her teeth. These flaws served to particularize her beauty. One's memory snagged on them.

"You're my first beard," she said thoughtfully.

"How was it?"

"Bristly."

"Like being with a lumberjack?"

"A lumberjack wouldn't whimper."

"Did I whimper?"

"Unless that was me."

Darcy sat up and peered around the room. Che Guevara stared down at her from the closet door, in his fierce mustache. My fertility goddesses stood ranked along the sill, squat figures with sagging breasts and hips round as swales. I waited for Darcy to ask me about them so I could recite my Peace Corps stories. (I'd saved a little girl's life! A goat had been killed in my honor!) But she only took another drag and covered her warm little breasts.

"Where are we again?"

"My apartment."

"The address, you dope."

"Why do you want the address?"

"For the cab."

"Oh please don't go. I'd rather if you stayed. Or I could drive you."

"No. I need to think about this."

"Can't we think together? I'd like to think with you."

"I'm not sure you're the best thing for my thought process."

Darcy rose from the bed and began collecting her clothes. I watched her move around the room. I wanted terribly for her to come close enough that I could take a bite of her tush, which trembled like a pale bell. But this was not going to happen. From the other room came the slithery sound of panty hose, the clasp of a bra.

"What's there to think about?" I called out. "Was this a mistake? Because I don't feel like this was a mistake."

Darcy reemerged looking combed and dangerous, like something from a winter catalogue. She took a last drag off her cigarette and dropped it in her wineglass. A horn sounded below, in the street.

"Can I at least walk you down?"

"You're sweet. I wish you wouldn't." She set her fingers to her throat and said, a little dreamily, "I'm going to have a rash tomorrow, from your beard."

I went to the window and watched her slip into the cab. There was something tragically illicit about the moment. I didn't know what to do. The golden thread between us had snapped. How had this happened? I threw open the window and bellowed: "Why do I feel like I've been taken advantage of?"

Darcy looked up. Her face shone behind the dark pane. Just before she laughed, her mouth pulled down slightly at the corners, which suggested, even in the midst of her gaiety, an irrevocable sadness. I was certain, gazing down through the soft tiers of snow, the smell of her rising up from my beard, that this sadness could be undone. This was my bright idea. I was, after all, a good liberal.

But then Darcy disappeared and I was left to moon liberally through the long white weekend, during which I spoke and ate and fucked dispiritedly with the woman I was dating, a good woman, with earnest rings of hair and a powerful devotion to social justice.

I called Darcy at the office and listened to her outgoing message, whose crisp, chirpy tones made me feel renounced, and left two excruciatingly casual messages, and took lunch at the bistro across from the Fund For Tradition, and one afternoon wandered over to Capitol Hill and kneeled in the cool Senate gallery, waiting like a parishioner. By week two my heart had dithered into a boyish panic. I left a final message on her machine telling her that I didn't understand what was going on but that I was hurt and confused and felt that something had been betrayed, the feelings that had passed between us, that these feelings felt real to me and that they didn't come along very often and shouldn't be squandered, and that if she felt any of these same things, even unsteadily, she owed it to herself, as well as just to common decency, to call me back, that dodging me was no solution, unless she was one of those people who offered intimacy and then withdrew, who, for lack of a better word, *used* people, in which case she was best not to call back at all. But that, if she was still, if she felt, even a little, I was sorry to sound petulant, I didn't mean to, but I was upset and if could she please call me back and here was my number, at which point a voice came on the line noting that my three minutes were up and would I like to leave the message, or re-record it, or erase the whole thing, which I did.

What was this thing between us, anyway? Just some Jungle Fever of the low political stripe. Who was Darcy Hicks, anyway? Maybe this was her secret fetish: sexing up the left and reporting the details back to her Republican overlords. On and on I went, the florid improvisations of the wounded heart.

And then, just as this clatter was subsiding, I saw her again. On C-SPAN. She stood at the edge of the frame as John McCain—fresh off his win in New Hampshire—rallied the troops in an Iowa VFW hall. Darcy kept drifting in and out of the picture. She was wearing a red dress and smiling desperately. McCain told the crowd he'd come to Elk Horn for one purpose: to discuss the plight of the small family farm, and the need for renewed agricultural subsidies.

The phone rang. It was late, one in the morning on a Tuesday.

"What's your address again?" Darcy said.

I wanted to say something caustic and clever but adrenaline had flushed my chest and all the words I had marshaled in my rehearsals for this moment seemed stingy and beside the point.

The line crackled. "Billy? Hurry up! My battery's going dead."

"Where are you?"

"That's what I'm asking you. Oh!" Darcy squealed, and there was a thump. Her phone began to cut out, so that I could hear her voice only in snatches, urgent little phonemes: *time, get, numb—*. The line went dead.

Twenty minutes later my buzzer rang. Darcy burst into my apartment. She was flushed, her lipstick was off-kilter. A purple fleece hat sat goofily on her head. She threw her arms around me and burrowed her cold cheeks into my neck. A noise of pleasure came from her throat, as if she were settling into a hot bath.

"Aren't you glad to see me?" she murmured.

I stood there trying not to relent.

"I'm just back in town," Darcy went on. "I was in Iowa. Trent sent me out on subsidies and ethanol production, and John, John McCain, he used one of my workups in his stump. And then he asked me—or Roger, his press guy—asked me to do advance work in South Carolina! Can you believe it? You have to meet John in person to get the whole picture. But those five years in Vietnam, I mean, he just cuts through all the bullshit. The man radiates charisma."

I found myself (rather unattractively) wishing to torture Senator John McCain.

Darcy pulled her hat off and her hair fell in a tangle.

"Are you proud of me?" she said.

"I'm a little confused actually."

"It's a confusing time," Darcy said breezily. "Election years always are. Aren't you going to kiss me? I know you're glad to see me." She nodded ever so slightly at my erection.

I tried to look indignant. "I left messages for you."

"I know I should have called. I'm sorry. Don't be mad at me. There was a lot going on. Not just Iowa. There were other things." She slipped her hands inside my pajamas and touched my ribs. "Are you cold, baby? You've got goose bumps. Can we lie down? I'm so tired. I've been thinking about lying down with you."

I was sore with the need for Darcy. She smelled of lilacs and gin; her body pressed forward. But I didn't like the way I'd been feeling, and I distrusted this erotic lobbying.

"What other things?" I said.

"I'm a loyal person. What I've been doing has been for us, okay? Just trust me, Billy. Don't you want to trust me?"

"Yeah. I mean, I want—"

"Then do. Just do. Quit asking questions and kiss me."

"I just want to know what we are."

Darcy let out a little shriek of frustration. "Would you stop being so *literal?* This is a love affair, Billy. Okay? Withstand a little doubt. I'm the one who's taking the risk here."

"Meaning what?"

"Stop being naive. The woman always loses power in a sexual relationship."

"Not always," I said.

Darcy sighed. She took her hands off me and stepped back. "I just flew four hours with a goddamn baby howling in my ear. I haven't slept more than three hours in the past two days. I'm expected to show up to work tomorrow, bright and early, to host a reception for Jack Fucking Kemp. I don't do this. I don't come over to men's houses. But I'm here, Billy. Do you understand? I am here. Now take me in your arms and *do something,* or I'm going home right now."

What Darcy enjoyed most was a good lathering between the thighs. As a lifelong liberal, this was one of my specialties. In some obscure but plausible fashion, I viewed the general neglect of the region as a bedrock of conservatism. The female sex was, in political terms, the equivalent of the inner city: a dark and mysterious zone, vilified by the powerful, derided as incapable of self-improvement, entrenched and smelly. Going down on a woman was a dirty business, humiliating, potentially infectious, best delegated to the sensitivos of the Left.

I relished the act, which I considered to be what Joe Lieberman would have termed, in his phlegmy rabbinical tone, a *mitzvah.* It required certain sacrifices. The deprivation of oxygen, to begin with. A certain ridiculousness of posture; cramping in the lower extremities. One had to engage with the process. There were no quick fixes.

This was especially true in Darcy's case. She was scandalized by the intensity of her desire, and highly aroused by this scandal. But the going was slow. If I told her "I want to kiss you there" she would grow flustered and glance about helplessly. Just act, was her point. Ditch all the soppy acknowledgment, the naming of things in the dark. The word *pussy* made her wince. (A tainted word, I admit, but one I employed with utmost fondness and in the spirit of fond excitements.)

I kissed my way down her body—the damp undersides of her breasts, her bumpy sternum, the belly she lamented not ridding herself of. Always, I could feel the tendons of her groin tensing. I nipped at them occasionally.

She perfumed herself elaborately, which meant withstanding an initial astringency, after which she tasted wonderfully, meaning strongly of herself, the brackish bouquet of her insides. I was careful not to linger in any one spot but to explore the entire intricate topography, the nerves flushed with blood and tingling mysteriously, while Darcy pressed herself back on the pillows and turned to face the wall and murmured the blessed nonsensical approvals of climax.

The body releases its electricity, merges with another, and together there is something like God in this pleasure. But afterward, in the quiet redolent air, there must also be offerings of truth. And so the mystery of love deepens.

Darcy's given name was Darlene. She'd grown up in Ashton, Pennsylvania, a rural township south of Allentown. Her grandpas had been farmers. Then the world had changed, grown more expensive and mechanical, and somehow less reliable. So her father, rather than inheriting dark fields of barley, worked for Archer Daniels Midland. (Her mother, it went without saying, was a homemaker.) All three of her sisters and her brother still lived in Ashton. She was an aunt eight times.

Darcy recognized that she was different from her family. But she was reluctant to speak too pointedly about these differences. Instead, she turned the Hicks clan into a comedy routine, delivering updates in the flat accent of her Grandpa Tuck.

Signs of her double life abounded. She dressed in Ann Taylor, but used a crock pot. She stored her birth-control pills in a bedside drawer, beside the worn green Bible she had been given in Sunday school. Her mantel displayed photos of the grip-and-grin with Arlen Specter, Robert Bork, Newt Gingrich. Only in the shadowed corner of her bedroom did one see a young, toothy Darcy, resplendent in acid wash and pink leg warmers, smiling from the seat of an old tractor on Grandpa Tuck's homestead. The photo was taken just before he sold the final acres to a chemical plant, back in '89.

As for me, I'd grown up outside Hartford. My parents had marched for Civil Rights and protested the war. Then they had kids, moved to a leafy suburb, and renovated an old Victorian. Their domestic and professional duties tired them out, left them susceptible to bourgeois enjoyments. But the way I remembered them—needed to remember them—was as young, beautiful radicals.

What we wanted from politics, in the end, was what we had been deprived of by our families. I hoped to create a world in which justice and compassion would be the enduring measure. Darcy sought permission to expand her horizons, to experience her prosperity without guilt. We both held to the notion that it mattered who won office and how they governed. Nothing, in the end, mattered more.

Yet it never would have occurred to us, not in a million years, that the 2000 election would turn volatile. The presidential candidates were a couple of second-raters, awkwardly hawking the same square yard of space, at the corner of Main and Centrist.

And so we lay about on weekends, scattering sheafs of newsprint onto the sunny hardwood floors of my apartment, lamenting (silently, to ourselves) the hopeless bias of the *Post* and *Times,* tumbling the stately avenues of downtown, drowning in happy wine and letting our messages stack up.

We were both too hooked on politics to ignore the subject entirely. But we had to be careful not to push too far into ideology. Darcy was altogether suspicious of the word. "Just a fancy way of saying policy aims," she insisted.

I disagreed. To me, the Left was a living force, animated by heroic and martyred ideas: Civil Rights. The War on Poverty. Christ Himself—as I argued in an unreadably earnest undergraduate paper—was a classic New Deal Democrat. Darcy listened to my ravings with a polite purse of her lips. She viewed me as quaint, I think.

But Darcy had her own dewy allegiances. Reagan, for instance. They'd named an airport after him. Now he had Alzheimer's and the news told stories of his decay, over which Darcy clucked. "He made it acceptable to love this country again," she told me. "Don't give me that snotty look, Billy. He was an American hero."

This was astounding to me: Ronald Reagan! The man who had allowed Big Business to run the country, slashed social programs, gorged the national debt on wacko military systems, funneled arms to Nicaraguan murderers, and just generally sodomized Mother Nature.

So, in other words, we learned to avoid policy aims.

By March Darcy was traveling nearly every week. She was unofficially on loan to the McCain campaign, which was full of reformist spunk but foundering in the polls. I expected Darcy to be devastated by the results of Super Tuesday, which all but assured Bush the nomination. But she emerged from her flight (a red-eye out of Atlanta) beaming.

"Kenny O'Brien talked to Roger about me. He wants me to do advance work for Dubya! Isn't that *amazing*!"

My reaction to this news was complicated. I was thrilled and impressed. Darcy was making a name for herself. But this would mean more travel for her, more prestige, more action. While I remained in D.C., plinking out obscure proposals on how to reduce recidivism, stewing over whether to vote for the Android or the Spoiler. And missing her.

Beyond envy, I felt genuinely unsettled. Darcy had been a rabid McCain supporter—one of his true believers. She had derided Bush as a semipro, a lollygagger. It was hard for me to fathom how she could now throw her support behind him.

"We fought the good fight," Darcy assured me. "The key is that we managed to push finance reform onto the agenda."

"You really think Shrub is going to do anything on that?" I said. "The guy raised fifty million before he even announced."

Darcy frowned. "Don't be so cynical," she said. "Have a little faith for a change. Oh, I'm hungry, Billy. Where can we get a burger at this hour?"

Winter limped into April and we barely noticed. The dirty slush glittered and the gutters lay ripe with magic. In early May the cherry blossoms reemerged along Pennsylvania and I turned twenty-seven. Darcy organized a celebration at a tapas bar in Foxhall Road, one of those places where the waiters are obliged to enforce a spirit of merriment by squirting rioja from boda bags into the mouths of particularly valued diners. Darcy, in her little cocktail dress, offered a toast, while my friends glanced in horror at the table beside us, where a pack of trashed dot-commers were plying the waitress to flash her tits.

Darcy considered the evening a triumph, and I hoped she was right. My friends were a glum and brainy lot, nonprofit warriors and outreach workers. They could see how smitten I was and spoke to Darcy with elaborate courtesy. But to them she must have appeared no different from the hundreds of other GOP tootsies cruising the capital in their jaunty hair ribbons.

I met Darcy's friends the following week, at a luncheon held in the executive dining room, on the second floor of the Fund's stately colonial. The maître d' grimaced politely at my sweater. He whisked into the cloakroom and reappeared with an elegant camel's hair sports coat.

Darcy waved to me and smiled, which instantly snuffed my doubt, made me hum a silent pledge of allegiance to our love. The men at her table wore matching dark green blazers, with an FFT in gold script over the breast pocket. Darcy stood out like a rose in a stand of rhododendron.

The servers were brisk Europeans, officious in their table-side preparation of chateaubriand. George F. Will delivered the keynote, wearily lamenting the "deracination of moral authority" to general mirth and light applause, though his platitudes were obscured by the sandblasting from next door, where workers were empaneling a new marble patio at the Saudi embassy.

I cannot remember the names of Darcy's colleagues, only that they seemed to have been cut from the same hearty block of wood. The older fellows evinced the serenity characteristic of a life spent in private clubs. The young guys imitated these manners. They were clean-shaven, deeply committed carnivores who seemed, in conversational lulls, to be searching the rich wainscoting for signs of a crew oar they might take up.

They all adored Darcy, that much was obvious, and chaffed her with careful paternalism.

"A remarkable young woman," said the gentleman on my left, the moment she had excused herself to the bathroom. "You are watching a future congressman from Pennsylvania."

"Congresswoman," I said, half to myself.

"Yes," he answered, poking at a rind of fat on his plate. "Darcy mentioned that about you."

At the brief reception after lunch, while the higher-ups clustered about Will, Darcy introduced me to her mentor. Trent was a thick blond fellow with the most marvelous teeth I had ever seen. "This your special friend, Hicks?" Trent said. "Good to meet you."

"Bill," I said.

"Bill. Good to meet you, Bill."

He gripped my hand and held it for a few beats. It occurred to me that Trent had served in the Armed Forces, possibly all four of them.

"Darcy tells me you've done some work for Bradley."

"Not really. A little volunteering."

"A good man," Trent said. "Principled. Shame he got ambushed by Gore. Not surprising, especially, but a shame. What're your plans for the election, Bill?"

"I'll probably be sitting this one out," I said.

Trent barked. "How long you been in the District, Bill? No such thing." He winked and drew Darcy against him. "You watch this one, Bill. She's going places."

Darcy blushed.

"You take care of her," Trent said.

"Darcy does a pretty good job of taking care of herself."

Trent dragged his knuckles across his chin and shot me a look of such naked disdain that I took a step backward. Then he wrapped Darcy in a bear hug, kissed her on the brow, and wished me well.

"He just seemed a little aggressive," I said to Darcy later, in her office.

"Nonsense. He's just protective."

"You know him better than me."

"Wait a second." Darcy's eyes—they were steel blue—flickered with her triumph. "You're jealous!"

"The guy was all over you, honey. And the way he behaved toward me—"

"He wasn't all over me. He was being *affectionate.*"

"Is that what they're calling it these days?"

Darcy began to laugh. She'd had three cups of punch and was still flying. I listened to her gleeful hiccups and watched the chandelier in the foyer glint. "Trent's LC," she said finally. "Log Cabin, Billy. He's gay."

She began laughing again.

Trent the Gay Republican? "He must be thrilled with Shrub's support of the sodomy laws in Texas."

"There you go again," Darcy said. She was imitating Reagan now. "Judging people. I thought you enlightened liberals didn't judge people."

Darcy traveled throughout spring and into summer, and this lent our relations an infatuated rhythm. My heart beat wildly as I waited for her plane to land. This was not her beauty acting upon me, the glamour of her ambitions, even the promise of sex, but the sense of good intention she radiated, a kindheartedness measured in the drowsy hours before she could assemble her public self. This was my favorite time: Darcy in the shades of dawn, warm with sleep, her hair scattered across the pillow.

There was an ease to her domestic rituals, the way she snipped coupons (which she would never use) and scrubbed her lonely appliances and listened sympathetically to the latest reports from Ashton. She fretted endlessly over what to pack for her trips. "I'm too fat for these slacks," she complained. "I'm one big, fat ass, Billy."

This was not true. If anything, Darcy was growing slimmer. But these sudden bouts of self-doubt were necessary to her maintenance. They were vestiges of her girlhood, of the awkward striver who lived behind the awesome machinery of her charm. They were the part of her that needed me.

I was a fool to watch the Republican Convention. But there was an element of morbid curiosity at work. I wanted to see Jesse Helms reborn as an emissary of tolerance. (What would he wear? A dashiki?) And besides, I had promised Darcy. She was attending as a Bush delegate from Pennsylvania.

What has always astounded me about the Republican psyche is its capacity for shamelessness. Here was the anti-immigration party parading its little brown ones across the rostrum, the party of Family Values showcasing its finest buttoned-down catamites. Here was Big Dick Cheney—who had voted against funding Head Start as a congressman—excoriating Clinton for not doing enough to educate oppressed children. On and on it went, and nobody exploded of hypocrisy!

Darcy called me each night, giddy with the sense of how well it was coming off. "Did you see me on CNBC?" she said. "Deb Borders interviewed me. Did you see Christie Whitman, Billy? Wasn't she amazing? Okay. Don't answer that. I miss you, Billy. Do you miss me? Do you?"

"Of course I do."

"Do you love me?" she said suddenly.

"You know I do."

"Say it."

"I love you, Darcy."

And I did. It was nothing I could help.

"I love you, Billy. I love you so much."

"Where are you?" I asked. "Are you in your room?"

"I'm on my bed."

And so we progressed, deeper into our thrilling disjunction.

By October the Bush people had taken Darcy on full-time. She was living out of a suitcase, returning to D.C. with purple stains under her eyes, sleeping twelve hours straight. I took it as my duty to offer her refuge in the cause of intimacy.

And Darcy returned this devotion. Even as the campaign drew to an end, she came at me in a dizzy operatic spin, ravished for affection, for a private domain in which she could shed the careful burnishings of her ascent. One evening, as we lay flushed on gin, she announced that she had a surprise for me and rose up on her haunches and slipped off her panties and knelt back. All that remained of her pubic hair was a single delicate stripe.

I felt touched to the point of tears. Here was this miraculous creature, tuckered beyond words, right here in my apartment on the eve of the election, flashing me her vaginal mohawk. She vamped gamely even as her eyelids drooped, and licked her lovely incisor and urged me forward. How could it possibly matter that she opposed gun control?

I called Darcy at 2:42 A.M. on election night. The networks had just issued their flop on Florida and Dan Rather—in an apparent caffeine psychosis—was urging America to give Dubya a big ole Texas-sized welcome to the White House.

Darcy was across town, at the Radisson. There were whoops in the background and the echoes of a bad jazz band.

"Congratulations," I said.

"Billy! Oh, you are so sweet!"

"Well, no one likes a sore loser."

"It was so close," Darcy said. "It's a shame anyone had to lose!"

There was a rush of sound and Darcy let out a happy scream. "Stop it! Stop!" She came back on the phone. "That was Trent."

"Can you come over?" I said. "I'd like to congratulate you in person."

Darcy drew in a breath. "I'd love to. That would be so nice. But I promised some people I'd stay here. At least until Dubya gives his speech."

I was quiet for a moment.

"Honey," she said. "Are you okay? Are you mad?"

I was maybe a little mad. But I knew how hard Darcy had worked for this, how much hope she'd pinned to the outcome. She had leapt toward the thick of the race, bravely, with her arms wide and her pretty little chest exposed, while I'd thrown up my hands in disgust and voted for Nader.

"No," I said. "I'm proud of you, Darce. You deserve this."

"I love you, Billy."

"I love you too," I said quietly. "You crazy Republican bitch."

She laughed. A chorus of deep voices swelled in the background and Darcy, carried away by some shenanigans, shrieked merrily.

I wondered sometimes why she didn't just settle for some GOP bohunk with a carapace of muscles and the proper worldview. She could have had her pick. We both knew that. But that's not how the heart works. It runs to deeper needs. "I'll try to come over after the speech," Darcy whispered. "I want to see you."

Two weeks later we were in Darcy's apartment, still trying to figure out what had happened. Al Gore was on CNN, imitating someone made of flesh.

"Why doesn't he give it up?" Darcy murmured.

"Why should he give up?" I said.

"Because he lost."

We had both assumed the election would bring an end to the tension. One or the other side would win, fair and square, and we would move on.

"You can't say he lost until they count all the votes," I said. "It's just too close. Can't you see that, honey?"

Darcy sighed. She'd cut her hair into a kind of bob, which made her look a little severe. "Why did Gore ask for recounts in only four counties? He's not interested in a full and accurate count. Admit it. He wants to count until he has the votes to win."

"They both want to win. It's called a race."

"Don't patronize me, Billy."

"I wouldn't patronize you if you didn't keep oversimplifying the situation."

Darcy clicked off the TV. "Why do you talk like that, Billy? Why do you make everything so personal?"

"Trying to impeach the president for getting a blowjob? That's not *personal?* Or DeLay sending his thugs down to Miami to storm the canvassing board? What is that? Politics as usual? Are you kidding me?"

Darcy shook her head; the edges of her new haircut sawed back and forth. "I can't talk with you about this stuff. You get too angry."

"You're as pissed as I am."

"No," she said. "I just want this to be over."

We didn't say anything else, but the mists of rage hung about us. And later on, after we had retired to the bedroom, this rage hid within our desire and charged out of our bodies in a way we hoped would bring us closure. We slammed against one another and gasped and clutched, did everything we could think to enthrall the other while at the same time hoping somewhat to murder, to die together, and woke instead, in the morning, bruised and contrite.

I agreed with Darcy, after all. I wanted the election to be over. I didn't want to be angry at her, because I loved her and that love was more important than any election. I honestly *tried* to ignore the dispute. What did I care? Gore had run an awful campaign. He deserved to lose.

Gradually, though, the radical truth was coming clear: more voters had gone to the polls in Florida intending to vote for him. The statisticians understood this, and the voting-machine wonks, and even the brighter reporters, the ones who bothered to think the matter through.

The Republican strategy was to obscure this truth, to prevent at all costs a closer inspection of the ballots. In doing so, they became opponents of democracy. (There is no other way to say this.) What amazed me was the gusto with which Bush executed this treason. His fixers lied incessantly and extravagantly. His allies stormed the cameras and frothed.

Us Democrats never quite grasped that we were in a street fight. We lacked the required viciousness, the mindless loyalty. This has always been the Achilles heel of the Left: we are too fond of our own decency, too fearful of our anger. When the blackjacks come out we quit the field and call it dignity.

The cold fog of December descended on the capital and I sat in my apartment glaring at CNN, and fantasized about putting a bullet in James Baker's skull. Darcy called out to me from the answering machine, her voice loosened by red wine. My name sounded vague and hopeful in her mouth.

And then, one night, just after the final certification of votes in Florida, a knock came at the door. There was Darcy, in her blue skirt and her lovely snaggled smile. She was breathing hard. I imagined for a moment that she had run from somewhere far away, from Georgetown perhaps, through the dark banished lowlands of Prince George County, or from the tawny plains of central Pennsylvania.

"We need to talk," she said.

She fell against me, smelling of gin and lilacs and cigarettes. Here she was, this soft person, soft all the way through. I felt terribly responsible.

"Where'd you come from?"

"That bar down the street."

"The Versailles?"

"Uh-huh."

"What were you doing there?"

She looked up into my face. "My friends say I should dump you."

"What do you say?"

"I don't know. You're a good lay." She tugged at my jeans. But this was only an imitation of lust, something borrowed from the booze. Her hands soon fell away. "Where the hell have you been?"

"I haven't been anywhere. I've been here. Look, I'm sorry. I haven't quite known what to do."

"You could start by returning my calls, okay? Okay, Mr. Fucking Sensitivity?" Darcy glanced into the living room, at the pizza boxes and heaps of clothing. She shook her head. Bush was on now, staring into the camera like a frightened monkey. "Please, Billy, don't tell me you're still moping about this election."

"It's more like constructive brooding."

Darcy plopped onto the couch. Her knees pressed together and her calves flared out like jousts. This lent her an antic quality, as if she might at any moment leap to her feet and burst into a tap-dance routine. "Why are you doing this to yourself?"

"I'm not doing anything to myself."

"I just don't understand why you have to hold this against me. I don't hold your views against you."

"That's because you're winning," I muttered.

"What?"

"You're winning. You can afford the luxury of grace. But I'll tell you what, if these undervotes ever get counted and Gore pulls ahead, you and the rest—"

"That will never happen," Darcy said sharply. She smoothed her skirt with the heel of her palm and took a deep breath. "You know as well as I do that if the situation were reversed, Gore would do the same thing as Bush."

"You may be right," I said. "But if he did that, he'd be wrong. And I hope I'd have the integrity to see that."

"And I *don't* have integrity?"

"I'm not saying that. What I'm saying is . . ."

But what *was* I saying? Wasn't I saying precisely that?

Darcy narrowed her eyes and waited for me to clarify myself.

"Look, I know you have a lot invested in Bush winning. You worked hard for him. And I realize we have different views on how to run things. I don't want you to be a liberal. But I'm talking about the underlying principle. Democracy means you do your best to look at all the ballots. You try to find the truth."

"Please, Billy. I came over here to talk about us."

"This *is* about us," I said. "We have to agree on the basic stuff. Truth. Fairness. I'm not talking about this damn election anymore. I don't even care who wins. They're both Republicans in my book. I'm talking about what you believe and what I believe."

"Would you listen to yourself?" Darcy said. "This is just politics, Billy. Christ. You're as bad as Gore."

"Don't reduce this to politics. Please. I want us to be able to agree here." I wasn't screaming exactly, but my voice kept throttling up because I could see where we were headed and it made my heart ache.

Darcy shook her head. "I knew this was a mistake. You don't even know what day it is today, do you?" She was speaking softly now, as she did in the sylvan hours, when the ruckus of her life gave way to frank disappointments. This made me want to hold her, to wrap myself along the railing of her hip.

"A year ago, Billy. We met a year ago tonight."

For a moment there it looked as if fairness might prevail. The Florida Supreme Court issued the ruling that should have come down in the beginning: recount the entire state, by hand. But then, of course, the U.S. Supreme Court stepped in to rule that, well, something or other involving equal protection and, more obscurely, the Constitution, and anyway there certainly wasn't enough time to clear this mess up—*such a mess*!—so, you know, don't blame us, we're only trying to help: Bush wins.

All over Washington, Republicans whooped it up. They'd managed to gain the White House and the only cost had been the integrity of every single civil institution in our country. What a bargain! I spent the evening swilling Jack and gingers, howling into Darcy's various machines, imagining I could taste her. Our situation was unclear. By which I mean: she was no longer returning my calls. At around one in the morning I drove to her apartment.

"Go away," she said, through the intercom. "You're drunk."

"I'm not drunk. I love you, honey. I wanna say sorry."

"I'm not going to talk with you, Billy."

"I don't wanna talk about that. I promise. Buzz me in, honey. *Please.*"

She was wearing an old nightgown, the cotton soft and pilled. Her face was a little puffy. Now it was my turn to fall against her, to kiss her brow and plead. Her body stiffened.

"I was wrong," I said. "I was a jerk. Nobody makes me feel like you. We fit, you know. Our bodies, we just fit."

She rose onto the balls of her feet. But she didn't push me away. "You're too angry," she said. "I don't like it when you get so angry."

I sank to my knees and hugged her waist. "I'm sorry. Something takes over. I start thinking too much."

It is true that Darcy was a Republican. But she was still a woman, and as such susceptible to forgiveness. I pressed my cheek against her and breathed warm air into her belly. Her muscles slowly softened.

"No more thinking, Billy. No more arguing. It's over now." With just her fingertips, she hoisted the hem of her nightgown. The tiny blond hairs at the top of her thighs stood on end. My tongue took up the taste of laundry soap. A thick pink scent came from the hollow below.

Could I have known, as she climbed onto the bed and opened herself to me, as I kissed that softest skin, that my anger would rise once again? But who can know these things? They are products of the past, of history finding an apt disguise in the moment. I wanted only to give my beloved this pleasure, to be forgiven. Why, then, as her knees fell open, as her breath bottomed into rasps and her flesh began to pulse, could I think only of James Baker? He rose from the darkest region of my love, his tongue twisted like an old piece of steak. Loathing shimmered around him like an aura. Why was I thinking of this man while Darcy lay open before me like a blossom?

Perhaps because (it occurred to me darkly) Darcy did not view Baker as a bad man at all. She had described him as a righteous man, not unlike her Grandpa Tuck. And now suddenly I imagined James Baker in the humble suit of a country preacher, presiding over my very own wedding.

Darcy was digging her fingers into the meat of my neck, murmuring *go go go*. Her body clenched. This was the life she wanted: a walloping orgasm and the sort of man who knew when to keep his mouth shut. I thought of my own parents, marching into the grim precincts of New Haven to register voters. They had done this. They had believed. My lips felt numb. I wasn't entirely sure I could breathe. Up above, the shuddering began. Darcy's thighs came together in a swirl. How I had loved this moment! The roar of the engines on the runway, the sudden flight. I closed my eyes and breathed in her body. But there was Baker again—and now he was winking at me.

I lifted my head.

Darcy's hands pawed the air. Her mouth puffed my name.

"The Supreme Court," I said, "has filed an emergency injunction."

"No, Billy. *Go.* I'm close." Darcy's eyes were pinched. Her hands had slipped to her breasts, which she gently cupped. Her hip bones stood out like tiny knobs. What in God's name was wrong with me?

"Billy. Come on. Not funny."

I could feel my throat knotting up with sorrow.

Darcy lifted her head from the pillows. Her eyes were starting to clear. "What exactly are you doing here?"

"Once the High Court rules, there are no more appeals."

Darcy drew back. "Do you have any idea how despicably you're behaving? Oh Billy, you really are a sad case." Darcy closed her legs and pulled a sheet across her chest, like a starlet. "The election is over. Don't you get it? *Over.*"

"That's not the issue," I said quietly.

"The issue?" Darcy's fists curled around the sheet. "Do you even know what the issue is anymore? The issue is us, okay? The issue is do you really love me. That's the issue, Billy."

Darcy waited for me to say something heroic. This seemed the thing to do, certainly, to renounce my stingy polemical heart, to affirm the primacy of love. What kind of liberal was I, anyway? And this is surely how it would have gone in the movies, where everything gets absolved in time for the credits. Though I loved Darcy, thrilled to the music of her body, stood in awe of her drive, I could not fathom how I was supposed to live with my disappointment in her.

Nor did I understand, exactly, how she could love me when she found my core beliefs naive and pitiable. Perhaps this was a uniquely Republican gift, the ability to ignore inconvenient contradictions. Or perhaps she was simply better at loving someone without judgment. All that matters is that I failed in that moment to tell her that I loved her.

"You should leave," Darcy said quietly. Her voice floated down in the dark. "Get out of here, Billy. Don't come back."

My friends told me I'd made the right decision. They were extremely reasonable and full of shit. I knew the truth, which was that Darcy was the most exciting lover I would ever take, because I always hated her a little, and never quite understood her, and because she forgave me this and loved me therefore more daringly, without relying on the congruence of our beliefs, the dull compliances of companionship.

I watched the inauguration simply to catch a glimpse of her. She was in the crowd beneath the podium. The camera caught her twice, a pretty woman with ruddy cheeks and a wide sad smile, gazing into the frozen rain.

Soon, she would rise to the office appointed by her talents and give her passion to another man. Eventually, she would move out to Bethesda or Arlington, where the stately oaks and pastures of blue grass survive. She would attach herself to the tasks of motherhood and governance with brilliant loyalty. And she would grow more achingly beautiful by the year, as our regrets inevitably do.

Washington was her town now. I understood that much. I lacked the guile, the gift for compromise, the ability to separate my wishes about the world from the cold facts of the place. I sat on my couch as the oaths were sworn and watched for Darcy's yellow hair, which flickered in the wind that swept across the capitol and then was gone.

The Fourth State of Matter

JO ANN BEARD

The collie wakes me up about three times a night, summoning me from a great distance as I row my boat through a dim, complicated dream. She's on the shoreline, barking. Wake up. She's staring at me with her head slightly tipped to the side, long nose, gazing eyes, toenails clenched to get a purchase on the wood floor. We used to call her the face of love.

She totters on her broomstick legs into the hallway and over the doorsill into the kitchen, makes a sharp left at the refrigerator—careful, almost went down—then a straightaway to the door. I sleep on my feet, in the cold of the doorway, waiting. Here she comes. Lift her down the two steps. She pees and then stands, Lassie in a ratty coat, gazing out at the yard.

In the porchlight the trees shiver, the squirrels turn over in their sleep. The Milky Way is a long smear on the sky, like something erased on a chalkboard. Over the neighbor's house, Mars flashes white, then red, then white again. Jupiter is hidden among the anonymous blinks and glitterings. It has a moon with sulfur-spewing volcanoes and a beautiful name: Io. I learned it at work, from the group of men who surround me there. Space physicists, guys who spend days on end with their heads poked through the fabric of the sky, listening to the sounds of the universe. Guys whose own lives are ticking like alarm clocks getting ready to go off, although none of us is aware of it yet.

The collie turns and looks, waits to be carried up the two steps. Inside the house, she drops like a shoe onto her blanket, a thud, an adjustment. I've climbed back under my covers already but her leg's stuck underneath her, we can't get comfortable. I fix the leg, she rolls over and sleeps. Two hours later I wake up again and she's gazing at me in the darkness. The face of love. She wants to go out again. I give her a boost, balance her on her legs. Right on time: 3:40 A.M.

There are squirrels living in the spare bedroom upstairs. Three dogs also live in this house, but they were invited. I keep the door of the spare bedroom shut at all times, because of the squirrels and because that's where the vanished husband's belongings are stored. Two of the dogs—the smart little brown mutt and the Labrador—spend hours sitting patiently outside the door, waiting for it to be opened so they can dismantle the squirrels. The collie can no longer make it up the stairs, so she lies at the bottom and snores or stares in an interested manner at the furniture around her.

I can take almost anything at this point. For instance, that my vanished husband is neither here nor there; he's reduced himself to a troubled voice on the telephone three or four times a day.

Or that the dog at the bottom of the stairs keeps having mild strokes which cause her to tilt her head inquisitively and also to fall over. She drinks prodigious amounts of water and pees great volumes onto the folded blankets where she sleeps. Each time this happens I stand her up, dry her off, put fresh blankets underneath her, carry the peed-on blankets down to the basement, stuff them into the washer and then into the dryer. By the time I bring them back upstairs they are needed again. The first few times this happened I found the dog trying to stand up, gazing with frantic concern at her own rear. I praised her and patted her head and gave her treats until she settled down. Now I know whenever it happens because I hear her tail thumping against the floor in anticipation of reward. In retraining her I've somehow retrained myself, bustling cheerfully down to the basement, arms drenched in urine, the task of doing load after load of laundry strangely satisfying. She is Pavlov and I am her dog.

I'm fine about the vanished husband's boxes stored in the spare bedroom. For now the boxes and the phone calls persuade me that things could turn around at any moment. The boxes are filled with thirteen years of his pack-rattedness: statistics textbooks that still harbor an air of desperation, smarmy suitcoats from the Goodwill, various old Halloween masks and one giant black papier-mâché thing that was supposed to be Elvis's hair but didn't turn out. A collection of ancient Rolling Stones T-shirts. You know he's turning over a new leaf when he leaves the Rolling Stones behind.

What I can't take are the squirrels. They come alive at night, throwing terrible parties in the spare bedroom, making thumps and crashes. Occasionally a high-pitched squeal is heard amid bumps and the sound of scrabbling toenails. I've taken to sleeping downstairs, on the blue vinyl dog couch, the sheets slipping off, my skin stuck to the cushions. This is an affront to two of the dogs, who know the couch belongs to them; as soon as I settle in they creep up and find their places between my knees and elbows.

I'm on the couch because the dog on the blanket gets worried at night. During the day she sleeps the catnappy sleep of the elderly, but when it gets dark her eyes open and she is agitated, trying to stand whenever I leave the room, settling down only when I'm next to her. We are in this together, the dying game, and I read for hours in the evening, one foot on her back, getting up only to open a new can of beer or take peed-on blankets to the basement. At some point I stretch out on the vinyl couch and close my eyes, one hand hanging down, touching her side. By morning the dog-arm has become a nerveless club that doesn't come around until noon. My friends think I'm nuts.

One night, for hours, the dog won't lie down, stands braced on her rickety legs in the middle of the living room, looking at me and slowly wagging her tail. Each time I get her situated on her blankets and try to stretch out on the couch she stands up, looks at me, wags her tail. I call my office pal, Mary, and wake her up. *"I'm weary,"* I say, in italics.

Mary listens, sympathetic, on the other end. "Oh my God," she finally says, "*what* are you going to do?"

I calm down immediately. "Exactly what I'm doing," I tell her. The dog finally parks herself with a thump on the stack of damp blankets. She sets her nose down and tips her eyes up to watch me. We all sleep then, for a bit, while the squirrels sort through the boxes overhead and the dog on the blanket keeps nervous watch.

I've called in tired to work. It's midmorning and I'm shuffling around in my long underwear, smoking cigarettes and drinking coffee. The whole house is bathed in sunlight and the faint odor of used diapers. The collie is on her blanket, taking one of her vampirish daytime naps. The other two dogs are being mild-mannered and charming. I nudge the collie with my foot.

"Wake up and smell zee bacons," I say. She startles awake, lifts her nose groggily, and falls back asleep. I get ready for the office.

"I'm leaving and I'm never coming back," I say, while putting on my coat. I use my mother's aggrieved, underappreciated tone. The little brown dog wags her tail, transferring her gaze from me to the table, which is the last place she remembers seeing toast. The collie continues her ghoulish sleep, eyes partially open, teeth exposed, while the Labrador, who understands English, begins howling miserably. She wins the toast sweepstakes and is chewing loudly when I leave, the little dog barking ferociously at her.

Work is its usual comforting green-corridored self. There are three blinks on the answering machine, the first from an author who speaks very slowly, like a kindergarten teacher, asking about reprints. "What am I, the village idiot?" I ask the room, taking down his number in large backward characters. The second and third blinks are from my husband, the across-town apartment dweller.

The first makes my heart lurch in a hopeful way. "I have to talk to you right *now*," he says grimly. "Where *are* you? I can never find you."

"Try calling your own house," I say to the machine. In the second message he has composed himself.

"I'm *fine* now," he says firmly. "Disregard previous message and don't call me back, please; I have meetings." Click, dial tone, rewind.

I feel crestfallen, the leaping heart settles back into its hole in my chest. I say *damn it* out loud, just as Chris strides into the office.

"What?" he asks defensively. He tries to think if he's done anything wrong recently. He checks the table for work; none there. He's on top of it. We have a genial relationship these days, reading the paper together in the mornings, congratulating ourselves on each issue of the journal. It's a space physics quarterly and he's the editor and I'm the managing editor. I know nothing about the science part; my job is to shepherd the manuscripts through the review process and create a journal out of the acceptable ones.

Christoph Goertz. He's hip in a professorial kind of way, tall and lanky and white-haired, forty-seven years old, with an elegant trace of accent from his native Germany. He has a great dog, a giant black outlaw named Mica who runs through the streets of Iowa City at night, inspecting garbage. She's big and friendly but a bad judge of character and frequently runs right into the arms of the dog catcher. Chris is always bailing her out.

"They don't understand dogs," he says.

I spend more time with Chris than I ever did with my husband. The morning I told him I was being dumped he was genuinely perplexed.

"He's leaving *you?*" he asked.

Chris was drinking coffee, sitting at his table in front of the chalkboard. Behind his head was a chalk drawing of a hip, professorial man holding a coffee cup. It was a collaborative effort; I drew the man and Chris framed him, using brown chalk and a straightedge. The two-dimensional man and the three-dimensional man stared at me intently.

"He's leaving *you?*" And for an instant I saw myself from their vantage point across the room—Jo Ann—and a small bubble of self-esteem percolated up from the depths. Chris shrugged. "You'll do fine," he said.

During my current turmoils, I've come to think of work as my own kind of zen practice, the constant barrage of paper hypnotic and soothing. Chris lets me work an erratic, eccentric schedule, which gives me time to pursue my nonexistent writing career. In return I update his publications list for him and listen to stories about outer space.

Besides being an editor and a teacher, he's the head of a theoretical plasma physics team made up of graduate students and research scientists. During the summers he travels all over the world telling people about the magnetospheres of various planets, and when he comes back he brings me presents—a small bronze box from Africa with an alligator embossed on the top, a big piece of amber from Poland with the wings of flies preserved inside it, and, once, a set of delicate, horrifying bracelets made from the hide of an elephant.

Currently he is obsessed with the dust in the plasma of Saturn's rings. Plasma is the fourth state of matter. You've got your solid, your liquid, your gas, and then your plasma. In outer space there's the plasmasphere and the plasmapause. I like to avoid the math when I can and put a layperson's spin on these things.

"Plasma is blood," I told him.

"Exactly," he agreed, removing the comics page and handing it to me.

Mostly we have those kinds of conversations around the office, but today he's caught me at a weak moment, tucking my heart back inside my chest. I decide to be cavalier.

"I wish my *dog* was out tearing up the town and my *husband* was home peeing on a blanket," I say.

Chris thinks the dog thing has gone far enough. "Why are you letting this go on?" he asks solemnly.

"I'm not *letting* it, that's why," I tell him. There are stacks of manuscripts everywhere and he has all the pens over on his side of the room. "It just *is,* is all. Throw me a pen." He does, I miss it, stoop to pick it up, and when I straighten up again I might be crying.

You have control over this, he explains in his professor voice. You can decide how long she suffers.

This makes my heart pound. Absolutely not, I cannot do it. And then I weaken and say what I really want. For her to go to sleep and not wake up, just slip out of her skin and into the other world.

"Exactly," he says.

I have an ex-beauty queen coming over to get rid of the squirrels for me. She has long red hair and a smile that can stop trucks. I've seen her wrestle goats, scare off a giant snake, and express a dog's anal glands, all in one afternoon. I told her on the phone that a family of squirrels is living in the upstairs of my house and there's nothing I can do about it.

"They're making a monkey out of me," I said.

So Caroline climbs in her car and drives across half the state, pulls up in front of my house, and gets out carrying zucchinis, cigarettes, and a pair of big leather gloves. I'm sitting outside with my sweet old dog, who lurches to her feet, staggers three steps, sits down, and falls over. Caroline starts crying.

"Don't try to give me zucchini," I tell her.

We sit companionably on the front stoop for a while, staring at the dog and smoking cigarettes. One time I went to Caroline's house and she was nursing a dead cat that was still breathing. At some point that afternoon I saw her spoon baby food into its mouth and as soon as she turned away the whole pureed mess plopped back out. A day later she took it to the vet and had it euthanized. I remind her of this.

"You'll do it when you do it," she says firmly.

I pick the collie up like a fifty-pound bag of sticks and feathers, stagger inside, place her on the damp blankets, and put the other two nutcases in the backyard. From upstairs comes a crash and a shriek. Caroline stares up at the ceiling.

"It's like having the Wallendas stay at your house," I say cheerfully. All of a sudden I feel fond of the squirrels and fond of Caroline and fond of myself for heroically calling her to help me. The phone rings four times. It's the husband, and his voice over the answering machine sounds frantic. He pleads with whoever Jo Ann is to pick up the phone.

"Please? I think I might be freaking out," he says. "Am I ruining my life here, or what? Am I making a *mistake?* Jo?" He breathes raggedly and sniffs into the receiver for a moment, then hangs up with a muffled clatter.

Caroline stares at the machine like it's a copperhead.

"Holy fuckoly," she says, shaking her head. "You're *living* with this crap?"

"He wants me to reassure him that he's strong enough to leave me," I tell her. "Else he won't have fun on his bike ride. And guess what; I'm too tired to." Except that now I can see him in his dank little apartment, wringing his hands and staring out the windows. He's wearing his Sunday hairdo with a baseball cap trying to scrunch it down. In his rickety dresser is the new package of condoms he accidentally showed me last week.

Caroline lights another cigarette. The dog pees and thumps her tail.

I need to call him back because he's suffering.

"You call him back and I'm forced to kill you," Caroline says. She exhales smoke and points to the phone. "That is evil shit," she says.

I tend to agree. It's blanket time. I roll the collie off onto the floor and put the fresh ones down, roll her back. She stares at me with the face of love. I get her a treat, which she chews with gusto and then goes back to sleep. I carry the blankets down to the basement and stuff them into the machine, trudge back up the stairs. Caroline has finished smoking her medicine and is wearing the leather gloves which go all the way to her elbows. She's staring at the ceiling with determination.

The plan is that I'm supposed to separate one from the herd and get it in a corner. Caroline will take it from there. Unfortunately, my nerves are shot, and when I'm in the room with her and the squirrels are running around all I can do is scream. I'm not even afraid of them, but my screaming button is stuck on and the only way to turn it off is to leave the room.

"How are you doing?" I ask from the other side of the door. All I can hear is Caroline crashing around and swearing. Suddenly there is a high-pitched screech that doesn't end. The door opens and Caroline falls out into the hall, with a gray squirrel stuck to her glove. Brief pandemonium and then she clatters down the stairs and out the front door and returns looking triumphant.

The collie appears at the foot of the stairs with her head cocked and her ears up. She looks like a puppy for an instant, and then her feet start to slide. I run down and catch her and carry her upstairs so she can watch the show. They careen around the room, tearing the ancient wallpaper off the walls. The last one is a baby, so we keep it for a few minutes, looking at its little feet and its little tail. We show it to the collie, who stands up immediately and tries to get it.

Caroline patches the hole where they got in, cutting wood with a power saw down in the basement. She comes up wearing a toolbelt and lugging a ladder. I've seen a scrapbook of photos of her wearing evening gowns with a banner across her chest and a crown on her head. Curled hair, lipstick. She climbs down and puts the tools away. We eat nachos.

"I only make food that's boiled or melted these days," I tell her.

"I know," she replies.

We smoke cigarettes and think. The phone rings again but whoever it is hangs up.

"Is it him?" she asks.

"Nope."

The collie sleeps on her blankets while the other two dogs sit next to Caroline on the couch. She's looking through their ears for mites. At some point she gestures to the sleeping dog on the blanket and remarks that it seems like just two days ago she was a puppy.

"She was never a puppy," I say. "She's always been older than me."

When they say good-bye, she holds the collie's long nose in one hand and kisses her on the forehead; the collie stares back at her gravely. Caroline is crying when she leaves, a combination of squirrel adrenaline and sadness. I cry, too, although I don't feel particularly bad about anything. I hand her the zucchini through the window and she pulls away from the curb.

The house is starting to get dark in that terrible early-evening twilit way. I turn on lights, get a cigarette, and go upstairs to the former squirrel room. The black dog comes with me and circles the room, snorting loudly, nose to floor. There is a spot of turmoil in an open box—they made a nest in some old disco shirts from the seventies. I suspect that's where the baby one slept. The mean landlady has evicted them.

Downstairs, I turn the lights back off and let evening have its way with me. Waves of pre-nighttime nervousness are coming from the collie's blanket. I sit next to her in the dimness, touching her ears, and listen for feet at the top of the stairs.

They're speaking in physics so I'm left out of the conversation. Chris apologetically erases one of the pictures I've drawn on the blackboard and replaces it with a curving blue arrow surrounded by radiating chalk waves of green.

"If it's plasma, make it in red," I suggest helpfully. We're all smoking illegally in the journal office with the door closed and the window open. We're having a plasma party.

"We aren't discussing *plasma,*" Bob says condescendingly. He's smoking a horrendously smelly pipe. The longer he stays in here the more it feels like I'm breathing small daggers in through my nose. He and I don't get along; each of us thinks the other needs to be taken down a peg. Once we had a hissing match in the hallway which ended with him suggesting that I could be fired, which drove me to tell him he was *already* fired, and both of us stomped into our offices and slammed our doors.

"I had to fire Bob," I tell Chris later.

"I heard," he says noncommittally. Bob is his best friend. They spend at least half of each day standing in front of chalkboards, writing equations and arguing about outer space. Then they write theoretical papers about what they come up with. They're actually quite a big deal in the space physics community, but around here they're just two guys who keep erasing my pictures.

Someone knocks on the door and we put our cigarettes out. Bob hides his pipe in the palm of his hand and opens the door.

It's Gang Lu, one of their students. Everyone lights up again. Gang Lu stands stiffly talking to Chris while Bob holds a match to his pipe and puffs fiercely; nose daggers waft up and out, right in my direction. I give him a sugary smile and he gives me one back. Unimaginable, really, that less than two months from now one of his colleagues from abroad, a woman with delicate, birdlike features, will appear at the door to my office and identify herself as a friend of Bob's. When she asks, I take her down the hall to the room with the long table and then to his empty office. I do this without saying anything because there's nothing to say, and she takes it all in with small, serious nods until the moment she sees his blackboard covered with scribbles and arrows and equations. At that point her face loosens and she starts to cry in long ragged sobs. An hour later I go back and the office is empty. When I erase the blackboard finally, I can see where she laid her hands carefully, where the numbers are ghostly and blurred.

Bob blows his smoke discreetly in my direction and waits for Chris to finish talking to Gang Lu, who is answering questions in a monotone—yes or no, or I don't know. Another Chinese student named Shan lets himself in after knocking lightly. He nods and smiles at me and then stands at a respectful distance, waiting to ask Chris a question.

It's like a physics conference in here. I wish they'd all leave so I could make my usual midafternoon spate of personal calls. I begin thumbing through papers in a businesslike way.

Bob pokes at his pipe with a bent paper clip. Shan yawns hugely and then looks embarrassed. Chris erases what he put on the blackboard and tries unsuccessfully to redraw my pecking parakeet. "I don't know how it goes," he says to me.

Gang Lu looks around the room idly with expressionless eyes. He's sick of physics and sick of the buffoons who practice it. The tall glacial German, Chris, who tells him what to do; the crass idiot Bob who talks to him like he is a dog; the student Shan whose ideas about plasma physics are treated with reverence and praised at every meeting. The woman who puts her feet on the desk and dismisses him with her eyes. Gang Lu no longer spends his evenings in the computer lab, running simulations and thinking about magnetic forces and invisible particles; he now spends them at the firing range, learning to hit a moving target with the gun he purchased last spring. He pictures himself holding the gun with both hands, arms straight out and steady; Clint Eastwood, only smarter. Clint Eastwood as a rocket scientist.

He stares at each person in turn, trying to gauge how much respect each of them has for him. One by one. Behind black-rimmed glasses, he counts with his eyes. In each case the verdict is clear: not enough.

The collie fell down the basement stairs. I don't know if she was disoriented and looking for me or what. But when I was at work she used her long nose like a lever and got the door to the basement open and tried to go down there except her legs wouldn't do it and she fell. I found her sleeping on the concrete floor in an unnatural position, one leg still awkwardly resting on the last step. I repositioned the leg and sat down next to her and petted her. We used to play a game called Maserati, where I'd grab her nose like a gearshift and put her through all the gears, first second third fourth, until we were going a hundred miles an hour through town. She thought it was funny.

Now I'm at work but this morning there's nothing to do, and every time I turn around I see her sprawled, eyes mute, leg bent upward. We're breaking each other's hearts. I draw a picture of her on the blackboard using brown chalk. I make Xs where her eyes should be. Chris walks in with the morning paper and a cup of coffee. He looks around the clean office.

"Why are you here when there's no work to do?" he asks.

"I'm hiding from my life, what else," I tell him. This sounds perfectly reasonable to him. He gives me part of the paper.

His mother is visiting from Germany, a robust woman of eighty who is depressed and hoping to be cheered up. In the last year she has lost her one-hundred-year-old mother and her husband of sixty years. She mostly can't be cheered up, but she likes going to art galleries so Chris has been driving her around the Midwest, to our best cities, showing her what kind of art Americans like to look at.

"How's your mom?" I ask him.

He shrugs and makes a flat-handed so-so motion.

We read, smoke, drink coffee, and yawn. I decide to go home.

"Good idea," he says encouragingly.

It's November 1, 1991, the last day of the first part of my life. Before I leave I pick up the eraser and stand in front of the collie's picture on the blackboard, thinking. I can feel him watching me, drinking his coffee. He's wearing a gold shirt and blue jeans and a gray cardigan sweater. He is tall and lanky and white-haired, forty-seven years old. He has a wife named Ulrike, a daughter named Karein, and a son named Goran. A dog named Mica. A mother named Ursula. A friend named me.

I erase the Xs.

Down the hall, Linhua Shan feeds numbers into a computer and watches as a graph is formed. The computer screen is brilliant blue, and the lines appear in red and yellow and green. Four keystrokes and the green becomes purple. More keystrokes and the blue background fades to the azure of a summer sky. The wave lines arc over it, crossing against one another. He asks the computer to print, and while it chugs along he pulls up a golf game on the screen and tees off.

One room over, at a desk, Gang Lu works on a letter to his sister in China. *The study of physics is more and more disappointing,* he tells her. *Modern physics is self-delusion* and *all my life I have been honest and straightforward, and I have most of all detested cunning, fawning sycophants and dishonest bureaucrats who think they are always right in everything.* Delicate Chinese characters all over a page. She was a kind and gentle sister, and he thanks her for that. He's going to kill himself. *You yourself should not be too sad about it, for at least I have found a few traveling companions to accompany me to the grave.* Inside the coat on the back of his chair are a .38–caliber handgun and a .22–caliber revolver. They're heavier than they look and weigh the pockets down. *My beloved elder sister, I take my eternal leave of you.*

The collie's eyes are almond-shaped; I draw them in with brown chalk and put a white bone next to her feet.

"That's better," Chris says kindly.

Before I leave the building I pass Gang Lu in the hallway and say hello. He has a letter in his hand and he's wearing his coat. He doesn't answer and I don't expect him to. At the end of the hallway are the double doors leading to the rest of my life. I push them open and walk through.

Friday afternoon seminar, everyone is glazed over, listening as someone explains something unexplainable at the head of the long table. Gang Lu stands up and leaves the room abruptly; goes down one floor to see if the chairman, Dwight, is sitting in his office. He is. The door is open. Gang Lu turns and walks back up the stairs and enters the meeting room again. Chris Goertz is sitting near the door and takes the first bullet in the back of the head. There is a loud popping sound and then blue smoke. Shan gets the second bullet in the forehead; the lenses of his glasses shatter. More smoke and the room rings with the popping. Bob Smith tries to crawl beneath the table. Gang Lu takes two steps, holds his arms straight out, and levels the gun with both hands. Bob looks up. The third bullet in the right hand, the fourth in the chest. Smoke. Elbows and legs, people trying to get out of the way and then out of the room.

Gang Lu walks quickly down the stairs, dispelling spent cartridges and loading new ones. From the doorway of Dwight's office: the fifth bullet in the head, the sixth strays, the seventh also in the head. A slumping. More smoke and ringing. Through the cloud an image comes forward—Bob Smith, hit in the chest, hit in the hand, still alive. Back up the stairs. Two scientists, young men, crouched over Bob, loosening his clothes, talking to him. From where he lies, Bob can see his best friend still sitting upright in a chair, head thrown back at an unnatural angle. Everything is broken and red. The two young scientists leave the room at gunpoint. Bob closes his eyes. The eighth and ninth bullets in his head. As Bob dies, Chris Goertz's body settles in his chair, a long sigh escapes his throat. Reload. Two more for Chris, one for Shan. Exit the building, cross two streets, run across the green, into building number two and upstairs.

The administrator, Anne Cleary, is summoned from her office by the receptionist. She speaks to him for a few seconds, he produces the gun and shoots her in the face. The receptionist, a young student working as a temp, is just beginning to stand when he shoots her in the mouth. He dispels the spent cartridges in the stairwell, loads new ones. Reaches the top of the steps, looks around. Is disoriented suddenly. The ringing and the smoke and the dissatisfaction of not checking all the names off the list. A slamming and a running sound, the shout of police. He walks into an empty classroom, takes off his coat, folds it carefully and puts it over the back of the chair. Checks his watch; twelve minutes since it began. Places the barrel against his right temple. Fires.

The first call comes at four o'clock. I'm reading on the bench in the kitchen, one foot on a sleeping dog's back. It's Mary, calling from work. There's been some kind of disturbance in the building, a rumor that Dwight was shot; cops are running through the halls carrying rifles. They're evacuating the building and she's coming over.

Dwight, a tall likable oddball who cut off his ponytail when they made him chair of the department. Greets everyone with a famous booming hello in the morning, studies plasma, just like Chris and Bob. Chris lives two and half blocks from the physics building; he'll be home by now if they've evacuated. I dial his house and his mother answers. She tells me that Chris won't be home until five o'clock, and then they're going to a play. Ulrike, her daughter-in-law, is coming back from a trip to Chicago and will join them. She wants to know why I'm looking for Chris; isn't he where I am?

No, I'm at home and I just had to ask him something. Could he please call me when he comes in.

She tells me that Chris showed her a drawing I made of him sitting at his desk behind a stack of manuscripts. She's so pleased to meet Chris's friends, and the Midwest is lovely, really, except it's very brown, isn't it?

It *is* very brown. We hang up.

The Midwest is very brown. The phone rings. It's a physicist. His wife, a friend of mine, is on the extension. Well, he's not sure, but it's possible that I should brace myself for bad news. I've already heard, I tell him, something happened to Dwight. There's a long pause and then his wife says, Jo Ann. It's possible that Chris was involved.

I think she means Chris shot Dwight. No, she says gently, killed too.

Mary is here. I tell them not to worry and hang up. I have two cigarettes going. Mary takes one and smokes it. She's not looking at me. I tell her about the phone call.

"They're out of it," I say. "They thought Chris was involved."

She repeats what they said: I think you should brace yourself for bad news. Pours whiskey in a coffee cup.

For a few minutes I can't sit down, I can't stand up. I can only smoke. The phone rings. Another physicist tells me there's some bad news. He mentions Chris and Bob and I tell him I don't want to talk right now. He says okay but to be prepared because it's going to be on the news any minute. It's 4:45.

"Now they're trying to stir Bob into the stew," I tell Mary. She nods; she's heard this, too. I have the distinct feeling there is something going on that I can either understand or not understand. There's a choice to be made.

"I don't understand," I tell Mary.

We sit in the darkening living room, smoking and sipping our cups of whiskey. Inside my head I keep thinking *Uh-oh,* over and over. I'm in a rattled condition; I can't calm down and figure this out.

"I think we should brace ourselves in case something bad has happened," I say to Mary. She nods. "Just in case. It won't hurt to be braced." She nods again. I realize that I don't know what *braced* means. You hear it all the time but that doesn't mean it makes sense. Whiskey is supposed to be bracing but what it is is awful. I want either tea or beer, no whiskey. Mary nods and heads into the kitchen.

Within an hour there are seven women in the dim living room, sitting. Switching back and forth between CNN and the special reports by the local news. There is something terrifying about the quality of the light and the way voices are echoing in the room. The phone never stops ringing, ever since the story hit the national news. Physics, University of Iowa, dead people. Names not yet released. Everyone I've ever known is checking in to see if I'm still alive. California calls, New York calls, Florida calls, Ohio calls twice. All the guests at a party my husband is having call, one after the other, to ask how I'm doing. Each time, fifty times, I think it might be Chris and then it isn't.

It occurs to me once that I could call his house and talk to him directly, find out exactly what happened. Fear that his mother would answer prevents me from doing it. By this time I am getting reconciled to the fact that Shan, Gang Lu, and Dwight were killed. Also an administrator and her office assistant. The Channel 9 newslady keeps saying there are six dead and two in critical condition. They're not saying who did the shooting. The names will be released at nine o'clock. Eventually I sacrifice all of them except Chris and Bob; they are the ones in critical condition, which is certainly not hopeless. At some point I go into the study to get away from the terrible dimness in the living room, all those eyes, all that calmness in the face of chaos. The collie tries to stand up but someone stops her with a handful of Fritos.

The study is small and cold after I shut the door, but more brightly lit than the living room. I can't remember what anything means. The phone rings and I pick up the extension and listen. My friend Michael is calling from Illinois for the second time. He asks Shirley if I'm holding up okay. Shirley says it's hard to tell. I go back into the living room.

The newslady breaks in at nine o'clock, and of course they drag it out as long as they can. I've already figured out that if they go in alphabetical order Chris will come first. Goertz, Lu, Nicholson, Shan, Smith. His name will come on first. She drones on, dead University of Iowa professors, lone gunman named Gang Lu.

Gang Lu. Lone gunman. Before I have a chance to absorb that she says, The dead are.

Chris's picture.

Oh no, oh God. I lean against Mary's chair and then leave the room abruptly. I have to stand in the bathroom for a while and look at myself in the mirror. I'm still Jo Ann, white face and dark hair. I have earrings on, tiny wrenches that hang from wires. In the living room she's pronouncing all the other names. The two critically wounded are the administrator and her assistant, Miya Sioson. The administrator is already dead for all practical purposes, although they won't disconnect the machines until the following afternoon. The student receptionist will survive but will never again be able to move more than her head. She was in Gang Lu's path and he shot her in the mouth and the bullet lodged in the top of her spine and not only will she never dance again, she'll never walk or write or spend a day alone. She got to keep her head but lost her body. The final victim is Chris's mother, who will weather it all with a dignified face and an erect spine, then return to Germany and kill herself without further words or fanfare.

I tell the white face in the mirror that Gang Lu did this, wrecked everything and killed all those people. It seems as ludicrous as everything else. I can't get my mind to work right, I'm still operating on yesterday's facts; today hasn't jelled yet. "It's a good thing none of this happened," I say to my face. A knock on the door and I open it.

The collie is swaying on her feet, toenails clenched to keep from sliding on the wood floor. Julene's hesitant face. "She wanted to come visit you," she tells me. I bring her in and close the door. We sit by the tub. She lifts her long nose to my face and I take her muzzle and we move through the gears slowly, first second third fourth, all the way through town, until what happened has happened and we know it has happened. We return to the living room. The second wave of calls is starting to come in, from those who just saw the faces on the news. Shirley screens. A knock comes on the door. Julene settles the dog down again on her blanket. It's the husband at the door, looking frantic. He hugs me hard but I'm made of cement, arms stuck in a down position.

The women immediately clear out, taking their leave, looking at the floor. Suddenly it's only me and him, sitting in our living room on a Friday night, just like always. I realize it took quite a bit of courage for him to come to the house when he did, facing all those women who think he's the Antichrist. The dogs are crowded against him on the couch and he's wearing a shirt I've never seen before. He's here to help me get through this. Me. He knows how awful this must be. Awful. He knows how I felt about Chris. Past tense. I have to put my hands over my face for a minute.

We sit silently in our living room. He watches the mute television screen and I watch him. The planes and ridges of his face are more familiar to me than my own. I understand that he wishes even more than I do that he still loved me. When he looks over at me, it's with an expression I've seen before. It's the way he looks at the dog on the blanket.

I get his coat and follow him out into the cold November night. There are stars and stars and stars. The sky is full of dead men, drifting in the blackness like helium balloons. My mother floats past in a hospital gown, trailing tubes. I go back inside where the heat is.

The house is empty and dim, full of dogs and cigarette butts. The collie has peed again. The television is flickering *Special Report* across the screen and I turn it off before the pictures appear. I bring blankets up, fresh and warm from the dryer.

After all the commotion the living room feels cavernous and dead. A branch scrapes against the house and for a brief instant I feel a surge of hope. They might have come back. And I stand at the foot of the stairs staring up into the darkness, listening for the sounds of their little squirrel feet. Silence. No matter how much you miss them. They never come back once they're gone.

I wake her up three times between midnight and dawn. She doesn't usually sleep this soundly but all the chaos and company in the house tonight have made her more tired than usual. The Lab wakes and drowsily begins licking her lower region. She stops and stares at me, trying to make out my face in the dark, then gives up and sleeps. The brown dog is flat on her back with her paws limp, wedged between me and the back of the couch.

I've propped myself so I'll be able to see when dawn starts to arrive. For now there are still planets and stars. Above the black branches of a maple is the dog star, Sirius, my personal favorite. The dusty rings of Saturn. Io, Jupiter's moon.

When I think I can't bear it for one more minute I reach down and nudge her gently with my dog-arm. She rises slowly, faltering, and stands over me in the darkness. My peer, my colleague. In a few hours the world will resume itself, but for now we're in a pocket of silence. We're in the plasmapause, a place of equilibrium, where the forces of the Earth meet the forces of the sun. I imagine it as a place of silence, where the particles of dust stop spinning and hang motionless in deep space.

Around my neck is the stone he brought me from Poland. I hold it out. *Like this?* I ask. Shards of fly wings, suspended in amber.

Exactly, he says.

Under the Radar

RICHARD FORD

On the drive over to the Nicholsons' for dinner—their first in some time—Marjorie Reeves told her husband, Steven Reeves, that she had had an affair with George Nicholson (their host) a year ago, but that it was all over with now and she hoped he—Steven—would not be mad about it and could go on with life.

At this point they were driving along Quaker Bridge Road where it leaves the Perkins Great Woods Road and begins to border the Shenipsit Reservoir, dark and shadowy and calmly mirrored in the late spring twilight. On the right was dense young timber, beech and alder saplings in pale leaf, the ground damp and cakey. Peepers were calling out from the watery lows. Their turn onto Apple Orchard Lane was still a mile on.

Steven, on hearing this news, began gradually and very carefully to steer their car—a tan Mercedes wagon with hooded yellow headlights—off of Quaker Bridge Road and onto the damp grassy shoulder so he could organize this information properly before going on.

They were extremely young. Steven Reeves was twenty-eight. Marjorie Reeves a year younger. They weren't rich, but they'd been lucky. Steven's job at Packard-Wells was to stay on top of a small segment of a larger segment of a rather small prefabrication intersection that serviced the automobile industry, and where any sudden alteration, or even the rumor of an alteration, in certain polymer-bonding formulas could tip crucial down-the-line demand patterns, and in that way affect the betting lines and comfort zones of a good many meaningful client positions. His job meant poring over dense and esoteric petrochemical-industry journals, attending technical seminars, flying to vendor conventions, then writing up detailed status reports and all the while keeping an eye on the market for the benefit of his higher-ups. He'd been a scholarship boy at Bates, studied chemistry, was the only son of a hard-put but upright lobstering family in Pemaquid, Maine, and had done well. His bosses at Packard-Wells liked him, saw themselves in him, and also in him saw character qualities they'd never quite owned—blond and slender callowness tending to gullibility, but backed by caution, ingenuity and a thoroughgoing, compact toughness. He was sharp. It was his seventh year with the company—his first job. He and Marjorie had been married two years. They had no children. The car had been his bonus two Christmases ago.

When the station wagon eased to a stop, Steven sat for a minute with the motor running, the salmon-colored dash lights illuminating his face. The radio had been playing softly—the last of the news, then an interlude for French horns. Responding to no particular signal, he pressed off the radio and in the same movement switched off the ignition, which left the headlights shining on the empty, countrified road. The windows were down to attract the fresh spring air, and when the engine noise ceased the evening's ambient sounds were waiting. The peepers. A sound of thrush wings fluttering in the brush only a few yards away. The noise of something falling from a small distance and hitting an invisible water surface. Beyond the stand of saplings was the west, and through the darkened trunks, the sky was still pale yellow with the day's light, though here on Quaker Bridge Road it was nearly dark.

When Marjorie said what she had just said, she'd been looking straight ahead to where the headlights made a bright path in the dark. Perhaps she'd looked at Steven once, but having said what she'd said, she kept her hands in her lap and continued looking ahead. She was a pretty, blonde, convictionless girl with small demure features—small nose, small ears, small chin, though with a surprisingly full-lipped smile which she practiced on everyone. She was fond of getting a little tipsy at parties and lowering her voice and sitting on a flowered ottoman or a burl tabletop with a glass of something and showing too much of her legs or inappropriate amounts of her small breasts. She had grown up in Indiana, studied art at Purdue. Steven had met her in New York at a party while she was working for a firm that did child-focused advertising for a large toymaker. He'd liked her bobbed hair, her fragile, wispy features, translucent skin and the slightly husky voice that made her seem more sophisticated than she was, but somehow convinced her she was, too. In their community east of Hartford, the women who knew Marjorie Reeves thought of her as a bimbo who would not stay married to sweet Steven Reeves for very long. His second wife would be the right wife for him. Marjorie was just a starter.

Marjorie, however, did not think of herself that way, only that she liked men and felt happy and confident around them and assumed Steven thought this was fine and that in the long run it would help his career to have a pretty, spirited wife no one could pigeonhole. To set herself apart and to take an interest in the community she'd gone to work as a volunteer at a grieving-children's center in Hartford, which meant all black. And it was in Hartford that she'd had the chance to encounter George Nicholson and fuck him at a Red Roof Inn until they'd both gotten tired of it. It would never happen again, was her view, since in a year it hadn't happened again.

For the two or possibly five minutes now that they had sat on the side of Quaker Bridge Road in the still airish evening, with the noises of spring floating in and out of the open window, Marjorie had said nothing and Steven had also said nothing, though he realized that he was saying nothing because he was at a loss for words. A loss for words, he realized, meant that nothing that comes to mind seems very interesting to say as a next thing to what has just been said. He knew he was a callow man—a boy in some ways, still—but he was not stupid. At Bates, he had taken Dr. Sudofsky's class on *Ulysses,* and come away with a sense of irony and humor and the assurance that true knowledge was a spiritual process, a quest, not a storage of dry facts—a thing like freedom, which you only fully experienced in practice. He'd also played hockey, and knew that knowledge and aggressiveness were a subtle and surprising and uncommon combination. He had sought to practice both at Packard-Wells.

But for a brief and terrifying instant in the cool padded semi-darkness, just when he began experiencing his loss for words, he entered or at least nearly slipped into a softened fuguelike state in which he began to fear that he perhaps *could* not say another word; that something (work fatigue, shock, disappointment over what Marjorie had admitted) was at that moment causing him to detach from reality and to slide away from the present, and in fact to begin to lose his mind and go crazy to the extent that he was in jeopardy of beginning to gibber like a chimp, or just to slowly slump sideways against the upholstered door and not speak for a long, long time—months—and then only with the aid of drugs be able merely to speak in simple utterances that would seem cryptic, so that eventually he would have to be looked after by his mother's family in Damariscotta. A terrible thought.

And so to avoid that—to save his life and sanity—he abruptly just said a word, any word that he could say into the perfumed twilight inhabiting the car, where his wife was obviously anticipating his reply to her unhappy confession.

And for some reason the word—phrase, really—that he uttered was "ground clutter." Something he'd heard on the TV weather report as they were dressing for dinner.

"Hm?" Marjorie said. "What was it?" She turned her pretty, small-featured face toward him so that her pearl earrings caught light from some unknown source. She was wearing a tiny green cocktail dress and green satin shoes that showed off her incredibly thin ankles and slender, bare brown calves. She had two tiny matching green bows in her hair. She smelled sweet. "I know this wasn't what you wanted to hear, Steven," she said, "but I felt I should tell you before we got to George's. The Nicholsons', I mean. It's all over. It'll never happen again. I promise you. No one will ever mention it. I just lost my bearings last year with the move. I'm sorry." She had made a little steeple of her fingertips, as if she'd been concentrating very hard as she spoke these words. But now she put her hands again calmly in her minty green lap. She had bought her dress especially for this night at the Nicholsons'. She'd thought George would like it and Steven, too. She turned her face away and exhaled a small but detectable sigh in the car. It was then that the headlights went off automatically.

George Nicholson was a big squash-playing, thick-chested, hairy-armed Yale lawyer who sailed his own Hinckley 61 out of Essex and had started backing off from his high-priced Hartford plaintiffs' practice at fifty to devote more time to competitive racket sports and senior skiing. George was a college roommate of one of Steven's firm's senior partners and had "adopted" the Reeveses when they moved into the community following their wedding. Marjorie had volunteered Saturdays with George's wife, Patsy, at the Episcopal Thrift Shop during their first six months in Connecticut. To Steven, George Nicholson had recounted a memorable, seasoning, summer spent hauling deep-water lobster traps with some tough old sea dogs out of Matinicus, Maine. Later, he'd been a Marine, and sported a faded anchor, ball and chain tattooed on his forearm. Later yet he'd fucked Steven's wife.

Having said something, even something that made no sense, Steven felt a sense of glum and deflated relief as he sat in the silent car beside Marjorie, who was still facing forward. Two thoughts had begun to compete in his reviving awareness. One was clearly occasioned by his conception of George Nicholson. He thought of George Nicholson as a gasbag, but also a forceful man who'd made his pile by letting very little stand in his way. When he thought about George he always remembered the story about Matinicus, which then put into his mind a mental picture of his own father and himself hauling traps somewhere out toward Monhegan. The reek of the bait, the toss of the ocean in late spring, the consoling monotony of the solid, tree-lined shore barely visible through the mists. Thinking through that circuitry always made him vaguely admire George Nicholson and, oddly, made him think he liked George even now, in spite of everything.

The other competing thought was that part of Marjorie's character had always been to confess upsetting things that turned out, he believed, not to be true: being a hooker for a summer up in Saugatuck; topless dancing while she was an undergraduate; heroin experimentation; taking part in armed robberies with her high-school boyfriend in Goshen, Indiana, where she was from. When she told these far-fetched stories she would grow distracted and shake her head, as though they were true. And now, while he didn't particularly think any of these stories was a bit truer, he did realize that he didn't really know his wife at all; and that in fact the entire conception of knowing another person—of trust, of closeness, of marriage itself—while not exactly a lie since it existed *someplace* if only as an idea (in his parents' life, at least marginally) was still completely out-of-date, defunct, was something typifying another era, now unfortunately gone. Meeting a girl, falling in love, marrying her, moving to Connecticut, buying a fucking house, starting a life with her and thinking you really knew anything about her—the last part was a complete fiction, which made all the rest a joke. Marjorie might as well have *been* a hooker or held up 7-Elevens and shot people, for all he really knew about her. And what was more, if he'd said any of this to her, sitting next to him thinking he would never know what, she either would not have understood a word of it or simply would've said, "Well, okay, that's fine." When people talked about the bottom line, Steven Reeves thought, they weren't talking about money, they were talking about what *this* meant, *this* kind of fatal ignorance. Money—losing it, gaining it, spending it, hoarding it—all that was only an emblem, though a good one, of what was happening here right now.

At this moment a pair of car lights rounded a curve somewhere out ahead of where the two of them sat in their station wagon. The lights found both their white faces staring forward in silence. The lights also found a raccoon just crossing the road from the reservoir shore, headed for the woods that were beside them. The car was going faster than might've been evident. The raccoon paused to peer up into the approaching beams, then continued on into the safe, opposite lane. But only then did it look up and notice Steven and Marjorie's car stopped on the verge of the road, silent in the murky evening. And because of that notice it must've decided that where it had been was much better than where it was going, and so turned to scamper back across Quaker Bridge Road toward the cool waters of the reservoir, which was what caused the car—actually it was a beat-up Ford pickup—to rumble over it, pitching and spinning it off to the side and then motionlessness near the opposite shoulder. "Yaaaahaaaa-yipeeee!" a man's shrill voice shouted from inside the dark cab of the pickup, followed by another man's laughter.

And then it became very silent again. The raccoon lay on the road twenty yards in front of the Reeveses' car. It didn't struggle. It was merely there.

"Gross," Marjorie said.

Steven said nothing, though he felt less at a loss for words now. His eyes, indeed, felt relieved to fix on the still corpse of the raccoon.

"Do we do something?" Marjorie said. She had leaned forward a few inches as if to study the raccoon through the windshield. Light was dying away behind the slender young beech trees to the west of them.

"No," Steven said. These were his first words—except for the words he took no responsibility for—since Marjorie had said what she'd importantly said and their car was still moving toward dinner.

It was then that he hit her. He hit her before he knew he'd hit her, but not before he knew he wanted to. He hit her with the back of his open hand without even looking at her, hit her straight in the front of her face, straight in the nose. And hard. In a way, it was more a gesture than a blow, though it was, he understood, a blow, he felt the soft tip of her nose, and then the knuckly cartilage against the hard bones of the backs of his fingers. He had never hit a woman before, and he had never even thought of hitting Marjorie, always imagining he *couldn't* hit her when he'd read newspaper accounts of such things happening in the sad lives of others. He'd hit other people, been hit by other people, plenty of times—tough Maine boys on the ice rinks. Girls were out, though. His father always made that clear. His mother, too.

"Oh, my goodness" was all that Marjorie said when she received the blow. She put her hand over her nose immediately, but then sat silently in the car while neither of them said anything. His heart was not beating hard. The back of his hand hurt a little. This was all new ground. Steven had a small rosy birthmark just where his left sideburn ended and his shaved face began. It resembled the shape of the state of West Virginia. He thought he could feel this birthmark now. His skin tingled there.

And the truth was he felt even more relieved, and didn't feel at all sorry for Marjorie, sitting there stoically, making a little tent of her hand to cover her nose and staring ahead as if nothing had happened. He thought she would cry, certainly. She was a girl who cried—when she was unhappy, when he said something insensitive, when she was approaching her period. Crying was natural. Clearly, though, it was a new experience for her to be hit. And so it called upon something new, and if not new then some strength, resilience, self-mastery normally reserved for other experiences.

"I can't go to the Nicholsons' now," Marjorie said almost patiently. She removed her hand and viewed her palm as if her palm had her nose in it. Of course it was blood she was thinking about. He heard her breathe in through what sounded like a congested nose, then the breath was completed out through her mouth. She was not crying yet. And for that moment he felt not even sure he *had* smacked her—if it hadn't just been a thought he'd entertained, a gesture somehow uncommissioned.

What he wanted to do, however, was skip to the most important things now, not get mired down in wrong, extraneous details. Because he didn't give a shit about George Nicholson or the particulars of what they'd done in some shitty motel. Marjorie would never leave him for George Nicholson or anyone like George Nicholson, and George Nicholson and men like him—high rollers with Hinckleys—didn't throw it all away for unimportant little women like Marjorie. He thought of her nose, red, swollen, smeared with sticky blood dripping onto her green dress. He didn't suppose it could be broken. Noses held up. And, of course, there was a phone in the car. He could simply make a call to the party. He pictured the Nicholsons' great rambling white-shingled house brightly lit beyond the curving drive, the original elms exorbitantly preserved, the footlights, the low-lit day court where they'd all played, the heated pool, the Henry Moore out on the darkened lawn where you just stumbled onto it. He imagined saying to someone—not George Nicholson—that Marjorie was ill, had thrown up on the side of the road.

The *right* details, though. The right details to ascertain from her were: *Are you sorry?* (he'd forgotten Marjorie had already said she was sorry) and *What does this mean for the future?* These were the details that mattered.

Surprisingly, the raccoon that had been cartwheeled by the pickup and then lain motionless, a blob in the near-darkness, had come back to life and was now trying to drag itself and its useless hinder parts off of Quaker Bridge Road and onto the grassy verge and into the underbrush that bordered the reservoir.

"Oh, for God's sake," Marjorie said, and put her hand over her damaged nose again. She could see the raccoon's struggle and turned her head away.

"Aren't you even sorry?" Steven said.

"Yes," Marjorie said, her nose still covered as if she wasn't thinking about the fact that she was covering it. Probably, he thought, the pain had gone away some. It hadn't been so bad. "I mean no," she said.

He wanted to hit her again then—this time in the ear—but he didn't. He wasn't sure why not. No one would ever know. "Well, which is it?" he said, and felt for the first time completely furious. The thing that made him furious—all his life, the very maddest—was to be put into a situation in which everything he did was wrong, when right was no longer an option. Now felt like one of those situations. "Which is it?" he said again angrily. "Really." He should just take her to the Nicholsons', he thought, swollen nose, bloody lips, all stoppered up, and let her deal with it. Or let her sit out in the car, or else start walking the 11.6 miles home. Maybe George could come out and drive her in his Rover. These were only thoughts, of course. "Which is it?" he said for the third time. He was stuck on these words, on this bit of barren curiosity.

"I was sorry when I told you," Marjorie said, very composed. She lowered her hand from her nose to her lap. One of the little green bows that had been in her hair was now resting on her bare shoulder. "Though not very sorry," she said. "Only sorry because I had to tell you. And now that I've told you and you've hit me in my face and probably broken my nose, I'm not sorry about anything—except that. Though I'm sorry about being married to you, which I'll remedy as soon as I can." She was still not crying. "So *now*, will you as a gesture of whatever good there is in you, get out and go over and do something to help that poor injured creature that those motherfucking rednecks maimed with their motherfucking pickup truck and then, because they're pieces of shit and low forms of degraded humanity, laughed about? Can you do that, Steven? Is that in your range?" She sniffed back hard through her nose, then expelled a short, deep and defeated moan. Her voice seemed more nasal, more midwestern even, now that her nose was congested.

"I'm sorry I hit you," Steven Reeves said, and opened the car door onto the silent road.

"I know," Marjorie said in an emotionless voice. "And you'll be sorrier."

When he had walked down the empty macadam road in his tan suit to where the raccoon had been struck and then bounced over onto the road's edge, there was nothing now there. Only a small circle of dark blood he could just make out on the nubbly road surface and that might've been an oil smudge. No raccoon. The raccoon with its last reserves of savage, unthinking will had found the strength to pull itself off into the bushes to die. Steven peered down into the dark, stalky confinement of scrubs and bramble that separated the road from the reservoir. It was very still there. He thought he heard a rustling in the low brush where a creature might be, getting itself settled into the soft grass and damp earth to go to sleep forever. Someplace out on the lake he heard a young girl's voice, very distinctly laughing. Then a car door closed farther away. Then another sort of door, a screen door, slapped shut. And then a man's voice saying "Oh no, oh-ho-ho-ho-ho, no." A small white light came on farther back in the trees beyond the reservoir, where he hadn't imagined there was a house. He wondered about how long it would be before his angry feelings stopped mattering to him. He considered briefly why Marjorie would admit this to him now. It seemed so odd.

Then he heard his own car start. The muffled-metal diesel racket of the Mercedes. The headlights came smartly on and disclosed him. Music was instantly loud inside. He turned just in time to see Marjorie's pretty face illuminated, as his own had been, by the salmon dashboard light. He saw the tips of her fingers atop the arc of the steering wheel, heard the surge of the engine. In the woods he noticed a strange glow coming through the trees, something yellow, something out of the low wet earth, a mist, a vapor, something that might be magical. The air smelled sweet now. The peepers stopped peeping. And then that was all.

From *Herzog*

SAUL BELLOW

It was now becoming clear to Herzog, himself incapable of making plans, how well Madeleine had prepared to get rid of him. Six weeks before sending him away, she had had him lease a house near the Midway at two hundred dollars a month. When they moved in, he built shelves, cleared the garden, and repaired the garage door; he put up the storm windows. Only a week before she demanded a divorce, she had his things cleaned and pressed, but on the day he left the house, she flung them all into a carton which she then dumped down the cellar stairs. She needed more closet space. And other things happened, sad, comical, or cruel, depending on one's point of view. Until the very last day, the tone of Herzog's relations with Madeleine was quite serious—that is, ideas, personalities, issues were respected and discussed. When she broke the news to him, for instance, she expressed herself with dignity, in that lovely, masterful style of hers. She had thought it over from every angle, she said, and she had to accept defeat. They could not make the grade together. She was prepared to shoulder some of the blame. Of course, Herzog was not entirely unprepared for this. But he had really thought matters were improving.

All this happened on a bright, keen fall day. He had been in the backyard putting in the storm windows. The first frost had already caught the tomatoes. The grass was dense and soft, with the peculiar beauty it gains when the cold days come and the gossamers lie on it in the morning; the dew is thick and lasting. The tomato vines had blackened and the red globes had burst.

He had seen Madeleine at the back window upstairs, putting June down for her nap, and later he heard the bath being run. Now she was calling from the kitchen door. A gust from the lake made the framed glass tremble in Herzog's arms. He propped it carefully against the porch and took off his canvas gloves but not his beret, as though he sensed that he would immediately go on a trip.

Madeleine hated her father violently, but it was not irrelevant that the old man was a famous impresario—sometimes called the American Stanislavsky. She had prepared the event with a certain theatrical genius of her own. She wore black stockings, high heels, a lavender dress with Indian brocade from Central America. She had on her opal earrings, her bracelets, and she was perfumed; her hair was combed with a new, clean part and her large eyelids shone with a bluish cosmetic. Her eyes were blue but the depth of the color was curiously affected by the variable tinge of the whites. Her nose, which descended in a straight elegant line from her brows, worked slightly when she was peculiarly stirred. To Herzog even this tic was precious. There was a flavor of subjugation in his love for Madeleine. Since she was domineering, and since he loved her, he had to accept the flavor that was given. In this confrontation in the untidy parlor, two kinds of egotism were present, and Herzog from his sofa in New York now contemplated them—hers in triumph (she had prepared a great moment, she was about to do what she longed most to do, strike a blow) and his egotism in abeyance, all converted into passivity. What he was about to suffer, he deserved; he had sinned long and hard; he had earned it. This was it.

In the window on glass shelves there stood an ornamental collection of small glass bottles, Venetian and Swedish. They came with the house. The sun now caught them. They were pierced with the light. Herzog saw the waves, the threads of color, the spectral intersecting bars, and especially a great blot of flaming white on the center of the wall above Madeleine. She was saying, "We can't live together anymore."

Her speech continued for several minutes. Her sentences were well formed. This speech had been rehearsed and it seemed also that he had been waiting for the performance to begin.

Theirs was not a marriage that could last. Madeleine had never loved him. She was telling him that. "It's painful to have to say I never loved you. I never will love you, either," she said. "So there's no point in going on."

Herzog said, "I do love you, Madeleine."

Step by step, Madeleine rose in distinction, in brilliance, in insight. Her color grew very rich, and her brows, and that Byzantine nose of hers, rose, moved; her blue eyes gained by the flush that kept deepening, rising from her chest and her throat. She was in an ecstasy of consciousness. It occurred to Herzog that she had beaten him so badly, her pride was so fully satisfied, that there was an overflow of strength into her intelligence. He realized that he was witnessing one of the very greatest moments of her life.

A Telephone Call

DOROTHY PARKER

Please, God, let him telephone me now. Dear God, let him call me now. I won't ask anything else of You, truly I won't. It isn't very much to ask. It would be so little to You, God, such a little, little thing. Only let him telephone now. Please, God. Please, please, please.

If I didn't think about it, maybe the telephone might ring. Sometimes it does that. If I could think of something else. If I could think of something else. Maybe if I counted five hundred by fives, it might ring by that time. I'll count slowly. I won't cheat. And if it rings when I get to three hundred, I won't stop; I won't answer it until I get to five hundred. Five, ten, fifteen, twenty, twenty-five, thirty, thirty-five, forty, forty-five, fifty. . . . Oh, please ring. Please.

This is the last time I'll look at the clock. I will not look at it again. It's ten minutes past seven. He said he would telephone at five o'clock. "I'll call you at five, darling." I think that's where he said "darling." I'm almost sure he said it there. I know he called me "darling" twice, and the other time was when he said good-bye. "Good-bye, darling." He was busy, and he can't say much in the office, but he called me "darling" twice. He couldn't have minded my calling him up. I know you shouldn't keep telephoning them—I know they don't like that. When you do that, they know you are thinking about them and wanting them, and that makes them hate you. But I hadn't talked to him in three days—not in three days. And all I did was ask him how he was; it was just the way anybody might have called him up. He couldn't have minded that. He couldn't have thought I was bothering him. "No, of course you're not," he said. And he said he'd telephone me. He didn't have to say that. I didn't ask him to, truly I didn't. I'm sure I didn't. I don't think he would say he'd telephone me, and then just never do it. Please don't let him do that, God. Please don't.

"I'll call you at five, darling." "Good-bye, darling." He was busy, and he was in a hurry, and there were people around him, but he called me "darling" twice. That's mine, that's mine. I have that, even if I never see him again. Oh, but that's so little. That isn't enough. Nothing's enough, if I never see him again. Please let me see him again, God. Please, I want him so much. I want him so much. I'll be good, God. I will try to be better, I will, if You will let me see him again. If You let him telephone me. Oh, let him telephone me now.

Ah, don't let my prayer seem too little to You, God. You sit up there, so white and old, with all the angels about You and the stars slipping by. And I come to You with a prayer about a telephone call. Ah, don't laugh, God. You see, You don't know how it feels. You're so safe, there on Your throne, with the blue swirling under You. Nothing can touch You; no one can twist Your heart in his hands. This is suffering. God, this is bad, bad suffering. Won't You help me? For Your Son's sake, help me. You said You would do whatever was asked of You in His name. Oh, God, in the name of Thine only beloved Son, Jesus Christ, our Lord, let him telephone me now.

I must stop this. I mustn't be this way. Look. Suppose a young man says he'll call a girl up, and then something happens, and he doesn't. That isn't so terrible, is it? Why, it's going on all over the world, right this minute. Oh, what do I care what's going on all over the world? Why can't that telephone ring? Why can't it, why can't it? Couldn't you ring? Ah, please, couldn't you? You damned, ugly, shiny thing. It would hurt you to ring, wouldn't it? Oh, that would hurt you. Damn you, I'll pull your filthy roots out of the wall, I'll smash your smug black face in little bits. Damn you to hell.

No, no, no. I must stop. I must think about something else. This is what I'll do. I'll put the clock in the other room. Then I can't look at it. If I do have to look at it, then I'll have to walk into the bedroom, and that will be something to do. Maybe, before I look at it again, he will call me. I'll be so sweet to him, if he calls me. If he says he can't see me tonight, I'll say, "Why, that's all right, dear. Why, of course it's all right." I'll be the way I was when I first met him. Then maybe he'll like me again. I was always sweet, at first. Oh, it's so easy to be sweet to people before you love them.

I think he must still like me a little. He couldn't have called me "darling" twice today, if he didn't still like me a little. It isn't all gone, if he still likes me a little; even if it's only a little, little bit. You see, God, if You would just let him telephone me, I wouldn't have to ask You anything more. I would be sweet to him, I would be gay, I would be just the way I used to be, and then he would love me again. And then I would never have to ask You for anything more. Don't You see, God? So won't You please let him telephone me? Won't You please, please, please?

Are You punishing me, God, because I've been bad? Are You angry with me because I did that? Oh, but, God, there are so many bad people—You could not be hard only to me. And it wasn't very bad; it couldn't have been bad. We didn't hurt anybody, God. Things are only bad when they hurt people. We didn't hurt one single soul; You know that. You know it wasn't bad, don't You, God? So won't You let him telephone me now? If he doesn't telephone me, I'll know God is angry with me. I'll count five hundred by fives, and if he hasn't called me then, I will know God isn't going to help me, ever again. That will be the sign. Five, ten, fifteen, twenty, twenty-five, thirty, thirty-five, forty, forty-five, fifty, fifty-five. . . . It was bad. I knew it was bad. All right, God, send me to hell. You think You're frightening me with Your hell, don't You? You think Your hell is worse than mine.

I mustn't. I mustn't do this. Suppose he's a little late calling me up—that's nothing to get hysterical about. Maybe he isn't going to call—maybe he's coming straight up here without telephoning. He'll be cross if he sees I have been crying. They don't like you to cry. He doesn't cry. I wish to God I could make him cry. I wish I could make him cry and tread the floor and feel his heart heavy and big and festering in him. I wish I could hurt him like hell.

He doesn't wish that about me. I don't think he even knows how he makes me feel. I wish he could know, without my telling him. They don't like you to tell them they've made you cry. They don't like you to tell them you're unhappy because of them. If you do, they think you're possessive and exacting. And then they hate you. They hate you whenever you say anything you really think. You always have to keep playing little games. Oh, I thought we didn't have to; I thought this was so big I could say whatever I meant. I guess you can't, ever. I guess there isn't ever anything big enough for that. Oh, if he would just telephone, I wouldn't tell him I had been sad about him. They hate sad people. I would be so sweet and so gay, he couldn't help but like me. If he would only telephone. If he would only telephone.

Maybe that's what he is doing. Maybe he is coming on here without calling me up. Maybe he's on his way now. Something might have happened to him. No, nothing could ever happen to him. I can't picture anything happening to him. I never picture him run over. I never see him lying still and long and dead. I wish he were dead. That's a terrible wish. That's a lovely wish. If he were dead, he would be mine. If he were dead, I would never think of now and the last few weeks. I would remember only the lovely times. It would be all beautiful. I wish he were dead. I wish he were dead, dead, dead.

This is silly. It's silly to go wishing people were dead just because they don't call you up the very minute they said they would. Maybe the clock's fast; I don't know whether it's right. Maybe he's hardly late at all. Anything could have made him a little late. Maybe he had to stay at his office. Maybe he went home, to call me up from there, and somebody came in. He doesn't like to telephone me in front of people. Maybe he's worried, just a little, little bit, about keeping me waiting. He might even hope that I would call him up. I could do that. I could telephone him.

I mustn't. I mustn't, I mustn't. Oh, God, please don't let me telephone him. Please keep me from doing that. I know, God, just as well as You do, that if he were worried about me, he'd telephone no matter where he was or how many people there were around him. Please make me know that, God. I don't ask You to make it easy for me—You can't do that, for all that You could make a world. Only let me know it, God. Don't let me go on hoping. Don't let me say comforting things to myself. Please don't let me hope, dear God. Please don't.

I won't telephone him. I'll never telephone him again as long as I live. He'll rot in hell, before I'll call him up. You don't have to give me strength, God; I have it myself. If he wanted me, he could get me. He knows where I am. He knows I'm waiting here. He's so sure of me, so sure. I wonder why they hate you, as soon as they are sure of you. I should think it would be so sweet to be sure.

It would be so easy to telephone him. Then I'd know. Maybe it wouldn't be a foolish thing to do. Maybe he wouldn't mind. Maybe he'd like it. Maybe he has been trying to get me. Sometimes people try and try to get you on the telephone, and they say the number doesn't answer. I'm not just saying that to help myself; that really happens. You know that really happens, God. Oh, God, keep me away from that telephone. Keep me away. Let me still have just a little bit of pride. I think I'm going to need it, God. I think it will be all I'll have.

Oh, what does pride matter, when I can't stand it if I don't talk to him? Pride like that is such a silly, shabby little thing. The real pride, the big pride, is in having no pride. I'm not saying that just because I want to call him. I am not. That's true, I know that's true. I will be big. I will be beyond little prides.

Please, God, keep me from telephoning him. Please, God. I don't see what pride has to do with it. This is such a little thing, for me to be bringing in pride, for me to be making such a fuss about. I may have misunderstood him. Maybe he said for me to call him up, at five. "Call me at five, darling." He could have said that, perfectly well. It's so possible that I didn't hear him right. "Call me at five, darling." I'm almost sure that's what he said. God, don't let me talk this way to myself. Make me know, please make me know.

I'll think about something else. I'll just sit quietly. If I could sit still. If I could sit still, maybe I could read. Oh, all the books are about people who love each other, truly and sweetly. What do they want to write about that for? Don't they know it isn't true? Don't they know it's a lie, it's a God-damned lie? What do they have to tell about that for, when they know how it hurts? Damn them, damn them, damn them.

I won't. I'll be quiet. This is nothing to get excited about. Look. Suppose he were someone I didn't know very well. Suppose he were another girl. Then I'd just telephone and say, "Well, for goodness' sake, what happened to you?" That's what I'd do, and I'd never even think about it. Why can't I be casual and natural, just because I love him? I can be. Honestly, I can be. I'll call him up, and be so easy and pleasant. You see if I won't, God. Oh, don't let me call him. Don't, don't, don't.

God, aren't You really going to let him call me? Are You sure, God? Couldn't You please relent? Couldn't You? I don't even ask You to let him telephone me this minute, God: only let him do it in a little while. I'll count five hundred by fives. I'll do it so slowly and so fairly, if he hasn't telephoned then, I'll call him. I will. Oh, please, dear God, dear kind God, my blessed Father in Heaven, let him call before then. Please, God. Please.

Five, ten, fifteen, twenty, twenty-five, thirty, thirty-five. . . .

Over the Hill

ANDRE DUBUS

1

Her hand was tiny. He held it gently, protectively, resting in her lap, the brocaded silk of her kimono against the back of his hand, the smooth flesh gentle and tender against his palm. He looked at her face, which seemed no larger than a child's, and she smiled.

"You buy me another drink?" she said.

"Sure."

He motioned to the bartender, who filled the girl's shot glass with what was supposedly whiskey, though Gale knew it was not and didn't care, then mixed bourbon and water for Gale, using the fifth of Old Crow that three hours earlier he had brought into the bar.

"I'll be right back," he said to the girl.

She nodded and he released her hand and slid from the stool.

"You stay here," he said.

"Sure I stay."

He walked unsteadily past booths where Japanese girls drank with sailors. In the smelly, closet-sized restroom he closed the door and urinated, reading the names of sailors and ships written on the walls, some of them followed by obscenities scrawled by a different, later hand. The ceiling was bare. He stepped onto the toilet and reaching up, his coat tightening at the armpits and bottom rib, he printed with a ballpoint pen, stopping often to shake ink down to the point again: *Gale Castete, Pvt. USMC, Marine Detachment, USS Vanguard Dec 1961.* He stood on the toilet with one hand against the door in front of him, reading his name. Then he thought of her face tilted back, the roots of her hair brown near the forehead when it was time for the Clairol again, the rest of it spreading pale blonde around her head, the eyes shut, the mouth half open, teeth visible, and the one who saw this now was not him—furiously he reached up to write an obscenity behind his name, then stopped; for reading it again, he felt a gentle stir of immortality, faint as a girl's whispering breath into his ear. He stepped down, was suddenly nauseated, and left the restroom, going outside into the alley behind the bar, where he leaned against the wall and loosened his tie and collar and raised his face to the cold air. Two Japanese girls entered the alley from a door to his left and walked past him as if he were not there, arms folded and hands in their kimono sleeves, their lowered heads jabbering strangely, like sea gulls.

He took out his billfold, which bulged with wide folded yen, and tried unsuccessfully to count it in the dark. He thought there should be around thirty-six thousand, for the night before—at sea—he had received the letter, and that morning when they tied up in Yokosuka he had drawn one hundred and fifty dollars, which was what he had saved since the cruise began in August because she wanted a Japanese stereo (and china and glassware and silk and wool and cashmere sweaters and a transistor radio) and in two more paydays she would have had at least the stereo. That evening he had left the slip with his money and two immediate goals: to get falling, screaming drunk and to get laid, two things he had not done on the entire cruise because he had had reason not to; or so he thought. But first he called home—Louisiana—to hear from her what his mother had already told him in the letter, and her vague answers cost him thirty dollars. Then he bought the Old Crow and went into the bar and the prettiest hostess came and stood beside him, her face level with his chest though he sat on a barstool, and she placed a hand on his thigh and said *Can I sit down?* and he said *Yes, would you like a drink?* and she said *Yes, sank you* and sat down and signaled the bartender and said *My name Betty-san* and he said *What is your Japanese name?* She told him but he could not repeat it, so she laughed and said *You call me Betty-san;* he said *Okay, I am Gale. Gale-san? Is girl's name. No,* he said, *it's a man's.*

Now he buttoned his collar and slipped his tie knot into place and went inside.

"You gone long time," she said. "I sink you go back ship."

"No. S'koshi sick. Maybe I won't go back ship."

"You better go. They put you in monkey house."

"Maybe so."

He raised his glass to the bartender and nodded at Betty, then looked at the cuff of his sleeve, at the red hashmark which branded him as a man with four years' service and no rank—three years in the Army and eighteen months in the Marines—although eight months earlier he had been a private first class, nearly certain that he would soon be a lance corporal, then walking back to the ship one night in Alameda, two sailors called him a jarhead and he fought them both and the next day he was reduced to private. He was twenty-four years old.

"I sink you have sta'side wife," Betty said.

"How come?"

"You all time quiet. All time sink sink sink."

She mimicked his brooding, then giggled and shyly covered her face with both hands.

"My wife is butterfly girl," he said.

"Dat's true?"

He nodded.

"While you in Japan she butterfly girl?"

"Yes."

"How you know?"

"My mama-san write me a letter."

"Dat's too bad."

"Maybe I take you home tonight, okay?"

"We'll see."

"When?"

"Bar close soon."

"You're very pretty."

"You really sink so?"

"Yes."

She brought her hands to her face, moved the fingertips up to her eyes.

"You like Japanese girl?"

"Yes," he said. "Very much."

2

Now he could not sleep and he wished they had not gone to bed so soon, for at least as they walked rapidly over strange, winding, suddenly quiet streets he had thought of nothing but Betty and his passion, stifled for four and a half months, but now he lay smoking, vaguely conscious of her foot touching his calf, knowing the Corporal of the Guard had already recorded his absence, and he felt helpless before the capricious forces which governed his life.

Her name was Dana. He had married her in June, two months before the cruise, and their transition from courtship to marriage involved merely the assumption of financial responsibility and an adjustment to conflicting habits of eating, sleeping, and using the bathroom, for they had been making love since their third date, when he had discovered that he not only was not her first, but probably was not even her fourth or fifth. In itself, her lack of innocence did not disturb him. His moral standards were a combination of Calvinism (greatly dulled since leaving home four and a half years earlier), the pragmatic workings of the service, and the ability to think rarely in terms of good and evil. Also, he had no illusions about girls and so on that third date he was not shocked. But afterward he was disturbed. Though he was often tormented by visions of her past, he never asked her about it and he had no idea of how many years or boys, then men, it entailed; but he felt that for the last two or three or even four years (she was nineteen) Dana had somehow cheated him, as if his possession of her was retroactive. He also feared comparison. But most disturbing of all was her casual worldliness: giving herself that first time as easily as, years before, high school girls had given a kiss, and her apparent assumption that he did not expect a lengthy seduction any more than he expected to find that she was a virgin. It was an infectious quality, sweeping him up, making him feel older and smarter, as if he had reached the end of a prolonged childhood. But at the same time he sensed his destruction and, for moments, he looked fearfully into her eyes.

They were blue. When she was angry they became suddenly hard, harder than any Gale had ever seen, and looking at them he always yielded, afraid that if he did not she would scream at him the terrible silent things he saw there. His memories of the last few days before the cruise—the drive in his old Plymouth from California to Louisiana, the lack of privacy in his parents' home—were filled with images of those eyes as they reacted to the heat and dust or a flintless cigarette lighter or his inability to afford a movie or an evening of drinking beer.

He took her home because in Alameda she had lived with her sister and brother-in-law (she had no parents: she told him they were killed in a car accident when she was fifteen, but for some reason he did not believe her) and she did not like her sister; she wanted to live alone in their apartment, but he refused, saying it was a waste of money when she could live with her sister or his parents without paying rent. They talked for days, often quarreling, and finally, reluctantly, she decided to go to Louisiana, saying even that would be better than her sister's. So he took her home, emerging from his car on a July afternoon, hot and tired but boyishly apprehensive, and taking her hand he led her up the steps and onto the front porch where nearly five years before, his father—a carpenter—had squinted down at him standing in the yard and said: *So you joined the Army. Well, maybe they can make something out of you. I shore couldn't do no good.*

3

Strange fish and octopus and squid were displayed uncovered in front of markets, their odors pervading the street. The morning was cold, damp, and gray: so much like a winter day in Louisiana that Gale walked silently with Betty, thinking of rice fields and swamps and ducks in a gray sky, and of the vanished faces and impersonal bunks which, during his service years, had been his surroundings but not his home.

They walked in the street, dodging through a succession of squat children with coats buttoned to their throats and women in kimonos, stooped with the weight of babies on their backs, and young men in business suits who glanced at Gale and Betty, and young girls who looked like bar hostesses and, like Betty, wore sweaters and skirts; men on bicycles, their patient faces incongruous with their fast-pumping legs, rode heedlessly through all of them, and small taxis sounded vain horns and braked and swerved and shifted gears until they had moved through the passive faces and were gone. Bars with American names were on both sides of the street. Betty entered one of the markets and, after pausing to look at the fish outside, Gale followed her and looked curiously at rows of canned goods with Japanese labels, then stepped into the street again. Above the market a window slid open and a woman in a kimono looked down at the street, then slowly laid her bedding on the market roof and, painfully, Gale felt the serenity of the room behind her. Betty came out of the market, carrying a paper bag.

"Now I make you sukiyaki," she said.

"Good. I need some shaving gear first."

"Okay. We go Japanese store."

"Where is it?"

"Not far. You sink somebody see you?"

"Naw. Everybody's on the ship now. They'll be out this afternoon."

"What they do when you go back? Put you in monkey house?"

"Right."

"When you go back?"

"Next week. Before she goes to sea."

"Maybe you better go now."

"They'd lock me up anyhow. One day over the bill or six, it doesn't matter."

"Here's store."

"You buy 'em. They wouldn't understand me."

"What you want?"

"Shaving cream, razor, and razor blades."

He gave her a thousand yen.

"Dat's too much."

"Keep the rest."

"Sank you. You nice man."

She went into the drugstore. He waited, then took her bags when she came out and, walking back to her house, treating her with deference and marveling at her femininity and apparent purity and honesty, he remembered how it was with Dana at first, how he had gone to the ship each morning feeling useful and involved with the world and he had had visions of himself as a salty, leather-faced, graying sergeant-major.

4

—and she was gone for a week before we could even find her and even when we got out there she told us she wasn't coming with us, she was going to stay with him and it took your daddy about a hour to talk her into coming with us and you know how mad he gets, I don't see how he didn't whip her good right there, that's what I felt like doing, and it's a good thing that boy wasn't there or I know your daddy woulda killed him. I don't know how long it was going on before, she used to go out at night in your car, she'd tell us she was going to a show and I guess we should have said no or followed her or something but you just don't know at the time, then Sunday she didn't come home and her suitcase was gone so I guess she packed it while I was taking a nap and stuck it in the car. I hate to be writing this but I don't know what else a mothers supposed to do when her boys wife is running around

like that. We'll keep her here til you tell us what your going to do, she don't have any money and daddy has the car keys. Tell us what your going to do, I hope its divorse because she's no good for you. I hate to say it but I could tell soon as I seen her, theres something about a girl of her kind and you just married too fast. Its no good around here, she stays in your room most of the time and just goes to the kitchen when she feels like it at all hours and gets something to eat by herself and I don't think we said three words since we got her back—

He returned the letter to his pocket, lighted a cigarette, poured another glass of dark, burning rum that a British sailor had left with Betty months before, and looked at his watch. It was seven o'clock; Betty had been gone an hour, promising to wake him when she came home from the bar. During the afternoon they had eaten sukiyaki, Betty kneeling on the opposite side of the low table, cooking and serving as he ate, shaking her head each time he asked her to eat instead of cook, assuring him that in Japan the woman ate last; he ate, sitting cross-legged on the floor until his legs cramped, then he straightened them and leaned back on one arm, the other hand proudly and adeptly manipulating a pair of chopsticks or lifting a tumbler of hot *sake* to his lips. After eating she turned on the television set and they sat on the floor and watched it for the rest of the afternoon. She reacted like a child: laughing, frowning, watching intently. He understood nothing and merely held her hand and smoked until near evening, when they watched an American Western with Japanese dialogue and he smiled.

Now he rose, brought the rum and his glass to the bedroom, undressed, went back to the living room for an ash tray and cigarettes, then lay in bed and pulled the blankets up to his throat. He lay in the dark, his hands on his belly, knowing that he could not take her back and could not divorce her; then he started drinking rum again, with the final knowledge that he did not want to live.

5

He stood in the detachment office, his legs spread, his hands behind his back, and stared at the white bulkhead behind the Marine captain. That afternoon, as his defense counsel told the court why he had gone over the hill, he had felt like crying and now, faced with compassion, he felt it again. But he would not. He had waited two weeks at sea for his court-martial and every night, sober and womanless and without mail, he had lain in bed with clenched jaws and finally slept without crying. Now he shut his eyes, then opened them again to the bulkhead and the voice.

"If you had told me about it, I would've got you off the ship. Emergency leave. I'd have flown you back. Why didn't you tell us?"

"I don't know, sir."

"All right, it's done. Now I want you to know what's going to happen. They gave you three months confinement today. We don't keep people in the ship's brig over thirty days, so you'll be sent to Yokosuka when we get back there and you'll serve the rest of your sentence in the Yokosuka brig. So we'll have to transfer you to the Marine Barracks at Yokosuka. When you get out of the brig, you'll report there for duty. Do you understand all that?"

"No, sir."

"What don't you understand?"

"When will I get back to the States?"

"You'll finish your overseas tour with the Barracks at Yokosuka. You'll be there about a year."

"A year, sir?"

"Yes. I'm sorry. But by the time you get out of the brig, the ship will be back in the States."

"Yes, sir."

"One other thing. You've worked in this brig. You know my policies and you know the duties of the turnkeys and prisoner chasers. While you're down there, I expect you to be a number one prisoner. Don't give your fellow Marines a hard time."

"Yes, sir."

"All right. If you need any help with your problem, let me know."

"Yes, sir."

He waited, blinking at the bulkhead.

"That's all," the captain said.

He clicked his heels together, pivoted around, and strode out. A chaser with a nightstick was waiting for him outside the door. Gale stopped.

"Son of a bitch," he whispered. "They're sending me to Yokosuka."

"Go to your wall locker and get your toilet articles and cigarettes and stationery," the chaser said.

Gale marched to his bunk, the chaser behind him, and squatted, opening the small bulkhead locker near the head of his bunk, which was the lower one, so that his hands were concealed by the two bunks above his and he was able to slide one razor blade from the case and hide it in his palm. He packed his shaving kit with one hand and brought the other to his waist and tucked the razor blade under his belt.

He rose and the chaser marched him to the brig on the third deck, where Fisher, the turnkey, took his shaving kit and stationery and cigarettes from him and put them in a locker.

"It's letter-writing time now," Fisher said. "You can sit on the deck and write a letter."

"Sir, Prisoner Castete would like to smoke."

"Only after meals. You missed the smoke break."

"Sir, Prisoner Castete will write a letter."

Fisher gave him his stationery and pen and he sat on the deck beside two sailors who glanced at him, then continued their writing.

He did not write. He sat for half an hour thinking of her scornful, angry, blue eyes looking at him or staring at the living room wall in Louisiana as she spoke loudly into the telephone:

What do you expect me to do when you're off on that damn boat? I bet you're not just sitting around over there in Japan.

No! I haven't done a damn thing. Goddamn it, Dana, I love you. Do you love me?

I don't know.

Do you love him?

I don't know.

What are you going to do?

What do you mean, what am I going to do?

Well, you have to do something!

It looks like I'm going to sit right here in this house.

That's not what—oh you goddamn bitch, you dirty goddamn bitch, how could you do it to me when I love you and I never even looked at these gooks, you're killing me, Dana, sonofabitch you're killing me—

Son. Son!

Mama?

She was going to hang up on you and you calling all the way from Japan and spending all that money—

Were you standing right there?

Yes, and I couldn't stand it, the way she was talking to you—

Why were you standing there?

Well, why shouldn't I be there when the phone rings in my own house and my boy's—

Never mind. Where's Dana?

In the bedroom, I guess. I don't know.

Let me talk to her.

She won't come.

You didn't ask her.

Gale, you're wasting time and money.

Mama, would you please call her to the damn phone?

All right, wait a minute.

What do you want?

Dana, we got to talk.

How can we talk when your mother's standing right here and you're across the ocean spending a fortune?

If I write you a letter, will you answer it?

Yes.

What?

Yes!

I got to know everything, all about it. Did you think you loved him?

I don't know.

Is he still hanging around?

No.

Dana, I love you. Have you ever run around on me before this?

No.

Why did you do it?

I told you I don't know! Why don't you leave me alone!

I'll write to you.

All right.

Bye. Answer my letter. I love you.

Bye.

The letter-writing period ended and he handed the blank paper and pen to Fisher, who started to say something but did not.

Gale did not start crying until after he was put into a cell and the door was locked behind him and he had unfolded his rubber mattress and was holding one end of it under his chin and with both hands was working it into a mattress cover and he thought of Dana, then of himself, preparing his bed in a cell thousands of miles away, then he started, the tears flowing soundlessly down his cheeks until he was blinded and could not see his hands or even the mattress and it seemed that he would never get the cover on it and he desperately wanted someone to do it for him and lay the mattress on the deck and turn back the blanket and speak his name. He dropped the mattress, threw the cover against the bulkhead, unfolded the blanket, and lay down and covered himself, then gingerly took the razor blade from under his belt, touching it to his left wrist, for a moment just touching, then pressing, then he slashed, knowing in that instant of cutting that he did not want to; that if he had, he would have cut an artery instead of the veins where now the blood was warm and fast, going down his forearm, and when it reached the inside of his elbow he said:

"Fisher."

But there was no answer, so he threw off the blanket and stood up, this time yelling it:

"Fisher!"

Fisher came to the door and looked through the bars and Gale showed him the wrist; he said sonofabitch and was gone, coming back with the keys and opening the door, pulling Gale out into the passageway and grabbing the wrist and tying a handkerchief around it, muttering.

"You crazy bastard. What are you? Crazy?"

Then he ran to the phone and dialed the dispensary, watching Gale, and when he hung up he said:

"Lie on your back. I oughta treat you for shock."

Gale lay on the deck and Fisher turned a waste basket on its side and rolled it under his legs, then threw a blanket over him.

"Son of a bitch!" he said. "They'll hang me. How'd you get that goddamn razor?"

6

The doctor was tall, with short gray hair and a thin gray mustache. He was a commander, so at least there was that much, at least they didn't send a lieutenant. The doctor filled his cup at the percolator, then faced Gale and looked at him, then came closer until Gale could smell the coffee.

"You didn't do a very good job, did you, son?"

"No, sir."

"Do you ever do a good job at anything?"

"No, sir."

The doctor's eyes softened and he raised his cup to his lips, watching Gale over its rim, then he lowered the cup and swallowed and wiped his mouth with the back of his hand.

"You go on and sleep now," he said, "without any more silly ideas. I'll see you tomorrow and we'll talk about it."

"Yes, sir."

Gale stepped into the passageway where the chaser was waiting and they marched down the long portside passageway, empty and darkened save for small red lights, Gale staring ahead, conscious of the bandage on his wrist as though it were an emblem of his uncertainty and his inability to change his life. He knew only that he faced a year of waiting for letters that would rarely come, three months of that in the brig where he would lie awake and wonder who shared her bed and, once released from the brig, he would have to return to Betty or find another girl so he would not have to think of Dana every night (although, resolving to do this, he already knew it would be in vain); and that, when he finally returned to the States, his life would be little more than a series of efforts to avoid being deceived and finally, perhaps years later, she would—with one last pitiless glare—leave him forever. All this stretched before him, as immutable as the long passageway where he marched now, the chaser in step behind him, yet he not only accepted it, but chose it. He figured that it was at least better than nothing.

From *Open House*

ELIZABETH BERG

I dress to bring in the morning paper. The new me. I once read that Martha Stewart never wears a bathrobe. Not that I like Martha Stewart, nobody likes Martha Stewart, I don't think even Martha Stewart likes Martha Stewart. Which actually makes me like her. But anyway, maybe she's onto something. You get up, you make your bed right away, you shower and dress. Ready. Armed. Fire.

I go into the kitchen to make a strong pot of coffee and to start Travis's breakfast. French toast he'll have today, made from scratch, cut diagonally; one piece lying artfully over the other; and I'll heat the syrup, serve it in the tiny flowered pitcher I once took from a room-service tray. I'll cut the butter pats into the shape of something. A whale, maybe, he likes whales. Or a Corvette. If that doesn't work, I'll make butter curls with a potato peeler.

I lay out a blue linen place mat at the head of the dining-room table, smooth it with the flat of my hands, add a matching cloth napkin pulled through a wooden ring. *Wedding gift.* I center a plate, lay out the silverware, then step back to regard my arrangement. I really think Travis will appreciate this.

My head hurts. My head hurts, my heart hurts, my heart hurts. I stand still for a moment, which is dangerous. So I go back into the kitchen, pull a dusty wineglass *wedding gift* down from the high cupboard above the refrigerator, wash it, and bring it to the dining room to center directly over the knife. Then I go back in the kitchen and select three oranges from the fruit bowl. I will squeeze them for juice just before he takes his seat.

Actually, Travis doesn't like fresh orange juice, but he's got to get used to elegance, because that's the way it's going to be from now on. Starting today. Well, starting last night, really, but Travis was asleep when the revolution started. I went to Bloomingdale's and charged a few things last night; that was the start; but when I got home, Travis had gone to bed.

I stand straighter, take in a deep breath. This is the first day. Every day that comes after this will be easier. Later, when I think of Travis sleeping, the thought will not pick up my stomach in its hands and twist it.

All right. Butter. The whale shape does not work, nor does the Corvette, but the butter curls do, more or less. I lay them carefully over ice chips in a small bowl, then bring them out to the dining room and place them to the right of his spoon. Is that where they go? There must be some incredibly expensive Martha Stewart book on table settings I can buy. Perhaps I'll hire a limo to take me to the bookstore, later—I don't really feel like driving. Perhaps I will take the limo to Martha's house. "I understand you're divorced," I'll say. "You seem to be doing all right."

Back in the kitchen, I gulp down another cup of coffee. Then I mix eggs and milk in a blue-and-yellow bowl *that tiny shop in Paris, our week-long vacation there, I stood at the window one morning after I'd gotten up and he came up behind me and put his arms around my middle, his lips to the back of my neck,* add a touch of vanilla, a sprinkle of sugar. I put a frying pan on the stove *put his lips to the back of my neck and we went back to bed,* lay out two slices of bread on a cutting board. These hands at the ends of my wrists remove the crusts. I'm not sure why. Oh, I know why. Because they're hard.

I sit down at the table. Stand up. Sit down. Concentrate on my breathing, that's supposed to help.

Actually, it does not.

I check my watch. Good, only five more minutes. I take off my apron and go upstairs to my bathroom. I brush my teeth again, put in my contacts, comb my hair, apply eyeliner, mascara, and a tasteful shade of red lipstick. I straighten the cowl neck of my new sweater. It's red, too—cashmere. I dab a little Joy—also new—behind my ears and on my wrists. Then I stand still, regard myself as objectively as possible in the mirror.

Well, I look just fine. Okay, circles under the eyes, big deal. The main thing is, what a wonderful change for Travis! Instead of him seeing me in my usual old bathrobe with the permanent egg stain on the left lapel, I am nicely dressed, made up, and ready to go. *Everything* will be different, starting today. Everything will be better.

I go into Travis's room. He is messily asleep; covers wrapped around one leg, pajama top hiked high on his back, pillows at odd angles, his arm hanging over one side of the bed.

"Travis?" I say softly, raising his shade. "It's seven o'clock." I sit down beside him, rub his back. "Travis?"

"I'm up," he says sleepily. Then, turning over quickly, eyes wide, "What *stinks?*" He puts his hand over his nose.

I stand; step back. "Perfume, it's . . . Listen, get dressed and come down for breakfast, okay? I'm making French toast."

No reaction.

"I mean, not the frozen kind. From scratch." *Please, Travis.*

He sits up, rubs his head. Two blond cowlicks stick up like devil horns. He is wearing one of David's T-shirts with his own pajama bottoms. The bottoms are too short for him, I see now. Well. No problem. Today I will replace them. Maybe Ralph Lauren makes pajama bottoms for kids. Silk ones. Monogrammed.

Travis yawns again, hugely, scratches his stomach. I look away, despairing of this too manly movement. It seems so recent that I had to step around imaginative arrangements of Legos—jagged-backed dinosaurs, secret space stations, tools for "surgery"—to wake him up. Now he hides a well-thumbed issue of *Playboy* under his bed. One day when Travis was at school, I inspected Miss August thoroughly. I felt like putting in a note for the next time he looked at her:

> Dear Travis, Please be advised that this is not a real woman. These are bought boobs, and pubic hair looks nothing like this in its natural state. This woman needs to find her life's work and not spend all of her time in front of a mirror. If you went out with her, you would soon be disappointed. Signed, a caring friend.

"I don't want French toast," Travis says. "I want Cheerios."

"You have Cheerios every day."

"Right. *Because,* you see, I *like* them."

Sarcastic. Like David. But he is smiling, saying this. It is David's smile, born again.

"Well, today is a special day," I tell him.

"How come?"

"We'll talk about that later."

"Okay, but I don't want French toast."

"Why don't you just try—"

"Pleeeeeeeease????"

My God. You'd think he was begging for a stay of execution.

"Fine." I make my mouth smile, make myself walk slowly down the stairs, one foot, then the other. I am wearing panty hose under my new jeans, and I feel the fabrics rubbing together as if each is questioning the other's right to be there.

I go into the family room *pipe tobacco* and turn the stereo on to the classical station. Ah, Mozart. Well, maybe not Mozart. But close enough. It's one of those guys. I'll take a music appreciation class. Somewhere. Then, getting ready to sit down to dinner with Travis some night I'll say, "Some Verdi, perhaps?"

"That's an idea," he'll answer. "But maybe Vivaldi would be better with lamb."

"You know, you're absolutely right," I'll say. I will have taught him this exquisite discrimination. As a famous man, Travis will say to the interviewer, "My mother changed wonderfully when my father left us. Our circumstances actually improved. Naturally I owe her everything."

In the dining room, I remove Travis's plate from the table, then go into the kitchen to pour Cheerios into a bowl. Too plain. I'll slice some banana on top in a most beautiful way. I pick up a knife, and some feeling comes over me that has me rush over to the kitchen table. I sit and hold the knife and try very hard to stifle a sob. *Not now. Later.* And then something occurs to me: David may change his mind. That's why he didn't insist on telling Travis himself, right away. He's not sure he even wants to do this. This is male menopause, early male menopause, it could be that, they get that just like they get their own version of PMS, they just don't admit it. He's been so moody, I haven't been good about listening to him, I haven't been willing to talk about a lot of things I do wrong. He could very well have needed to just act out this way, scare himself a little—well, scare both of us—and now he'll come back and we'll just straighten this out. Men! I get up, Lucy Ricardo.

I take a banana from the fruit bowl, slice it evenly, ignore the feeling of a finger tapping my shoulder. *Sam? He's not coming back.*

I look at my watch, pour milk into the pitcher I was going to use for the syrup. Then I pick a pink blossom off the begonia plant on the kitchen windowsill to rest beside his plate. I carry everything out to the dining room, carefully arrange it, then lean against the doorjamb. Outside, the sun shines. Birds call. Cars pass with the windows down, people's elbows hanging out.

I am exhausted.

It will be a few minutes before Travis comes down. I need to do something.

I go into the basement to start a load of wash. When I begin separating, I find a pair of David's boxer shorts, the blue ones, and, God help me, I bury my face in them for the smell of him.

I look up and see my sewing machine. I bring his shorts over to it. Then, using a hidden seam, I sew the fly shut. With great care, I do this, with tenderness. Then I go back to the pile of laundry and get some of his fancy socks and sew the tops of them shut.

I have a lot of David's clothes to choose from; he packed last evening like he was only going on a business trip for a couple of days. And I sat on the bed watching him, thinking *Why is he packing? Where is he going? Why must he do it like this, does he think he's in a movie? What can I say to stop this, isn't there something to say to stop this?* But I couldn't say anything. I felt paralyzed. And when he finally stood at the doorway of the bedroom and said, "I'll call you," I'd waved. Waved! Then, from the bedroom window, I'd watched him drive away, marveling at his cool efficiency in signaling at the corner.

I could not stay in the house alone. I would not stay in the house. Travis was gone—he went to his friend Ben's house every Thursday after school to eat dinner and do homework. He liked going there because that family had three dogs and a cat, whereas, as Travis frequently liked to point out, he had nothing, not even ants. I called my mother, telling her briefly what had happened and asking her to come over and wait for Travis to get home. And then I got in the car and drove to the mall and charged and charged and charged.

When I got home my mother assured me that, as requested, she had not said anything to Travis. Amazingly, she said little to me, either. "We'll talk later, honey," she said, and I answered in what I hoped was a noncommittal way. I was so grateful she had come. I wanted so much for her to go.

I come up from the laundry room and find Travis seated at the dining-room table, delicately picking the banana off his Cheerios. "How come I'm eating out here?" he asks.

"For fun."

"Can I have some orange juice?"

"Oh! Yes, I forgot, I'll go make it right now."

". . . You're making it?"

"Yes. You're having fresh-squeezed orange juice."

"I don't like fresh-squeezed orange juice. I mean, I'm *sorry*, but you *know* I don't like it. It's got all that stuff floating around that bumps into your teeth. Plus I don't like *bananas* on my cereal, *either*."

"Travis. Listen to me. You must try new things every now and then. Sometimes you have learned to like things in your sleep."

"Are we out of Tropicana?"

"Yes, we are."

He gets up and goes to the refrigerator, peers in, triumphantly pulls out a carton of juice. "It's right here, Mom, practically full! We're not out of it! See?"

I take the carton from him, upend it over the sink. "Now we are."

We stand there. Finally, "*Je*sus!" he says. "What's wrong with *you?*"

Let's see. Let's see. What to do.

"Come with me," I say. I lead him to the dining room, point to his chair. "Finish your cereal, okay? It's almost time to go."

I sit down with him, take in a breath. "I'm sorry about the orange juice, Travis. I'm really sorry I did that. That wasn't right."

I clasp my hands together, stare at him. He has a bit of sleep stuck in one corner. "Wipe your left eye," I tell him. "You need to wash your face a little better in the morning. And, listen, I don't want you saying 'Jesus' like that."

"*You* do." He wipes at his right eye.

"Other eye."

"*Dad* does. *He* does it all the time."

I sit still. Outside, I see the wind lift up a branch, rock it. Then let it go.

Finally, I say, "I don't care who does it, Travis. It's not okay for you to do it. Don't say it anymore."

"Fine."

I lean back in my chair, sigh.

"What's *wrong?*" he asks.

"There is something wrong."

"I *said.*"

"Right. But I don't want you to worry. I'm going to talk to you about it, okay? But I think it would be best if we waited until after school."

"Are you . . . going somewhere, Morn?"

I don't answer right away. I don't know. Am I?

Worried now, "How come you're all dressed already? Are you going to the doctor or something?" Someone in Travis's grade had lost his mother recently. The knowledge festered among the kids, spooked them terribly despite the carefully planned programs presented by the guidance counselors.

There, I am suddenly grounded. It is such sweet, wavelike relief. "Oh, sweetie, no, it's nothing like that. It's nothing like that. I'm sorry, I know I'm acting . . . I'm just tired. But we'll talk later. I'll be fine." I smile brightly. "So! Did you like eating breakfast this way?"

"What way?"

"Well . . . You know, out here in the dining room. Fancy dishes . . ."

"Yeah, I guess so. Yeah! It was nice. Thanks, Mom."

Oh, what am I doing? Why am I making him take care of *me?*

Travis picks up his book bag, then shifts his shoulders, seeming to adjust himself inside himself, a gesture I love.

"Can I kiss you good-bye?" I ask.

Our old joke. Every morning I ask him this, and every morning (since he turned nine, anyway) he makes a face as though I were asking him if I could spoon cold oatmeal into his ear. But now he nods yes and my stomach does an unpleasant little somersault. I put my lips to his cheek. And he kisses me back—pecks at my cheek and then quickly turns away.

So. He knows. They are absolutely right, kids always know. When he comes home from school today and I tell him that David has moved out, he will nod sadly and say, "I thought so." And then he will start making *F*s.

I watch him walk down the sidewalk toward school. His jacket collar is half up, half down. His jeans are slightly too long; they bunch up over the top of his sneakers. His book bag carries papers with his earnest script, his own thoughts about the material he is assigned to read. He is just beginning to become himself. He is too young to have to face what he is going to have to face, it will shape him too much, quash his tender optimism. It's unfair, it's so *unfair!* That's what I should have told David: do what you have to do. But don't walk out on Travis. For God's sake. Ruin my world if you have to, but don't ruin his, too.

Back in the kitchen, I take a sip from my coffee. It's gone cold; a ring of congealed cream visible at the outside edge. Look how fast things turn. I dump the coffee out, then throw the cup in the trash. I never want to see that cup again. "David," I say, very softly. Like a prayer. "David," I say again, and lean against the wall to cry. It helps. It's so funny, how it helps. Stress hormones get released when you cry, that's why it works. It's amazing how smart the body is. Though maybe we could do without loving. I think it's overrated, and I think it's too hard. You should only love your children; that is necessary, because otherwise you might kill them. But to love a man? It's overrated, and it's too hard and I will never, ever do it again.

Well. What I will do now is make a list. There's a lot to think about, so much to do. I'll go outside, I'll sit out there where it's so much bigger, where there is no roof to fall in on your head and make you brain damaged, should you survive.

At three-thirty, I am sitting on the sofa in the family room, waiting for Travis. I've had a nap, I'm fine. Well, I've had a couple of naps. The waking-up part, that's hard. *What's . . .* ? Oh. Oh, *yes.*

One thing I want to be sure of is that Travis does not blame himself in any way. I believe I should start with that. Out loud, I practice. "Travis, sweetie, I need to tell you some things that will be hard for you to hear." Yes. Good. "But what I want you to understand, and to remember the whole time I'm talking, is this: all of this is about your *father and me.* This decision. It has nothing to do with you. You are such a good boy." Yes.

No. No. This starting with a negative. It will scare him. Start with something positive. "Travis, as I'm sure you know, both your father and I love you very much." No. That will scare him, too. Oh, what then? *Guess what, Travis? Your father left us and now we get to have a whole new life! Do you want a dog? I was never the one who objected to pets, you know. Do you want a Newfoundland? I think they weigh about five hundred pounds, do you want one of them?*

The door opens and Travis comes in, sees me from the hallway.

"Hi, Mom." *The last normal thing.*

"Oh. Hi! Hi, honey."

He regards me warily. "Are you . . . ?"

"I'm fine!"

He nods, heads toward the kitchen.

"What are you doing?"

"Getting a snack. Do you want some pretzels?"

"No, thanks." I cross my legs, fold my hands on my lap. Uncross my legs.

"Travis?"

"Yeah?"

"Why don't you put your pretzels in a bowl, okay?"

Silence.

"Travis?"

He comes into the room, holding the bag of pretzels. "What do I need a bowl for? The bag is fine, I always eat out of the bag."

"Well, it's . . ." *Inelegant,* is what I want to say. I would like to say that, I have always liked that word. And I have to tell him that we need to make some changes here; things are going to change. But, "The bag is fine," I say. And then, "Could you come here, please?"

He walks over slowly, sits beside me, offers me the bag of pretzels.

"No, thanks."

"They're a little stale."

"Travis," I begin.

"I know. You're getting a divorce." He looks up at me, sighs.

I sit back, smile.

"Aren't you?"

"Well, yes, we just—"

"I figured."

". . . You figured."

"Yeah."

"Why?"

He puts his finger in his ear, experimentally, it seems. Twists it.

"Travis?"

"Huh?"

"*Why* did you 'figure'?"

"I don't know. Everybody gets divorced."

"Oh no. Not everyone. There are many, many happy marriages. I'm sure you'll have one. But your father and I have decided that . . . yes, we want a divorce, and so we're going to be living apart from one another. Starting . . . Well, actually starting last night."

"Where is he?"

"He's close by, he's at a hotel in town, he called me this afternoon. And he'll be calling you tonight, Travis, he told me to tell you he'd be calling you after dinner. And that he will be seeing you very soon."

"What time?"

"Pardon?"

"What time will he call?"

"I don't think he said that. I think he just said after dinner."

"Yeah, but what does that *mean,* what *time* does that mean?"

"Um . . . Okay. It must . . . I think about seven, right around seven. All right?"

"Why is he at a *hotel?"*

Beats me. "He . . . Well, you know, honey, when people decide they aren't going to be together any longer, they often need a little time apart, to think about things."

"But you're getting divorced!"

"Yes."

"So you'll *be* apart!"

"Yes, but—there just sometimes has to be this—"

"Whatever. I don't care."

"Oh, Travis, I'm so sorry."

He shrugs, inspects his thumb, the wall. "It's all right." His right knee starts bouncing up and down and I have to stop myself from stopping it.

When Travis was six, he fell off a jungle gym and hurt his arm. The X-ray technician kept telling him to hold his arm a certain way—it required a kind of twisting. Travis kept saying he couldn't do it, and the impatient tech finally went into the room with him and *made* his arm go the way she wanted it to. "Now, *keep* it like that until I get the picture," I heard her say. When Travis came out of the room, he had tears in his eyes, and when he saw me, he began crying. A little later, when the X-rays were hung, the doctor saw that there was a break right where the tech had been twisting. "That must have *hurt*," the doctor said, "holding your arm that way." Travis nodded gravely. He wasn't crying anymore. He'd been given a lollipop and a sticker that said *I just got an X-ray!*

"Travis, it's not all right. I want you to know that Dad and I both know that. And we also want you to understand that this decision had nothing to do with you." *I just got taken off the hook for my parents' divorce!*

"I know that."

"Do you?"

"Yeah. Why would it have to do with me?"

"Well, that's absolutely right, Travis. We both love you very much, and we will both continue to be your parents. It's just that Dad and I can't live together anymore."

"Why?"

"Well . . ." *Sometimes people, even when they really love each other, they kind of grow apart. And it becomes very hard to . . .* "Because your father is a very, very selfish person who thinks only of himself. Always has, always will. He deserted me, Travis, just like that. I had no idea he was so unhappy. I don't know what I'm going to do. I don't know what to do. I really hate him for this. I *hate* him!" I put my hand to my mouth, start to cry. "Oh, Travis, I'm sorry."

"I'm going upstairs to my room for a while."

"Wait. I—"

"Mom, please?"

"Yes, all right." A weight attaches itself to my chest, sinks in. And in. Maybe it's a heart attack. I hope it is.

Travis walks quickly up the stairs. I hear his door close. I hold one of my hands with the other, stare out the window. Sit there. Sit. When I see the sun beginning to go down, I head up to his bedroom. On the pretense of asking what he'd like for dinner.

Tomorrow morning I will call someone for help.

To think that I asked David to let me be the one to tell Travis, and to let me be alone, telling him. I should have known better. I don't blame David for leaving me, I would like to leave me, too. I would like to step into the body of a woman who does not get lost going around the block, who does not smell of garlic for three days after she eats it, who can make conversation with David's clients at a restaurant rather than going into the ladies' room to sit in the stall and find things in her purse to play with. David has never liked my mother, who is just plain foolish, or my best friend, Rita, who does not censor her thoughts enough to suit him. Gray hair is popping out all over my head, I have become intimately acquainted with cellulite, and just last week, I awakened to hear myself snoring. I want to leave, too. But I can't.

I go upstairs and knock on Travis's door. There is a moment. Then he calls, "Come in," and I can feel the relief clear to the edges of my scalp.

Final Touches

DAN O'BRIEN

Peter and Marvin sat at the table in Peter's kitchen drinking coffee. It was Tuesday morning, the day before Peter was supposed to leave for California. Marvin wore an oily baseball cap pulled low, shading his dark eyes and stubbly cheeks. There was nothing on the table but a flowered china sugar bowl. Diane had not taken it when she left because the lid was broken. Once in a while, as they talked and drank their coffee, one of them would glance into the otherwise bare living room at the shiny black studio grand piano and comment on how heavy it looked.

Peter had a little headache. He had had a headache almost every Tuesday morning since Marvin got arrested for DWI. In addition to the week in the county jail, Marvin had been directed to go to AA meetings on Monday nights. It was part of his sentence. He had to go, but he wasn't allowed to drive. His license had been suspended, and Peter had to pick him up and drive him into town and wait while Marvin went to the AA meeting. There was no place to wait in Vermillion except the Charcoal Lounge. So while Marvin listened to testimonials from old winos about the pitfalls of alcohol, Peter drank draft beers and chased them with peppermint schnapps.

In return Marvin helped Peter when he needed it. Today Peter needed help packing and loading the piano into the pickup.

"I wish I was still in jail," Marvin said.

"Why?"

"So I wouldn't have to help you move that piano." He glanced into the living room.

"It won't be that bad," Peter said.

"Don't bullshit me. I helped you unpack it. I know how bad it's going to be."

"You were drunk that day."

"So were you."

"It'll be easier sober."

"Nothing's easier sober."

"More coffee?"

Marvin nodded and held his cup out. "How's she doing?"

"Who?"

"Come on."

"She sounds all right on the phone. She's got friends out there," Peter said. He wanted to tell Marvin that Diane was living with someone already, but he couldn't. "She's got friends in California."

"Friends?"

"A doctor that we used to know in Sioux Falls."

Marvin nodded. "Say," he said, "you got a little something to hop this up a bit?" He held up the coffee cup and smiled an innocent, missing-tooth smile.

"I thought you were supposed to lay off that stuff."

"Just when I'm driving. One more DWI and it's the state slammer. But I ain't driving." He squinted at Peter. "You could use a shot yourself."

Peter took the bottle of Windsor from the cupboard. He broke the seal and poured a shot or so into each cup. He felt a pang of embarrassment, a touch of remorse. He never thought he'd find himself drinking before noon. The time they'd unpacked the piano had been different. It had been the middle of the afternoon and very hot. Besides, Diane had drunk the beer with them, a kind of celebration for the new piano. He'd been hung over for days, hadn't had another drink for a month. But a lot had changed in the last five years. He looked at the brown liquid in the bottom of his cup. Marvin was watching him but Peter didn't drink.

"I didn't ask when you picked me up because I didn't want to know, but is that piece of junk in the back of your pickup the crate for the piano?"

"Yep."

Marvin drank.

It was December and the South Dakota countryside looked cold. There had been snow several times in the last few weeks. There was still an inch or so on the ground where the wind couldn't get at it. Peter could see the mailbox out the front window, its silverness gone gray in the light. He thought about the letter from Diane. She'd said it was eighty-two degrees. She'd said there was a palm tree in their yard and that oranges and tangerines grew in the backyard. Peter had trouble imagining oranges on trees. Impersonating apples, he thought. Orange trees in Diane's backyard; it was hard to believe, especially when Peter looked out the window and saw the bare oaks and ash trees around the house and the pasture. Diane had loved those trees, or said that she did. Now he was planning a trip to take what was left of hers to California.

It had been part of the divorce; she got the piano. It made sense. What could Peter do with a piano? He could listen to someone else play it, and he could help move it. So that part seemed right. What troubled him was the part that left the delivery of the piano—an assumption, really—up to him. He didn't want to go to California. He didn't want to see Doctor Price again. He wasn't sure he wanted to see Diane again. But he had agreed to deliver the piano when she got settled. Well, the letter said that she was settled so he should bring it out. Just like that, as if it was fifty miles, or across town. Probably she didn't realize how far South Dakota was from California. Maybe she didn't know that the Rocky Mountains were in the way. Marvin had finished off his coffee and set the cup down on the table. "More?" Peter asked.

Marvin nodded and Peter filled the cup halfway, topping it off with Windsor. "Ain't you drinking?" Marvin asked, pointing to Peter's cup. Peter shook his head. "Not yet." They moved into the living room and sat on the floor. They watched the piano, pretending to be thinking about how they were going to attack it. They could hear the wind outside, could feel the dampness and the cold.

In a few minutes Marvin asked if Peter had a crescent wrench. Peter said he did. A while later Peter said that he had borrowed a dolly from Bob Cramer at the furniture store. Marvin said that would help.

Then, finally, as if a silent order had been given, they both rose to their feet. "Suppose we ought to bring the fucking crate in first," Marvin said.

The house faced south, and when they stepped out onto the porch that Peter had built he remembered the nights Diane and he had slept out there wrapped warm in the zip-together sleeping bags and watched the constellations. Orion was always his favorite. Sometime before midnight on early winter nights he used to appear in the sky to the south. He had always been easy for Peter to find. He could remember pointing him out to Diane, stretching his naked arm out into the cold air with Diane sighting along it from where she snuggled her head against his shoulder. Their breath had frozen as they whispered to each other. It had been a long time since he'd looked for Orion, a couple of years at least.

They stood on the porch and finished off their coffee. Then they stepped down and across the yard to the pickup truck. Peter hopped up into the bed and pushed the crate toward Marvin. It was an old crate he'd picked up in Vermillion at the furniture store. It had been in the back for years. "Been that long since I sold a real grand piano," Cramer had said. The wood was broken in several places and nails stuck out at odd angles. Marvin moaned when the weight shifted from the pickup to him. Peter jumped down and slid his end to where he could get a grip on it. The crate wasn't heavy but it was awkward. The wind buffeted it slightly as they made their way to the front door. When they got it inside they set it down gently. "Time for more coffee. More Windsor," Marvin said. He filled his cup and handed Peter's to him.

They sat down again and looked at the crate alongside the piano. "What d'you suppose it weighs?" Marvin said.

"Six hundred," said Peter.

"At least."

Marvin mused on the weight of the piano. "That'd be over twelve sacks of hog feed." A second later, "Three engine blocks. Two 700-80 tractor tires. Christ." He sipped and thought. "Maybe we could move it in pieces."

"The legs come off."

"Big deal."

Again they rose, pulled the piano out away from the wall, and walked around it. "We take a leg off first and set that side down on the floor," Peter said.

"Left foreleg or single rear?"

"Left fore, I figure."

"Then single rear."

"Yeah, and the right foreleg last. Then it's flat on the floor," Peter said. "We slide the crate around right beside it and tip the whole thing up and in."

"Simple," Marvin said, "if we had six guys to help." He walked around the piano one more time. "Better take them pedals off first," he said and pointed, "or Diane won't have nothing for her feet to do."

Peter took the pedals off and loosened the first leg while Marvin refilled their cups. This time he skipped the coffee. "Take ahold of this corner," Peter said; "I'm going to take the leg off."

"Oh sure, you think I'm going to hold the corner of that thing all by myself?"

"Just until I get the leg off and can get up to help you lower it."

"Jesus." Marvin put the cups down and braced himself at the corner of the piano. "Make it snappy," he said.

Peter knocked the leg out of the socket where it had been bolted and for an instant Marvin held the piano corner alone. "Hurry! Jesus! Hurry! Ahhh, whew!" And they lowered it to the floor together.

They sipped at their Windsors and studied the tilted piano. "Diane said to have it moved professionally."

"Now you tell me."

"Two hundred bucks just to drive down from Sioux Falls, crate it up, and load it into the pickup."

"You're going to owe me a hundred when this is over. Two hundred counting when we brought it in."

"The freight people put it on the porch for us, remember?"

"Hundred and fifty."

"Forget it."

The next two legs were easier, and in no time the piano was flat on the floor. It looked as though the legs had crashed through the floor. Now they moved the crate up along the straight side of the piano. "And we just tip it up and in," Peter said.

"Going to need some padding," Marvin said.

Peter looked. Of course; he remembered the foam rubber that had come with it. He sipped on his drink and thought. "Blankets, stuff like that," Marvin said. There wasn't much left in the house. Diane had taken most of it. Not that she'd stolen it; it was hers. Peter really didn't have a use for more than one blanket. There were a few burlap sacks in the barn, they could use them. And in the basement, sure, Diane had missed the sleeping bags.

"There are sacks in the tack room," Peter said. "I'll get an old sleeping bag from the basement."

There were a few spiderwebs on the stairway. Water had leaked in from the last fall storm. When they moved in, there had been no concrete floor. The house had been abandoned in the middle of renovation, two years before they bought it. The basement had been dug but they had never gotten around to pouring the floor. Peter had done it himself. That was before he'd met Marvin, before they'd met anyone, really. They'd just driven out from Ohio, seen this place, liked it, put all their savings down on it, and moved in. He remembered spending most of the night on his hands and knees troweling the cement, with Diane sitting on the basement steps helping where she could, bringing him snacks, and talking about how great it was going to be. Before they put the floor in the basement it had a smell like something Peter had never smelled before—decay, moisture trapped in the earth with no chance of escape. It had been a perfect habitat for salamanders. That had been a big reason they'd been able to afford the place. Nobody wanted to live above a salamander den.

But now it smelled like a basement. His basement. Their basement. The salamanders were gone. There were rough shelves along one wall where the sleeping bags were. They'd bought them together, made them from kits, really, left-hand zipper for him, right-hand for her. The bags had always been kept together in one sack. He'd keep the sack, he thought. But by rights one of the sleeping bags was hers. Finding it protecting the piano would be a nice surprise for her.

He brought both bags upstairs and found that Marvin was into the Windsor again. Peter glanced at the clock on the stove. It was almost two o'clock. They stuffed the crate with feed sacks and Diane's sleeping bag. They lined it up perfectly so that the piano would tip right into it. Then they moved to the other side of the piano, hiked their pants up, took deep breaths, and squared their stances. They bent down and Peter counted backward from five. To their amazement it worked. The piano went right in. Peter went for the crate lid and a hammer while Marvin, still skeptical, kept one hand against the piano and slurped his Windsor with the other. They slipped the legs into the corner of the crate and nailed the lid in place. Then they sat down on the floor, leaning against the crate lid as if there were a tiger inside.

"A-fuckin'-mazing," Marvin said.

"A breeze."

"Now all we got to do is get it into the truck."

They strapped the crate to the dolly and rolled it easily out the front door. The sky showed signs of clearing but was still gray. There were three front steps and it seemed that the only way to get the piano down was for one person to push from the rear while the other lowered the front gradually. "I'll push," Marvin said.

They eased it down the first step and the center of the crate hung up. "Push hard," Peter said.

"You sure?"

"Push."

Marvin pushed and the front of the crate came off the next two steps, banged against the sidewalk, swayed as if it might tip over, and finally lodged halfway to ground level. For a moment it seemed certain that the piano would go over. "I wish I was still in jail," Marvin said.

"We're okay, the dolly just slipped. Come around and help me get it back on."

They lifted together and the dolly went back on. Then, more slowly this time, they moved the rear of the crate onto the sidewalk. They smiled at each other and wheeled it out to the pickup. The tailgate was down and hit the piano crate about midway up.

"Jesus," Marvin said. "Six hundred pounds four feet straight up."

"We need a jack or a ramp or something."

"We need a drink," Marvin said.

The bottle was half gone.

"If we were at my place we could use my winch."

"But I don't have a winch."

"How about a tractor with a loader?"

"I'd have to borrow one from a neighbor. Besides, if we dropped it . . ."

Peter winced at the thought.

"We'll never push it up a ramp. Like BBs up a rat's ass."

Peter agreed. "Probably break a two-by-ten. We'll have to use a jack."

"We'll be crushed," Marvin said, nearly to himself. He splashed more whiskey into his cup and reached over to fill Peter's.

"There are some cement blocks out by the shed. If we leave the dolly on, jack one end up, and back the pickup under it, then we can jack the other end up and block it. When it's level we just back the pickup the rest of the way and she rolls right in."

"We'll be crushed," Marvin said again. "They won't find us till the county man comes to plow the road."

The jack sank into the soft driveway but only a few inches. When the piano started up it went fast. Marvin steadied it, throwing blocks up as they went as a precaution against its slipping off the jack. By the time the edge of the crate looked high enough to get the pickup under it, the jack had nearly worked its way out from under the lip where Peter had hooked it. "Get in and back her up," Peter said, "quick."

The tailgate slipped under the tilted edge of the crate with little to spare. "I'm going to let her down," Peter said. "You ready?"

"Jesus, Jesus." Marvin put both hands on the crate. "Slow, now," he said.

When Peter began to lower the jack it slipped and the crate fell onto the tailgate. It fell only two inches but the pickup sagged and a faint, sick chord sounded from within. Marvin didn't break and run. He stayed right there and steadied it. "Jesus, Jesus." And the piano crate did not fall; it stood solidly, just as they had planned, with one end firmly on the ground and the other on the tailgate of the pickup.

They raised the rear of the crate very carefully, blocking it with every crank of the jack. Finally it was suspended three and a half feet off the ground, the front on the tailgate of the pickup and the rear on a stack of cement blocks. It loomed against the afternoon sky, the top eight feet off the ground. Now it was a matter of one of them holding the piano in place while the other slowly backed the pickup. The plan was for it to roll right in, but it seemed too high off the ground to Peter, too wobbly, too much chance for an accident. Now he was afraid. What if it tipped and fell? It would be smashed, totally ruined. He imagined the sound it would make as it hit the ground. What would Diane say? Would she think that he'd done it on purpose? Subconsciously?

But now it was too late.

"Who's holding and who's driving?"

Peter shrugged

"It's Diane's piano," Marvin said. "If it's going to crush somebody seems like it ought to be you."

Peter nodded. "Okay," he said.

When Marvin started the pickup the piano trembled. The crate was just thin enough for him to put an outstretched arm and hand on each side and press his chest and cheek against the rear. He braced himself and closed his eyes as Marvin started back. He could feel some pressure and could hear the dolly wheels begin to roll along the bed of the pickup. When the tailgate knocked the pile of cement blocks down Peter grasped at the crate desperately, but the piano was already loaded. He felt Marvin turn the engine off and saw him get out, slam the door, and head for the house.

He was back in seconds with the bottle. "Un-fuckin'-believable," he said.

They drank the whiskey while Peter tied the piano into the pickup. Peter wasn't sure how it had happened but he was giddy now and getting drunk. He lashed the piano in tight. He tied half-hitches between sips of whiskey. Marvin didn't help. He walked around the pickup, holding the bottle by the neck and shaking his head. He held the bottle up and they toasted each other. "When you pull up out there in California with this rig, that doctor is going to have about twenty-five of his friends lined up to help unload it," he said. "They're going to look up at that fucking whale and say, 'Why, Peter, however did you get it up there?'" He laughed and drank from the bottle. "Tell 'em your old pal Marvin helped."

They sat on the porch as the sun went down. They watched the piano and finished the bottle of Windsor. It was getting very cold. Peter sat leaning against the railing along the steps. "It'll be a long trip," he said. "Might take me a week." He could see the evening star now. "Look there," he said, pointing. "Going to be clear and cold tonight." He turned but Marvin was gone.

When he went into the house he found Marvin asleep on the floor where the piano had been. The sleeping bag was still where he'd left it. He took it from the sack and went back outside. He climbed up into the pickup bed and laid his sleeping bag out on top of the piano crate. The bag was cold against his skin and the crate not very wide. He lay quietly on his back with his head turned toward the south. He thought that his mind would be full, but nothing came. He would wait, he thought, until Orion swung up from the southern sky and the stars began to sparkle and do their dance in the cold December night.

My Stuff

ROGER HART

Time was I could fix anything with my fist or foot. *Bamm,* the furnace started. *Bamm,* the refrigerator quit humming. Cindy didn't like it, but there wasn't much she could say when it worked. Take the time the lawn mower died in the tall, gummy grass where the neighbor's dog unloaded in our yard. A Saturday morning. Hot and humid with bugs flying in my ears and biting my back where the sweaty T-shirt stuck, and this rank odor coming up from all that dog crap. The mower coughed, choked, then stopped. Blue smoke and steam came from underneath. I pulled the starter rope. Nothing. I yanked again and again until I thought my damn arm would fall off, then grabbed the mower by the handle and spun around like a hammer thrower in the Olympics. I grunted, let go. A flying lawn-mower. It hit the trunk of the silver maple. Moldy grass, rusty lawn mower parts and maple bark littered the ground. I swore at the son of a bitch, then let it lie there, bleed lubricants, while I went in the house, had a beer, maybe two.

Cindy said, "Look what you've done to the tree, look at that tree," then said that it was too early to drink, and I said I was on daylight savings time, which was pretty clever considering the heat, bug bites, and the mower not working. I waited awhile, watched cartoons with Jake, then went outside and tried again, pulled the rope. Flames six inches long shot out the exhaust. The engine roared like the Saturn V taking off for the moon. I could have mowed down the lilacs, roses and rhododendrons if I'd wanted.

Cindy didn't like my swearing either, but I said, "Hey, a man's got to talk."

Ohio summers can be bad but winters are worse. Snow, cloudy days, fog, the lack of light, the cold wet wind blowing off Lake Erie. Muscles tense from slipping on ice, people get moody, think bad thoughts.

I drive for the county, a snowplow in the winter, an asphalt truck in the summer. Winter of '76, our worst winter ever, I knocked off thirty-two mailboxes. A record. That winter Cindy hit me but it wasn't because of what I did to the mailboxes, although she didn't like that either. I was tired from plowing all night and when I opened the refrigerator door things fell out. It was like food and bottles and bowls attacking me. I put my foot inside and began to stir things around, kick this and kick that, fight back. More things fell out: A-1 Sauce, milk, orange juice, leftover lasagna. Cindy came out of nowhere, knocked me away, almost knocked me off my feet. She was crying and yelling at me to stop and the chocolate syrup was running out onto the floor, and my foot wouldn't, couldn't, stop kicking.

Later, we cleaned up the mess and fixed the broken refrigerator shelf and wiped the tomato juice off the stove where it splattered, but the red stains on the wall and the way the shelf tilted always reminded us.

Cindy taught fifth grade, made greeting cards, sold them at craft shows. After our problems, after I had moved into this apartment, she sent me a card that had a buckeye leaf—Ohio, the Buckeye State—on the front of it. Inside, the card said, "Be-leaf in yourself."

Three hundred bucks a month and the bedroom has a tiny jail-size window, but it doesn't matter because I don't have a bed. I sleep on the couch in the living room, listen to television and people sounds from the apartment below. The phone in the kitchen doesn't work because of problems with wires in the wall, and, when I moved in, the silverware drawer was littered with marijuana seeds. O.K., his real name is Oscar Kurt but he goes by O.K., said the seeds were from the previous tenant, a man he had not liked. O.K. is the manager of the apartments. O.K. and his wife. He said he was sorry for not cleaning out the seeds when he painted the apartment and that I should toss them out. "No," he said, "better burn them or flush them down the toilet so they don't sprout somewhere and cause a problem." O.K. gets a tumor in his head but that hasn't happened yet in this story.

Alone in the apartment. A boring life except for planting those marijuana seeds and sometimes watching the woman in 214 undress behind her thin curtains. With binoculars, I can see tan lines almost.

Jake! What a boy. When he was four we went ice skating. He was a natural. Glide, cut, glide. A speed skater, another Eric Heiden. He'd skate towards me and I'd spread my legs, and he'd skate through. Swoosh! We were like the United States hockey team beating the Russians. Following year, we went skating and he was even better, but he had grown and when he tried to skate between my legs, his head smashed me in the balls and I nearly died out there on the ice, another broken winter thing.

Jake doesn't talk to me much since this last bad winter when Cindy and I had our differences. I try calling him, but my phone sometimes doesn't work, and if Cindy answers, she goes on and on about "my problems." I dial anyway, punch the wall, wait, swear, then walk to the gas station on the corner and stand in the phone booth, stand on broken glass and sticky spilled pop, breathe in the stink of cigarette butts and hear the cars, trucks and vans going down the street. A crummy place to talk to your kid. I press the phone tight to my ear and yell things at the passing cars and trucks, give them the finger while I listen to the phone ring.

"Yes," she says, Jake's mom, like she knew it was me that was going to call. "Yes? Yes?" like she'd already said it a dozen times and this was the last.

"Jake, please," I say.

"Your stuff," Cindy says.

"My stuff?" I ask.

"Your stuff," she says, and then, "You going to Jake's soccer game?"

I say, "Yes, of course, and what about my stuff, and can I speak to Jake?" I shift my weight. Glass crunches.

"You said that last game," she says, and then she says a *friend* will be at the game with her and that Jake can not come to the phone.

"Where's Jake?" I ask.

"It's *Les, Les* from the fire department. You know him, Les Huddle."

"Les?" I ask. I want to talk with Jake but this Les talk has me confused.

She says, "Yes, Les," and that I shouldn't forget my stuff, that it will be in the trunk of her car, and before I can ask for Jake one more time, she hangs up.

"Les?" I say. "Les?" I say it to the cars going down the street. I feel as if I've been smacked and scraped by a snowplow. Cindy seeing a Les. I get a pain in the middle of my forehead, like I was stung there by a wasp. I'm a Les, too.

I head back to the apartment and am followed by a dumped-off dog. Brown, curly hair down its back. Big paws, sharp, white pup teeth. "Go home," I say. "Go home." She sniffs my shoe. "Go," I repeat. "Go on. GIT!" I slam my foot on the ground. She stares, brown eyes rimmed with red, a hungover dog.

I give her a bath in my tub and then a bowl of stale cereal that she scarfs down. The apartment's hot, real hot because it's on the second floor, which is cheaper, and because it's August, but the dog shivers like she's about to freeze, so I take her outside in the sun. She does her chores on the grass, then sits on the toe of my boot. Back inside, I throw a ripped jacket on the floor, and she starts a nap.

O.K. comes, knocks on the door, says he saw me with a dog, and he saw it making a pile out there on the lawn where the little kids play, and we can't have that, can we?

I say I'll clean it up and point at her sleeping on the jacket, the spot in the sun, tell him how the dog is gone as soon as she finishes her nap. I jerk my thumb at the door. "Out of here," I say.

O.K. says, sure, sure, waves his hand in the air like he's shooing mosquitoes, slurs his words, says he has a headache, then shakes his head like a hound with a bug in its ear. Sure.

August. The marijuana plants are ten inches high, and Cindy's seeing another Les.

Jake thinks I don't like soccer because I ask the wrong questions, say the wrong things like, "kick a goal," when that isn't his thing to do, and I have missed the first three games. Cindy says he's angry because I left him. She jabs that word, *left,* like a knife in my gut. *Left,* RIP! *Left,* SLASH! Cindy says that Jake's full of anger and will have to work it out. "He's a good kid," she says. "You left him, but he's a good kid."

I get a kick out of soccer: balls bouncing off heads, referees waving yellow cards in front of faces—those who've sworn or tried to hurt somebody. "There, take that," the referee says, holds the yellow card above the player's head so everyone can see who the guilty one is. Jake hasn't gotten any yellow cards, although he's been warned.

I got the big red card from Cindy. Out of the game! A red card. The worst. Not a divorce really, a dissolution, although Cindy called it a "dis-illusion."

Doris sleeps beside the couch in a cardboard TV box I got out of the Dumpster. I got the couch for nothing, found it in the middle of the Shoreway while plowing. Dropped by someone moving, someone trying to escape Ohio winters. One cushion has tire marks, but the couch is comfortable so I don't bother buying a bed.

Doris—I named her after Cindy's mother—rides in the truck with me to the game. It's raining hard and the turning this way and that makes Doris sick. Real sick. Soggy cereal all over the floor. She gets a guilty look after she tosses but I don't say anything. I've been there. I think fresh air, roll the window down and push her head out, hold it there until we get to the school. When we stop, I throw the floor mat out in the parking lot; Doris licks from a puddle to wash that bad taste out of her mouth, then climbs back in the truck to get some sleep.

I squish through the grass toward the sidelines. Soggy socks, wet feet, Jake on the field, pretending not to look for me. Cindy and her new Les with a clot of friends in the bleachers, chummy beneath their umbrellas. Cindy motions me over and says, "Les, this is Les."

We say, "Hi, Les," at the same time. It sounds funny in the wet. Cordial. I can feel the others taking time out to watch so they can see how the mechanics of these things work. I say I think we'll win this one, start to tell them about Doris, but they turn away, don't answer. I'm not part of the clot, but I sit close enough to be part of the cheering when good things happen and to hear kind things said about Jake.

Cindy hangs onto Les Two, holds his hand, rubs his back, his neck, punches his arm, puts her head on his shoulder. If Doris could see it, she'd get sick again. I sit and wonder if Cindy ever says, "Les," thinking me, but it being Les him. He wouldn't know, but she would. Maybe that's why she hangs onto him so, trying to make up for thinking the wrong Les.

I start to climb higher for a better view and slip on the damn bleacher steps. Aluminum. Whoops! Just like that. I go down three, four, maybe more steps. Boom, boom, boom. Hurt my damn hip and I want to say the f-word twenty times which I'm trying to give up on account of the way Jake has picked it up and is using at the wrong times.

People in the clot say, "Ooh, are you okay?" and "Be careful there." Then they give each other the secret look because they think it's the beer. No one invites me to sit with them, hide under their umbrella. My pants, wet and cold, cling to my leg.

I no sooner stop my moaning than the other team bounces the ball off a head and into the net.

Back and forth, up and down the field, knees pumping, elbows flying. Jake gets knocked down, his feet tripped from under him. "Hey, hey," I yell. Jake jumps up, kicks the ball, runs, slides, kicks again. "Way to go, Wright!" I yell. I say "Wright" so he hears it, his last name, remembers how good it sounds. "Way to go, Jake," Cindy yells, a shriek that almost stops the game.

My hip throbs, and I worry that I've broken something but I watch the game anyway. Jake's team is running down the field like looters in L.A. when the referee blows the whistle, throws his arms up and gives the ball to Fairport. Once, twice, three times it happens. No one says what for, and I can't stand the not knowing so I turn to the umbrellas and ask, "What's going on?"

My hip bone hurts like hell, and I'm nearly drowning in the rain, but I need to know.

"Jake's offsides," someone throws out. I don't know offsides. I'd know if it were football, but soccer players run everywhere, no huddle, no *hut, hut*. I nod at the umbrellas and pretend I understand.

People say Jake and I walk alike. We roll along, our legs swinging back and forth like wet noodles, our asses not doing anything fancy except bringing up the rear. I figure Jake and I'll stop at McDonald's after the game, grab some hamburgers and fries, maybe a couple vanilla shakes, too. We'll wet noodle walk in together, and people will nod and smile. We'll scatter packs of sugar on the table, move them this way and that, and he'll explain offsides. Jake and me, his dad.

Fairport scores four more, Jake's team none. Game over, rain coming down. Jake and the others drift across the field, wet and muddy but no one in a hurry.

"Nice game," I say.

Jake gives me the dirty look, the one he's learned from his mother.

"Let's get something to eat," I say.

"Too tired," he says.

We walk toward the parking lot, me on one side, Cindy and the new Les on the other. She puts her hand on Jake's back, which isn't a good thing to do as that is one of the first things that'll get you called candy-ass, and Jake has enough of a burden with those offsides.

"A milkshake?" I ask.

"I'm tired," Jake answers, staring at the ground, at his feet going slop, slop, in the puddles.

"Next time," I say.

"What?" says Jake.

Cindy throws her hands in the air. "Your stuff," she says. "I have a box of your stuff in the trunk."

But this is no time for stuff talking. I slap Jake on the back. "Next time we'll get something to eat."

"Oh," Jake says, and he climbs into the other Les's car. The trunk lid is up, waiting, and Cindy is standing there with her hands on her hips, but I need to get Doris home, so I wave good-bye and head out.

When I get to the apartments, an ambulance is backed up to O.K.'s, the red flasher lights bouncing off wet windshields, the brick walls and everyone's windows. Curtains are pulled back, and flat-nosed faces stare out. A dozen or so people stand in the parking lot and watch, hold themselves tight.

The radio hums, and the medical people talk back and forth, but I don't know what's happening. It's like the offsides. They slide a stretcher inside the ambulance, and O.K.'s wife tries to climb in too. "O.K.," some guy says and two women give him a dirty look. Doris and I stand with the group on the corner. Feels good to be part of a knot, but feels bad for O.K., who is not. My hip hurts like hell, but it isn't the time to tell anyone, hope for a little sympathy. No one knows what's wrong but we stand and talk, me and a guy from another building and a young woman from the apartment below mine who runs every morning. Tom. Rita. Rita lets Doris lick her face.

Next day, Rita knocks on my door. "What's your story," Rita asks. Rita looks nineteen, wears snug jeans and scratches Doris's belly with red fingernails.

I tell her I nearly broke my damn hip and the phone doesn't work when the apartment is hot, and she says that O.K. has a brain tumor, a big sucker. She hands me a card to sign and asks if I want to chip in for some flowers. She bends over and pets Doris again; the blouse gapes open. Skimpy, black bra. I give twenty bucks, wish I could give more.

The brain tumor scares me. Cindy used to yell that I must have a brain tumor the way I acted. A week passes, two. Can't get it out of my mind, his tumor, maybe mine. Gives me a headache. I think maybe I've got something ugly growing inside, that living here in the apartment has caused it. Cindy used to say that the drinking would kill my liver, but here's a tumor popping up in O.K.'s head for no reason.

So. I'm sipping beer and thinking and I dial Cindy to say I've waited long enough and I want my stuff. The phone won't work, and I start yelling and swearing and beating on the wall. Doris runs to the corner by the stove and shakes. I say, come here, but she can't for all the shaking. I punch the wall and I think she's going to drop dead of a heart attack.

I try dialing again and Les answers and I forget what I'm going to say. "Hello? Hello?" he goes and then the forgotten thought comes to me and I say, "May I speak to Cindy?"

Les Two tells Cindy it's me for her, then whispers that I've been drinking, like he doesn't think I can hear and like he could tell over the phone, which shows what a jerk he is.

Cindy says, "Yes," and I say the manager of the apartments is back, and she asks where he's been, and I tell her about the brain tumor and that it had nothing to do with drinking. She asks if I am alone and can she talk freely. I say, yes, except for Doris.

Cindy waits for me to say who Doris is. I wish I'd named Doris *Cindy,* just so Cindy could know what it's like for me. Her seeing another Les. But I don't tell her who Doris is and she—Cindy, not Doris—says it's too bad about the brain tumor, and she's tired of carrying my stuff around in the back of her car, and if I don't get it soon she is going to pitch it out.

I say, "I have to see Jake, we need time together." Doris trembles in the corner. "Come here," I say, but Doris sticks to the corner like she's nailed there. Cindy says no way she is coming to my place.

I tell her I want to speak to Jake, and she says not to push him, that he's tired and angry and I need to give him space. "Come here," I repeat. I move toward Doris and she squats, pees a puddle on the floor.

"No!" Cindy answers.

I say she doesn't sound too upset about O.K.'s tumor and tell her Doris is trembling, shaking like a buckeye leaf in the corner, and Cindy asks if I'm drinking but doesn't give me time to answer. The line goes dead. Maybe Cindy, maybe the heat.

I could punch the wall again. I could yank the phone out. I want to and I would except Doris has this shaking problem and is going to flood the apartment downstairs if she doesn't get control of herself. I stand there wondering what's wrong with Doris. I get a handful of Sugar Pops off the table, drop some on the floor. She doesn't move.

I toss a Sugar Pop in her direction which lands in the puddle and Doris ignores it, just stands hunched over in that wet spot. I toss another Sugar Pop across the floor, another. One bounces off her head and she doesn't even notice. I cross the kitchen, almost pull the damn phone cord out of the wall because it's wrapped around my arm and I forgot to hang up. Doris trembles. First O.K., now Doris. I hold her tight, stick her nose in my armpit and after a few minutes the shaking stops.

Because the phone's not working I don't get many calls: "Hey, Les, come on over. The game's on, and there's plenty of beer," or, "Dad, want to go see the Browns?" So I walk Doris mornings and nights along the railroad tracks that run behind the apartment. I figure if she tires herself out she won't chew on the electric cords or steal garbage from the wastebasket and will get over the nervous condition I suspect she has.

I walk the rails and think how the tracks go nowhere, not to Dallas, not to Santa Fe. No place like that. No place different from this.

Doris has instincts. She'll sneak up on bottles and beer cans, freeze, lift a paw. Her point isn't the best, being young and mostly retriever, but somewhere in her blood she knows: one paw up, tail out, body stiff, nose sniffing the air. She holds her head high, looks up in the night sky like she's seeing birds except her eyes are on the moon and stars. An astronomer dog almost. While we walk, I talk, tell her things. "Doris, the moon," I say and I tilt her head in my hands until I think she sees it.

Sometimes I let Doris pull the leash while I lean back and study the sky, find the constellations. Long time back, Cindy was surprised

I knew them, Ursa Major, Cygnus, Cassiopeia, the Horse Head Nebula, there in Orion, in the belt. Amazing stuff. "How do you know them?" she'd ask, like I might not be smart enough. I taught her ten constellations and the names of certain stars. On summer nights, we'd lie in the drive, look at them through a telescope I had, a telescope still wrapped in garbage bags in the basement of the house where I used to live.

After the next under-the-lights night soccer game, I tell Jake, "I have someone I want you to meet." As we walk to the parking lot you can see the wheels turning in his head, him thinking it's some woman, which tells you something about the stories his mother has put in his head. Cindy looks angry, Les Two smug. I open the tailgate, and Doris jumps out.

"That's Doris?" Cindy asks.

"Doris," I say, "meet Jake."

For a second, Jake grins, although they lost the game. "You need a leash," he says.

"You can't keep her in the apartment, can you?" Cindy says. "I mean, I don't see how you can keep her in the apartment."

Instead of saying she's a cute dog or something like how Jake will have fun with her when he comes to visit, she starts off talking about the problems. She glances at the other Les like he might help her with this, like he might chime in and say, "Can't keep a dog in the apartment."

But he stands there not knowing what to say.

Her seeing another Les is not a good thing—not that Lesses are bad apples or anything like that. But, if he, Les Two, did something stupid and Cindy said to the teachers at school or to the women she walks with, "Les lost his job," or "Les lost three hundred dollars playing poker," or "Les was drunk again last night," I don't want people confusing which Les it was. And Jake. What if he hears someone say, "That Les, what an asshole"?

By the time O.K. comes home from the hospital the leaves are off the trees, it's snowed twice, Jimmy C. has lost the White House job to

Ronnie "Wagon Train" Reagan, Jake's team has lost ten games, Doris can find Venus almost, and Cindy has heard talk, wants to know if I am living with that young girl.

Rita offered to take care of Doris when I was plowing snow, and I said that would be fine, but she is not the other woman Cindy thinks she is although it would be okay with me if she was. I barely know Rita other than catching the glimpse of her lace bra and some of what was in it.

It's good to talk to a dog, tell them stories. They pick up more than you think. I tell Doris things. I tell her about Jake skating between my legs, and how soccer season is over. No more games, I say.

We walk along the tracks and there are things I want to tell her that I don't know the words for. "Look, look," I say, pointing to the sky. "Millions of stars. Millions." I sit on the rails, pull Doris to my side. Doris puts her cheek, smooth and soft, against mine, her breath warm, our eyes on the night sky. Orion, Lyra, the Big Dipper. I show her Polaris, the North star, and explain that it's the one to use if she's ever lost.

The cold from the rail I'm sitting on creeps through my pants, my butt goes tingly then numb, and I tell Doris it's time for us to move on. Six in the morning, stumbling down the tracks, me and Doris, chunky gravel loose underfoot, cold December kicking off Lake Erie. The moon huge at the end of the rails.

Doris. What a dog. I could say, *fetch moon,* and she'd try. She'd bounce on those hind legs and snap at the cold night air until she passed out. I could tell Doris to fetch the moon but I don't. Doris is young and doesn't understand distance.

The End of the Relationship

WILL SELF

"Why the hell don't you leave him if he's such a monster?" said Grace. We were sitting in the Café Delancey in Camden Town, eating *croques m'sieurs* and slurping down cappuccino. I was dabbing the sore skin under my eyes with a scratchy piece of toilet paper—trying to stop the persistent leaking. When I'd finished dabbing I deposited the wad of salty stuff in my bag, took another slurp and looked across at Grace.

"I don't know," I said. "I don't know why I don't leave him."

"You can't go back there—not after this morning. I don't know why you didn't leave him immediately after it happened . . ."

That morning I'd woken to find him already up. He was standing at the window, naked. One hand held the struts of the venetian blind apart, while he squinted down on to the Pentonville Road. Lying in bed I could feel the judder and hear the squeal of the traffic as it built up to the rush hour.

In the half-light of dawn his body seemed monolithic: his limbs columnar and white, his head and shoulders solid capitals. I stirred in the bed and he sensed that I was awake. He came back to the side of the bed and stood looking down at me. "You're like a little animal in there. A little rabbit, snuggled down in its burrow."

I squirmed down further into the duvet and looked up at him, puckering my lip so that I had goofy, rabbity teeth. He got back into bed and curled himself around me. He tucked his legs under mine. He lay on his side—I on my back. The front of his thighs pressed against my haunch and buttock. I felt his penis stiffen against me as his fingers made slight, brushing passes over my breasts, up to my throat and face and then slowly down. His mouth nuzzled against my neck, his tongue licked my flesh, his fingers poised over my nipples, twirling them into erection. My body teetered, a heavy rock on the edge of a precipice.

The rasp of his cheek against mine; the too peremptory prodding of his cock against my mons; the sense of something casual and off-hand about the way he was caressing me. Whatever—it was all wrong. There was no true feeling in the way he was touching me; he was manipulating me like some giant dolly. I tensed up—which he sensed; he persisted for a short while, for two more rotations of palm on breast, and then he rolled over on his back with a heavy sigh.

"I'm sorry—"

"It's OK."

"It's just that sometimes I feel that—"

"It's OK, really, please don't."

"Don't what?"

"Don't talk about it."

"But if we don't talk about it we're never going to deal with it. We're never going to sort it all out."

"Look, I've got feelings too. Right now I feel like shit. If you don't want to, don't start. That's what I can't stand, starting and then stopping—it makes me sick to the stomach."

"Well, if that's what you want." I reached down to touch his penis; the chill from his voice hadn't reached it yet. I gripped it as tightly as I could and began to pull up and down, feeling the skin un- and re-peel over the shaft. Suddenly he recoiled.

"Not like that, ferchrissakes!" He slapped my hand away. "Anyway I don't want that. I don't want . . . I don't want . . . I don't want some bloody hand relief!"

I could feel the tears pricking at my eyes. "I thought you said—"

"What does it matter what I said? What does it matter what I do . . . I can't convince you, now can I?"

"I want to, I really do. It's just that I don't feel I can trust you any more . . . not at the moment. You have to give me more time."

"Trust! Trust! I'm not a fucking building society, you know. You're not setting an account up with me. Oh fuck it! Fuck the whole fucking thing!"

He rolled away from me and pivoted himself upright. Pulling a pair of trousers from the chair where he'd chucked them the night before, he dragged his legs into them. I dug deeper into the bed and looked out at him through eyes fringed by hair and tears.

"Coffee?" His voice was icily polite.

"Yes please." He left the room. I could hear him moving around downstairs. Pained love made me picture his actions: unscrewing the percolator, sluicing it out with cold water, tamping the coffee grains down in the metal basket, screwing it back together again and setting it on the lighted stove.

When he reappeared ten minutes later, with two cups of coffee, I was still dug into the bed. He sat down sideways and waited while I struggled upward and crammed a pillow behind my head. I pulled a limp corner of the duvet cover over my breasts. I took the cup from him and sipped. He'd gone to the trouble of heating milk for my coffee. He always took his black.

"I'm going out now. I've got to get down to Kensington and see Steve about those castings." He'd mooched a cigarette from somewhere and the smoking of it, and the cocking of his elbow, went with his tone: officer speaking to other ranks. I hated him for it.

But hated myself more for asking, "When will you be back?"

"Later . . . not for quite a while." The studied ambiguity was another put-down. "What're you doing today?"

"N-nothing . . . meeting Grace, I s'pose."

"Well, that's good, the two of you can have a really trusting talk—that's obviously what you need." His chocolate drop of sarcasm was thinly candy-coated with sincerity.

"Maybe it is . . . look . . ."

"Don't say anything, don't get started again. We've talked and talked about this. There's nothing I can do, is there? There's no way I can convince you—and I think I'm about ready to give up trying."

"You shouldn't have done it."

"Don't you think I know that? Don't you think I fucking know that?! Look, do you think I enjoyed it? Do you think that? 'Cause if you do, you are fucking mad. More mad than I thought you were."

"You can't love me . . ." A wail was starting up in me; the saucer chattered against the base of my cup. "You can't, whatever you say."

"I don't know about that. All I do know is that this is torturing me. I hate myself—that's true enough. Look at this. Look at how much I hate myself!"

He set his coffee cup down on the varnished floorboards and began to give himself enormous open-handed clouts around the head. "You think I love myself? Look at this!" (clout) "All you think about is your-own-fucking-self, your own fucking feelings." (clout) "Don't come back here tonight!" (clout) "Just don't come back, because I don't think I can take much more."

As he was saying the last of this he was pirouetting around the room, scooping up small change and keys from the table, pulling on his shirt and shoes. It wasn't until he got to the door that I became convinced that he actually was going to walk out on me. Sometimes these scenes could run to several entrances and exits. I leapt from the bed, snatched up a towel, and caught him at the head of the stairs.

"Don't walk out on me! Don't walk out, don't do that, not that." I was hiccupping, mucus and tears were mixing on my lips and chin. He twisted away from me and clattered down a few stairs, then he paused and turning said, "You talk to me about trust, but I think the reality of it is that you don't really care about me at all, or else none of this would have happened in the first place." He was doing his best to sound furious, but I could tell that the real anger was dying down. I sniffed up my tears and snot and descended toward him.

"Don't run off, I do care, come back to bed—it's still early." I touched his forearm with my hand. He looked so anguished, his face all twisted and reddened with anger and pain.

"Oh, fuck it. Fuck it. Just fuck it." He swore flatly. The flap of towel that I was holding against my breast fell away, and I pushed the nipple, which dumbly re-erected itself, against his hand. He didn't seem to notice, and instead stared fixedly over my shoulder, up the stairs and into the bedroom. I pushed against him a little more firmly. Then he took my nipple between the knuckles of his index and forefinger and pinched it, quite hard, muttering, "Fuck it, just fucking fuck it."

He turned on his heels and left. I doubled over on the stairs. The sobs that racked me had a sickening component. I staggered to the bathroom and as I clutched the toilet bowl the mixture of coffee and mucus streamed from my mouth and nose. Then I heard the front door slam.

"I don't know why."

"Then leave. You can stay at your own place—"

"You know I hate it there. I can't stand the people I have to share with—"

"Be that as it may, the point is that you don't need him, you just think you do. It's like you're caught in some trap. You think you love him, but it's just your insecurity talking. Remember," and here Grace's voice took on an extra depth, a special sonority of caring, "your insecurity is like a clever actor, it can mimic any emotion it chooses to and still be utterly convincing. But whether it pretends to be love or hate, the truth is that at bottom it's just the fear of being alone."

"Well why should I be alone? You're not alone, are you?"

"No, that's true, but it's not easy for me either. Any relationship is an enormous sacrifice . . . I don't know . . . Anyway, you know that I was alone for two years before I met John, perhaps you should give it a try?"

"I spend most of my time alone anyway. I'm perfectly capable of being by myself. But I also need to see him . . ."

As my voice died away I became conscious of the voice of another woman two tables away. I couldn't hear what she was saying to her set-faced male companion, but the tone was the same as my own, the exact same plangent composite of need and recrimination. I stared at them. Their faces said it all: his awful detachment, her hideous yearning. And as I looked around the café at couple after couple, each confronting one another over the marble table tops, I had the beginnings of an intimation.

Perhaps all this awful mismatching, this emotional grating, these Mexican stand-offs of trust and commitment, were somehow in the air. It wasn't down to individuals: me and him, Grace and John, those two over there . . . It was a contagion that was getting to all of us; a germ of insecurity that had lodged in all our breasts and was now fissioning frantically, creating a domino effect as relationship after relationship collapsed in a rubble of mistrust and acrimony.

After he had left that morning I went back to his bed and lay there, gagged and bound by the smell of him in the duvet. I didn't get up until eleven. I listened to Radio Four, imagining that the deep-timbred, wholesome voices of each successive presenter were those of ideal parents. There was a discussion program, a gardening panel discussion, a discussion about books, a short story about an elderly woman and her relationship with her son, followed by a discussion about it. It all sounded so cultured, so eminently reasonable. I tried to construct a new view of myself on the basis of being the kind of young woman who would consume such hearty radiophonic fare, but it didn't work. Instead I felt quite weightless and blown out, a husk of a person.

The light quality in the attic bedroom didn't change all morning. The only way I could measure the passage of time was by the radio, and the position of the watery shadows that his metal sculptures made on the magnolia paint.

Eventually I managed to rouse myself. I dressed and washed my face. I pulled my hair back tightly and fixed it in place with a loop of elastic. I sat down at his work table. It was blanketed with loose sheets of paper, all of which were covered with the meticulous plans he did for his sculptures. Elevations and perspectives, all neatly shaded and the dimensions written in using the lightest of pencils. There was a mess of other stuff on the table as well: sticks of flux, a broken soldering iron, bits of acrylic and angled steel brackets. I cleared a space amidst the evidence of his industry and taking out my notebook and biro, added my own patch of emotion to the collage:

> I do understand how you feel. I know the pressure that you're under at the moment, but you must realize that it's pressure that *you* put on *yourself.* It's not me that's doing it to you. I do love you and I want to be with you, but it takes time to forgive. And what you did to me was almost unforgivable. I've been hurt before and I don't want to be hurt again. If you can't understand that, if you can't understand how I feel about it, then it's probably best if we don't see one another again. I'll be at the flat this evening, perhaps you'll call?

Out in the street the sky was spitting at the pavement. There was no wind to speak of, but despite that each gob seemed to have an added impetus. With every corner that I rounded on my way to King's Cross I encountered another little cyclone of rain and grit. I walked past shops full of mouldering stock that were boarded up, and empty, derelict ones that were still open.

On the corner of the Caledonian Road I almost collided with a dosser wearing a long, dirty overcoat. He was clutching a bottle of VP in a hand that was blue with impacted filth, filth that seemed to have been worked deliberately into the open sores on his knuckles. He turned his face to me and I recoiled instinctively. It was the face of a myxomatosic rabbit ("You're like a little animal in there. A little rabbit, snuggled down in its burrow"), the eyes swollen up and exploding in a series of burst ramparts and lesions of diseased flesh. His nose was no longer nose-shaped.

But on the tube the people were comforting and workaday enough. I paid at the barrier when I reached Camden Town and walked off quickly down the High Street. Perhaps it was the encounter with the dying drunk that had cleansed me, jerked me out of my self-pity, because for a short while I felt more lucid, better able to look honestly at my relationship. While it was true that he did have problems, emotional problems, and was prepared to admit to them, it was still the case that nothing could forgive his conduct while I was away visiting my parents.

I knew that the woman he had slept with lived here in Camden Town. As I walked down the High Street I began—at first almost unconsciously, then with growing intensity—to examine the faces of any youngish women that passed me. They came in all shapes and sizes, these suspect lovers. There were tall women in floor-length linen coats; plump women in stretchy slacks; petite women in neat, two-piece suits; raddled women in unravelling pullovers; and painfully smart women, Sindy dolls: press a pleasure-button in the small of their backs and their hair would grow.

The trouble was that they all looked perfectly plausible candidates for the job as the metal worker's anvil. Outside Woolworth's I was gripped by a sharp attack of nausea. An old swallow of milky coffee reentered my mouth as I thought of him, on top of this woman, on top of that woman, hammering himself into them, bash after bash after bash, flattening their bodies, making them ductile with pleasure.

I went into Marks & Sparks to buy some clean underwear and paused to look at myself in a full-length mirror. My skirt was bunched up around my hips, my hair was lank and flecked with dandruff, my tights bagged at the knees, my sleeve-ends bulged with snot-clogged Kleenex. I looked like shit. It was no wonder that he didn't fancy me anymore, that he'd gone looking for some retouched vision.

"Come on," said Grace, "let's go. The longer we stay here, the more weight we put on." On our way out of the café I took a mint from the cut-glass bowl by the cash register and recklessly crunched it between my molars. The sweet pain of sugar-in-cavity spread through my mouth as I fumbled in my bag for my purse. "Well, what are you going to do now?" It was only three-thirty in the afternoon but already the sky over London was turning the shocking bilious color it only ever aspires to when winter is fast encroaching.

"Can I come back with you, Grace?"

"Of course you can, silly, why do you think I asked the question?" She put her arm about my shoulder and twirled me round until we were facing in the direction of the tube. Then she marched me off, like the young emotional offender that I was. Feeling her warm body against mine I almost choked, about to cry again at this display of caring from Grace. But I needed her too much, so I restrained myself.

"You come back with me, love," she clucked. "We can watch telly, or eat, or you can do some work. I've got some pattern cutting I've got to finish by tomorrow. John won't be back for ages yet . . . or I tell you what, if you like we can go and meet him in Soho after he's finished work and have something to eat there—would you like that?" She turned to me, flicking back the ledge of her thick blonde fringe with her index finger—a characteristic gesture.

"Well, yes," I murmured, "whatever."

"OK." Her eyes, turned toward mine, were blue, frank. "I can see you want to take it easy."

When we left the tube at Chalk Farm and started up the hill toward where Grace lived, she started up again, wittering on about her and John and me; about what we might do and what fun it would be to have me stay for a couple of nights; and about what a pity it was that I couldn't live with them for a while, because what I really needed was a good sense of security. There was something edgy and brittle about her enthusiasm. I began to feel that she was overstating her case.

I stopped listening to the words she was saying and began to hear them merely as sounds, as some ambient tape of reassurance. Her arm was linked in mine, but from this slight contact I could gain a whole sense of her small body. The precise slope and jut of her full breasts, the soft brush of her round stomach against the drape of her dress, the infinitesimal gratings of knee against nylon, against nylon against knee.

And as I built up this sense of Grace-as-body, I began also to consider how her bush would look as you went down on her. Would the lips gape wetly, or would they tidily recede? Would the cellulite on her hips crinkle as she parted her legs? How would she smell to you, of sex or cinnamon? But, of course, it wasn't any impersonal "you" I was thinking of—it was a highly personal *him.* I joined their bodies together in my mind and tormented myself with the hideous tableau of betrayal. After all, if he was prepared to screw some nameless bitch, what would have prevented him from shitting where I ate? I shuddered. Grace sensed this, and disengaging her arm from mine returned it to my shoulders, which she gave a squeeze.

John and Grace lived in a thirties council block halfway up Haverstock Hill. Their flat was just like all the others. You stepped through the front door and directly into a long corridor, off which were a number of small rooms. They may have been small, but Grace had done everything possible to make them seem spacious. Furniture and pictures were kept to an artful minimum, and the wooden blocks on the floor had been sanded and polished until they shone.

Grace snapped on floor lamps and put a Mozart concerto on the CD. I tried to write in my neglected journal, timing my flourishes of supposed insight to the ascending and descending scales. Grace set up the ironing board and began to do something complicated, involving sheets of paper, pins, and round, worn fragments of chalk.

When the music finished, neither of us made any move to put something else on, or to draw the curtains. Instead we sat in the off-white noise of the speakers, under the opaque stare of the dark windows. To me there was something intensely evocative about the scene: two young women sitting in a pool of yellow light on a winter's afternoon. Images of my childhood came to me; for the first time in days I felt secure.

When John got back from work, Grace put food-in-a-foil-tray in the oven, and tossed some varieties of leaves. John plonked himself down on one of the low chairs in the sitting room and propped the *Standard* on his knees. Occasionally he would give a snide laugh and read out an item, his intent being always to emphasise the utter consistency of its editorial stupidity.

We ate with our plates balanced on our knees, and when we had finished, turned on the television to watch a play. I noticed that John didn't move over to the sofa to sit with Grace. Instead, he remained slumped in his chair. As the drama unfolded I began to find these seating positions quite wrong and disquieting. John really should have sat with Grace.

The play was about a family riven by domestic violence. It was well acted and the jerky camerawork made it grittily real, almost like documentary. But still I felt that the basic premise was overstated. It wasn't that I didn't believe a family with such horrors boiling within it could maintain a closed face to the outside world, it was just that these horrors were so relentless.

The husband beat up the wife, beat up the kids, got drunk, sexually abused the kids, raped the wife, assaulted social workers, assaulted police, assaulted probation officers, and all within the space of a week or so. It should have been laughable—this chronically dysfunctional family—but it wasn't. How could it be remotely entertaining while we all sat in our separate padded places? Each fresh on-screen outrage increased the distance between the three of us, pushing us still further apart. I hunched down in my chair and felt the waistband of my skirt burn across my bloated stomach. I shouldn't have eaten all that salad—and the underdone garlic bread smelt flat and sour on my own tongue. So flat and sour that the idea even of kissing myself was repulsive, let alone allowing him to taste me.

The on-screen husband, his shirt open, the knot of his tie dragged halfway down his chest, was beating his adolescent daughter with short, powerful clouts around the head. They were standing in her bedroom doorway, and the camera stared fixedly over her shoulder, up the stairs and into the bedroom, where it picked up the corner of a pop poster, pinned to the flowered wallpaper. Each clout was audible as a loud "crack!" in the room where we sat. I felt so remote, from Grace, from John, from the play . . . from him.

I stood up and walked unsteadily to the toilet at the end of the corridor. Inside I slid the flimsy bolt into its loop and pushed the loosely stacked pile of magazines away from the toilet bowl. My stomach felt as if it were swelling by the second. My fingers when I put them in my mouth were large and alien. My nails scraped against the sides of my throat. As I leant forward I was aware of myself as a vessel, my curdled contents ready to pour. I looked down into the toilet world and there—as my oatmeal stream splashed down—saw that someone had already done the same. Cut out the nutritional middlewoman, that is.

After I'd finished I wiped around the rim of the toilet with hard scraps of paper. I flushed and then splashed my cheeks with cold water. Walking back down the corridor towards the sitting room, I was conscious only of the ultra-sonic whine of the television; until, that is, I reached the door:

"Don't bother." (A sob.)

"Mr. Evans . . . are you in there?"

"You don't want me to touch you?"

"Go away. Just go away . . ."

"It's just that I feel a bit wound up. I get all stressed out during the day—you know that. I need a long time to wind down."

"Mr. Evans, we have a court order that empowers us to take these children away."

"It's not that—I know it's not just that. You don't fancy me any more, you don't want to have sex anymore. You've been like this for weeks."

"I don't care if you've got the bloody Home Secretary out there. If you come in that door, I swear she gets it!"

"How do you expect me to feel like sex? Everything around here is so bloody claustrophobic. I can't stand these little fireside evenings. You sit there all hunched up and fidgety. You bite your nails and smoke away with little puffs. Puff, puff, puff. It's a total turn-off."

(*Smash!*) *"Oh my God. For Christ's sake! Oh Jesus . . ."*

"I bite my nails and smoke because I don't feel loved, because I feel all alone. I can't trust you, John, not when you're like this—you don't seem to have any feeling for me."

"Yeah, maybe you're right. Maybe I don't. I'm certainly fed up with all of this shit . . ."

I left my bag in the room. I could come back for it tomorrow when John had gone to work. I couldn't stand to listen—and I didn't want to go back into the room and sit down with them again, crouch with them, like another vulture in the moldering carcass of their relationship. I couldn't bear to see them reassemble the uncommunicative blocks of that static silence. And I didn't want to sleep in the narrow spare bed, under the child-sized duvet.

I wanted to be back with him. Wanted it the way a junky wants a hit. I yearned to be in that tippy, creaky boat of a bed, full of crumbs and sex and fag ash. I wanted to be framed by the basketry of angular shadows the naked bulb threw on the walls, and contained by the soft basketry of his limbs. At least we felt something for each other. He got right inside me—he really did. All my other relationships were as superficial as a salutation—this evening proved it. It was only with him that I became a real person.

Outside in the street the proportions were all wrong. The block of flats should have been taller than it was long—but it wasn't. Damp leaves blew against, and clung to my ankles. I'd been sitting in front of the gas fire in the flat and my right-hand side had become numb with the heat. Now this wore off—like a pain—leaving my clammy clothes sticking to my clammy flesh.

I walked for a couple of hundred yards down the hill, then a stitch stabbed into me and I felt little pockets of gas beading my stomach. I was level with a tiny parade of shops which included a cab company. Suddenly I couldn't face the walk to the tube, the tube itself, the walk back from the tube to his house. If I was going to go back to him I had to be there right away. If I went by tube it would take too long and this marvelous reconciliatory feeling might have soured by the time I arrived. And more to the point there might not be a relationship there for me to go back to. He was a feckless and promiscuous man, insecure and given to the grossest and most evil abuses of trust.

The jealous agony came over me again, covering my flesh like some awful hive. I leant up against a shopfront. The sick image of him entering some other. I could feel it so vividly that it was as if I was him: my penis snagging frustratingly against something . . . my blood beating in my temples . . . my sweat dripping on to her upturned face . . . and then the release of entry . . .

I pushed open the door of the minicab office and lurched in. Two squat men stood like bookends on either side of the counter. They were both reading the racing form. The man nearest to me was encased in a tube of caramel leather. He twisted his neckless head as far round as he could. Was it my imagination, or did his eyes probe and pluck at me, run up my thighs and attempt an imaginative penetration, rapid, rigid and metallic. The creak of his leather and the cold fug of damp, dead filter tips, assaulted me together.

"D'jew want a cab, love?" The other bookend, the one behind the counter, looked at me with dim-sum eyes, morsels of pupil packaged in fat.

"Err . . . yes, I want to go up to Islington, Barnsbury."

"George'll take yer—woncha, George?" George was still eyeing me around the midriff. I noticed—quite inconsequentially—that he was wearing very clean, blue trousers, with razor-sharp creases. Also that he had no buttocks—the legs of the trousers zoomed straight up into his jacket.

"Yerallright. C'mon, love." George rattled shut his paper and scooped a packet of Dunhill International and a big bunch of keys off the counter. He opened the door for me and as I passed through I could sense his fat black heart, encased in leather, beating behind me.

He was at the back door of the car before me and ushered me inside. I squidged halfway across the seat before collapsing in a nerveless torpor. But I knew that I wouldn't make it back to him unless I held myself in a state of no expectancy, no hope. If I dared to picture the two of us together again, then when I arrived at the house he would be out. Out fucking.

We woozed away from the curb and jounced around the corner. An air freshener shaped like a fir tree dingled and dangled as we took the bends down to Chalk Farm Road. The car was, I noticed, scrupulously clean and poisonous with smoke. George lit another Dunhill and offered me one, which I accepted. In the molded divider between the two front seats there sat a tin of travel sweets. I could hear them schussing round on their caster-sugar slope as we cornered and cornered and cornered again.

I sucked on the fag and thought determinedly of other things: figure skating; Christmas sales; the way small children have their mittens threaded through the arms of their winter coats on lengths of elastic; Grace . . . which was a mistake, because this train of thought was bad magic. Grace's relationship with John was clearly at an end. It was perverse to realize this, particularly after her display in the café, when she was so secure and self-possessed in the face of my tears and distress. But I could imagine the truth: that the huge crevices in their understanding of each other had been only temporarily papered over by the thrill of having someone in the flat who was in more emotional distress than they. No, there was no doubt about it now, Grace belonged to the league of the self-deceived.

George had put on a tape. The Crusaders—or at any rate some kind of jazz funk, music for glove compartments. I looked at the tightly bunched flesh at the back of his neck. It was malevolent flesh. I was alone in the world really. People tried to understand me, but they completely missed the mark. It was as if they were always looking at me from entirely the wrong angle and mistaking a knee for a bald pate, or an elbow for a breast.

And then I knew that I'd been a fool to get into the cab, the rapist-mobile. I looked at George's hands, where they had pounced on the steering wheel. They were flexing more than they should have been, flexing in anticipation. When he looked at me in the office he had taken me for jailbait, thought I was younger than I am. He just looked at my skirt—not at my sweater; and anyway, my sweater hides my breasts, which are small. He could do it, right enough, because he knew exactly where to go and the other man, the man in the office, would laughingly concoct an alibi for him. And who would believe me anyway? He'd be careful not to leave anything inside me . . . and no marks.

We were driving down a long street with warehouses on either side. I didn't recognize it. The distances between the street lamps were increasing. The car thwacked over some shallow depressions in the road, depressions that offered no resistance. I felt everything sliding toward the inevitable. He used to cuddle me and call me "little animal," "little rabbit." It should happen again, not end like this, in terror, in violation.

Then the sequence of events went awry. I subsided sideways, sobbing, choking. The seat was wide enough for me to curl up on it, which is what I did. The car slid to a halt. "Whassermatter, love?" Oh Jesus, I thought, don't let him touch me, please don't let him touch me, he can't be human. But I knew that he was. "C'mon, love, whassermatter?" My back in its suede jacket was like a carapace. When he penetrated me I'd rather he did it from behind, anything not to have him touch and pry at the soft parts of my front.

The car pulls away once more. Perhaps this place isn't right for his purposes, he needs somewhere more remote. I'm already under the earth, under the soft earth . . . The wet earth will cling to my putrid face when the police find me . . . when they put up the loops of yellow tape around my uncovered grave . . . and the WPC used to play me when they reconstruct the crime will look nothing like me . . . She'll have coarser features, but bigger breasts and hips . . . something not lost on the grieving boyfriend . . . Later he'll take her back to the flat, and fuck her standing up, pushing her ample, smooth bum into the third shelf of books in his main room (some Penguin classics, a couple of old economics text books, my copy of *The House of Mirth*), with each turgid stroke.

I hear the door catch through these layers of soft earth. I lunge up, painfully slow, he has me . . . and come face to face with a woman. A handsome woman, heavily built, in her late thirties. I relapse back into the car and regard her at crotch level. It's clear immediately—from the creases in her jeans—that she's George's wife.

"C'mon love, whassermatter?" I crawl from the car and stagger against her, still choking. I can't speak, but gesture vaguely towards George, who's kicking the front wheel of the car, with a steady "chok-chok-chok." "What'd 'e do then? Eh? Did he frighten you or something? You're a bloody fool, George!" She slaps him, a roundhouse slap—her arm, traveling ninety degrees level with her shoulder. George still stands, even glummer now, rubbing his cheek.

In terrorist-siege-survivor-mode (me clutching her round the waist with wasted arms) we turn and head across the parking area to the exterior staircase of a block of flats exactly the same as the one I recently left. Behind us comes a Dunhill International, and behind that comes George. On the third floor we pass a woman fumbling for her key in her handbag—she's small enough to eyeball the lock. My savior pushes open the door of the next flat along and pulls me in. Still holding me by the shoulder she escorts me along the corridor and into an overheated room.

"Park yerself there, love." She turns, exposing the high, prominent hips of a steer and disappears into another room, from where I hear the clang of aluminium kettle on iron prong. I'm left behind on a great scoop of upholstery—an armchair wide enough for three of me—facing a similarly outsize television screen. The armchair still has on the thick plastic dress of its first commercial communion.

George comes in, dangling his keys, and without looking at me crosses the room purposively. He picks up a doll in Dutch national costume and begins to fiddle under its skirt. "Git out of there!" This from the kitchen. He puts the doll down and exits without looking at me.

"C'mon, love, stick that in your laugh hole." She sets the tea cup and saucer down on a side table. She sits alongside me in a similar elephantine armchair. We might be a couple testing out a new suite in some furniture warehouse. She settles herself, yanking hard at the exposed pink webbing of her bra, where it cuts into her. "It's not the first time this has happened, you know," she slurps. "Not that George would do anything, mind, leastways not in his cab. But he does have this way of . . . well, frightening people, I s'pose. He sits there twirling his bloody wheel, not saying anything and somehow girls like you get terrified. Are you feeling better now?"

"Yes, thanks, really it wasn't his fault. I've been rather upset all day. I had a row with my boyfriend this morning and I had been going to stay at a friend's, but suddenly I wanted to get home. And I was in the car when it all sort of came down on top of me . . ."

"Where do you live, love?"

"I've got a room in a flat in Kensal Rise, but my boyfriend lives in Barnsbury."

"That's just around the corner from here. When you've 'ad your tea I'll walk you back."

"But what about George—I haven't even paid him."

"Don't worry about that. He's gone off now, anyway he could see that you aren't exactly loaded . . . He thinks a lot about money, does George. Wants us to have our own place an' that. It's an obsession with him. And he has to get back on call as quickly as he can or he'll miss a job, and if he misses a job he's in for a bad night. And if he has a bad night, then it's me that's on the receiving end the next day. Not that I hardly ever see him, mind. He works two shifts at the moment. Gets in at three-thirty in the afternoon, has a kip, and goes back out again at eight. On his day off he sleeps. He never sees the kids, doesn't seem to care about 'em . . ."

She trails off. In the next room I hear the high aspiration of a child turning in its sleep.

"D'jew think 'e's got some bint somewhere? D'jew think that's what these double shifts are really about?"

"Really, I don't know—"

"'E's a dark one. Now, I am a bit too fat to frolic, but I make sure he gets milked every so often. YerknowhatImean? Men are like bulls really, aren't they? They need to have some of that spunk taken out of them. But I dunno . . . Perhaps it's not enough. He's out and about, seeing all these skinny little bints, picking them up . . . I dunno, what's the use?" She lights a cigarette and deposits the match in a freestanding ash-tray. Then she starts yanking at the webbing again, where it encases her beneath her pullover. "I'd swear there are bloody fleas in this flat. I keep powdering the mutt, but it doesn't make no difference, does it, yer great ball of dough."

She pushes a slippered foot against the heaving stomach of a moldering Alsatian. I haven't even noticed the dog before now—its fur merges so seamlessly with the shaggy carpet. "They say dog fleas can't live on a human, yer know, but these ones are making a real effort. P'raps they aren't fleas at all . . . P'raps that bastard has given me a dose of the crabs. Got them off some fucking brass, I expect, whad'jew think?"

"I've no idea really—"

"I know it's the crabs. I've even seen one of the fuckers crawling up me pubes. Oh gawd, dunnit make you sick. I'm going to leave the bastard—I am. I'll go to Berkhamsted to my Mum's. I'll go tonight. I'll wake the kids and go tonight . . . "

I need to reach out to her, I suppose, I need to make some sort of contact. After all she has helped me—so really I ought to reciprocate. But I'm all inhibited. There's no point in offering help to anyone if you don't follow through. There's no point in implying to anyone the possibility of some fount of unconditional love if you aren't prepared to follow through . . . To do so would be worse than to do nothing. And anyway . . . I'm on my way back to sort out my relationship. That has to take priority.

These justifications are running through my mind, each one accompanied by a counter argument, like a subtitle at the opera, or a stock market quotation running along the base of a television screen. Again there's the soft aspiration from the next room, this time matched, shudderingly, by the vast shelf of tit alongside me. She subsides. Twisted face, foundation cracking, folded into cracking hands. For some reason I think of Atrixo.

She didn't hear me set down my cup and saucer. She didn't hear my footfalls. She didn't hear the door. She just sobbed. And now I'm clear, I'm in the street and I'm walking with confident strides toward his flat. Nothing can touch me now. I've survived the cab ride with George—that's good karma, good magic. It means that I'll make it back to him and his heartfelt, contrite embrace.

Sometimes—I remember as a child remembers Christmas—we used to drink a bottle of champagne together. Drink half the bottle and then make love, then drink the other half and make love again. It was one of the rituals I remember from the beginning of our relationship, from the springtime of our love. And as I pace on up the hill, more recollections hustle alongside. Funny how when a relationship is starting up you always praise the qualities of your lover to any third party there is to hand, saying, "Oh yes, he's absolutely brilliant at X,Y, and Z . . ." and sad how that tendency dies so quickly. Dies at about the same time that disrobing in front of one another ceases to be embarrassing . . . and perhaps for that reason ceases to be quite so sexy.

Surely it doesn't have to be this way? Stretching up the hill ahead of me, I begin to see all of my future relationships, bearing me on and up like some escalator of the fleshly. Each step is a man, a man who will penetrate me with his penis and his language, a man who will make a little private place with me, secure from the world, for a month, or a week, or a couple of years.

How much more lonely and driven is the serial monogamist than the serial killer? I won't be the same person when I come to lie with that man there, the one with the ginger fuzz on his white stomach; or that one further up there—almost level with the junction of Barnsbury Road—the one with the round head and skull cap of thick, black hair. I'll be his "little rabbit," or his "baby-doll," or his "sex goddess," but I won't be me. I can only be me . . . with him.

Maybe it isn't too late? Maybe we can recapture some of what we once had.

I'm passing an off-license. It's on the point of closing—I can see a man in a cardigan doing something with some crates toward the back of the shop. I'll get some champagne. I'll turn up at his flat with the bottle of champagne, and we'll do it like we did it before.

I push open the door and venture inside. The atmosphere of the place is acridly reminiscent of George's minicab office. I cast an eye along the shelves—they are pitifully stocked, just a few cans of lager and some bottles of cheap wine. There's a cooler in the corner, but all I can see behind the misted glass are a couple of isolated bottles of Asti Spumante. It doesn't look like they'll have any champagne in this place. It doesn't look like my magic is going to hold up. I feel the tears welling up in me again, welling up as the offie proprietor treads wearily back along the lino.

"Yes, can I help you?"

"I . . . oh, well, I . . . oh, really . . . it doesn't matter . . ."

"Ay-up, love, are you all right?"

"Yes . . . I'm sorry . . . it's just . . ."

He's a kindly, round ball of a little man, with an implausibly straight toothbrush mustache. Impossible to imagine him as a threat. I'm crying as much with relief—that the offie proprietor is not some cro-magnon—as I am from knowing that I can't get the champagne now, and that things will be over between me and him.

The offie proprietor has pulled a handkerchief out of his cardigan pocket, but it's obviously not suitable, so he shoves it back in and picking up a handi-pack of tissues from the rack on the counter, he tears it open and hands one to me, saying, "Now there you go, love, give your nose a good blow like, and you'll feel better."

"Thanks." I mop myself up for what seems like the nth time today. Who would have thought the old girl had so much salt in her?

"Now, how can I help you?"

"Oh, well . . . I don't suppose you have a bottle of champagne?" It sounds stupid, saying that rich word in this zone of poor business opportunity.

"Champagne? I don't get much of a call for that round here." His voice is still kindly, he isn't offended. "My customers tend to prefer their wine fortified—if you know what I mean. Still, I remember I did have a bottle out in the store room a while back. I'll go and see if it's still there."

He turns and heads off down the lino again. I stand and look out at the dark street and the swishing cars and the shuddering lorries. He's gone for quite a while. He must trust me—I think to myself. He's left me here in the shop with the till and all the booze on the shelves. How ironic that I should find trust here, in this slightest of contexts, and find so little of it in my intimate relationships.

Then I hear footsteps coming from up above, and I am conscious of earnest voices:

"Haven't you shut up the shop yet?"

"I'm just doing it, my love. There's a young woman down there wanting a bottle of champagne, I just came up to get it."

"Champagne! Pshaw! What the bloody hell does she want it for at this time of night?"

"I dunno. Probably to drink with her boyfriend."

"Well, you take her bottle of champagne down to her and then get yourself back up here. I'm not finished talking to you yet."

"Yes, my love."

When he comes back in I do my best to look as if I haven't overheard anything. He puts the bifocals that hang from the cord round his neck on to his nose and scrutinises the label on the bottle: "Chambertin Demi-sec. Looks all right to me—good stuff as I recall."

"It looks fine to me."

"Good," he smiles—a nice smile. "I'll wrap it up for you . . . Oh, hang on a minute, there's no price on it, I'll have to go and check the stock list."

"Brian!" This comes from upstairs, a great bellow full of imperiousness.

"Just a minute, my love." He tilts his head back and calls up to the ceiling, as if addressing some vengeful goddess, hidden behind the fire-resistant tiles.

"Now, Brian!" He gives me a pained smile, takes off his bi-focals and rubs his eyes redder.

"It's my wife," he says in a stage whisper, "she's a bit poorly. I'll check on her quickly and get that price for you. I shan't be a moment."

He's gone again. More footsteps, and then Brian's wife says, "I'm not going to wait all night to tell you this, Brian, I'm going to bloody well tell you now—"

"But I've a customer—"

"I couldn't give a monkey's. I couldn't care less about your bloody customer. I've had it with you, Brian—you make me sick with your stupid little cardigan and your glasses. You're like some fucking relic—"

"Can't this wait a minute—"

"No, it bloody can't. I want you out of here, Brian. It's my lease and my fucking business. You can sleep in the spare room tonight, but I want you out of here in the morning."

"We've discussed this before—I know we have. But now I've made my decision."

I take the crumpled bills from my purse. Twenty quid has to be enough for the bottle of Chambertin. I wrap it in a piece of paper and write on it "Thanks for the champagne." Then I pick up the bottle and leave the shop as quietly as I can. They're still at it upstairs: her voice big and angry; his, small and placatory.

I can see the light in the bedroom when I'm still two hundred yards away from the house. It's the Anglepoise on the windowsill. He's put it on so that it will appear like a beacon, drawing me back into his arms.

I let myself in with my key, and go on up the stairs. He's standing at the top, wearing a black sweater that I gave him and blue jeans. There's a cigarette trailing from one hand, and a smear of cigarette ash by his nose, which I want to kiss away the minute I see it. He says, "What are you doing here, I thought you were going to stay at your place tonight?"

I don't say anything, but pull the bottle of champagne out from under my jacket, because I know that'll explain everything and make it all all right.

He advances toward me, down a couple of stairs, and I half-close my eyes, waiting for him to take me in his arms, but instead he holds me by my elbows and looking me in the face says, "I think it really would be best if you stayed at your place tonight, I need some time to think things over—"

"But I want to stay with you. I want to be with you. Look, I brought this for us to drink . . . for us to drink while we make love."

"That's really sweet of you, but I think after this morning it would be best if we didn't see one another for a while."

"You don't want me any more—do you? This is the end of our relationship, isn't it? Isn't that what you're saying?"

"No, I'm not saying that, I just think it would be a good idea if we cooled things down for a while."

I can't stand the tone of his voice. He's talking to me as if I were a child or a crazy person. And he's looking at me like that as well—as if I might do something mad, like bash his fucking brains out with my bottle of Chambertin Demi-sec. "I don't want to cool things down, I want to be with you. I need to be with you. We're meant to be together—you said that. You said it yourself!"

"Look, I really feel it would be better if you went now. I'll call you a cab—"

"I don't want a cab!"

"I'll call you a cab and we can talk about it in the morning—"

"I don't want to talk about it in the morning, I want to talk about it now. Why won't you let me stay, why are you trying to get rid of me?"

And then he sort of cracks. He cracks and out of the gaps in his face come these horrible words, these sick, slanderous, revolting words, he isn't him anymore, because he could never have said such things. He must be possessed.

"I don't want you here!" He begins to shout and pound the wall. "Because you're like some fucking emotional Typhoid Mary. That's why I don't want you here. Don't you understand, it's not just me and you, it's everywhere you go, everyone you come into contact with. You've got some kind of bacillus inside you, a contagion—everything you touch you turn to neurotic ashes with your pick-pick-picking away at the fabric of people's relationships. That's why I don't want you here. Tonight—or any other night!"

Out in the street again—I don't know how. I don't know if he said more of these things, or if we fought, or if we fucked. I must have blacked out, blacked out with the sheer anguish of it. You think you know someone, you imagine that you are close to them, and then they reveal this slimy pit at their core . . . this pit they've kept concreted over. Sex is a profound language, all right, and so easy to lie in.

I don't need him—that's what I have to tell myself: I don't need him. But I'm bucking with sobs and the needing of him is all I can think of. I'm standing in the dark street, rain starting to fall, and every little thing: every gleam of chromium, serration of brick edge, mush of waste paper, thrusts its material integrity in the face of my lost soul.

I'll go to my therapist. It occurs to me—and tagged behind it is the admonition: why didn't you think of this earlier, much earlier, it could have saved you a whole day of distress?

Yes, I'll go to Jill's house. She always says I should come to her place if I'm in real trouble. She knows how sensitive I am. She knows how much love I need. She's not like a conventional therapist—all dispassionate and uncaring. She believes in getting involved in her clients' lives. I'll go to her now. I need her now more than I ever have.

When I go to see her she doesn't put me in some garage of a consulting room, some annex of feeling. She lets me into her warm house, the domicile lined with caring. It isn't so much therapy that Jill gives me, as acceptance. I need to be there now, with all the evidence of her three small children spread about me: the red plastic crates full of soft toys, the finger paintings sellotaped to the fridge, the diminutive coats and jackets hanging from hip-height hooks.

I need to be close to her and also to her husband, Paul. I've never met him—of course, but I'm always aware of his after-presence in the house when I attend my sessions. I know that he's an architect, that he and Jill have been together for fourteen years, and that they too have had their vicissitudes, their comings-together and fallings-apart. How else could Jill have such total sympathy when it comes to the wreckage of my own emotions? Now I need to be within the precincts of their happy cathedral of a relationship again. Jill and Paul's probity, their mutual relinquishment, their acceptance of one another's foibles—all of this towers above my desolate plain of abandonment.

It's OK, I'm going to Jill's now. I'm going to Jill's and we're going to drink hot chocolate and sit up late, talking it all over. And then she'll let me stay the night at her place—I know she will. And in the morning I'll start to sort myself out.

Another cab ride, but I'm not concentrating on anything, not noticing anything. I'm intent on the vision I have of Jill opening the front door to her cozy house. Intent on the homely vision of sports equipment loosely stacked in the hall, and the expression of heartfelt concern that suffuses Jill's face when she sees the state I'm in.

The cab stops and I pay off the driver. I open the front gate and walk up to the house. The door opens and there's Jill: "Oh . . . hi . . . it's you."

"I'm sorry . . . perhaps I should have called?" This isn't at all as I imagined it would be—there's something lurking in her face, something I haven't seen there before.

"It's rather late—"

"I know, it's just, just that . . . " My voice dies away. I don't know what to say to her, I expect her to do the talking, to lead me in and then lead me on, tease out the awful narrative of my day. But she's still standing in the doorway, not moving, not asking me in.

"It's not altogether convenient . . ." And I start to cry—I can't help it, I know I shouldn't, I know she'll think I'm being manipulative (and where does this thought come from, I've never imagined such a thing before), but I can't stop myself.

And then there is the comforting arm around my shoulder and she does invite me in, saying, "Oh, all right, come into the kitchen and have a cup of chocolate, but you can't stay for long. I'll have to order you another mini cab in ten minutes or so."

"What's the matter then? Why are you in such a state?"

The kitchen has a proper grown-up kitchen smell, of wholesome ingredients, well-stocked larders and fully employed wine racks. The lighting is good as well: a bell-bottomed shade pulled well down on to the wooden table, creating an island in the hundred-watt sun.

"He's ending our relationship—he didn't say as much, but I know that that's what he meant. He called me 'an emotional Typhoid Mary,' and all sorts of other stuff. Vile things."

"Was this this evening?"

"Yeah, half an hour ago. I came straight here afterward, but it's been going on all day, we had a dreadful fight this morning."

"Well," she snorts, "isn't that a nice coincidence?" Her tone isn't nice at all. There's a hardness in it, a flat bitterness I've never heard before.

"I'm sorry?" Her fingers are white against the dark brown of the drinking-chocolate tin, her face is all drawn out of shape. She looks her age—and I've never even thought what this might be before now. For me she's either been a sister or a mother or a friend. Free-floatingly female, not buckled into a strait-jacket of biology.

"My husband saw fit to inform me that our marriage was over this evening . . . oh, about fifteen minutes before you arrived, approximately . . . " Her voice dies away. It doesn't sound malicious—her tone, that is, but what she's said is clearly directed at me. But before I can reply she goes on. "I suppose there are all sorts of reasons for it. Above and beyond all the normal shit that happens in relationships: the arguments, the Death of Sex, the conflicting priorities, there are other supervening factors." She's regaining her stride now, beginning to talk to me the way she normally does.

"It seems impossible for men and women to work out their fundamental differences nowadays. Perhaps it's because of the uncertainty about gender roles, or the sheer stress of modern living, or maybe there's some still deeper malaise of which we're not aware."

"What do you think it is? I mean—between you and Paul." I've adopted her tone—and perhaps even her posture. I imagine that if I can coax some of this out of her then things will get back to the way they should be, roles will re-reverse.

"I'll tell you what I think it is"—she looks directly at me for the first time since I arrived—"since you ask. I think he could handle the kids, the lack of sleep, the constant money problems, my moods, his moods, the dog shit in the streets and the beggars on the Tube. Oh yes, he was mature enough to cope with all of that. But in the final analysis what he couldn't bear was the constant stream of neurotics flowing through this house. I think he called it 'a babbling brook of self-pity.' Yes, that's right, that's what he said. Always good with a turn of phrase is Paul."

"And what do you think?" I asked—not wanting an answer, but not wanting her to stop speaking, for the silence to interpose.

"I'll tell you what I think, young lady." She gets up and, placing the empty mugs on the draining board, turns to the telephone. She lifts the receiver and says as she dials, "I think that the so-called 'talking cure' has turned into a talking disease, that's what I think. Furthermore, I think that given the way things stand this is a fortuitous moment for us to end our relationship too. After all, we may as well make a clean sweep of it . . . Oh, hello. I'd like a cab, please. From 27 Argyll Road . . . Going to . . . Hold on a sec—" She turns to me and asks with peculiar emphasis, "Do you know where you're going to?"

Making Arrangements

ELIZABETH BOWEN

Six days after Margery's departure, a letter from her came for Hewson Blair. That surprised him; he had not expected her to write: surely the next move should be his? Assuming this, he had deliberated comfortably—there was time, it had appeared, for sustained deliberation—and now Margery had pounced back upon him suddenly. It was like being spoken to when he was settling down to a stiff book in the evening; Margery had often done this.

He remembered as he scrutinized the postmark that the last time she had written to him was from Switzerland, last Christmas. She always said she found him difficult to write to—why write now, then, when she might be better occupied? Hewson never sneered; his face lacked the finer mobility and his voice the finer inflections: he turned over the unopened letter, felt that it was compact and fat, and pinched the corners thoughtfully.

He found the name of a riverside hotel printed on the flap of the envelope, and re-read this several times with amazement, unable to conceive how a young woman who had gone away with somebody else to a riverside hotel—with white railings, Hewson imagined, and geraniums swinging in baskets, and a perpetual, even rushing past of the water—could spare some hours of her time there writing to her husband. Unless, of course, she simply wanted to tell him about Leslie.

Of course, she must have a considerable amount to say about Leslie after having lived with him under necessarily restricted conditions for the last six days. She had always told Hewson about her many friends, at great length, and as he was not interested in these people the information went in at one ear and out at the other. He imagined that Leslie was the one with the cello, though he might have been the one with the golf handicap—he could not say.

If she wanted to come back—he was slitting open the envelope carefully, and this made him pause a moment—if she wanted to come back he must write briefly and say he was sorry, he could not have her, he had made other arrangements. His sister was coming to keep house for him tomorrow, and the servants were even now getting ready the spare room.

Hewson had just come in, having got away a little earlier than usual from the office, where people were beginning to know, and to speak to him awkwardly with scared faces. He had not, of course, been near the club. In stories, people who were treated as Margery had treated him threw up everything and went abroad; but Hewson did not care for traveling, and it would be difficult to leave his business just at present. He had never seen very much of Margery, his wheels went round without her; all this, if one could regard it rationally, came down to a few readjustments in one's menage and a slight social awkwardness which one would soon outgrow.

Parkins had just made up the library fire; she was drawing the curtains noiselessly across the windows. Hewson wondered what she had thought of Margery's letter as she placed it, lonely, gleaming and defiant, on the silver salver on to which Margery had so often flung her gloves. Margery would fling her gloves on to the salver and her furs across the oak chest and swing humming into the library to read her letters by the fire. She would settle down over them like a cat over a saucer of milk, bend and smile and murmur over each, rustling the paper; and one by one drop them, crumpled, into the grate. Margery was a person who dealt summarily with her husks; bit through direct to the milk kernel of things and crunched delectably.

Tonight the grate was very tidy. Hewson watched Parkins' back and felt the room unbearably crowded.

"That's all right," he said. "That will do. Thank you, Parkins."

He stood with his back to the fire, watching Parkins narrowly until he had left the room. Then he let Margery out of the envelope.

"It does seem funny to be writing to you again," Margery wrote. "I haven't for such ages—that note I left on the mantelpiece doesn't count, of course. Wasn't it dramatic, leaving a note like that! I couldn't help laughing; it just shows how true novels really are.

"Dear Hewson, there are several things, quite a lot, that I want sent after me at once. As I expect you saw, I didn't take more than my dressing-case. I know you will make all arrangements—you are so awfully good at that sort of thing. I suppose there are rather a lot of arrangements—I mean, like getting the divorce and sending my clothes on and writing to tell people; and I expect you would rather give away the dogs.

"We don't quite know how long a divorce takes or how one gets it, but as I told Leslie, who often gets rather depressed about all this fuss, you will be able to arrange it all beautifully. We are going abroad till it is all over; Leslie is so fearfully sensitive. We want to go quite soon, so I should be so much obliged if you could send those clothes off to me at once. I enclose a list.

"Leslie says he thinks I am perfectly wonderful, the way I think of everything, and I suppose it really is rather wonderful, isn't it, considering you always made all the arrangements. It just shows what one can do if one is put to it. Leslie would like to send a message; he feels he can't very well send his love, but he asks me to say how sorry he is for any inconvenience this will cause you, but that he is sure you cannot fail to feel, as we do, that it is all for the best. Leslie is fearfully considerate.

"Dear Hewson, I think you are too sweet, and you know I have always liked you. I feel quite homesick sometimes in this horrid hotel, but it's no good being sentimental, is it? We never suited each other a bit, and I never quite knew what you wanted me for. I expect you will be fearfully happy now and settle down again and marry some fearfully nice girl and get the rock-garden really nice without my horrid dogs to come and scratch it up. Now, about the clothes . . ."

Directions followed.

As Hewson read this letter he remembered Leslie (though he still could not say whether he was the one with the cello or the golf handicap), a young man with a very fair short mustache and flickering lashes, who liked his port. It seemed quite right that such a fair young man should admire Margery, who was dark. Many people had, indeed, admired Margery, which gratified Hewson, who had married her. Many more people praised her clothes, which still further gratified Hewson, who had paid for them. When he married Margery he stamped himself as a man of taste (and a man of charm, too, to have secured her), and he rose still higher in the estimation of his friends; while even men who had thought him a dull dog in the army or at Oxford began coming to the house again.

It was all very nice, and Hewson often found himself arrested in a trance of self-congratulation; when he came in in the evenings, for instance, and found firelight flooding and ebbing in the white-paneled hall and more cards on the table, and heard Parkins moving about in the dining room, here through the slit of the door the glass and silver on the table sparkled under the low inverted corolla of the shade. Sometimes he would have to put his hand before his mouth, and pass for yawning, to conceal the slow smile that crept irresistibly across his face; as when he stood beside the really good gramophone and changed the records of thudding music for Margery and her friends to dance to. She danced beautifully with her slim, balanced partners; they moved like moths, almost soundlessly, their feet hissing faintly on the parquet. Hewson's hand brushed across the switchboard, lights would spring up dazzlingly against the ceiling and pour down opulently on to the amber floor to play and melt among the shadows of feet. This had all been very satisfactory.

Hewson never conceived or imagined, but he intended; and his home had been all that he had intended. He had a sense of fitness and never made an error in taste. He was not amusing, he did not intend to be an amusing man; but he had always intended to marry an amusing wife, a pretty little thing with charm. He considered that Margery was becoming to him, which indeed she was. He had a fine fair impassive face with the jaw in evidence and owl's eyebrows; he stood for dark oak and white paneling, good wine, and billiard-tables. Margery stood for watercolors, gramophones, and rosy chintz. They had made a home together with all this; none of these elements was lacking, and thus their home had, rightly, the finality of completeness.

Tonight he dined early, and, though eating abstractedly, ate well. He knew the importance of this. They had taken out all the leaves, the table had shrunk to its smallest. Margery had often been away or out, and this evening was in no way different from many others. They brought his coffee to the table, and after coffee he went upstairs, slowly, turning out all but one of the hall lights behind him. He carried Margery's letter, and paused on the landing to look through the list again, because he had decided to get the things packed up tonight and sent off early tomorrow. As he did not wish to give Emily or Parkins Margery's letter (the list being punctuated by irrelevancies), he proposed to get the shoes and dresses out himself and leave them on the bed for Emily or Parkins to pack.

Yes, Margery was not unperceptive; he really did like making arrangements. The sense of efficiency intoxicated him, like dancing. He liked going for a thing methodically and getting it done; jotting down lists on pieces of paper and clipping the papers together and putting them away in the one inevitable drawer.

"You can't think what Hewson's like!" Margery would exult to their friends, waving a glass dessert spoon at him from her end of the table. "He does everything and finds everything and puts everything away and sends everything off. He's absolutely amazing!"

At this, all the way down the table the shirt-fronts and pink quarter-faces veered intently toward Margery would veer round, guffawing, toward Hewson, and become three-quarter faces, twinkling over with mirth, while the ladies, tittering deprecatingly, swayed toward Hewson, their mirth drawn out into a sigh. "You must forgive us, Mr. Blair," they implied; "but your wife is really *so* amusing!" And Hewson sat on solidly and kept the wine going.

Margery's room sprang into light nakedly; the servants had taken away the pink shades. The curtains were undrawn, and Emily, with a housemaid's one cannot say how conscious sense of the dramatic, had dropped a sheet over the mirror and swathed the dressing-table: bowls and bottles here and there projected, glacial, through the folds. The room was very cold and Hewson thought of ordering a fire, then recoiled in shyness from the imagined face of Emily or Parkins. He had not entered Margery's room since her departure—he preferred to think of it as a departure rather than a flight, an ignominious scurrying-forth unworthy of the home and husband that she left. He preferred to feel that if his wife sinned, she would sin like a lady.

Margery's directions were minute, though perhaps a trifle incoherent. Hewson sat down on the sofa along the end of the bed to study the list in the light of imminent activity. He must revise it systematically, making it out into headings: "Contents of wardrobe, contents of chest by window, contents of dressing-table drawers." Something caught his eye; he started. Margery's pink slippers, overlooked by Emily, peeped out at him from under the valance of the bed.

From the slippers, connections of ideas brought round his eyes to the fireplace again; he had never seen it black on a chilly evening; Margery had had everything, this was a really good room. She would never have a room like this again; Leslie would not be able to give it to her. What could have been the attraction? . . . Well, that was a blind alley; it was no good wandering down there.

She had written: "I never quite knew what you wanted me for."

That statement amazed Hewson; it simply amazed him. He got up and walked round the room, staring at the shining furniture, challenging the pictures, thinking of the library fire, the dancing-floor under the downpour of light, the oval table in the dining room compassed about for him always with an imaginary crowd of faces. Surely the sense of inclusion in all this should have justified Margery's existence to her. It was not as if he had ever bothered her to give him anything. He had assumed quite naturally that this sense of being cognate parts of a whole should suffice for both of them. He still could not understand where this had failed her.

He could not conceive what Leslie had held out to her, and what she had run to grasp.

Hewson advanced toward his reflection in the wardrobe mirror, and they stood eyeing one another sternly; then their faces softened. "Lonely fellow," Hewson condescended. The ghost of one of his old happy trances returned to his reflection; he saw the slow smile spread across its face, its fine face. That she should have fallen short of this . . .

He tugged at the handle of the wardrobe door, and his reflection swung toward him, flashed in the light and vanished. From the dusk within, cedar-scented and cavernous, Margery leaped out to him again as she had leaped up out of the envelope. There were so many Margerys in there, phalanx on, and the scent of her rushed out to fill this room, depose the bleak regency of Emily, and make the pictures, the chairs, the chintzes, the shadows in the alcove, suddenly significant. He drew out his fountain pen, detached a leaf from his notebook and headed it: "Contents of Wardrobe."

If he had been a different type of man Margery's chameleon quality would, he knew, have irritated him; the way she took color from everything she put on, and not only took color but became it, while shadowing behind all her changes an immutable, untouched, and careless self. Now the black dress—Hewson took it down and carried it over to the bed, and its long draperies swept the carpet, clinging to the pile, and seemed to follow him reluctantly—you would have said the black dress was the very essence, the expression of the innermost of her, till you met her in the flame-color.

He took down the flame-color next, and could hardly help caressing it as it lay across his arms, languishing and passive. The shimmer and rustle of it, the swinging of its pendent draperies round his feet, filled him with a sharp nostalgia, though they stood to him for nothing in particular—there had been that evening in the billiard-room.

He laid the dress down reverently on the bed, like a corpse, and folded its gauzy sleeves across its bosom.

He was less tender with the one that followed, a creamy, slithery thing with a metallic brilliance that slipped down into his hands with a horrible wanton willingness. He had always felt an animosity toward it since they drove together to that dance. It slid and shone round Margery's limbs as though she were dressed in quicksilver; more beautiful than all the rest, more costly also, as Hewson knew. He let it drip down from his arms on to the bed and creep across the counterpane like a river.

He was summary, too, with the velvety things that followed, weighed down by their heavy fur hems. They were evenings at home to him, *tête-à-têtes* with their faint, discomfortable challenge; Margery tilting back her chin to yawn, or lolling sideways out of her chair to tickle her dog in the stomach, or shuffling illustrated papers. She would say: "Talk to me, Hewson. Hewson, do talk . . . " And later: "Hewson, I suppose evenings at home are good for one. I'm so sleepy. That does show, doesn't it, how I need sleep?"

He worked more quickly after this, carrying the dresses one by one across the room, laying them on the bed, and pausing after each to compare his list with Margery's. Sometimes the name of a color, the description of a stuff, would puzzle him, and he pored above the two lists with bent brows, unable to make them tally. Reluctantly he would inscribe a question mark. He heard ten strike, and began working even faster. He had still to make arrangements with the chauffeur: he liked to be in bed himself by half-past eleven, and he didn't approve of keeping the servants late.

Then, leaning deep into the cupboard, he saw the red dress, melting away into the shadows of the cedar-wood. It hung alone in one corner with an air of withdrawal. Hewson reached out, twitched it down; it hung limp from his hands, unrustling, exhaling its own perfume of chiffon. He stepped back; it resisted for an infinitesimal second, then, before he could release the tension on it, tore with a long soft sound.

It came out into the light of the room hanging jagged and lamentable, the long hem trailing. Hewson had torn it, torn the red dress; of all her dresses. He looked at it in fear and a kind of defiant anger. He assured himself the stuff was rotten; she had not worn it for so long. Had, indeed, Margery's avoidance of the red dress been deliberate?

With what motive, Hewson wondered, had this unique presentation of herself been so definitely eschewed? Did it make her shy—was she then conscious that it stood for something to be forgotten? He could never have believed this of Margery; he was startled to find that he himself should suspect it. Yet he returned to this: she had never worn the red dress since *that* occasion. He had watched for it speechlessly those ensuing weeks, evening after evening, but it had never appeared again. And here he had found it, hanging in the deepest shadow, trying to be forgotten.

Margery had put the red dress down on her list; she had underlined it. It was one of the dresses she wanted to take away to Leslie. Now it was torn, irreparably torn; she would never be able to wear it.

Hewson wondered whether Margery would be angry. He quailed a little, feeling the quick storm of her wrath about him; windy little buffets of derision and a fine sting of irony. She would certainly be angry when she knew, and go sobbing with rage to Leslie: Hewson wondered whether Leslie would be adequate. He debated whether he should pack the dress. Well, since it had admittedly stood for that to Margery as well as to himself, let her have it as it was! Hewson's wits stirred—this should be his comment. Why should he let her go to Leslie with that dress, the dress in which Hewson had most nearly won her? It had been pacific, their relationship; neither of them would have admitted a crescendo, a climax, a decrescendo; but there had been a climax, and the red dress shone in both their memories to mark it. He did not think he would let the Margery who lived for Leslie wear the red dress of his own irreclaimable Margery.

Smiling and frowning a little with concentration, he eyed the thing, then gripped the folds in both hands and tore the dress effortlessly from throat to hem, refolded it, and tore again. A fine dust of silk crimsoned the air for a moment, assailed his nostrils, made him sneeze. He laid the dead dress gently down among the other dresses and stood away, looking down at them all.

These were all his, his like the room and the house. Without these dresses the inner Margery, unfostered, would never have become perceptible to the world. She would have been like a page of music written never to be played. All her delightfulness to her friends had been in this expansion of herself into forms and colors. Hewson had fostered this expansion, as it now appeared, that Leslie might ultimately be delighted. From the hotel by the river the disembodied ghost of Margery was crying thinly to him for her body, her innumerable lovely bodies. Hewson expressed this to himself concisely and heavily, as a man should, as he stood looking down at the bed, half smiling, and said, "She has commited suicide."

From boyhood, Hewson had never cared for any thoughts of revenge. Revenge was a very wild kind of justice, and Hewson was a civilized man. He believed in the Good, in the balance of things, and in an eventual, tremendous payday. At once, the very evening Margery had left him, he had felt the matter to be out of his hands, and, wondering quite impartially how much she would be punished, had sat down almost at once to write and make arrangements with his sister. He had not, these last few days, felt sorrowful, venomous, or angry, because he had not felt at all; the making of these and other arrangements had too fully occupied him. He had always very lucidly and reasonably contended that the importance of mere feeling in determining a man's line of action is greatly overrated.

Now, looking down, he watched the dresses, tense with readiness to fall upon them if they stirred and pin them down and crush and crush and crush them. If he could unswervingly and unsparingly hold them in his eyes, he would be able to detect their movements, the irrepressible palpitation of that vitality she had infused into them. They lay there dormant; only the crimson dress was dead. He bent, and touched the creamy trickle of the ball-dress; his finger dinted it and a metallic brightness spurted down the dint, filling it like a tide. He drew back his finger, cold yet curiously vibrant from the contact. The folds were cool; and yet he had expected, had expected . . . He brought down his outspread hands slowly; they paused, then closed on handfuls of the creamy stuff that trickled icily away; between his fingers.

The dress lay stretched out and provocative and did not resist him, and Hewson with dilated eyes stared down at it and did not dare to breathe.

He turned and crossed the room on tiptoe, peered out into the darkness of the trees, then drew the blinds down. He glanced round secretly and stealthily at the pictures; then he went over to the door and peered out, listening intently, onto the landing. Silence there and silence through the house. Shutting the door carefully behind him, he returned to the bedside.

It seemed to him, as he softly, inexorably approached them, that the swirls, rivers, and luxuriance of silk and silver, fur and lace and velvet, shuddered as he came. His shadow drained the color from them as he bent over the bed.

Half an hour later, Hewson once more crossed the landing and went up to the box-room to look for Margery's trunk. He was intent and flushed, and paused for a moment under the light to brush some shreds of silver from his sleeve. He seemed unconscious that a wraith of flame-colored chiffon drifted away from his shoulder as he walked, hung in the air, and settled on the carpet behind him. He came down again from the box-room breathing hard, bent beneath the trunk, and as he re-entered the bedroom something black and snake-like lying across the threshold wound round his feet and nearly entangled him. Approaching the bed, his steps were once more impeded; sometimes he was walking ankle-deep.

He pitched the trunk down in a clear space, propped it open and began to pack. Many of the fragments, torn too fine, were elusive; he stooped with the action of a gleaner to gather them in armfuls, then thrust them down into the trunk. The silks—they seemed still sentient—quivered under his touch; the velvets lay there sullenly, and sometimes, when he heaped them in, dripped out over the edge of the box again. Here and there an end of fur ruffled into deeper shadows under his excited breath. When he had amassed everything, Hewson beat with the flat of his hands upon the pile to make it level, spread tissue over it, and locked the trunk. Then he rang for Parkins and sat down to wait. He re-read Margery's list once again, folded it, and put it away in his pocket-book.

That night, Lippit the chauffeur received his instructions. He was to take Mrs. Blair's box to the station at half-past eight the following morning, and dispatch it to the given address per luggage in advance, having taken to the same station a ticket to be afterward destroyed. This extravagance Hewson deplored, but the exigencies of the railway company demanded it. The trunk was strapped and corded and placed in the back hall in readiness for its early departure, and Hewson, seated comfortably at his table by the library fire, printed out two labels in neat black characters, then himself affixed them to the handles of the trunk.

"Would there be anything more, sir?" inquired Parkins, standing at attention.

"No, not tonight," said Hewson courteously. "I am sorry to have kept you late, Parkins: you had better go to bed."

"Thank you, sir."

"And oh, Parkins!"

"Sir?"

"You had better ask Emily to sweep out Mrs. Blair's room again tonight. The carpet needs sweeping; she should pay particular attention to the carpet."

Hearing the hall clock strike eleven, Hewson turned the lights out, quenched the astonished face of Parkins and went upstairs to bed.

Marching Through Delaware

BRUCE JAY FRIEDMAN

One night, driving from Washington to New York, Valurian, for the first time in his life, passed through the state of Delaware, and felt a sweet and weakening sensation in his stomach when he realized that Carla Wilson lived nearby. All he would have to do is sweep off one of the highway exits; at most she would be half an hour away. Twenty-two years before, at a college in the West, he had loved her for a month; then, in what appeared to be a young and thoughtless way, she had shut the door abruptly in his face. Much later, he became fond of saying it was a valuable thing to have happen and that he was grateful to her for providing him with that lovely ache of rejection. But in truth, and particularly at the time, it was no picnic. He remembered her now as being thin-lipped and modest of bosom, but having long, playful legs and an agonizingly sexual way of getting down on floors in a perfect Indian squat. She had no control over her laugh; it was musical, slightly embarrassed and seemed to operate on machinery entirely separate from her. She had an extraordinary Eastern finishing-school accent, although to his knowledge she had attended no Eastern finishing school. She was an actress; he reviewed her plays for the local newspaper. Members of the drama group, some of whom had been in Pittsburgh repertory, referred to him as the "village idiot."

Although she often did starring roles, the most he ever awarded her was a single line of faint praise. On one occasion, he said she handled the role of Desdemona "adequately." He was quietly insane about her; in his mind, the paltry mentions were a way of guarding against any nepotistic inclinations. It was a preposterous length to go to; she never complained or appeared to take notice of it.

Although he remembered quite sharply the night he got his walking papers, he had only disconnected, bedraggled recollections of time actually spent with her. She wore black ordinarily, had a marvelous dampness to her and trembled without control the first time they danced together. "Are you all right?" he kept asking. "Have you perhaps caught a chill?" There were some walks through town, one during which a truck backfired, causing Valurian to clutch at her arm as though it were a guardrail. "Oh, my God," she said, surprised, delighted and not at all to demean him, "I thought I was being protected." Her mother swooped down upon them one day, a great ship of a woman, catching Valurian in terrible clothes, needing a shave. In a restaurant, lit by ice-white fixtures, she spoke in an international accent and told them of her cattle investments and of killings at racetracks around the world; Valurian, still embarrassed about his shadowy face, prayed for the dinner to end. Later, he took them back to his rooming house and lit a fire; turning toward them, he saw that Carla had hopped into her mother's lap and gone to sleep in it like a little girl. He had never slept with her, although she gave him massive hints that it would be perfectly all right, indeed, highly preferred. "Oh, I'd love to be in a hotel somewhere," she would say as they danced. Or she would begin her trembling and say, rather hopelessly, "When I feel this way, whatever you do, don't take me out to some dark section of the woods." Ignoring the bait, he gave her aristocratic looks, as though he were an impeccable tennis star and she was insulting him by the inferior quality of her play. In truth, her dampness, the black skirts, the Indian squats, all were furnacelike and frightening to him. A boy named Harbinger had no such problems. She alerted him to Harbinger, saying she had run into the cutest fellow who lived in town and always hung his argyle socks out on the line where the girls could see them. It was as though she were giving him a last chance to get her into hotels or to sweep her out to cordoned-off sections of the woods. But he had always seen his affair with Carla—could he dignify it with that phrase?—as a losing battle, with perhaps a few brief successful forays before the final rout. One night, for example, he surprised her by batting out a few show tunes on the piano, singing along, too, through a megaphone, a talent he had kept up his sleeve. She almost tore his head off with her kisses, although, in retrospect, they were on the sisterly side. Toward the very end, he showed up on her dormitory steps with an alligator handbag, a Christmas gift she didn't quite know what to make of. Inevitably, she summoned him one day to talk over an ominous "little something"; polishing up his white buck shoes, he walked the length of the campus to her dormitory where she told him she had stayed out all night with the argyles boy and that she would not be seeing Valurian anymore. He called her a shithead and for weeks afterward regretted being so clumsy and uncharming. There began for him a period of splendid agony. The first night, he was unable to eat and told a German exchange student—who had suffered many a rejection of his own—that any time he couldn't get fried chicken down he was really in trouble. A week later, he strolled by to see Carla as though nothing had happened; she told him that Harbinger was more in the picture than ever. She started off to rehearsals and he tailed her; she broke into a run, and he jogged right after her, as though it were perfectly normal to have conversations at the trot. On another occasion, he lay in wait for her outside the theater, grabbed her roughly and said, "Off to the woods we go. I have something to show you, something I'd been unwilling to show you before."

"What's that?" she asked, teasing him.

"You'll see," he said. But she wrenched herself away, an indication that Harbinger had already shown her plenty. He stayed away then for several months, taking up with a green-eyed Irish girl who had great torpedoing breasts, thought all easterners were authentic gangsters and with no nonsense about it simply whisked him off to the woods. One night, before graduation, he went to a dance, feeling fine about being with the Irish girl, until Carla showed up with the argyles man. He continued to dance, but it was as though his entire back were frozen stiff. He saw her only one more time, paying her a good-bye visit and asking if he might have a picture. "No," she said. "I don't understand it," he said, "a lousy picture." But she held fast—and that was that.

He left school, went through the army as a second lieutenant in grain supply and then, for ten years or so, led a muted, unspectacular life, gathering in a living wage by doing many scattered fragments of jobs. He was fond of saying he "hit bottom" at age thirty, but, in truth, all that happened was that he developed asthma, got very frightened about it, saw a psychiatrist and, in the swiftest treatment on record, came upon a great springing trampoline of confidence that was to propel him, asthma and all, into seven years crowded with triumphs in the entertainment world—a part in a play that worked out well, a directing job that turned out even more attractively, films, more plays, television work and ultimately a great blizzard of activity that took a staff to keep track of.

From time to time, he had heard a little about her, not much—that she had gotten married quickly (not to the argyles man), had a child, gotten divorced. That she had settled in Delaware and never left. Although from time to time the thought of her flew into his mind, it was never a question of his wallowing in this particular memory. Valurian had little cause to feel slighted by love. Along with the chain of professional triumphs had come a series of romantic ones, a series of women, each attractive in her own way, ones that Carla no doubt had seen in films and read about in columns. He had as much confidence with women as he did with his work. He *owned* women. When he thought of Carla at all, it was never to wonder what she was up to, but to speculate on whether she read his reviews, the interviews with him, the column mentions. What indeed could she really have been up to all those years? In Delaware. Bridge? Scrabble? The Johnny Carson show? Getting a taste of the sweet life via the *Times* theater section? The marriage, no doubt, had been to an accountant. Or was it a stockbroker? Saturday nights, spell that nites, with three or four other young marrieds, Delaware young marrieds, young married Delaware swingers at Delaware's top nite spot. He could imagine those couples, too. The jokes. The talk about switching. And salves. Bedroom salves. They all used bedroom salves. She had been divorced. After that, she had probably tried to land another second-rater. She loved the theater; no doubt she'd go after a local theater notable this time, one who whipped together Chekhov plays and was terribly temperamental. Wore heavy Shetland sweaters. Get rid of the taste of that routine stockbrokering first marriage. What *really* could she have been doing with her time? Did she have any idea that Valurian had been to the White House? That, indeed, he was driving back from the White House now. And that it wasn't his first trip. He'd met De Gaulle. Did she know that he had slept with actresses whose names would make her gasp? That he *turned down* dinner invitations from Leonard Bernstein. Lennie Bernstein. How could he explain to her that the only sadness in his life was that the circle of important people he had yet to meet was an ever-shrinking one and soon to be nonexistent? Oh, she had read about him, all right. How could she have escaped knowing about him, following his career? Everyone knew about him. And when you consider her special interest in Valurian . . . she probably kept a scrapbook. Far from a preposterous notion. How many lonely, divorced nights had she spent kicking herself for not having spotted the seeds of it in him, his possibilities? How close she had come to an extraordinary life and never, at the time, realized it for a moment. What did that say about her judgment? She probably wondered about that every day of her life. Hadn't she loved the theater? He owned the theater. He *was* the theater. And whom had she passed him up for: An argyles man. Every time she thought of that little stunt, she probably chewed at her wrists in agony. And she had *summoned* him to give him the news. And then refused to give him a picture. *She,* get this, hadn't wanted to give *Andrew Valurian* a picture. It was almost too much for the mind to comprehend. It would take a computer to handle that one. Well, she was probably in a constant sweat about it, night after night in Delaware. In Delaware, mind you. How she must have punished herself all those years. And here he was, Valurian, coming back from the White House on his way to a party at Sardi's that was probably going to bore him to death. How many years of her life would she trade to show up at that party? On his arm. Two, five, a decade? To top it all off, he was only half an hour's drive away from her at most. God, if she knew that . . . If he ever drove by and called on her, stopped at her dreary, divorced Delaware house, at the very least she'd go right into shock. Faint dead away on the spot. More likely, she'd tear off her clothes and fly at his groin. Would she in a million years be able to find her voice? Never. So she would probably just kneel at his feet and pray and let it go at that. The poor lost miserable wretch.

Oh well, he thought, screw her, and drove off for the big city.

Lamb to the Slaughter

ROALD DAHL

The room was warm and clean, the curtains drawn, the two table lamps alight—hers and the one by the empty chair opposite. On the sideboard behind her, two tall glasses, soda water, whiskey. Fresh ice cubes in the Thermos bucket.

Mary Maloney was waiting for her husband to come home from work.

Now and again she would glance up at the clock, but without anxiety, merely to please herself with the thought that each minute gone by made it nearer the time when he would come. There was a slow smiling air about her, and about everything she did. The drop of the head as she bent over her sewing was curiously tranquil. Her skin—for this was her sixth month with child—had acquired a wonderful translucent quality, the mouth was soft, and the eyes, with their new placid look, seemed larger, darker than before.

When the clock said ten minutes to five, she began to listen, and a few moments later, punctually as always, she heard the tires on the gravel outside, and the car door slamming, the footsteps passing the window, the key turning in the lock. She laid aside her sewing, stood up, and went forward to kiss him as he came in.

"Hullo darling," she said.

"Hullo," he answered.

She took his coat and hung it in the closet. Then she walked over and made the drinks, a strongish one for him, a weak one for herself; and soon she was back again in her chair with the sewing, and he in the other, opposite, holding the tall glass with both his hands, rocking it so the ice cubes tinkled against the side.

For her, this was always a blissful time of day. She knew he didn't want to speak much until the first drink was finished, and she, on her side, was content to sit quietly, enjoying his company after the long hours alone in the house. She loved to luxuriate in the presence of this man, and to feel—almost as a sunbather feels the sun—that warm male glow that came out of him to her when they were alone together. She loved him for the way he sat loosely in a chair, for the way he came in a door, or moved slowly across the room with long strides. She loved the intent, far look in his eyes when they rested on her, the funny shape of the mouth, and especially the way he remained silent about his tiredness, sitting still with himself until the whiskey had taken some of it away.

"Tired, darling?"

"Yes," he said. "I'm tired." And as he spoke, he did an unusual thing. He lifted his glass and drained it in one swallow although there was still half of it, at least half of it left. She wasn't really watching him, but she knew what he had done because she heard the ice cubes falling back against the bottom of the empty glass when he lowered his arm. He paused a moment, leaning forward in the chair, then he got up and went slowly over to fetch himself another.

"I'll get it!" she cried, jumping up.

"Sit down," he said.

When he came back, she noticed that the new drink was dark amber with the quantity of whiskey in it.

"Darling, shall I get your slippers?"

"No."

She watched him as he began to sip the dark yellow drink, and she could see little oily swirls in the liquid because it was so strong.

"I think it's a shame," she said, "that when a policeman gets to be as senior as you, they keep him walking about on his feet all day long."

He didn't answer, so she bent her head again and went on with her sewing; but each time he lifted the drink to his lips, she heard the ice cubes clinking against the side of the glass.

"Darling," she said. "Would you like me to get you some cheese? I haven't made any supper because it's Thursday."

"No," he said.

"If you're too tired to eat out," she went on, "it's still not too late. There's plenty of meat and stuff in the freezer, and you can have it right here and not even move out of the chair."

Her eyes waited on him for an answer, a smile, a little nod, but he made no sign.

"Anyway," she went on, "I'll get you some cheese and crackers first."

"I don't want it," he said.

She moved uneasily in her chair, the large eyes still watching his face. "But you *must* have supper. I can easily do it here. I'd like to do it. We can have lamb chops. Or pork. Anything you want. Everything's in the freezer."

"Forget it," he said

"But darling, you *must* eat! I'll fix it anyway, and then you can have it or not, as you like."

She stood up and placed her sewing on the table by the lamp.

"Sit down," he said. "Just for a minute, sit down."

It wasn't till then that she began to get frightened.

"Go on," he said. "Sit down."

She lowered herself back slowly into the chair, watching him all the time with those large, bewildered eyes. He had finished the second drink and was staring down into the glass, frowning.

"Listen," he said. "I've got something to tell you."

"What is it, darling? What's the matter?"

He had now become absolutely motionless, and he kept his head down so that the light from the lamp beside him fell across the upper part of his face, leaving the chin and mouth in shadow. She noticed there was a little muscle moving near the corner of his left eye.

"This is going to be a bit of a shock to you, I'm afraid," he said. "But I've thought about it a good deal and I've decided the only thing to do is tell you right away. I hope you won't blame me too much."

And he told her. It didn't take long, four or five minutes at most, and she sat very still through it all, watching him with a kind of dazed horror as he went further and further away from her with each word.

"So there it is," he added. "And I know it's kind of a bad time to be telling you, but there simply wasn't any other way. Of course I'll give you money and see you're looked after. But there needn't really be any fuss. I hope not anyway. It wouldn't be very good for my job."

Her first instinct was not to believe any of it, to reject it all. It occurred to her that perhaps he hadn't even spoken, that she herself had imagined the whole thing. Maybe, if she went about her business and acted as though she hadn't been listening, then later, when she sort of woke up again, she might find none of it had ever happened.

"I'll get the supper," she managed to whisper, and this time he didn't stop her.

When she walked across the room she couldn't feel her feet touching the floor. She couldn't feel anything at all—except a slight nausea and a desire to vomit. Everything was automatic now—down the steps to the cellar, the light switch, the deep freeze, the hand inside the cabinet taking hold of the first object it met. She lifted it out, and looked at it. It was wrapped in paper, so she took off the paper and looked at it again.

A leg of lamb.

All right then, they would have lamb for supper. She carried it upstairs, holding the thin bone-end of it with both her hands, and as she went through the living room, she saw him standing over by the window with his back to her, and she stopped.

"For God's sake," he said, hearing her, but not turning round. "Don't make supper for me. I'm going out."

At that point, Mary Maloney simply walked up behind him and without any pause she swung the big frozen leg of lamb high in the air and brought it down as hard as she could on the back of his head.

She might just as well have hit him with a steel club.

She stepped back a pace, waiting, and the funny thing was that he remained standing there for at least four or five seconds, gently swaying. Then he crashed to the carpet.

The violence of the crash, the noise, the small table overturning, helped bring her out of the shock. She came out slowly, feeling cold and surprised, and she stood for a while blinking at the body, still holding the ridiculous piece of meat tight with both hands.

All right, she told herself. So I've killed him.

It was extraordinary, now, how clear her mind became all of a sudden. She began thinking very fast. As the wife of a detective, she knew quite well what the penalty would be. That was fine. It made no difference to her. In fact, it would be a relief. On the other hand, what about the child? What were the laws about murderers with unborn children? Did they kill them both—mother and child? Or did they wait until the tenth month? What did they do?

Mary Maloney didn't know. And she certainly wasn't prepared to take a chance.

She carried the meat into the kitchen, placed it in a pan, turned the oven on high, and shoved it inside. Then she washed her hands and ran upstairs to the bedroom. She sat down before the mirror, tidied her hair, touched up her lips and face. She tried a smile. It came out rather peculiar. She tried again.

"Hullo Sam," she said brightly, aloud.

The voice sounded peculiar too.

"I want some potatoes please, Sam. Yes, and I think a can of peas."

That was better. Both the smile and the voice were coming out better now. She rehearsed it several times more. Then she ran downstairs, took her coat, went out the back door, down the garden, into the street.

It wasn't six o'clock yet and the lights were still on in the grocery shop.

"Hullo Sam," she said brightly, smiling at the man behind the counter.

"Why, good evening, Mrs. Maloney. How're *you?*"

"I want some potatoes please, Sam. Yes, and I think a can of peas."

The man turned and reached up behind him on the shelf for the peas.

"Patrick's decided he's tired and doesn't want to eat out tonight," she told him. "We usually go out Thursdays, you know, and now he's caught me without any vegetables in the house."

"Then how about meat, Mrs. Maloney?"

"No, I've got meat, thanks. I got a nice leg of lamb from the freezer."

"Oh."

"I don't much like cooking it frozen, Sam, but I'm taking a chance on it this time. You think it'll be all right?"

"Personally," the grocer said, "I don't believe it makes any difference. You want these Idaho potatoes?"

"Oh yes, that'll be fine. Two of those."

"Anything else?" The grocer cocked his head on one side, looking at her pleasantly. "How about afterward? What you going to give him for afterward?"

"Well—what would you suggest, Sam?"

The man glanced around his shop. "How about a nice big slice of cheesecake? I know he likes that."

"Perfect," she said. "He loves it."

And when it was all wrapped and she had paid, she put on her brightest smile and said, "Thank you, Sam. Goodnight."

"Goodnight, Mrs. Maloney. And thank *you*."

And now, she told herself as she hurried back, all she was doing now, she was returning home to her husband and he was waiting for his supper; and she must cook it good, and make it as tasty as possible because the poor man was tired; and if, when she entered the house, she happened to find anything unusual, or tragic, or terrible, then naturally it would be a shock and she'd become frantic with grief and horror. Mind you, she wasn't *expecting* to find anything. She was just going home with the vegetables. Mrs. Patrick Maloney going home with the vegetables on Thursday evening to cook supper for her husband.

That's the way, she told herself. Do everything right and natural. Keep things absolutely natural and there'll be no need for any acting at all.

Therefore, when she entered the kitchen by the back door, she was humming a little tune to herself and smiling.

"Patrick!" she called. "How are you, darling?"

She put the parcel down on the table and went through into the living room; and when she saw him lying there on the floor with his legs doubled up and one arm twisted back underneath his body, it really was rather a shock. All the old love and longing for him welled up inside her, and she ran over to him, knelt down beside him, and began to cry her heart out. It was easy. No acting was necessary.

A few minutes later she got up and went to the phone. She knew the number of the police station, and when the man at the other end answered, she cried to him, "Quick! Come quick! Patrick's dead!"

"Who's speaking?"

"Mrs. Maloney. Mrs. Patrick Maloney."

"You mean Patrick Maloney's dead?"

"I think so," she sobbed. "He's lying on the floor and I think he's dead."

"Be right over," the man said.

The car came very quickly, and when she opened the front door, two policemen walked in. She knew them both—she knew nearly all the men at that precinct—and she fell right into Jack Noonan's arms, weeping hysterically. He put her gently into a chair, then went over to join the other one, who was called O'Malley, kneeling by the body.

"Is he dead?" she cried.

"I'm afraid he is. What happened?"

Briefly, she told her story about going out to the grocer and coming back to find him on the floor. While she was talking, crying and talking, Noonan discovered a small patch of congealed blood on the dead man's head. He showed it to O'Malley, who got up at once and hurried to the phone.

Soon, other men began to come into the house. First a doctor, then two detectives, one of whom she knew by name. Later, a police photographer arrived and took pictures, and a man who knew about fingerprints. There was a great deal of whispering and muttering beside the corpse, and the detectives kept asking her a lot of questions. But they always treated her kindly. She told her story again, this time right from the beginning, when Patrick had come in, and she was sewing, and he was tired, so tired he hadn't wanted to go out for supper. She told how she'd put the meat in the oven—"it's there now, cooking"—and how she'd slipped out to the grocer for vegetables, and come back to find him lying on the floor.

"Which grocer?" one of the detectives asked.

She told him, and he turned and whispered something to the other detective, who immediately went outside into the street.

In fifteen minutes he was back with a page of notes, and there was more whispering, and through her sobbing she heard a few of the whispered phrases—". . . acted quite normal . . . very cheerful . . . wanted to give him a good supper . . . peas . . . cheesecake . . . impossible that she . . ."

After a while, the photographer and the doctor departed and two other men came in and took the corpse away on a stretcher. Then the fingerprint man went away. The two detectives remained, and so did the two policemen. They were exceptionally nice to her, and Jack Noonan asked if she wouldn't rather go somewhere else, to her sister's house perhaps, or to his own wife who would take care of her and put her up for the night.

No, she said. She didn't feel she could move even a yard at the moment. Would they mind awfully if she stayed just where she was until she felt better. She didn't feel too good at the moment, she really didn't.

Then hadn't she better lie down on the bed? Jack Noonan asked.

No, she said. She'd like to stay right where she was, in this chair. A little later perhaps, when she felt better, she would move.

So they left her there while they went about their business, searching the house. Occasionally one of the detectives asked her another question. Sometimes Jack Noonan spoke at her gently as he passed by. Her husband, he told her, had been killed by a blow on the back of the head administered with a heavy blunt instrument, almost certainly a large piece of metal. They were looking for the weapon. The murderer may have taken it with him, but on the other hand he may've thrown it away or hidden it somewhere on the premises.

"It's the old story," he said. "Get the weapon, and you've got the man."

Later, one of the detectives came up and sat beside her. Did she know, he asked, of anything in the house that could've been used as the weapon? Would she mind having a look around to see if anything was missing—a very big spanner, for example, or a heavy metal vase.

They didn't have any heavy metal vases, she said.

"Or a big spanner?"

She didn't think they had a big spanner. But there might be some things like that in the garage.

The search went on. She knew that there were other policemen in the garden all around the house. She could hear their footsteps on the gravel outside, and sometimes she saw the flash of a torch through a chink in the curtains. It began to get late, nearly nine she noticed by the clock on the mantel. The four men searching the rooms seemed to be growing weary, a trifle exasperated.

"Jack," she said, the next time Sergeant Noonan went by. "Would you mind giving me a drink?"

"Sure I'll give you a drink. You mean this whiskey?"

"Yes please. But just a small one. It might make me feel better."

He handed her the glass.

"Why don't you have one yourself," she said. "You must be awfully tired. Please do. You've been very good to me."

"Well," he answered. "It's not strictly allowed, but I might take just a drop to keep me going."

One by one the others came in and were persuaded to take a little nip of whiskey. They stood around rather awkwardly with the drinks in their hands, uncomfortable in her presence, trying to say consoling things to her. Sergeant Noonan wandered into the kitchen, came out quickly and said, "Look, Mrs. Maloney. You know that oven of yours is still on, and the meat still inside."

"Oh *dear* me!" she cried. "So it is!"

"I better turn it off for you, hadn't I?"

"Will you do that, Jack? Thank you so much."

When the sergeant returned the second time, she looked at him with her large, dark, tearful eyes. "Jack Noonan," she said.

"Yes?"

"Would you do me a small favor—you and these others?"

"We can try, Mrs. Maloney."

"Well," she said. "Here you all are, and good friends of dear Patrick's too, and helping to catch the man who killed him. You must be terribly hungry by now because it's long past your suppertime, and I know Patrick would never forgive me, God bless his soul, if I allowed you to remain in his house without offering you decent hospitality. Why don't you eat up that lamb that's in the oven. It'll be cooked just right by now."

"Wouldn't dream of it," Sergeant Noonan said.

"Please," she begged. "Please eat it. Personally I couldn't touch a thing, certainly not what's been in the house when he was here. But it's all right for you. It'd be a favor to me if you'd eat it up. Then you can go on with your work again afterward."

There was a good deal of hesitating among the four policemen, but they were clearly hungry, and in the end they were persuaded to go into the kitchen and help themselves. The woman stayed where she was, listening to them through the open door, and she could hear them speaking among themselves, their voices thick and sloppy because their mouths were full of meat.

"Have some more, Charlie?"

"No. Better not finish it."

"She *wants* us to finish it. She said so. Be doing her a favor."

"Okay then. Give me some more."

"That's a hell of a big club the guy must've used to hit poor Patrick," one of them was saying. "The doc says his skull was smashed all to pieces just like from a sledgehammer."

"That's why it ought to be easy to find."

"Exactly what I say."

"Whoever done it, they're not going to be carrying a thing like that around with them longer than they need."

One of them belched.

"Personally, I think it's right here on the premises."

"Probably right under our very noses. What you think, Jack?"

And in the other room, Mary Maloney began to giggle.

The Camping Ground

DALLAS ANGGUISH

The Longland twins used to do everything together—including me. They were lanky blonds with blue eyes and perfect tans developed over hours of creek swimming. They were healthy lads with large appetites, evidenced by the endless bounty of their lunch boxes. Their appetite for sexual fun and games was equally awe-inspiring.

By the summer of 1983, I had been their regular sexual experiment for some twelve months. We were all fifteen. That year the annual school bonding activity, a time-honored tradition in our all-boys' school, was to take the form of a weekend camp. In this instance camping appealed to us more than it usually would, because it offered the opportunity to be close to each other day in and day out.

It was with visions of a romantic lakeside getaway that I endured the hellish hour-and-a-half drive from school to the camp. The driver, Brother Mac, was notorious both for a mean hand at the strap and homicidal driving tendencies.

We arrived at Camp Robertson shaken but invigorated. The Longland twins, like small children, always happy to be frightened, whooped in scary unison, "Now the real fun begins!" They always did have a talent for understatement.

The other boys found them strange, but I found them interesting, and attractive. The thing is, if they weren't identical twins, and they didn't behave like clairvoyant clones, they would have been perfectly acceptable to the others. They were good looking, athletic, masculine, not sissy in any way. And taken on their own they seemed just like all regular boys—a little hyperactive but normal. But put them together and you got spooky, you got weird, and no one really likes spooky and weird, except for me, but I didn't have much choice. I was considered spooky myself, or more to the point, poofy.

Being outcasts, it was only right—or so the teachers thought—that the Longland twins and I be placed in the same hut. We didn't object to this particular management decision. Unfortunately the hut we were assigned slept eight persons and the teachers had decided to put every last one of the school's misfits in the same hut. And purely by coincidence I'm sure, the hut was the furthest from the rest of the camp. We were the leper colony, put far enough away so as not to infect the others, but not so far away that we couldn't be monitored and prevented from having fun.

Our little colony included the following: Chris Bird, who apart from being a seething pot of hormones, had been in the same grade for three years; Thic Phat and Nhat Phat, two Vietnamese Buddhist refugees whose poor English and heathen faith, not to mention their names, gave them little chance of acceptance at all; Julian Day, a red-haired and freckled sissy boy with a sense of humor so well developed that everyone found him funny. Then there were the Longland twins, handsome in a duplicate way, and sort of disconcertingly sexual; and last, but by no means least, myself—captain of the sissy squad. I was a stringy boy, not too ugly, not too much of a weakling but enough of a meekling, enough of a queer, to be well and truly disapproved of. Altogether we were seven, leaving one spare bed which I assumed would remain so. It turned out I was wrong about that, delightfully wrong.

As we unpacked I heard Brother Mac's distinctive Irish voice from outside the hut saying, "I'm really sorry about this, son, but it's the only available bed. If only your parents hadn't got you here so late."

This apology said a lot. It said that whoever was being brought to fill the empty bed was not of the same caliber as the rest of us; it said that as far as Brother Mac was concerned this boy didn't deserve to be thrown in with us. My curiosity peaked. I stopped unpacking and watched to see which teen god was to be lodged with the lepers.

What happened next unfolded in slow motion. Striding into the hut with a surety that said, I own even this place, this humpy of hopelessness, was Antonio Libera, the A-list boy of A-list boys, captain of the swimming team, vice-captain of the football team, and class captain. He moved like a projection on a screen, slow as grass growing, and with a grace, a fluidity, that made it look like he was rolling on castors.

Antonio Libera was Italian in all the best ways—olive in complexion, espresso brown eyes and muscular. All real sissies swooned when he walked by, as the cloud of teen sweat and Old Spice that followed him everywhere enveloped us and spoke of the cruel perfection of his Italian genes. To make matters worse Antonio Libera was a nice guy, never condescending or rude. He didn't speak to us because he had no need to, not because he thought we were unworthy of his company. He had nothing in common with us. He was sporty—we spent most of our time cowering in the library; he had a plethora of friends—we only had each other. In essence, he lived in a world so far removed from ours—from mine—that we didn't even speak the same language, couldn't possibly communicate.

The hut went silent when he entered, and he, used to this kind of obeisance, didn't notice a thing. With the kind of nonchalant lightheartedness for which he was famous, he said, "Hey fellas, good day for it!"

Good day for what? I asked myself. For having my heart squeezed mercilessly by fate? For having the object of my, quite considerable, obsession walk within range of touch?

I bit my tongue and it bled as he said to me, "I suppose I'll be bunking next to you." I knew then that, though I didn't believe in God, some higher power had my happiness in mind.

The Longland twins, though mostly thinking of themselves, also had me in mind. That night, after a savagely disappointing meal in the canteen, we were all shuffled off to bed in preparation for the big day to follow—an excursion to the top of a hill, and an afternoon of canoeing.

I have always been fussy about cleaning my teeth, but for once in my life I wished I had ignored my personal hygiene and gone straight to bed because while I was off in the shower block cleaning my teeth, Antonio had changed into his pajamas—damn, damn, damn, to have seen that!—and gotten into bed. I determined not to clean my teeth for the duration of the camp. When I returned, most of the boys were already in bed, except for Julian who was flirting outrageously with Chris. The Phats, sitting up in their beds as if waiting for permission to go to sleep, were watching Julian's display with Buddhist detachment.

Antonio lay in his bed, in blue striped pajamas, which were exactly the right color for his skin, looking peacefully at the ceiling. His bed was between mine and the wall and when I wanted to change I became acutely aware that there was nothing to shield me if he accidentally looked my way. I hesitated, but feeling conspicuous just standing there, turned my back to him and proceeded to quickly change.

Perhaps too quickly. I found myself tangled in my pajamas and when I'd finally got into them, realized that I'd completely misbuttoned the shirt. I turned to slip into bed before anyone noticed my mistake and as I did so saw Antonio turn his eyes away.

Had he been looking at me? Or had he simply glanced in my direction as I turned around, or, worst of all these possibilities, had he been looking at me because of my clumsy inability to dress myself? My mind went wild with thoughts along these lines and was still doing so well after the lights went out.

I had come to no conclusion when, at a time in the night when the only sounds were teenage boys sleeping, I felt someone lift my covers and slide in beside me, warm as a water bottle. It was so dark I couldn't quite make out who it was. Before I knew it, his hands were under my shirt.

I thought it was Antonio, or rather hoped it was him, and as the dark face nuzzled into my neck I felt sure of it. Wanting confirmation of my hopes I asked, "Is that you?"

"Yes it's me," one said, as the other one slid in as well and echoed, "And me too." The Longland twins, of course, how could I have thought, even for a moment, that Antonio, my Apollo, could have ever lowered himself to crawl into bed with me, with a nothing.

I lay there and let them do what they wanted. When they were finished they slipped out of my bed and I turned over on my stomach, buried my head in the pillow and cried myself to sleep.

Breakfast was horror, after which we were assembled for our walk up the hill, which was also hell. My mother omitted to pack sneakers, packing a pair of loafers instead. This annoyed all and sundry—loafers just weren't kosher, and although I was quite adept at the art of nonconformity, my feet conformed to the general rule that hiking in loafers is painful and exhausting. The only person who didn't seem annoyed by my loafers was Antonio himself who, dropping back for a moment to chat to one of the teachers, flashed that light smile of his and said ever so casually as he passed by, "You need to be lighter in your loafers."

I nearly fell on my face. Was he flirting with me? Or was he being derisive? All of a sudden marching up that hill in those ridiculous loafers didn't seem quite so terrible, because when I reached the top Antonio would be there, glowing with perspiration, maybe with his shirt off, and I could go up to him, return that familiar smile and there would be no looking back, for either of us.

Things never work out as planned. The Longland boys bushwhacked me before I reached the summit. Before I knew it they'd dragged me into the shrubbery and we were involved in some strange act, the configuration of which I could hardly work out myself. By the time the twins were finished the rest of the class were coming back down the hill. As I pulled on my clothes, I saw Antonio, with three or four other A-listers in tow, hurtling down the hillside at an unbelievable speed. My loafers weren't built for those kinds of speeds; I knew I could never catch up. I decided then that I would hate my mother forever onwards.

Lunch was hell as well. The regular boys decided to initiate a food fight, designating Julian Day as target. I would have been targeted also if I hadn't been skulking at the back of the canteen well out of view, nursing a freshly rebroken heart.

The food fight quickly got out of hand and soon dozens of boys had joined in. They launched everything they could at Julian—even plastic cups and utensils—and before long he was cowering, mortally humiliated, on the filthy canteen floor.

I was not surprised by this act of brutality—regular boys are defined by them, it is proof of their regularity—but I was surprised to see that Antonio did not participate. He cheered at first but then, when it became clear that it wasn't a good humored food fight but a malicious assault, he turned his back on it and quietly ate his lunch. I could see Antonio's face from where I was hiding; he was using all of his mental capacities to block out the fracas going on around him. I looked straight into his eyes. He saw me and looked straight into mine and in that moment a kind of empathy passed between us. Revelation! Antonio Libera, though perhaps not one of us, was not one of them. Our eyes had met, we had communicated, and I saw this as a brilliant opportunity—a doorway to friendship and, if I had my way, to a multitude of other things.

But first there was an afternoon of canoeing, and confronting my intense fear of water, and what lay under it. The Longlands quickly donned their life-jackets and boarded their canoe, shoving off with a perfunctory wave in my direction, too excited by the prospect of an afternoon on the water to take my fears into consideration. I then realized something: the canoes were built for two and I was the only one left. I wouldn't have to go out on the water after all!

This thought had just formed when Antonio waved me over. "It looks like it's me and you," he said. "We're in the same boat."

What an ironic choice of words, I thought, as he picked up my life-jacket and held it up for me, offering to help me put it on. I slipped in my arms and he buckled it up, pulling so tightly on the straps that my breath was forced out with each tug.

Antonio took charge, shoving off with a resonant grunt, taking up the paddle to propel us swiftly, and terrifyingly, far from the shore. He directed the canoe into a small cove lined on either side by tall gum trees, where he stopped paddling and let the canoe drift. An uneasy silence descended in which he stared at the water as we drifted along and I, not knowing what to think or do, stared at his beautiful form.

Soon the canoe came to a stop, bobbing gently up and down in the middle of the cove. I felt that I had to say something; too long a time had passed in which we'd said nothing. Soon he would begin to think that I was dumb, mute, and unworthy of his attention.

"This is a lovely spot," I said, knowing as soon as I said it that it would have been better if I hadn't said anything at all. He looked at me and smiled an uncomfortable smile. He didn't answer but rather put his hands in the water and scooped up a handful and wet his face and hair, shaking off the loose droplets like some animal might, showering me with cold spray. He ran his fingers through his hair, pushing the wet strands away from his face.

"It's hot isn't it," he said. And I said, "Yes"—just yes—in a small frightened voice. All was quiet again.

He looked at me. I looked at his feet, brown and perfect like the rest of him. I had to say something so I said that the trees by the shore were gorgeous.

He smiled, less uncomfortably. "You use a lot of words most guys wouldn't," he said.

I felt sick. It was true, only homosexuals use adjectives. I chose not to speak again; the condemned should not push their luck. A moment passed in which I waited for him to cast me overboard. He didn't. He sat there, looking at me with either confusion or amusement. And then he said, "Is it true what they say about you?"

I wanted to run but couldn't. At least four metres of murky water lay between me and land. I contemplated beating myself to death with the paddles but, thinking this too Marquis de Sade even for me, decided against it. I pondered strangling myself with the straps of my life jacket, the straps Antonio bound me up with, like roast meat. I decided to simply die of shame, the longer route to annihilation, but nevertheless effective.

He waited for an answer and I, feeling defeated, asked, "Whatever do you mean?"

"Well," he began hesitantly, "everyone says that you're a poof."

"Surely not everyone," I said.

"Yes, everyone," he jibed, and I sat there like a stuffed goose, silenced.

"Well, I wouldn't put it past you," he offered, a smile sneaking across his chiseled face.

I didn't understand. I said, "What do you mean?" and he said it again, "I wouldn't put it past you."

I still didn't know exactly what he meant; what couldn't he pass by me? Did he mean that his body was like smelling salts to me, awakening my full queer potential when passed under my nose? I decided this was what he meant, and felt that he was probably right.

"No, you probably shouldn't put it past me," I whispered.

"I beg your pardon," he asked.

"Nothing," I said.

He picked up the paddle and set to work, taking us out of the cove and into the larger body of the lake. We paddled around for a while, Antonio displaying his physical prowess as I displayed my prowess at reclining elegantly in the sun.

Way too soon we heard Brother Mac blowing his whistle, calling us back. Antonio made sounds of disappointment but being who he was, ever obedient, promptly turned the canoe to shore and took us in. As I climbed out of the canoe, more love sick than sea sick, I listened with disinterest as Brother Mac told us we were now to attend a trust-forming workshop, after which we would eat dinner and then retire.

I had no need of a trust-forming workshop. I trusted Antonio wholly. I watched as he threw off his life jacket, and headed back to the camping ground.

During the trust-forming workshop we were divided into teams. Due to the shortage of teachers, our team—the lepers—was forced to undertake all the trust-forming games without guidance. What do sissies need trust for anyhow? (Or so the teachers must have thought.)

Having no clear idea what we were supposed to be doing, my team meandered back towards our hut. The Longland boys came up behind me as I walked by the toilet block, deftly steering me inside and into a shower cubicle.

It was quite stunning how proficient at undressing a person the twins were. They seemed to operate with a single will, psychically coordinating the task, knowing without verbal communication who was to undo which button, who was to tackle the zipper as the other maneuvered arms out of sleeves, or undid a buckle. They had my shirt off, my fly undone, and their lips all over my bare chest before I could muster the strength to tell them to stop.

These adventures with the Longlands were mostly enjoyable but I couldn't continue, given Antonio, given my certainty that he and I were soul mates, or at the very minimum destined to spend at least one moment in each other's arms.

The twins were surprised when I finally managed to voice a less than forceful "No," which I followed with a slightly firmer, "I don't want to."

"What's the matter?" said one. "Why don't you want to?" asked the other.

"I just don't want to anymore," I said.

"Anymore?" they asked in spooky unison. I told them that there were to be no more little adventures between us. They looked annoyed, pissed off that I should deny them what they felt was their right.

"My body is my own!" I said feebly, mimicking my feminist Aunty Leeta whose big leg hairs acted as proof that her body was indeed her own, and pointing out that despite what they thought I was not a possession but an individual with a right and a need to determine my own destiny. They snarled and levelled me with hateful eyes, before walking out, leaving me alone with the drip, drip, drip of the taps echoing against the concrete walls.

I stood there for the longest time, listening to that drip, drip, drip, feeling guilty for dumping the twins, trying to reassure myself that I did the right thing. For some reason the phrase, "A bird in the hand is better than two in the bush" ran through my mind. I'd had two birds in the hand and I discarded them for one in the bush, if indeed Antonio was a bird at all, if you get my meaning. Antonio may be utterly and awfully straight, though some part of me tried to believe that he wasn't. I had no proof that he liked boys at all, even less evidence that he liked me in particular.

I was still pondering these things when I heard someone enter. I looked through the crack of the shower door to see a flash of bare back, deep brown in color. I knew immediately who it was, it was Antonio. I hid in the back of the cubicle, not wanting him to think I was lurking in the toilets like some pervert. I peeked through the crack of the door again to see him washing his face, and splashing water over his chest.

I decided to escape while he was preoccupied, quietly opening the door and sneaking towards the entrance. Just at that moment I heard the taps go off.

I quickly spun around, to pretend I was just entering, and came face to face with him.

"Hey," he said.

"Hey," I replied, my eyes involuntarily wandering down his body. He asked me how I'd liked the workshop. I said I didn't and he said, "Yeah, we just ended up playing footy."

My eyes searched out his belly button. I am much in awe of a good belly button, and found Antonio's to be small and perfectly round, a fleshy whirlpool threatening to suck me in and consume me. My eyes froze on it, refused to move.

"What are you looking at?" he asked nervously, a kind of accusation, feeling perhaps that I had violated him somehow.

"I'm acquainting myself with your crushing perfection," I said, before I had time to rethink it. He looked down at the floor, then back up into my eyes.

"I don't know what you mean," he said quietly, "but I think I'm glad I don't." There was a hint of fear in his voice which I found both surprising and empowering. He walked past me, his shoulder gently grazing mine as he went by. I was left with the drip, drip, drip thinking, Now you've done it, now he knows for sure you're a pansy!

But then again, wasn't that the point?

* * *

I didn't see him again until dinner. He was sitting with the usual cast of crims. This time I chose not to hide at the back of the canteen and took a seat in his direct line of sight. I felt sure that he hadn't told anyone of our run-in in the amenities building, and that he wouldn't. The more I analysed that sound of fear in his voice, the more I interpreted it as a fear of his own desire, a fear of crossing over from regularity to irregularity.

Let's face it, he had a lot to lose: he was the popular boy of the school. If it were discovered that he wasn't exactly what he pretended to be, his fall would be great. There's nothing so loathed as a traitor. Being a fag is one thing, turning fag is altogether worse. I felt a small pang of guilt for so desperately wanting Antonio to take that dive. I ate my dinner with a conspicuous contentment; I wanted him to know that I didn't regret what I'd said, and that I had no fear of repercussion. On the inside I was filled with fear—that he might hate me forever; that he might get a posse together and lynch me outside the toilet block, "Cause that's what fags deserve," they would say to the police, who would nod in agreement.

After dinner, Brother Mac commissioned me and the Phats to clean up the canteen. It must have taken us at least an hour. When we finished we went back to the hut, only to find the lights out and everyone quiet. The Phats deftly found their beds and went to sleep. I stumbled about in the dark, finding my bed more by accident than skill. I couldn't see, but Antonio seemed to be asleep, or at least not moving. Damn, I thought, foiled again.

As I fluffed my pillow I looked once more over to Antonio's bed. He was sitting up. He seemed to be looking in my direction. I stopped still. He continued to sit there, and as my eyes adjusted to the dark I could make out that he was looking straight at me. I felt a surge of confidence: he was interested in me, but this confidence was quickly undermined by the thought that perhaps he was about to accost me for having so repeatedly affronted his straightness.

I gathered the courage to ask him how long he'd been watching me.

"Since you came in," he said. I asked why and he said nothing. I settled back on my pillow, not knowing what else to do. I could hear him breathing, hear small movements of his body. I looked over at him, willing him to speak, willing him to say what I wanted to hear, "I've been watching you because I love you."

He didn't say that. He said, "Why were you looking at me earlier, in the toilets?"

I sat stunned for a second, then gathered courage and said that I was looking at him because I was acquainting myself with his crushing perfection. He took that in, along with a deep breath. I was now able to make out his shape in the dark. He was shirtless, and the moonlight slid over his body like quicksilver. I could see a look of consternation on his face. He went to say something else but stopped himself. I wanted to know what was going to happen; I thought that I would die from waiting, die from wanting. I closed my eyes, a reflex action to somehow close out some of the hope and dread.

When I reopened them he was standing over my bed, his firm sculptured torso casting a deep shadow over me, plunging me into scintillating blackness.

"Can I get in?" he asked.

"Yes," I said, thinking Yes! Yes! Yes! Yes! Yes!

He climbed in beside me, his body occupying the bed like an invading army, forcing me to diminish myself so that he would fit, forcing me to adhere to his body, echoing its every curve, like cling wrap. His chest pushed against mine, causing me to inhale when he did, exhale when he did. He was warm, nearly hot, and I felt his heat spread to the bedclothes and to my skin and deep inside me, to my organs, warming my bones. Our faces were centimeters apart, he looked deeply into my eyes. I wanted to tell him how much I had wanted this, how long I had dreamt it, how much scheming and plotting had been necessary to get to that moment, how many little heart failures I'd endured when I thought it might never happen.

Instead, I asked if he had enough room. "Yes," he said, "plenty." I seized the day, kissed him on his heavy lips, drew out his tongue and massaged it with my own, running my hands over his chest, paying homage to his nipples, moving downward to explore with trembling fingers the shallow cave of his belly button. He kissed me hard, mimicking with his hands what I did with mine, turning to bite my neck as I reached into his pants, moving his hips to welcome my grip, groaning loudly into my ear.

It was then I heard him say it—"No . . . stop . . . " He took my hand from his pants and placed it on his chest instead. I asked what was wrong, thinking that perhaps he had second thoughts, perhaps he felt he'd made a mistake.

"Nothing's wrong," he said, "I don't want to do it here . . . I make too much noise when I come."

"Is that all? We can be quiet," I whispered, and told him if he couldn't I would gag him with my hand.

He said, "No . . . I want to do it when we're alone."

He kissed me again, hard and this time very long. Then he said, "Can we stay here together for a while, just hugging and stuff?" I whispered yes, whispered it into his mouth as we kissed again.

We stayed that way until dawn, drifting in and out of sleep, and then he got out of my bed and into his own, a glorious figure in the dawn twilight, brown and solid and disheveled. We lay on our sides watching each other as our room mates began to stir from their sleep.

Nothing mattered anymore. All that I thought about was the smell of him, the taste of him, the hardness and strength and vulnerability of his body. So it didn't matter that breakfast was bland and beige, that the regulars controlled the world. It didn't matter that I was an outcast, a leper, thrown into the company of other outcasts I despised. It didn't matter that the Longland boys hated me and sent venomous glances in my direction as often as they took breath. It didn't matter that in the light of day Antonio sat at table with the baboons, with the average and forgettable ones, because in the end it was all a charade and he would be with me when it mattered, in our quiet moments. I didn't bother to finish my breakfast, I felt sustained by my love of Antonio. I headed off to the showers while the other boys finished eating, wanting to make myself pristine for my next encounter with my Italian god.

I undressed and got under the shower with thoughts of Antonio dominating my mind. I was wondering when we could be alone. The camp would end that afternoon, but there would be plenty of opportunities in the future. Perhaps I could invite him to stay over the holidays, or maybe he would invite me to stay with him. I soaped myself up and lathered my hair. I closed my eyes and pictured him as I massaged my scalp but before I'd finished, I heard the distinct sounds of bare footsteps. I realized I'd not latched the door. Before I could open my eyes, a hand covered them. Whoever it was held me firmly from behind. I thought it was Antonio and did not resist when his hands slid down to my genitals. He worked me over for a while, still covering my eyes with his free hand. Before I could come he let go. I quickly rinsed the suds from my hair and turned to ask why he'd stopped.

It was the Longlands, both naked and clearly excited. "We thought you'd change your mind," they said in unison. I told them to fuck off. I went to get dressed and as I reached for my towel I heard someone else enter. The Longlands and I didn't have time to scatter or cover ourselves before the person who entered saw all three of us standing together, naked and with erections. It was Antonio Libera! He turned and walked out immediately, without a word. I hastily got dressed and ran after him.

I caught up with him by the lake. He was sitting on the sand staring at the tiny waves on the water's surface. He looked both very angry and very sad. He got up and walked away when I tried to sit down beside him. I followed him, my loafers filling with sand and slowing me down.

"Wait," I yelled.

"Why?" he answered. "You already got off today, you don't need me."

I caught up with him and grabbed his arm. He swung around and said, "Don't touch me, faggot!" with an anger in his voice that stopped me still. No one had ever spoken to me with such violence, not in all the years of boys' school, and it frightened me, terrified me.

He walked away, I dared not follow him, and when he had nearly gone out of sight he turned and shouted back, "Don't ever touch me again! Faggot!" And with those words he discarded me. My soul died in that moment, my body and mind remaining only as zombies, half dead things with no reason or purpose.

I looked out onto the waters of the lake, hoping to cast myself out to be chewed up and swallowed deep down, to be digested by burning fluids, fishy acids, until there was nothing left of me at all to feel the pain of being dumped by my only true love.

I wandered back toward the camping ground, certain that I would never know joy again. I staggered into the hut, a mindless thing with no sense of what it might do. The Longlands were there, packing their things in preparation for the afternoon's journey back to town. They had not dressed since their shower and were wearing pristine white towels about their waists. I should have hated them but I was too weak to hate, too weak for anything but desperate longing. I sat on my bed in despair. They did not acknowledge me.

In my sadness I found myself looking at their bodies. Memories of what it was like to be with them assailed me. I experienced a kind of home sickness for their shape, their smell, the feel of them.

I shook it off. I was disgusted with myself: no more than five minutes since my soul mate dumped me and I was already turning elsewhere for satisfaction. I felt crazy, out of control, insane.

But that's what happens when you get dumped isn't it? You search for reassurance or affirmation anywhere you can, no matter how debasing, no matter how opposite it might be to what you'd want if you were in your right mind.

And it's not true what they say, that time heals all wounds. The wounds just add up, until our hearts are like voodoo objects, littered with pins and punctures. I didn't know that then but even if I had I wouldn't have done anything differently. I wouldn't be who I am if I had.

Fever

RAYMOND CARVER

Carlyle was in a spot. He'd been in a spot all summer, since early June when his wife had left him. But up until a little while ago, just a few days before he had to start meeting his classes at the high school, Carlyle hadn't needed a sitter. He'd been the sitter. Every day and every night he'd attended to the children. Their mother, he told them, was away on a long trip.

Debbie, the first sitter he contacted, was a fat girl, nineteen years old, who told Carlyle she came from a big family. Kids loved her, she said. She offered a couple of names for reference. She penciled them on a piece of notebook paper. Carlyle took the names, folded the piece of paper, and put it in his shirt pocket. He told her he had meetings the next day. He said she could start to work for him the next morning. She said, "Okay."

He understood that his life was entering a new period. Eileen had left while Carlyle was still filling out his grade reports. She'd said she was going to Southern California to begin a new life for herself there. She'd gone with Richard Hoopes, one of Carlyle's colleagues at the high school. Hoopes was a drama teacher and glass-blowing instructor who'd apparently turned his grades in on time, taken his things, and left town in a hurry with Eileen. Now, the long and painful summer nearly behind him, and his classes about to resume, Carlyle had finally turned his attention to this matter of finding a baby-sitter. His first efforts had not been successful. In his desperation to find someone—anyone—he'd taken Debbie on.

In the beginning, he was grateful to have this girl turn up in response to his call. He'd yielded up the house and children to her as if she were a relative. So he had no one to blame but himself, his own carelessness, he was convinced, when he came home early from school one day that first week and pulled into the drive next to a car that had a big pair of flannel dice hanging from the rearview mirror. To his astonishment, he saw his children in the front yard, their clothes filthy, playing with a dog big enough to bite off their hands. His son, Keith, had the hiccups and had been crying. Sarah, his daughter, began to cry when she saw him get out of the car. They were sitting on the grass, and the dog was licking their hands and faces. The dog growled at him and then moved off a little as Carlyle made for his children. He picked up Keith and then he picked up Sarah. One child under each arm, he made for his front door. Inside the house, the phonograph was turned up so high the front windows vibrated.

In the living room, three teenaged boys jumped to their feet from where they'd been sitting around the coffee table. Beer bottles stood on the table and cigarettes burned in the ashtray. Rod Stewart screamed from the stereo. On the sofa, Debbie, the fat girl, sat with another teenaged boy. She stared at Carlyle with dumb disbelief as he entered the living room. The fat girl's blouse was unbuttoned. She had her legs drawn under her, and she was smoking a cigarette. The living room was filled with smoke and music. The fat girl and her friend got off the sofa in a hurry.

"Mr. Carlyle, wait a minute," Debbie said. "I can explain."

"Don't explain," Carlyle said. "Get the hell out of here. All of you. Before I throw you out." He tightened his grip on the children.

"You owe me for four days," the fat girl said, as she tried to button her blouse. She still had the cigarette between her fingers. Ashes fell from the cigarette as she tried to button up. "Forget today. You don't owe me for today. Mr. Carlyle, it's not what it looks like. They dropped by to listen to this record."

"I understand, Debbie," he said. He let the children down onto the carpet. But they stayed close to his legs and watched the people in the living room. Debbie looked at them and shook her head slowly, as if she'd never laid eyes on them before. "Goddamnit, get out!" Carlyle said. "Now. Get going. All of you."

He went over and opened the front door. The boys acted as if they were in no real hurry. They picked up their beer and started slowly for the door. The Rod Stewart record was still playing. One of them said, "That's my record."

"Get it," Carlyle said. He took a step toward the boy and then stopped.

"Don't touch me, okay? Just don't touch me," the boy said. He went over to the phonograph, picked up the arm, swung it back, and took his record off while the turntable was still spinning.

Carlyle's hands were shaking. "If that car's not out of the drive in one minute—one minute—I'm calling the police." He felt sick and dizzy with his anger. He saw, really saw, spots dance in front of his eyes.

"Hey, listen, we're on our way, all right? We're going," the boy said.

They filed out of the house. Outside, the fat girl stumbled a little. She weaved as she moved toward the car. Carlyle saw her stop and bring her hands up to her face. She stood like that in the drive for a minute. Then one of the boys pushed her from behind and said her name. She dropped her hands and got into the backseat of the car.

"Daddy will get you into some clean clothes," Carlyle told his children, trying to keep his voice steady. "I'll give you a bath, and put you into some clean clothes. Then we'll go out for some pizza. How does pizza sound to you?"

"Where's Debbie?" Sarah asked him.

"She's gone," Carlyle said.

* * *

That evening, after he'd put the children to bed, he called Carol, the woman from school he'd been seeing for the past month. He told her what had happened with his sitter.

"My kids were out in the yard with this big dog," he said. "The dog was as big as a wolf. The baby-sitter was in the house with a bunch of her hoodlum boyfriends. They had Rod Stewart going full blast, and they were tying one on while my kids were outside playing with this strange dog." He brought his fingers to his temples and held them there while he talked.

"My God," Carol said. "Poor sweetie, I'm so sorry." Her voice sounded indistinct. He pictured her letting the receiver slide down to her chin, as she was in the habit of doing while talking on the phone. He'd seen her do it before. It was a habit of hers he found vaguely irritating. Did he want her to come over to his place? she asked. She would. She thought maybe she'd better do that. She'd call her sitter. Then she'd drive to his place. She wanted to. He shouldn't be afraid to say when he needed affection, she said. Carol was one of the secretaries in the principal's office at the high school where Carlyle taught art classes. She was divorced and had one child, a neurotic ten-year-old the father had named Dodge, after his automobile.

"No, that's all right," Carlyle said. "But thanks. *Thanks,* Carol. The kids are in bed, but I think I'd feel a little funny, you know, having company tonight."

She didn't offer again. "Sweetie, I'm sorry about what happened. But I understand your wanting to be alone tonight. I respect that. I'll see you at school tomorrow."

He could hear her waiting for him to say something else. "That's two baby-sitters in less than a week," he said. "I'm going out of my tree with this."

"Honey, don't let it get you down," she said. "Something will turn up. I'll help you find somebody this weekend. It'll be all right, you'll see."

"Thanks again for being there when I need you," he said. "You're one in a million, you know."

"'Night, Carlyle," she said.

After he'd hung up, he wished he could have thought of something else to say to her instead of what he'd just said. He'd never talked that way before in his life. They weren't having a love affair, he wouldn't call it that, but he liked her. She knew it was a hard time for him, and she didn't make demands.

After Eileen had left for California, Carlyle had spent every waking minute for the first month with his children. He supposed the shock of her going had caused this, but he didn't want to let the children out of his sight. He'd certainly not been interested in seeing other women, and for a time he didn't think he ever would be. He felt as if he were in mourning. His days and nights were passed in the company of his children. He cooked for them—he had no appetite himself—washed and ironed their clothes, drove them into the country, where they picked flowers and ate sandwiches wrapped up in waxed paper. He took them to the supermarket and let them pick out what they liked. And every few days they went to the park, or else to the library, or the zoo. They took old bread to the zoo so they could feed the ducks. At night, before tucking them in, Carlyle read to them—Aesop, Hans Christian Andersen, the Brothers Grimm.

"When is Mama coming back?" one of them might ask him in the middle of a fairy tale.

"Soon," he'd say. "One of these days. Now listen to this." Then he'd read the tale to its conclusion, kiss them, and turn off the light.

And while they'd slept, he had wandered the rooms of his house with a glass in his hand, telling himself that, yes, sooner or later, Eileen would come back. In the next breath, he would say, "I never want to see your face again. I'll never forgive you for this, you crazy bitch." Then, a minute later, "Come back, sweetheart, please. I love you and need you. The kids need you, too." Some nights that summer he fell asleep in front of the TV and woke up with the set still going and the screen filled with snow. This was the period when he didn't think he would be seeing any women for a long time, if ever. At night, sitting in front of the TV with an unopened book or magazine next to him on the sofa, he often thought of Eileen. When he did, he might remember her sweet laugh, or else her hand rubbing his neck if he complained of a soreness there. It was at these times that he thought he could weep. He thought, You hear about stuff like this happening to other people.

Just before the incident with Debbie, when some of the shock and grief had worn off, he'd phoned an employment service to tell them something of his predicament and his requirements. Someone took down the information and said they would get back to him. Not many people wanted to do housework *and* baby-sit, they said, but they'd find somebody. A few days before he had to be at the high school for meetings and registration, he called again and was told there'd be somebody at his house first thing the next morning.

That person was a thirty-five-year-old woman with hairy arms and run-over shoes. She shook hands with him and listened to him talk without asking a single question about the children—not even their names. When he took her into the back of the house where the children were playing, she simply stared at them for a minute without saying anything. When she finally smiled, Carlyle noticed for the first time that she had a tooth missing. Sarah left her crayons and got up to come over and stand next to him. She took Carlyle's hand and stared at the woman. Keith stared at her, too. Then he went back to his coloring. Carlyle thanked the woman for her time and said he would be in touch.

That afternoon he took down a number from an index card tacked to the bulletin board at the supermarket. Someone was offering baby-sitting services. References furnished on request. Carlyle called the number and got Debbie, the fat girl.

Over the summer, Eileen had sent a few cards, letters, and photographs of herself to the children, and some pen-and-ink drawings of her own that she'd done since she'd gone away. She also sent Carlyle long, rambling letters in which she asked for his understanding in this matter—*this matter*—but told him that she was happy. Happy. As if, Carlyle thought, happiness was all there was to life. She told him that if he really loved her, as he said he did, and as she really believed—she loved him, too, don't forget—then he would understand and accept things as they were. She wrote, "That which is truly bonded can never become unbonded." Carlyle didn't know if she was talking about their own relationship or her way of life out in California. He hated the word *bonded.* What did it have to do with the two of them? Did she think they were a corporation? He thought Eileen must be losing her mind to talk like that. He read that part again and then crumpled the letter.

But a few hours later he retrieved the letter from the trash can where he'd thrown it, and put it with her other cards and letters in a box on the shelf in his closet. In one of the envelopes, there was a photograph of her in a big, floppy hat, wearing a bathing suit. And there was a pencil drawing on heavy paper of a woman on a riverbank in a filmy gown, her hands covering her eyes, her shoulders slumped. It was, Carlyle assumed, Eileen showing her heartbreak over the situation. In college, she had majored in art, and even though she'd agreed to marry him, she said she intended to do something with her talent. Carlyle said he wouldn't have it any other way. She owed it to herself, he said. She owed it to both of them. They had loved each other in those days. He knew they had. He couldn't imagine ever loving anyone again the way he'd loved her. And he'd felt loved, too. Then, after eight years of being married to him, Eileen had pulled out. She was, she said in her letter, "going for it."

After talking to Carol, he looked in on the children, who were asleep. Then he went into the kitchen and made himself a drink. He thought of calling Eileen to talk to her about the baby-sitting crisis, but decided against it. He had her phone number and her address out there, of course. But he'd only called once and, so far, had not written a letter. This was partly out of a feeling of bewilderment with the situation, partly out of anger and humiliation. Once, earlier in the summer, after a few drinks, he'd chanced humiliation and called. Richard Hoopes answered the phone. Richard had said, "Hey, Carlyle," as if he were still Carlyle's friend. And then, as if remembering something, he said, "Just a minute, all right?"

Eileen had come on the line and said, "Carlyle, how are you? How are the kids? Tell me about yourself." He told her the kids were fine.

But before he could say anything else, she interrupted him to say, "I know *they're* fine. What about *you?*" Then she went on to tell him that her head was in the right place for the first time in a long time. Next she wanted to talk about his head and his karma. She'd looked into his karma. It was going to improve any time now, she said. Carlyle listened, hardly able to believe his ears. Then he said, "I have to go now, Eileen." And he hung up. The phone rang a minute or so later, but he let it ring. When it stopped ringing, he took the phone off the hook and left it off until he was ready for bed.

He wanted to call her now, but he was afraid to call. He still missed her and wanted to confide in her. He longed to hear her voice—sweet, steady, not manic as it had been for months now—but if he dialed her number, Richard Hoopes might answer the telephone. Carlyle knew he didn't want to hear that man's voice again. Richard had been a colleague for three years and, Carlyle supposed, a kind of friend. At least he was someone Carlyle ate lunch with in the faculty dining room, someone who talked about Tennessee Williams and the photographs of Ansel Adams. But even if Eileen answered the telephone, she might launch into something about his karma.

While he was sitting there with the glass in his hand, trying to remember what it had felt like to be married and intimate with someone, the phone rang. He picked up the receiver, heard a trace of static on the line, and knew, even before she'd said his name, that it was Eileen.

"I was just thinking about you," Carlyle said, and at once regretted saying it.

"See! I knew I was on your mind, Carlyle. Well, I was thinking about you, too. That's why I called." He drew a breath. She *was* losing her mind. That much was clear to him. She kept talking. "Now listen," she said. "The big reason I called is that I know things are in kind of a mess out there right now. Don't ask me how, but I know. I'm sorry, Carlyle. But here's the thing. You're still in need of a good housekeeper and sitter combined, right? Well, she's practically right there in the neighborhood! Oh, you may have found someone already, and that's good, if that's the case. If so, it's supposed to be that way. But see, just in case you're having trouble in that area, there's this woman who used to work for Richard's mother. I told Richard about the potential problem, and he put himself to work on it. You want to know what he did? Are you listening? He called his mother, who used to have this woman who kept house for her. The woman's name is Mrs. Webster. She looked after things for Richard's mother before his aunt and her daughter moved in there. Richard was able to get a number through his mother. He talked to Mrs. Webster today. Richard did. Mrs. Webster is going to call you tonight. Or else maybe she'll call you in the morning. One or the other. Anyway, she's going to volunteer her services, if you need her. You might, you never can tell. Even if your situation is okay right now, which I hope it is. But some time or another you might need her. You know what I'm saying? If not this minute, some other time. Okay? How are the kids? What are they up to?"

"The children are fine, Eileen. They're asleep now," he said. Maybe he should tell her they cried themselves to sleep every night. He wondered if he should tell her the truth—that they hadn't asked about her even once in the last couple of weeks. He decided not to say anything.

"I called earlier, but the line was busy. I told Richard you were probably talking to your girlfriend," Eileen said and laughed. "Think positive thoughts. You sound depressed," she said.

"I have to go, Eileen." He started to hang up, and he took the receiver from his ear. But she was still talking.

"Tell Keith and Sarah I love them. Tell them I'm sending some more pictures. Tell them that. I don't want them to forget their mother is an artist. Maybe not a great artist yet, that's not important. But, you know, an artist. It's important they shouldn't forget that."

Carlyle said, "I'll tell them."

"Richard says hello."

Carlyle didn't say anything. He said the word to himself—*hello*. What could the man possibly mean by this? Then he said, "Thanks for calling. Thanks for talking to that woman."

"Mrs. Webster!"

"Yes. I'd better get off the phone now. I don't want to run up your nickel."

Eileen laughed. "It's only money. Money's not important except as a necessary medium of exchange. There are more important things than money. But then you already know that."

He held the receiver out in front of him. He looked at the instrument from which her voice was issuing.

"Carlyle, things are going to get better for you. I *know* they are. You may think I'm crazy or something," she said. "But just remember."

Remember what? Carlyle wondered in alarm, thinking he must have missed something she'd said. He brought the receiver in close. "Eileen, thanks for calling," he said.

"We have to stay in touch," Eileen said. "We have to keep all lines of communication open. I think the worst is over. For both of us. I've suffered, too. But we're going to get what we're supposed to get out of this life, both of us, and we're going to be made *stronger* for it in the long run."

"Good night," he said. He put the receiver back. Then he looked at the phone. He waited. It didn't ring again. But an hour later it did ring. He answered it.

"Mr. Carlyle." It was an old woman's voice. "You don't know me, but my name is Mrs. Jim Webster. I was supposed to get in touch."

"Mrs. Webster. Yes," he said. Eileen's mention of the woman came back to him. "Mrs. Webster, can you come to my house in the morning? Early. Say seven o'clock?"

"I can do that easily," the old woman said. "Seven o'clock. Give me your address."

"I'd like to be able to count on you," Carlyle said.

"You can count on me," she said.

"I can't tell you how important it is," Carlyle said.

"Don't you worry," the old woman said.

The next morning, when the alarm went off, he wanted to keep his eyes closed and keep on with the dream he was having. Something about a farmhouse. And there was a waterfall in there, too. Someone, he didn't know who, was walking along the road carrying something. Maybe it was a picnic hamper. He was not made uneasy by the dream. In the dream, there seemed to exist a sense of well-being.

Finally, he rolled over and pushed something to stop the buzzing. He lay in bed a while longer. Then he got up, put his feet into his slippers, and went out to the kitchen to start the coffee.

He shaved and dressed for the day. Then he sat down at the kitchen table with coffee and a cigarette. The children were still in bed. But in five minutes or so he planned to put boxes of cereal on the table and lay out bowls and spoons, then go in to wake them for breakfast. He really couldn't believe that the old woman who'd phoned him last night would show up this morning, as she'd said she would. He decided he'd wait until five minutes after seven o'clock, and then he'd call in, take the day off, and make every effort in the book to locate someone reliable. He brought the cup of coffee to his lips.

It was then that he heard a rumbling sound out in the street. He left his cup and got up from the table to look out the window. A pickup truck had pulled over to the curb in front of his house. The pickup cab shook as the engine idled. Carlyle went to the front door, opened it, and waved. An old woman waved back and then let herself out of the vehicle. Carlyle saw the driver lean over and disappear under the dash. The truck gasped, shook itself once more, and fell still.

"Mr. Carlyle?" the old woman said, as she came slowly up his walk carrying a large purse.

"Mrs. Webster," he said. "Come on inside. Is that your husband? Ask him in. I just made coffee."

"It's okay," she said. "He has his thermos."

Carlyle shrugged. He held the door for her. She stepped inside and they shook hands. Mrs. Webster smiled. Carlyle nodded. They moved out to the kitchen. "Did you want me today, then?" she asked.

"Let me get the children up," he said. "I'd like them to meet you before I leave for school."

"That'd be good," she said. She looked around his kitchen. She put her purse on the drainboard.

"Why don't I get the children?" he said. "I'll just be a minute or two."

In a little while, he brought the children out and introduced them. They were still in their pajamas. Sarah was rubbing her eyes. Keith was wide awake. "This is Keith," Carlyle said. "And this one here, this is my Sarah." He held on to Sarah's hand and turned to Mrs. Webster. "They need someone, you see. We need someone we can count on. I guess that's our problem."

Mrs. Webster moved over to the children. She fastened the top button of Keith's pajamas. She moved the hair away from Sarah's face. They let her do it. "Don't you kids worry, now," she said to them. "Mr. Carlyle, it'll be all right. We're going to be fine. Give us a day or two to get to know each other, that's all. But if I'm going to stay, why don't you give Mr. Webster the all-clear sign? Just wave at him through the window," she said, and then she gave her attention back to the children.

Carlyle stepped to the bay window and drew the curtain. An old man was watching the house from the cab of the truck. He was just bringing a thermos cup to his lips. Carlyle waved to him, and with his free hand the man waved back. Carlyle watched him roll down the truck window and throw out what was left in his cup. Then he bent down under the dash again—Carlyle imagined him touching some wires together—and in a minute the truck started and began to shake. The old man put the truck in gear and pulled away from the curb.

Carlyle turned from the window. "Mrs. Webster," he said, "I'm glad you're here."

"Likewise, Mr. Carlyle," she said. "Now you go on about your business before you're late. Don't worry about anything. We're going to be fine. Aren't we, kids?"

The children nodded their heads. Keith held on to her dress with one hand. He put the thumb of his other hand into his mouth.

"Thank you," Carlyle said. "I feel, I really feel a hundred percent better." He shook his head and grinned. He felt a welling in his chest as he kissed each of his children good-bye. He told Mrs. Webster what time she could expect him home, put on his coat, said good-bye once more, and went out of the house. For the first time in months, it seemed, he felt his burden had lifted a little. Driving to school, he listened to some music on the radio.

During first-period art-history class, he lingered over slides of Byzantine paintings. He patiently explained the nuances of detail and motif. He pointed out the emotional power and fitness of the work. But he took so long trying to place the anonymous artists in their social milieu that some of his students began to scrape their shoes on the floor, or else clear their throats. They covered only a third of the lesson plan that day. He was still talking when the bell rang.

In his next class, watercolor painting, he felt unusually calm and insightful. "Like this, like this," he said, guiding their hands. "Delicately. Like a breath of air on the paper. Just a touch. Like so. See?" he'd say and felt on the edge of discovery himself. "*Suggestion* is what it's all about," he said, holding lightly to Sue Colvin's fingers as he guided her brush. "You've got to work with your mistakes until they look intended. Understand?"

As he moved down the lunch line in the faculty dining room, he saw Carol a few places ahead of him. She paid for her food. He waited impatiently while his own bill was being rung up. Carol was halfway across the room by the time he caught up with her. He slipped his hand under her elbow and guided her to an empty table near the window.

"God, Carlyle," she said after they'd seated themselves. She picked up her glass of iced tea. Her face was flushed. "Did you see the look Mrs. Storr gave us? What's wrong with you? Everybody will know." She sipped from her iced tea and put the glass down.

"The hell with Mrs. Storr," Carlyle said. "Hey, let me tell you something. Honey, I feel light-years better than I did this time yesterday. Jesus," he said.

"What's happened?" Carol said. "Carlyle, tell me." She moved her fruit cup to one side of her tray and shook cheese over her spaghetti. But she didn't eat anything. She waited for him to go on. "Tell me what it is."

He told her about Mrs. Webster. He even told her about Mr. Webster. How the man'd had to hot-wire the truck in order to start it. Carlyle ate his tapioca while he talked. Then he ate the garlic bread. He drank Carol's iced tea down before he realized he was doing it.

"You're nuts, Carlyle," she said, nodding at the spaghetti in his plate that he hadn't touched.

He shook his head. "My *God,* Carol. God, I feel good, you know? I feel better than I have all summer." He lowered his voice. "Come over tonight, will you?"

He reached under the table and put his hand on her knee. She turned red again. She raised her eyes and looked around the dining room. But no one was paying any attention to them. She nodded quickly. Then she reached under the table and touched his hand.

That afternoon he arrived home to find his house neat and orderly and his children in clean clothes. In the kitchen, Keith and Sarah stood on chairs, helping Mrs. Webster with gingerbread cookies. Sarah's hair was out of her face and held back with a barrette.

"Daddy!" his children cried, happy, when they saw him.

"Keith, Sarah," he said. "Mrs. Webster, I—" But she didn't let him finish.

"We've had a fine day, Mr. Carlyle," Mrs. Webster said quickly. She wiped her fingers on the apron she was wearing. It was an old apron with blue windmills on it and it had belonged to Eileen. "Such beautiful children. They're a treasure. Just a treasure."

"I don't know what to say." Carlyle stood by the drain-board and watched Sarah press out some dough. He could smell the spice. He took off his coat and sat down at the kitchen table. He loosened his tie.

"Today was a get-acquainted day," Mrs. Webster said. "Tomorrow we have some other plans. I thought we'd walk to the park. We ought to take advantage of this good weather."

"That's a fine idea," Carlyle said. "That's just fine. Good. Good for you, Mrs. Webster."

"I'll finish putting these cookies in the oven, and by that time Mr. Webster should be here. You said four o'clock? I told him to come at four."

Carlyle nodded, his heart full.

"You had a call today," she said as she went over to the sink with the mixing bowl. "Mrs. Carlyle called."

"Mrs. Carlyle," he said. He waited for whatever it was Mrs. Webster might say next.

"Yes. I identified myself, but she didn't seem surprised to find me here. She said a few words to each of the children."

Carlyle glanced at Keith and Sarah, but they weren't paying any attention. They were lining up cookies on another baking sheet.

Mrs. Webster continued. "She left a message. Let me see, I wrote it down, but I think I can remember it. She said, 'Tell him'—that is, tell you—'what goes around, comes around.' I think that's right. She said you'd understand."

Carlyle stared at her. He heard Mr. Webster's truck outside.

"That's Mr. Webster," she said and took off the apron. Carlyle nodded.

"Seven o'clock in the morning?" she asked.

"That will be fine," he said. "And thank you again."

That evening he bathed each of the children, got them into their pajamas, and then read to them. He listened to their prayers, tucked in their covers, and turned out the light. It was nearly nine o'clock. He made himself a drink and watched something on TV until he heard Carol's car pull into the drive.

Around ten, while they were in bed together, the phone rang. He swore, but he didn't get up to answer it. It kept ringing.

"It might be important," Carol said, sitting up. "It might be my sitter. She has this number."

"It's my wife," Carlyle said. "I know it's her. She's losing her mind. She's going crazy. I'm not going to answer it."

"I have to go pretty soon anyway," Carol said. "It was real sweet tonight, honey." She touched his face.

* * *

It was the middle of the fall term. Mrs. Webster had been with him for nearly six weeks. During this time, Carlyle's life had undergone a number of changes. For one thing, he was becoming reconciled to the fact that Eileen was gone and, as far as he could understand it, had no intention of coming back. He had stopped imagining that this might change. It was only late at night, on the nights he was not with Carol, that he wished for an end to the love he still had for Eileen and felt tormented as to why all of this had happened. But for the most part he and the children were happy; they thrived under Mrs. Webster's attentions. Lately, she'd gotten into the routine of making their dinner and keeping it in the oven, warming, until his arrival home from school. He'd walk in the door to the smell of something good coming from the kitchen and find Keith and Sarah helping to set the dining-room table. Now and again he asked Mrs. Webster if she would care for overtime work on Saturdays. She agreed, as long as it wouldn't entail her being at his house before noon. Saturday mornings, she said, she had things to do for Mr. Webster and herself. On these days, Carol would leave Dodge with Carlyle's children, all of them under Mrs. Webster's care, and Carol and he would drive to a restaurant out in the country for dinner. He believed his life was beginning again. Though he hadn't heard from Eileen since that call six weeks ago, he found himself able to think about her now without either being angry or else feeling close to tears.

At school, they were just leaving the medieval period and about to enter the Gothic. The Renaissance was still some time off, at least not until after the Christmas recess. It was during this time that Carlyle got sick. Overnight, it seemed, his chest tightened and his head began to hurt. The joints of his body became stiff. He felt dizzy when he moved around. The headache got worse. He woke up with it on a Sunday and thought of calling Mrs. Webster to ask her to come and take the children somewhere. They'd been sweet to him, bringing him glasses of juice and some soda pop. But he couldn't take care of them. On the second morning of his illness, he was just able to get to the phone to call in sick. He gave his name, his school, department, and the nature of his illness to the person who answered the number. Then he recommended Mel Fisher as his substitute. Fisher was a man who painted abstract oils three or four days a week, sixteen hours a day, but who didn't sell or even show his work. He was a friend of Carlyle's. "Get Mel Fisher," Carlyle told the woman on the other end of the line. "Fisher," he whispered.

He made it back to his bed, got under the covers, and went to sleep. In his sleep, he heard the pickup engine running outside, and then the backfire it made as the engine was turned off. Sometime later he heard Mrs. Webster's voice outside the bedroom door.

"Mr. Carlyle?"

"Yes, Mrs. Webster." His voice sounded strange to him. He kept his eyes shut. "I'm sick today. I called the school. I'm going to stay in bed today."

"I see. Don't worry, then," she said. "I'll look after things at this end."

He shut his eyes. Directly, still in a state between sleeping and waking, he thought he heard his front door open and close. He listened. Out in the kitchen, he heard a man say something in a low voice, and a chair being pulled away from the table. Pretty soon he heard the voices of the children. Sometime later—he wasn't sure how much time had passed—he heard Mrs. Webster outside his door.

"Mr. Carlyle, should I call the doctor?"

"No, that's all right," he said. "I think it's just a bad cold. But I feel hot all over. I think I have too many covers. And it's too warm in the house. Maybe you'll turn down the furnace." Then he felt himself drift back into sleep.

In a little while, he heard the children talking to Mrs. Webster in the living room. Were they coming inside or going out? Carlyle wondered. Could it be the next day already?

He went back to sleep. But then he was aware of his door opening. Mrs. Webster appeared beside his bed. She put her hand on his forehead.

"You're burning up," she said. "You have a fever."

"I'll be all right," Carlyle said. "I just need to sleep a little longer. And maybe you could turn the furnace down. Please, I'd appreciate it if you could get me some aspirin. I have an awful headache."

Mrs. Webster left the room. But his door stood open. Carlyle could hear the TV going out there. "Keep it down, Jim," he heard her say, and the volume was lowered at once. Carlyle fell asleep again.

But he couldn't have slept more than a minute, because Mrs. Webster was suddenly back in his room with a tray. She sat down on the side of his bed. He roused himself and tried to sit up. She put a pillow behind his back.

"Take these," she said and gave him some tablets. "Drink this." She held a glass of juice for him. "I also brought you some Cream of Wheat. I want you to eat it. It'll be good for you."

He took the aspirin and drank the juice. He nodded. But he shut his eyes once more. He was going back to sleep.

"Mr. Carlyle," she said.

He opened his eyes. "I'm awake," he said. "I'm sorry." He sat up a little. "I'm too warm, that's all. What time is it? Is it eight-thirty yet?"

"It's a little after nine-thirty," she said.

"Nine-thirty," he said.

"Now I'm going to feed this cereal to you. And you're going to open up and eat it. Six bites, that's all. Here, here's the first bite. Open," she said. "You're going to feel better after you eat this. Then I'll let you go back to sleep. You eat this, and then you can sleep all you want."

He ate the cereal she spooned to him and asked for more juice. He drank the juice, and then he pulled down in the bed again. Just as he was going off to sleep, he felt her covering him with another blanket.

The next time he awoke, it was afternoon. He could tell it was afternoon by the pale light that came through his window. He reached up and pulled the curtain back. He could see that it was overcast outside; the wintry sun was behind the clouds. He got out of bed slowly, found his slippers, and put on his robe. He went into the bathroom and looked at himself in the mirror. Then he washed his face and took some more aspirin. He used the towel and then went out to the living room.

On the dining-room table, Mrs. Webster had spread some newspaper, and she and the children were pinching clay figures together. They had already made some things that had long necks and bulging eyes, things that resembled giraffes, or else dinosaurs. Mrs. Webster looked up as he walked by the table.

"How are you feeling?" Mrs. Webster asked him as he settled onto the sofa. He could see into the dining-room area, where Mrs. Webster and the children sat at the table.

"Better, thanks. A little better," he said. "I still have a headache, and I feel a little warm." He brought the back of his hand up to his forehead. "But I'm better. Yes, I'm better. Thanks for your help this morning."

"Can I get you anything now?" Mrs. Webster said. "Some more juice or some tea? I don't think coffee would hurt, but I think tea would be better. Some juice would be best of all."

"No, no thanks," he said. "I'll just sit here for a while. It's good to be out of bed. I feel a little weak is all. Mrs. Webster?"

She looked at him and waited.

"Did I hear Mr. Webster in the house this morning? It's fine, of course. I'm just sorry I didn't get a chance to meet him and say hello."

"It was him," she said. "He wanted to meet you, too. I asked him to come in. He just picked the wrong morning, what with you being sick and all. I'd wanted to tell you something about our plans, Mr. Webster's and mine, but this morning wasn't a good time for it."

"Tell me what?" he said, alert, fear plucking at his heart.

She shook her head. "It's all right," she said. "It can wait."

"Tell him what?" Sarah said. "Tell him what?"

"What, what?" Keith picked it up. The children stopped what they were doing.

"Just a minute, you two," Mrs. Webster said as she got to her feet.

"Mrs. Webster, Mrs. Webster!" Keith cried.

"Now see here, little man," Mrs. Webster said. "I need to talk to your father. Your father is sick today. You just take it easy. You go on and play with your clay. If you don't watch it, your sister is going to get ahead of you with these creatures."

Just as she began to move toward the living room, the phone rang. Carlyle reached over to the end table and picked up the receiver.

As before, he heard faint singing in the wire and knew that it was Eileen. "Yes," he said. "What is it?"

"Carlyle," his wife said, "I know, don't ask me how, that things are not going so well right now. You're sick, aren't you? Richard's been sick, too. It's something going around. He can't keep anything on his stomach. He's already missed a week of rehearsal for this play he's doing. I've had to go down myself and help block out scenes with his assistant. But I didn't call to tell you that. Tell me how things are out there."

"Nothing to tell," Carlyle said. "I'm sick, that's all. A touch of the flu. But I'm getting better."

"Are you still writing in your journal?" she asked. It caught him by surprise. Several years before, he'd told her that he was keeping a journal. Not a diary, he'd said, a journal—as if that explained something. But he'd never shown it to her, and he hadn't written in it for over a year. He'd forgotten about it.

"Because," she said, "you ought to write something in the journal during this period. How you feel and what you're thinking. You know, where your head is at during this period of sickness. Remember, sickness is a message about your health and your well-being. It's telling you things. Keep a record. You know what I mean? When you're well, you can look back and see what the message was. You can read it later, after the fact. Colette did that," Eileen said. "When she had a fever this one time."

"Who?" Carlyle said. "What did you say?"

"Colette," Eileen answered. "The French writer. You know who I'm talking about. We had a book of hers around the house. *Gigi* or something. I didn't read *that* book, but I've been reading her since I've been out here. Richard turned me on to her. She wrote a little book about what it was like, about what she was thinking and feeling the whole time she had this fever. Sometimes her temperature was a hundred and two. Sometimes it was lower. Maybe it went higher than a hundred and two. But a hundred and two was the highest she ever took her temperature and wrote, too, when she had the fever. Anyway, she wrote about it. That's what I'm saying. Try writing about what it's like. Something might come of it," Eileen said and, inexplicably, it seemed to Carlyle, she laughed. "At least later on you'd have an hour-by-hour account of your sickness. To look back at. At least you'd have that to show for it. Right now you've just got this discomfort. You've got to translate that into something usable."

He pressed his fingertips against his temple and shut his eyes. But she was still on the line, waiting for him to say something. What could he say? It was clear to him that she was insane.

"Jesus," he said. "Jesus, Eileen. I don't know what to say to that. I really don't. I have to go now. Thanks for calling," he said.

"It's all right," she said. "We have to be able to communicate. Kiss the kids for me. Tell them I love them. And Richard sends his hellos to you. Even though he's flat on his back."

"Good-bye," Carlyle said and hung up. Then he brought his hands to his face. He remembered, for some reason, seeing the fat girl make the same gesture that time as she moved toward the car. He lowered his hands and looked at Mrs. Webster, who was watching him.

"Not bad news, I hope," she said. The old woman had moved a chair near to where he sat on the sofa.

Carlyle shook his head.

"Good," Mrs. Webster said. "That's good. Now, Mr. Carlyle, this may not be the best time in the world to talk about this." She glanced out to the dining room. At the table, the children had their heads bent over the clay. "But since it has to be talked about sometime soon, and since it concerns you and the children, and you're up now, I have something to tell you. Jim and I, we're getting on. The thing is, we need something more than we have at the present. Do you know what I'm saying? This is hard for me," she said and shook her head. Carlyle nodded slowly. He knew that she was going to tell him she had to leave. He wiped his face on his sleeve. "Jim's son by a former marriage, Bob—the man is forty years old—called yesterday to invite us to go out to Oregon and help him with his mink ranch. Jim would be doing whatever they do with minks, and I'd cook, buy the groceries, clean house, and do anything else that needed doing. It's a chance for both of us. And it's board and room and then some. Jim and I won't have to worry anymore about what's going to happen to us. You know what I'm saying. Right now, Jim doesn't have anything," she said. "He was sixty-two last week. He hasn't had anything for some time. He came in this morning to tell you about it himself, because I was going to have to give notice, you see. We thought—*I* thought—it would help if Jim was here when I told you." She waited for Carlyle to say something. When he didn't, she went on. "I'll finish out the week, and I could stay on a couple of days next week, if need be. But then, you know, for sure, we really have to leave, and you'll have to wish us luck. I mean, can you imagine—all the way out there to Oregon in that old rattletrap of ours? But I'm going to miss these little kids. They're so precious."

After a time, when he still hadn't moved to answer her, she got up from her chair and went to sit on the cushion next to his. She touched the sleeve of his robe. "Mr. Carlyle?"

"I understand," he said. "I want you to know your being here has made a big difference to me and the children." His head ached so much that he had to squint his eyes. "This headache," he said. "This headache is killing me."

Mrs. Webster reached over and laid the back of her hand against his forehead. "You still have some fever," she told him. "I'll get more aspirin. That'll help bring it down. I'm still on the case here," she said. "I'm still the doctor."

"My wife thinks I should write down what this feels like," Carlyle said. "She thinks it might be a good idea to describe what the fever is like. So I can look back later and get the message." He laughed. Some tears came to his eyes. He wiped them away with the heel of his hand.

"I think I'll get your aspirin and juice and then go out there with the kids," Mrs. Webster said. "Looks to me like they've about worn out their interest with that clay."

Carlyle was afraid she'd move into the other room and leave him alone. He wanted to talk to her. He cleared his throat. "Mrs. Webster, there's something I want you to know. For a long time, my wife and I loved each other more than anything or anybody in the world. And that includes those children. We thought, well, we *knew* that we'd grow old together. And we knew we'd do all the things in the world that we wanted to do, and do them together." He shook his head. That seemed the saddest thing of all to him now—that whatever they did from now on, each would do it without the other.

"There, it's all right," Mrs. Webster said. She patted his hand. He sat forward and began to talk again. After a time, the children came out to the living room. Mrs. Webster caught their attention and held a finger to her lips. Carlyle looked at them and went on talking. Let them listen, he thought. It concerns them, too. The children seemed to understand they had to remain quiet, even pretend some interest, so they sat down next to Mrs. Webster's legs. Then they got down on their stomachs on the carpet and started to giggle. But Mrs. Webster looked sternly in their direction, and that stopped it.

Carlyle went on talking. At first, his head still ached, and he felt awkward to be in his pajamas on the sofa with this old woman beside him, waiting patiently for him to go on to the next thing. But then his headache went away. And soon he stopped feeling awkward and forgot how he was supposed to feel. He had begun his story somewhere in the middle, after the children were born. But then he backed up and started at the beginning, back when Eileen was eighteen and he was nineteen, a boy and girl in love, burning with it.

He stopped to wipe his forehead. He moistened his lips.

"Go on," Mrs. Webster said. "I know what you're saying. You just keep talking, Mr. Carlyle. Sometimes it's good to talk about it. Sometimes it has to be talked about. Besides, I want to hear it. And you're going to feel better afterward. Something just like it happened to me once, something like what you're describing. Love. That's what it is."

The children fell asleep on the carpet. Keith had his thumb in his mouth. Carlyle was still talking when Mr. Webster came to the door, knocked, and then stepped inside to collect Mrs. Webster.

"Sit down, Jim," Mrs. Webster said. "There's no hurry. Go on with what you were saying, Mr. Carlyle."

Carlyle nodded at the old man, and the old man nodded back, then got himself one of the dining-room chairs and carried it into the living room. He brought the chair close to the sofa and sat down on it with a sigh. Then he took off his cap and wearily lifted one leg over the other. When Carlyle began talking again, the old man put both feet on the floor. The children woke up. They sat up on the carpet and rolled their heads back and forth. But by then Carlyle had said all he knew to say, so he stopped talking.

"Good. Good for you," Mrs. Webster said when she saw he had finished. "You're made out of good stuff. And so is she—so is Mrs. Carlyle. And don't you forget it. You're both going to be okay after this is over." She got up and took off the apron she'd been wearing. Mr. Webster got up, too, and put his cap back on.

At the door, Carlyle shook hands with both of the Websters.

"So long," Jim Webster said. He touched the bill of his cap.

"Good luck to you," Carlyle said.

Mrs. Webster said she'd see him in the morning then, bright and early as always.

As if something important had been settled, Carlyle said, "Right!"

The old couple went carefully along the walk and got into their truck. Jim Webster bent down under the dashboard. Mrs. Webster looked at Carlyle and waved. It was then, as he stood at the window, that he felt something come to an end. It had to do with Eileen and the life before this. Had he ever waved at her? He must have, of course, he knew he had, yet he could not remember just now. But he understood it was over, and he felt able to let her go. He was sure their life together had happened in the way he said it had. But it was something that had passed. And that passing—though it had seemed impossible and he'd fought against it—would become a part of him now, too, as surely as anything else he'd left behind.

As the pickup lurched forward, he lifted his arm once more. He saw the old couple lean toward him briefly as they drove away. Then he brought his arm down and turned to his children.

Grateful acknowledgment is made to the following for permission to reprint previously copyrighted material:

Steve Almond, "How to Love a Republican," from *My Life in Heavy Metal*. Copyright © 2002 by Steve Almond. Reprinted by permission of Grove/Atlantic, Inc.

Dallas Angguish, "The Camping Ground," from *Dumped* (Australian edition). Copyright © 2000 by Dallas Angguish. Reprinted by permission of Black Inc., Australia.

Noah Baumbach, "The Zagat History of My Last Relationship," copyright © 2002. Reprinted by permission of Noah Baumbach. Originally published in *The New Yorker*.

Jo Ann Beard, "The Fourth State of Matter," from *Boys of My Youth*. Copyright © 1998 by Jo Ann Beard. Reprinted with the permission of Little, Brown and Company, Inc.

Saul Bellow, excerpt from *Herzog*. Copyright © 1961, 1963, 1964 by Saul Bellow. Reprinted with the permission of Viking Penguin, a division of Penguin Putnam Inc. and The Wylie Agency, Inc.

Elizabeth Berg, excerpt from *Open House*. Copyright © 2000 by Elizabeth Berg. Reprinted with the permission of Random House, Inc.

Elizabeth Bowen, "Making Arrangements," from *Collected Stories*. Copyright © 1981 by Curtis Brown, Ltd., literary executors of the Estate of Elizabeth Bowen. Reprinted with the permission of Alfred A. Knopf, a division of Random House, Inc.

Raymond Carver, "Fever," from *Cathedral*. Copyright © 1981, 1982, 1983 by Raymond Carver. Reprinted with the permission of Alfred A. Knopf, a division of Random House, Inc.

Roald Dahl, "Lamb to the Slaughter," from *The Best of Roald Dahl* (New York: Vintage, 1990). Copyright © 1953 by Roald Dahl. Reprinted with the permission of David Higham Associates, Ltd.

Andre Dubus, "Over the Hill," from *Separate Flights*. Copyright © 1975 by Andre Dubus. Reprinted with the permission of David R. Godine, Publisher, Inc.

Richard Ford, "Under the Radar," from *A Multitude of Sins*. Copyright © 2001 by Richard Ford. Reprinted with the permission of Alfred A. Knopf, a division of Random House, Inc. Originally published in *The New Yorker*.

Bruce Jay Friedman, "Marching Through Delaware," from *The Collected Short Fiction of Bruce Jay Friedman*. Copyright © 1997 by Bruce Jay Friedman. Reprinted by permission of Grove/Atlantic, Inc.

Roger Hart, "My Stuff," from *Erratics*, published by Texas Review Press. Copyright © 2001 by Roger Hart. Reprinted with permission of Roger Hart.

Lorrie Moore, "Willing," from *Birds of America*. Copyright © 1998 by Lorrie Moore. Reprinted with the permission of Alfred A. Knopf, a division of Random House, Inc.

Alice Munro, "The Spanish Lady," from *Something I've Been Meaning to Tell You*. Copyright © 1974 by Alice Munro. Reprinted with the permission of the author.

Haruki Murakami, "UFO in Kushiro," from *After the Quake: Stories*. Copyright © 2002 by Haruki Murakami. Reprinted with the permission of Alfred A. Knopf, a division of Random House, Inc. Originally published in *The New Yorker.*

Dan O'Brien, "Final Touches," from *Eminent Domain*. Copyright © 1987 by Dan O'Brien. Reprinted with the permission of the University of Iowa Press.

Dorothy Parker, "A Telephone Call," from *The Portable Dorothy Parker*. Copyright © 1928 and renewed © 1956 by Dorothy Parker. Reprinted with the permission of Viking Penguin, a division of Penguin Putnam Inc.

Lucinda Rosenfeld, excerpt from "Pablo Miles" in *What She Saw*. Originally published as "The Male Gaze" from *The New Yorker* (June 2000). Copyright © 2000 by Lucinda Rosenfeld. Reprinted with the permission of Random House, Inc.

Will Self, "The End of the Relationship," from *Grey Area*. Copyright © 1994 by Will Self. Reprinted by permission of Grove/Atlantic, Inc.

William Trevor, "Access to the Children," from *The Collected Stories of William Trevor*. Copyright © 1992 by William Trevor. Reprinted with the permission of Penguin Putnam Inc. and Sterling Lord Literistic.

Tobias Wolff, excerpt from *This Boy's Life*. Copyright © 1989 by Tobias Wolff. Reprinted by permission of Grove/Atlantic, Inc.